To Ben Bryant —
Best Wishes —
Michael Terry

SO SHINE
BEFORE MEN

SO SHINE
BEFORE MEN

A Novel by
Michael Terry

First Fiction Series

SUNSTONE
PRESS
SANTA FE

Sunstone books may be purchased for educational, business, or sales promotional use. For information please write: Special Markets Department, Sunstone Press, P.O. Box 2321, Santa Fe, New Mexico 87504-2321.

FIRST EDITION

10 9 8 7 6 5 4 3 2 1

Library of Congress Cataloging-in-Publication Data:
Terry, Michael, 1946–
    So shine before men: a novel / by Michael Terry.—1st ed.
        p. cm.
    ISBN: 0-86534-346-2
        1. Washington (D.C.)—Fiction. I. Title.

PS3620.E77 S6 2002
813' .6—dc21   2001057749

Published in

SUNSTONE PRESS
Post Office Box 2321
Santa Fe, NM 87504-2321 / USA
(505) 988-4418 / *orders only* (800) 243-5644
FAX (505) 988-1025
www.sunstonepress.com

To my family—Joan, Agnes and Luke—whose
patience with me always greatly exceeds
my profound love for them.

Thanks to . . .

Dave and Pam Anderson, Mary Ashmun, The Averys,
Jim Breazeale, Christie and George Hamilton,
Elizabeth Ferrall, The Forrest Forum, Samantha Jernigan,
Ooze Johnson, Robert Kissling, Jan and David Kollock,
Wayne Lewis, Suzy Mallory, Sammie Mashall, Frances Martin,
Bruce Miller, Jesse and Sandy Morgan, Anne Piper, Gayle Rose,
Mike Rose, Jennifer Satre, Glenda Shorb, Belinda, Luther and
Three Sticks Terry, and Ferrell Varner

. . . for their advice, support and caring.

You are the light of the world.
A city set on a hill cannot be hid. Nor do men light a lamp and put it
under a bushel, but on a stand, and it gives light to all in the house.
Let your light so shine before men, that they may see your good works
and give glory to your Father who is in heaven.

Matthew 5:14

HOUSE SPEAKER FOUND DEAD AT CLUB

Victim of Apparent Sauna Accident

By CLAYTON ROSECROFT

WASHINGTON, Oct. 30 (AP)—Representative Henry L. Berkhardt (Dem – Ariz) was discovered dead this morning at his private club here in the Nation's Capital. Berkhardt, Speaker of the House of Representatives, was the victim of an apparent accident. He was found in a sauna room on the third floor of the prestigious Downtown Capital Club.

A custodial employee of the club, Desmond Wilson, is reported to have discovered the Speaker at approximately seven-thirty a.m. (EST) as Wilson was preparing the club's health and fitness center for the day. Wilson, who was unavailable for comment, reportedly called 911 to report the incident. An emergency rescue team was unable to resuscitate the Speaker and, according to sources at the scene, Berkhardt was pronounced dead at 7:58 a.m.

A spokeswoman for Capital police stated, "We are very early into our investigation of this tragic death. Mr. Wilson, who found the body and called for emergency aid, is cooperating fully and is not a suspect at this time. While the investigation is ongoing, preliminary indications are that it was accidental."

Other reports say that Capital police have called in the Federal Bureau of investigation to assist in analyzing the accident scene. No representative of the FBI was available for comment.

Speaker Berkhardt, 63, served as a U.S. Representative from Arizona's 14th district for 19 years. He was widely regarded as an adroit mediator of hotly contested legislative issues. In particular, he promoted legislative solutions on Western water rights, and sought find common ground among ranchers and agricultural interests, environmental advocates, and influential groups representing the interests of sportsmen, hunters, and fishermen.

Berkhardt was also known for his ardent advocacy of the historical rights of Arizonan and other Native American tribes. A vocal critic of both Republicans and Democrats with respect to what he termed "historical moral wrongs," he persistently and vigorously sought "redress" for the tribes, in particular for return of federal land held sacred by the Indians.

9

1

On this late September night Ellie, wearing her crisp white housekeeper's dress, shuffled to the phone. "May I tell the Senator who is calling, please? Yes, sir . . . just a moment."

Before she could notify him, Senator Reginald Edward Calvin's booming Southern voice echoed down the marble steps of the double spiral staircase in the front hallway.

"Who is it, Ellie?"

Ellie, an elderly black woman, lived in the housekeeper's quarters of the venerable townhouse, just around the corner from Twenty-ninth and N. She was from Mississippi and, for fourteen years, had worked for the Senator and his wife, raising her children along side of theirs. Like the Senator, and unlike the many thousands of others who serve here, she remained unchanged by her years in Washington.

Life in Washington changes the soul. No matter how frequently politicians and their families return to their home states, their tenures in the nation's capital render them Washingtonians . . . permanently. The transformation is usually gradual, but no less inescapable.

Despite their superficial regional differences, legislators here eventually give in to the juggernaut. This city bleeds out all traces of home.

They become Gores and Gingrichs. They inexorably lose the traces of their provinciality. They become transformed, from elected representatives to cardboard bureaucrats.

These capital residents thus become a unique genre, not evil, but nonetheless corrupted. After a time Washington, most are inured to the bureaucratization of self, sleepwalking through term after term, roused only when some upstart with more energy and ideas than money, threatens their incumbency.

Some, like Bernard Cartwright, the Republican Presidential campaign chairman, suffer a more precipitous descent, not the more common gradual erosion. Despite, or perhaps because of, his importance, Cartwright became critically afflicted by his authority and self-importance.

And incumbent President Williams, the man whom Cartwright presumably served, was too long in recognizing that his campaign chairman had become a pustule . . . and too long in cutting out this abscess.

Ellie's boss, the Mississippi Senator, was one of the rare men who had defied the forces of Washington. He was different. He maintained Mississippi not only in his voice and his demeanor, but also in his attitude and in his heart. After years in Washington, despite his graying hair and widening waist, he had never succumbed. His soul was still as pure as that of the little boy who worked and played—each with equal intensity—on the family's Delta farm.

"It's the White House, sir. A Mr. Harwood," Ellie answered, her frail voice bouncing back up the marble stairs. At the top, a tall, stately gentleman with salt-and-pepper hair and a long self-assured stride, picked up the phone.

"This is Senator Calvin."

Stanley Harwood immediately felt the Deep South in the Senator's voice. Without a "good evening," Harwood began. "This is Stanley Harwood from the White House. The President has asked me to meet with you on a matter of the greatest urgency."

"Yes, Mr. Harwood, I got a message earlier from the President's office telling me to expect your call. When do you want to try to get together?"

"Right now, if you don't mind, Senator." Harwood was polite, but direct.

"Can you tell me the nature of the meeting, Mr. Harwood? It's getting to be quite late."

"No sir, I'm sorry. The President has asked me to discuss this directly and personally with you. I can assure you, sir, that this is a matter of the greatest urgency."

"You repeat yourself, Mr. Harwood. When can you be here?"

"About four minutes, sir."

"Four minutes? You must be in a phone booth on M Street!"

"Yes, sir. In the lobby of the Four Seasons, to be exact."

"Well, then, if you've gotten this far, you might as well complete the trip, don't you think? You know where I am? Just down the street from the Synagogue?"

"Yes, sir. I'm going to walk up the hill now."

2

At seventy-four and older than anyone else in history to run for a second term, the President knew that he was liked by the people, perhaps even loved. Well, maybe not loved, but liked and respected. And trusted.

Isn't that all that matters, he thought, trying unsuccessfully to convince himself, *not love, but respect and trust? But, historically, don't the people elect men whom they do not love, that they do not even like? What do the voters want . . . personality, promises? Everything off the menu? Do they not seek either vision or action . . . but is not one without the other worthless? Or dangerous?*

President Ralph Waldo Emerson Williams could not sleep. He got out of bed and walked through the darkness to the window and looked out over the blackness of Washington.

The city was deserted and dark, an appropriate metaphor, he thought, for his re-election campaign. But, in a couple of hours, with daylight, the capital would be refreshed, alive and active for another day. The city-desert would bloom.

And the campaign-desert? My campaign just needs a good rain, a good soaking, to force the waiting seeds and blossoms. It needs the cleansing wash of an unexpected desert storm. But the campaign-sky is arid and cloudless. My campaign is the Sahara of campaigns, he thought.

He brushed his hair flat with his fingers, walked to the end of the bed, picked up his robe and put it on. For a long time he stared at his wife. It made him feel good to know how well she slept. Whatever their problems, Phyllis did not take them to bed with her. Through forty-seven years of marriage, he never ceased to envy her ability to compartmentalize the issues in their lives. "We'll get through it," she would say, "it's nothing to lose sleep over."

Phyllis Williams never trivialized a problem. But she had her own unique way of dimensioning its seriousness relative to the things she loved in her life: God, herself, her family, and her fellow humans. And, if asked, she would admit that this is the specific order in which she loved those things. Were she not so disarmingly honest, for a president's wife she would have been a media disaster. Instead, while her public image was alternately a paradox and an asset, it was never negative.

President Williams resumed his worrying as he walked toward the door of the darkened bedroom.

As the Democratic candidate for the Presidency, surely Frank Moore is a worthy opponent. But is he the one to lead America? What do the People want in a President? What do they expect?

What can Man do best? What is his function? Moore as our nation's President? Perhaps it's the Democrats' time. And O'Malley . . . on my own ticket, my own running mate. Again! What are the purposes of such men? If Aristotle was right, and moral virtue is a matter of reason and balance—the avoidance of extremes—then these men are the opposite. They are the epitome of the imperfect soul, the opposite of the Mean.

The President smiled at the possibilities with the word "mean."

Who could have done more than I have? Who is fairer than I am? And I'm not tired. I am a young seventy-four. Sure, I'm not a fighter, not in the classic sense, but I can rise to the challenge, I can scrap with the best of them. Didn't I get campaign finance reform enacted? And Congress to pass, despite its collective kicking and screaming, health care reform legislation that was both effective and cost-efficient?

I'm not lying down after a single term. I can make this happen. This is no time for philosophy. I must overcome this penchant for introspection . . . I must fight this philosopher that lives inside of me.

The President walked out of the family quarters, into the second floor hallway, past a wide-awake Secret Service agent. "Good morning, Mr. President, or good night, I guess. It's late, sir. Do you have work to do?"

"Can't sleep, Fred. I'm going down to my office."

"Yes, sir, Mr. President. I'd walk with you, but my assignment requires me to stay here. Procedures, you know. Do you mind waiting here for a second, and I'll buzz Milbury. You must be escorted, sir."

"No, I'm okay. Just walking and thinking . . . going to head down-stairs."

Like his peers, the agent was a well-trained, no-nonsense professional. He knew that under a 1917 law, the Secret Service kept a protective eye on all members of the Presidential family. More important, he knew that Congress, after the Kennedy assassination, enacted legislation requiring that the President and his family be accompanied by an agent at all times, the only exception being when they were actually in their second-floor-west private living quarters. And even the President himself did not have the power to contradict the requirements of this law.

"Mr. President, sir," the agent replied, "with all due respect, I need to ask you to remain here for a second until I can get an escort for you. I'm very sorry, sir," he apologized, as he pulled his handset from his coat pocket to alert his supervisor.

Williams shrugged. He respected the law's intent, despite the minor burdens it imposed. But, he respected the agent's responsibilities more than the law, and he would not deign to make things difficult for a man who stuck to his assignment and the rules governing it. And the President's attitude extended to everyone, including the White House's eighty-one domestic and maintenance employees, some of whom mopped and shined the six-hundred thousand square feet of wood floors and vacuumed the twenty-five thousand square feet of carpet.

The President reflected on the tireless efforts of the unsung staff that made the White House—part family residence, part official place of business—work efficiently. A separate staff of accountants routinely separated family expenses for which the President was personally responsible—personal maids, laundry, valets, and other domestic help; personal telephone calls; private or family events and parties.

In less than a minute, Tom Milbury appeared, and the President, now accompanied, resumed his walk, downstairs and past the rabbit warren of staff and secretaries' offices. He ignored the light switch, and entered a darkened Oval Office. Moving to the window, he leaned on the sill, arms extended and elbows locked, and stared out.

This is a time for action. It's not too late. The polls are right, I've slipped badly . . . now even behind. But I can come back from a deficit of this magnitude. How could I have kept Bernie Cartwright on as campaign chairman this long? He's a disaster and I know it. No ideas, no strategy. How to recover? There's no plan, no direction. And I can't get one in place in the weeks that remain. After that, it's moot.

The dark office and early morning hour heightened the President's reflective mood.

I'm not one of those blamers, one of those victims. Numbers are numbers and, right now the numbers are saying I'm not the guy this time. Whatever it takes, I've still got ten weeks. Ten weeks is an eternity in a Presidential election campaign . . . or am I kidding myself?

Why can't Cartwright get anything moving? What the heck have those guys been doing? Okay, maybe Moore's a worthy candidate, but he's not close to being presidential. He's all platitudes. Plus, he has more skeletons in his closet than the Smithsonian, and the press treats him like a saint.

The word 'entropy' returned to him from an engineering class at Stanford.

Entropy: steady degradation. It's an engineer's word: but shouldn't entropy be a philosopher's word? It's a negative word . . . a 'glass is half-empty' word. Entropy and the Williams/O'Malley campaign were synonymous, he thought. *Entropy 'R' Us.*

He laughed to himself, relieved that, despite his campaign debacle, his usual sense of humor had not been baked into dross. Even if it was black, at least a little humor remained.

Entropy 'R' Us! We need new campaign buttons! Ennui . . . On We . . . On We Go, Ennui Go.

The President smiled.

'Entropy 'R' Us. Ennui Go.' Ennui: weariness and dissatisfaction. What a shame that O'Malley wouldn't get it. Look up 'entropy' in Webster's and there's our picture. Our showing in the polls is the definition of entropy. Our sails are torn. We have no course, no compass. Where's our vision, our energy, our meaning? Slipping in the polls, me brooding, and no compass.

"Uh, excuse me, Mr. President? Are you okay?"

The President jerked from his contemplation, and spun.

"Oh it's you, Milbury."

"Yes, I'm sorry I startled you, sir, I just wanted to stick my head back in and make sure you're okay."

"Sure, Milbury, I'm fine. Just thinking about things."

"Well, sir, I'm just outside the door, if you need me."

Tom Milbury adjusted his earpiece slightly and moved toward the door.

The President caught the agent before he could leave. "Milbury, who are you going to vote for?"

"Vote for, Mr. President?"

"Yes, Agent Milbury. Who you are going to vote for."

Milbury turned and paused. The President and Milbury were friends, but now both were equally uncomfortable.

"Why you, Mr. President. I'm voting Williams/O'Malley all the way."

"And why are you doing that Milbury?"

"I'm sorry, but I'm not sure if I get your drift, sir."

"It's easy, Milbury. There are two major parties and a few others. Why are you going to vote—in a little more than two months—for the Republicans, 'all the way' as you put it?"

Agent Milbury raised his right hand nervously, and again fumbled with his earpiece. He was comfortable with the President as a person. Everyone was. He felt uncomfortable, as many did, with the President's intellectualism. He felt like he was entering a debate, one that he was guaranteed to lose. Milbury decided to cut it short.

"I'm voting for the Republicans because of you, Mr. President."

"And what about me?"

"Well, sir, you're a good guy. I think you ought to stay President. You're good for the country. I've been in the Secret Service a long time, and I've known some of your predecessors pretty well. They were nice too, but not real and genuine like you are, sir."

"Go on, Agent Milbury."

"Well, you may be a little spacey sometimes, sir . . . I mean, you're a great guy, full of brilliant ideas. More important, you're somebody I know I can trust in this office. Otherwise, I wouldn't even be talking to you like this.

You've had a tough go this past year or so, but no one ever doubts where you're coming from."

"Thanks, Milbury. You really know how to make an old man . . . an old President, feel good. Except maybe for the spacey part," the President laughed.

"Well, sir, I'm sorry to say it, but I'm around you a lot and I can see you dying inside, especially these past few weeks. I'm not so sure if you're not too good for the job. Maybe this job *needs* a liar. Maybe that's what it takes to succeed."

Tom Milbury took two steps toward Williams. Closing the space between them seemed to heighten his honesty. "What I mean is, I'm not sure if the people deserve you, sir. For sure they don't know what a good man they've got. Particularly, if they read the newspapers. You and the President I read about in the Washington Post are two entirely different people."

"Your candor is really surprising."

"Well sir, I'm just a senior agent, but you asked, Mr. President, you asked."

"I sure did. One final thing . . . do you think I'm going to win?"

Milbury craned his neck and shifted his weight from one foot to the other. "No sir, I sure don't. Not the way things are going now."

"So I'm dead, huh?"

"Well sir, first of all, we agents just hate the image you just created: dead Presidents. It's really bad for our job security."

The President laughed like he hadn't in months.

"Milbury, I think you're feeling pretty secure in your job!"

"Not so much sir, I just think you needed a laugh."

"Okay, good job. Anyway, I'm a goner, huh?"

"Bad choice of words again, Mr. President!"

"I give up, Milbury. Just give it to me straight."

"Mr. President, unless you can figure out some way to make the waters part, turn water into wine, well, you know those Bible miracles better than me. The fact is that no one sees how you can do it this late and this far behind. It's only ten weeks to Election Day . . . and, you seem to be the only one around here who's worried."

"Seriously? How about O'Malley?"

"Well, sir, win or lose, he figures he's okay. You lose, at your age, we know you're not coming back. You're going to the ranch in Ojai and relax."

"Not too bad for second place, huh Milbury?"

"You bet . . . I'd sure take an assignment out there. Anyway, you lose, and O'Malley, he's the leader of the Party. He blames the loss on you and comes back next time, four years later, as the Presidential candidate. He's got that figured out. This is a win/win for him." Senior Agent Milbury caught himself. "Sir, I'm way out of line with these comments. It's three-thirty in the morning, I'm b.s.ing with the President. I hope none of this gets repeated, sir. I'm trying to help."

"Don't worry, Milbury, you are."

"I guess I should go, Mr. President, unless you need me for something else."

"No, no . . . thanks. You've been a big help. I may be regarded as the philosopher, but I'm sure you're the wiser man."

"I sincerely doubt it, but thanks. Shout if you need anything, sir."

The President was alone again. Milbury's interruption had not de-railed his musings, only heightened them.

Damn Cartwright, why can't that man stick to a published itinerary? He's got to get back and manage these last few weeks from here. Does he want to win this thing or not? Some days I wonder. He acts like he doesn't give a damn. Milbury's right.

Is it too late to dump Cartwright? What would the RNC say? Has it ever been done? O'Malley has surely turned into a liability. Dump your incumbent VP from the ticket? Impossible! The convention was just two weeks ago! Eagleton? If only O'Malley would profess to some mental disability, that is, other than what's already obvious. If anyone ever needed shock therapy, it's him.

Dump Cartwright. How the Post would have a field day with that! But, maybe now, bad publicity would be better than none at all. Dump Cartwright. It would look too desperate, send the wrong signal. Dump Cartwright. It's got a really good ring to it. I need to make a change, maybe that's it. Dump Cartwright.

President Williams was more perplexed than angry. His world was upside down, and there was no Atlas to right it. This man of wisdom and ideas was adrift, entrapped in an action age which has no time for philosophers. He lived in a time that scorned and ridiculed its do-gooders. The Digital Age had no time for thinkers.

Throughout a summer of rudderless campaigning, President Williams had grown tired. Never having had a temper, now one surfaced. And his anger was like a new pair of shoes bought too small. There was not only physical discomfort, but self-criticism and resentment, too. His undirected, diffused anger was unsettling, but oddly, it felt constructive.

3

Harwood's call left the Senator more bemused than concerned. Visits like these were hardly unheard of: the air attack on Libya, the Panama Canal "initiative", the Yugoslavia bombing, Afghanistan . . . too many to recall. Something's breaking, he thought, probably in the Middle East. That made the most sense. And the President, as a courtesy, was informing key members of the Foreign Relations Committee.

Yes, he had seen this many times. The White House sent a staffer over to meet personally with the Committee members. But he had never heard of this Harwood before . . . it would be highly unusual to send a junior staff member. The Senator's interest was piqued.

Any Senator with a couple of terms under his belt understood the protocol: a smart, young, West Wing staffer, with a thousand-page thesis and a couple of scholarly articles in print—maybe even a stint at the Carter Center under his belt—would show up. He'd cover the background information in copious detail, and inform the Senator of what had already been done without consulting Congress—then explain that everyone in the administration was on board—the Defense Secretary, CIA Director, National Security Administration, etc. The White House would not ask the Committee's advice or seek its permission. They would assume the high ground, and politely inform Congress of what had to be done. Inevitably, they'd call it a "conflict", not a "war." Still, the Senator wondered why they hadn't sent a car for him. Why was this Harwood walking up the hill?

Whatever it was tonight, as Chairman of the Committee, the Senator might have expected a telephone call from the President himself, or at least from Charles Whittingham, the President's Chief of Staff.

Rec Calvin chuckled to himself. The President was obviously desperate. With eight weeks to go to Election Day, the timing was perfect for the Administration to manufacture an international incident. Bomb something, settle something. Make war, bring peace. Wag the dog, throw some smart bombs into downtown Kabul. Get some positive press for a change. Stop thinking, start acting, shine now, and do it quickly. Capture the momentum, rather than fade away after a single term.

But even a healthy dose of old fashioned Republican shoot 'em up Jingoism wouldn't help the President now. Countdown . . . fifty days . . . forty-nine. Only a miracle would bail Williams out now, and the Lord wasn't going to dispense any favors for the Republicans this year. If Williams was sending up prayers, they were surely going unanswered.

The Mississippi Senator mused on Harwood. Maybe his name was vaguely familiar . . . a junior staffer, a wannabe, another Pennsylvania Avenue-techie-drone?

After brief reflection, considering that this Harwood fellow was the emissary, the Senator concluded that the meeting was even more perfunctory than he might have originally surmised.

He was wrong.

4

The tuxedoed maitre d' held the chair and Cartwright dropped into his seat. The table was as instructed, discreetly separate.

Though they had not met here for a couple of months, Bernard Cartwright luxuriated in Denver's Petroleum Club. He loved the good life and for him the Petroleum Club symbolized it: fine art, crisp white tablecloths, rich wines, and richer people. And, while being eight points behind in the polls wasn't some people's idea of "the good life", he could now enjoy a couple of hours of comfort at this oasis away from Washington. And maybe a special dividend.

Here, Cartwright was, for a few golden hours, unreachable. The growing campaign debacle could be set aside. His driver would wait on Sixteenth Street, read the Denver Post twice through, and sleep. His pilot, copilot, and assistant would nap at jetCenter's pilot lounge. And Cartwright would make the necessary moves to appear to be working hard at raising campaign funds from the wealthiest Republican donor in the country. He was not a man at peace, but on this stop from his Western tour, he would pretend for a fleeting moment. That would have to do.

He pushed his nose deep into his glass, breathed deeply, exhaled, and took his first taste of the Caymus '85 Cabernet, which, like his host, had been at the table awaiting his arrival. Cartwright loved this wine. He *thought* he liked its taste, but he *knew* that it was $275 on the Petroleum Club wine list. He approached this dinner with a combination of trepidation, lust, and curiosity. After a taste of wine, he leaned back in his chair and sighed.

Across the table sat, silently, Chris Weiner, his host. They had normally been careful enough to meet privately, but tonight Weiner had refused.

When Weiner was elected to The Club, it was an historical triple first:

the first Los Angeles resident, the first *nouveau riche*, and the first woman. God, how beautiful this woman was, and how the old-timers hated the *nouveau riche*, Cartwright thought. Oh, how they hated accepting a non-Denver, non-Colorado native, a Beverly Hills resident of all things, one who had the gall to make the oxymoronic claim of an L.A. home and being class and society, as well.

Her admission to The Club spawned the resignations of nearly thirty members. However, as a local society columnist cracked at the time, those who quit were all white Protestant men over eighty who had lost most of their oil money. And, anyway, most of them would have "resigned" from The Club pretty soon, that is, at their Maker's request, not any sort of "voluntary resignation." He turned the knife with, "A resignation from The Club with a simultaneous resignation from the temporal world."

And, after all, Weiner owned the skyscraper where The Club was ensconced on the top floor, and she was convinced, not without merit, that her being The Club's landlord accorded clout. She had purchased the building out of Chapter Seven, before the members knew the trustee was even considering a deal. They were both frothing with fury and pathetically helpless.

Today, the Petroleum Club was not The Club of forty-two-dollar-a-barrel oil, but of twenty-dollar oil; of the new reality of the oil business, where government had ceased to dispense like candy whopping tax benefits for solar and wind power, leaving those technologies to, as it were, twist slowly in the wind. So, the *nouveau riche*, however distasteful the experience, must be dealt with. And, as Chris Weiner, a second generation business child parroting her father's words, often had said, "I may be nouveau, but at least I'm plenty god damn riche!"

Weiner worked hard for her father, the founder of Weiner Oil and Exploration. She was an only child, but not a pampered one. She knew the oil business and she was tougher than a diamond drill bit. She had worked on the rigs in West Texas and the Gulf, and managed his exploration and engineering departments. At the River and Bohemian Clubs, she had argued the fallacies related to the capital intensity of vertically integrated distribution with the chairmen of Mobil and Shell. With a degree in petroleum engineering from the University of Texas, summa cum laude, and as a Baker Scholar MBA from

Harvard, she soon became the Weiner Companies' chief strategist.

Weiner was every bit as accomplished technically as she was in the field. Working with Luke Ristorek, a young Berkeley drilling engineer, she had taken to heart the work of Vincken and Anderson, and invented drilling processes that altered the cost dynamics of the entire industry. To the shock of old drilling hands, her research and development work demolished the prevailing wisdom on constant rock stress and constant penetration rate drilling. Her refinements of constant cutting performance theory, or CCP, resulted in radical new drill bit designs, garnering her eight patents, and cutting by twenty-five percent the time spent rotating on bottom and tripping in and out of hole.

Moreover, Weiner was a globalist, an acknowledged expert in international economics and geo-politics. She was the equal of—probably superior to—any man who ever pulled on a pair of boots. And she knew it.

In 1980, when her father died, the spot price of Texas crude was twenty-two dollars a barrel. She was his sole heir. Within six months, the price had risen to over thirty dollars. For several years, she had, as the Texas rig hands would say, "suspicioned" the relative price of oil, believing, if viscerally, that oil was not intrinsically worth its current price. Her increasing anxiety drove her already manic desire for success and money—and long weekends immersed in studying strategic supply and demand relationships of the business.

She delved into geo-history and analyzed the religious fervor of the Saud family. She read and re-read the Koran for insights into the stability of the Middle East producers. Within a few minutes, her assistant could rouse the Secretary of Energy—at any hour of the day or night.

Finally, when her mind was nearly made up, she arranged to meet with Marvin Davis and Harvard's Cromwell Crum. One hot day, her jet struggled out of the thin summer air of Aspen and flew to Cambridge. After the meeting with Crum, she re-crossed the country for dinner with Davis in L.A.

Then, late that night, she unequivocally reached two simple conclusions: one, that both of these men were absolutely brilliant thinkers; and, two, that she would immediately liquefy the entirety of her oil holdings.

It was reported that, including joint ventures, overrides, participations, and partnerships, Weiner controlled seventy-million barrels of oil, though the secrecy of her organization precluded any high-confidence estimates. Six months and sixty-million in fees to CSFB and Goldman Sachs later, the Weiner family holdings, which had taken her father more than fifty years to establish, were liquidated and converted into nearly two and one- half billion dollars in cash, at an average price of thirty-four dollars and fifty cents a barrel. The prestigious Oil Trader Monthly was to remark later that the Weiner disposition was the sole industry example of perfect timing.

Chris Weiner was the first businesswoman to be on the front of Time Magazine above the caption "Ingenious or Insane? Wonder Woman Weiner Cashes Out!" The IRS delighted at the receipt of capital gain taxes totaling over three-hundred million dollars.

In 1988, after seven years on the sidelines, she moved again. Oil prices crashed, dropping over fifty percent from their 1981 peak. After the payment of another twenty million in legal and investment banking fees, Weiner bought back most of her family's holdings for five-hundred million dollars. Not bad, was the dry retort throughout the oil patch: nearly two billion in cash, net after taxes, and she still had her original properties.

Then, as if to prove to the world that her fortune was the result of consummate skill rather than some sort of transcendent luck, she reprised her performance of the Eighties. This time, the headlines of Forbes, Fortune, and the Journal trumpeted, "The Second Time Around", "Dual Fool", and "Cash Lass." In twenty-four months, she had sold her properties again, this time to Awahnee Oil, at an average price of twenty-one dollars a barrel. Awahnee paid with the proceeds of a four-billion-dollar junk convertible bond issue that was in default by the middle of 1994. With spot prices at $15, Weiner then tendered for the convertibles, engineering a take-over that left her back in control of over three-hundred million barrels.

Despite her financial engineering brilliance, above all, her passion was in the ground. Though Weiner Oil had good marketing and distribution, she had always, as she put it, "loved being in the dirt" . . . drilling for oil.

"There's nothing like digging a hole in a nice piece of ground. Maybe there's something in there, maybe not. If you're smarter than the next guy, there'll be something in the hole you've dug. If you don't like what's in there, you fill it in and move on. But knowing that you've got something special down there in the ground . . . well, there's no other feeling like it."

At the age of thirty-seven, Chris Weiner had assured her longevity, if not permanence, in the Forbes 400. And as a woman, younger than Gates and a lot younger than Buffett, she was all the more unique. Her social aggressiveness was more Trump-like than Buffet-like or Gates-like. Mostly, she possessed enormous wealth and power. And, perhaps not unlike either Gates or Buffet, but certainly less subtly, Weiner wanted that wealth and power to make things happen for her.

She had not always been a political activist, but by this point in her life, as if incurably infected by the unfathomable dimensions of her personal wealth, she had evolved intense political goals. At least she represented them as political goals. Whatever her motivation and accompanying emotions, if they were not always consistent or rational, they were always intense.

Cartwright finished his first glass of wine before he and Weiner had exchanged a dozen sentences. He felt the glow that even this little alcohol imparted to his aching body. His dinner partner was, as usual, brooding and contemplative.

As the waiter began to refill his glass, the maitre d' returned to the table, handing him a small envelope with the Petroleum Club seal embossed on the flap, his name written in calligraphy on the front. Weiner silently noted the Club's motto, three Latin words: *Gubernatio, Divitiae, Integritas*: Leadership, Wealth, Integrity. Well, one out of three ain't bad, she mused.

Cartwright tore the envelope open, read the note, and audibly gasped.

"What is it, Bernie?"

"It's the President. He wants me back . . . tonight. Something is really wrong."

"You'd better call right now."

"How the hell did he find me?"

Weiner taunted, "For Christ's sake, Bernie, he's the President! What do you mean, how did he find you? You're absolutely losing it. And everything I see tells me that we are absolutely losing this race . . . and ten million of my money."

"Nine million, Chris."

"Nine million, then. Soft money, hard money . . . who cares? For that price you'd just better deliver on things, Bernie. I want this election won, but mostly I want to be certain that our Mr. Vice President O'Malley will follow through on our deal. I've made a very . . . very big investment in him. He'd better not let us down."

"Look, Chris, we've been over this a thousand times."

"You look, Bernie! Let me put it to you straight," Weiner corrected. "In the first campaign, you had it easy. Williams was swept into office by people who wanted a change, a breath of fresh air. Plus, the Democrats nearly self-destructed. Hell, they shot themselves in the foot every time they possibly could. They didn't know what to do with a man like Williams. Now, he's hardly an adroit politician, but he gets things done by the force of his character, God forbid. But that's as far as it goes. Yeah, he's a great guy . . . la dee dah . . . the outsider, the former professor, using big words and expressing deep thoughts . . . la dee fucking dah. This year, you're in the shit, Bernie. You are over your head, and Governor Moore is a power to be reckoned with. The Democrats want this bad, they've got a strong candidate in Moore, and they are taking no prisoners. They started chipping away at Williams this summer . . . now they're taking big chunks out of him, and he doesn't know how to respond. Your precious campaign is not only stalled, it's in reverse. And the only ones who seem to be missing the point are the two most important people, you and Williams."

"It's not that bad, Chris."

"Would you kindly shut up, and let me finish? Now, even though I've got a lot invested in Williams and the Republicans, I really don't care if he gets thrown out or not. I've got a lot invested with the Democrats too, so I'm covered. But, I am not, I repeat not, covered on this tax legislation initiative of mine. I have to have action on that. You need to make this casino thing happen . . . and happen fast. Do you hear me?"

"First, O'Malley's the same stupid Mick he was when he was a freshman in Congress . . . the intelligence of a potato and the morals of a snake . . . or is it the intelligence of a snake and the morals of a potato? Either way, it's a great combination! We may've even overpaid him and his contacts on the Hill. Don't worry, he'll deliver. If nothing else, he understands that political deals are broken only at, how shall I put it, great personal expense."

"Well, you tell O'Malley that if he doesn't come through on that tax, we'll go to those shamrock cronies of his across the pond . . . and sic them on him!"

"Chris, we agreed not to bring O'Malley's 'foreign friends' into this."

"Right now, nobody gets left out of this, Bernie. Now, you'd better call your boss. I'm worried."

"Chris, stop worrying, we're covered." Cartwright's tone suddenly softened. He folded the phone message, unconsciously placed it in his shirt pocket, and leaned slowly forward, lowering his eyes. "Are we going to have time for a little extra activity tonight?"

Cartwright stared at Weiner's décolleté, fantasizing how she dressed tonight. Her routine: the sheer black bikini panties; the black, front-hook demi-bra, just thin enough that he could see her erect nipples forming a distinct outline through her diaphanous dress; black hose and black heels; finished with a massive diamond necklace and earrings. Cartwright fidgeted and waited for an answer, squirming in his chair like a schoolboy fighting an erection at the class bell.

Weiner's only acknowledgment was to arch her back and pull her shoulders back, making her breasts even more prominent. She touched her top lip with her tongue, responding implacably, "You'd better call your boss, Bernie. We're here on business tonight, serious business."

Cartwright pushed his chair from the table and stood.

"I could be here for a couple of more hours, Chris. It's been quite a while."

Weiner continued to ignore Cartwright's adolescent supplications, while feigning desire. "Soon though . . . I want you in me real soon." Then, abandoning any trace of subtlety, she leaned forward so that her cleavage was even more visible, slowly wet her lips again, and whispered, "Call your boss, Bernie. You don't want to keep the President waiting."

Cartwright walked past the maitre d's rostrum, nodded mechanically, stepped into one of the private phone booths, and dialed. He waited to be transferred twice and then gave the White House operator his security code.

"Can you hold, Mr. Cartwright?"

"Yes, of course I can hold," he responded with some agitation. There were a couple of audible clicks, and Cartwright passed the moment worrying about his situation. Before he could marshal any more anxiety, President Williams came on the line.

"Bernie, what are you doing in Denver?"

"I'm on my way back from the California State campaign meeting which, by the way, went very well. We're really cooking in California, sir."

"I hope so." The President was clearly peeved. "After all, it's my home state. If we were behind there, I'd really be worried."

"We're not taking anything for granted . . . we're pulling out all the stops."

"So . . . what about Denver?"

"I stopped here to have dinner with Chris Weiner, sir."

"Weiner's awfully slick for me, Bernie. Be careful."

"With all due respect, Mr. President, she's our largest contributor. All told, through her PACs, arm-twisting, and other relationships I can't discuss, she's been responsible for about five million."

"Well, I appreciate that, Bernie, but I don't like that 'other relationships I can't discuss' kind of talk. We've been over this before. Everything we do has to be on the up and up . . . completely so . . . nothing gray."

"Yes, sir, absolutely."

"Now, you've got a lot more to do than court a single contributor who is already doing the most she can. We need to spend time planning the final push. And, you need to stay in better touch, too."

"Yes, Mr. President, I know. But things have really kept me going."

The Philosopher's patience was wearing thin. "Listen, Bernie, I want you back here tonight. I want to convene an all-hands meeting first thing tomorrow."

"It's already eleven there, sir. I've filed a flight plan to leave here at six a.m. I can be in your office before noon tomorrow."

The President was uncharacteristically short. "I know what your flight plan is. Now, please get your team together for a comprehensive campaign strategy review."

Son of a bitch, why do I keep underestimating this man, Cartwright thought.

The President reflected briefly on his meeting with Stanley Harwood and Harwood's challenge. "Look, Bernie," the President directed, "contact your staff while you're in the air, and come straight here to start getting the meeting organized."

"Yes, sir, on my way." Cartwright held the receiver to his ear until he heard a distinct click and the dial tone following the disconnect. Then he allowed himself to curse out loud in the privacy of the carpeted booth. "Shit!" he spat.

As he stomped past the maitre d', a waiter with a white napkin folded over his arm asked, "Is everything alright, Mr. Cartwright?"

Cartwright, mute, glared, turned, and marched back to the table. Chris Weiner was sitting as he had left her, the level in her wineglass unchanged. She stared at him with an unemotional gaze. Without sitting down, Cartwright lifted his glass and gulped down half.

"I'm afraid I have to get back, Chris."

"Sorry you can't stay, Bernie. The waiter says the osso bucco is fabulous."

From her matter-of-fact tone, Cartwright could not tell if Weiner was teasing him or not, making him even more uncomfortable than his brief talk with the President.

Weiner continued, "The President must have something pretty important if he needs you back in Washington in the middle of the night," she added.

"No problem, Chris. It's just getting close and we've probably gotten some new polling numbers."

"If that's true, which I sincerely doubt, then the numbers are not good."

Weiner's tongue crossed slowly across her upper lip, paused at the corner of her mouth, then moved to the lower lip, her mouth half parted. She looked down at the table and reached for her wineglass, took a sip, and looked back up at Bernard Cartwright. Her voice was level and controlled, but her eyes squinted, reflecting anger welling inside her.

"I am really worried, Bernie. You cannot let this thing slip away. Jesus, it's September, and instead of improving, it's looking worse every week. And I don't get the sense you're feeling good about it, either. You have got to get a hold of this thing. Get with O'Malley as soon as you get back. I want to have a detailed plan of where we're going from here on out. Quick. Don't screw this up, Bernie."

Cartwright, still standing across the table from Weiner, shifted from foot to foot.

"Don't worry, Chris, we've got a lot working. Timing is everything. O'Malley's coming back in New England and the First Lady is hitting the bricks for the women's vote. And we're getting some new endorsements from Hollywood. Just wait'll you see. We got three rap stars just about to come on board. When they come over, the numbers on the kids and the blacks are going to totally turn around."

"Yeah, Bernie. Big turnout: kids, blacks, and rap stars!" Chris Weiner's fury moved to disgust. She had been hearing this litany for too long. Just wait, just wait, it'll be great, blah, blah, blah. "SOS, Bernie. Same old shit."

Weiner looked down, poked at her shrimp cocktail, and dabbed a huge shrimp into the cocktail sauce in the middle of her gold trimmed hors d'oeuvre plate. She held the skewered shrimp above her plate, then pointed it at Cartwright, ignoring the thick red sauce dripping onto the white tablecloth. "Your driver's waiting, Bernie."

"Look, Chris, it may be an hour before I leave. Let's just stop off at your hotel for a little, uh, personal time."

Weiner's voice was transformed. Now came a different tone, sweet and lustful. "Oh, Bernie, you know I love the way you do it to me. But we can't keep the President waiting, can we?" She slowly sucked the shrimp from its little fork and, more slowly, chewed it. "Bye Bernie," she said.

5

As he reached the eight stone steps up to Senator Calvin's front door, Stan Harwood checked his watch. He had measured the distance carefully, the twelve hundred plus strides, but neglected to consider the uphill walk, costing him half a minute more than he had calculated.

Standing on the sidewalk of diagonally-laid bricks, he paused to inspect the house again . . . the freshly painted iron handrails, their curves ending at matching quaint, obsolete bootscrapes; the worn brick at the first floor bearing vestiges of where ivy had been pulled away; the dark green shutters and coach lamps; the width of the house—double or triple that of surrounding ones—so that the residence was more mansion than townhouse.

Pulling his necktie tight, he wiped the corners of his mouth, took a deep breath, and firmly pushed the brass doorbell. Ellie greeted Harwood politely, and ushered him through the foyer to the library at the foot of the marble stairs.

"Make yourself comfortable, Mr. Harwood. Senator Calvin will be right with you." She excused herself and softly closed the library door. He was glad to have a moment alone. For the middle of September, it was unseasonably warm in Washington, and a patina of sweat covered his brow. Also, he appreciated having a couple of minutes to study the room.

Harwood wouldn't surprise Rec Calvin in one respect: he was young. His aquiline nose somehow contradicted his otherwise preppy good looks and tousled blond hair. His suit was custom made, set off by tailored buttonholes, English style shaping to the jacket, and pleated trousers. His tie was Hermes and his shirt was tapered and discreetly monogrammed in a pastel color. This was clearly not a typical Foggy Bottom bureaucrat in a three hundred-dollar department store suit. A lean frame and a leaner look complemented Harwood's sartorial aspect.

He was more calm and composed than would be expected, given the import of the moment. The nature of the offer he was to make tonight would make even the oldest Washington hands jittery. But, it never occurred to Harwood that others would be nervous. He knew he was the expert. He designed the plan, he knew it would work. And, he knew it was the right thing to do.

Harwood absorbed the surroundings. This was definitely the library of a Lodge, an Astor, a Phipps, or at least fashioned to look that way. It was hard to believe that Senator Calvin was a Catholic, Harwood thought. This library shouted Episcopalian, or better yet, Anglican: rich, oiled wood, not the veneer crap of modern builder's "dream" houses. Solid walnut.

He noted the leather bound classics, not too neatly lined on the shelves, disarranged just enough to impart the impression of use. Overstuffed leather chairs, carefully well worn. Fox hunting prints. A photograph of the Senator with a group of camouflage-dressed, gray-haired men, probably corporate lobbyists, on a hunting trip, their bounty spread on the ground in front of the first row of kneeling men. An oil painting of a presumed ancestor in a dark blue suit. Beneath his feet, Harwood considered the huge Tabriz, slightly faded with the look of genteel, careful use. The rug had that "this was left in my grandmother's will . . . it's been in the family for generations" look. The entire library was obviously the work of a professional decorator, but very effective, Harwood thought. He took a final look around, sat down, and waited.

The Senator had done very well, he thought. And he was about to do a lot better.

6

When House Speaker Henry Berkhardt rapped on the door of room 617 of the Grant Hotel, the men had been waiting for almost two hours. Nick opened the door, while Willie jumped to his feet as the Speaker entered.

"Welcome, Mr. Speaker. Thanks for coming over," Willie cried. Shaking hands with Berkhardt, Willie introduced himself as Roger Crespo. "And this is my associate, Joseph Taylor."

As a seasoned politician, Berkhardt had seen every ilk of lobbyist, but these men seemed less sophisticated than most, their rough edges immediately apparent in their thick New York accents and cheap suits. It takes all kinds, the Speaker thought.

"Glad to meet you, gentlemen."

"Good to meet you too, sir. Before we get started, can I fix you a drink?"

"No thanks, I'll just have a bottled water, if you've got one."

"Too early, Mr. Speaker?" asked Willie, though he knew the answer. "How about a grapefruit juice? No water, I'm afraid."

"That's fine, Mr. Crespo. I understand you're representing people interested in some of my proposed legislation."

Handing the Speaker his glass of juice, Willie replied, "Yes sir, and I'm sorry we had to be so careful about this. Our client insists on keeping a low profile until we've gotten a little further down the road. He's got concerns about publicity and, because of the amount of money he's got, his personal safety, too."

"I'm accustomed to working with lobbyists and family advisors. And lots of times, I need the confidentiality, as well. So, tell me something about your plans."

"Well, Mr. Speaker, our client—a family from the Seattle area . . . Microsoft money—is interested in a couple of different areas. They originally hired us to look into how they could put their money to work in the area of water rights, particularly the issues with river damming and salmon restoration. But after researching some of your work, they're interested in supporting the repurchase of sacred Indian lands held by the Federal government."

"That's wonderful, gentlemen. These efforts take a combination of activism, vision and—I'm afraid it's reality—lots of money."

"Well, that's what we're here for, sir," Willie responded enthusiastically.

Willie and Nick studied the Speaker, carefully observing how, after only a few sips of juice, his speech slowed, and his head nodded, ever so slightly.

"Let me freshen that up for you," Nick insisted, as he grabbed Berkhardt's glass, walked across the room, secretly adding more clear liquid before pouring more juice.

As the Speaker rambled about pet legislation, the men mechanically offered a series of "uh huhs' and "yes sirs," until Berkhardt had consumed his second glass.

After a half-hour of drinking, the Speaker slumped and prattled on about the travails of being Speaker of the House. Another thirty minutes later, Willie said to his partner, "I think we're there, little buddy!" Then, turning to the Speaker, he said, "Let's go for a little walk, shall we, Congressman Berkhardt?"

The Speaker mumbled incoherently, as Willie pulled him to his feet. "Wipe the prints, Nick. Just the places we touched."

As Willie held the Speaker in a standing position, his little partner hustled around the room, selectively wiping the only spots where the men had previously agreed to place their hands. When his chore was complete, he rushed to help Willie support the Speaker. Holding a handkerchief, he opened the hotel door and glanced over his shoulder for a last check of the room. Then the men half-dragged Berkhardt out of the room, down the hall and, after a brief wait for the elevator, descended to the basement parking level.

"Help me get him in, Nick!"

The men struggled the limp body of the Speaker into the back of a van. "Let's go," Willie cried. "I'll follow you . . . no illegal turns, no speeding!

Just follow the route we laid out . . . I'll be right behind you."

Nick jumped behind the wheel of the van, as Willie unlocked the Speaker's car, climbed in, and started it up. As the van rolled cautiously up the parking ramp and turned left onto the street, Willie stayed close behind.

A block from their destination, Willie left Berkhardt's car in a "No Parking—Tow Away" zone, made sure that it was left unlocked, and strode methodically toward the club where Nick waited by the side door.

"Okay, unlock the door," Willie directed. It took only seconds for Nick to unlock the club's side door and return to the van. Immediately, the two men pulled their prey from the van, and carried him—upright, their shoulders propping Berkhardt—up the back stairs to the club's third floor gym.

"Whew, he's heavy," Nick complained.

Without a further word, they lay him down outside the sauna. Nick stripped the Congressman, while Willie moved to the sauna's controls, cranking up the heat to the maximum.

"You got the tube and stuff?"

"Yeah," answered Nick, pulling from his pocket a long plastic tube and a plastic bag. After having knelt over Berkhardt to get his shirt and undershorts off, Nick quickly stood, unzipped his pants, and urinated into the plastic bag. Peeing, he looked over his shoulder to see his partner manipulating the sauna controls. "How're we doing on time, Willie?"

"Good. Just get your stuff done and let's get out of here!"

While Nick drained the Speaker's bladder and made the swap, Willie folded Berkhardt's clothes, every few seconds glancing around to assure that no one was coming. "You pretty close to done?"

"Got it! Now help me lift him in."

Willie picked up the Speaker's shoulders and the men dragged him into the already-hot sauna. "Lay him down easy, and let's blow."

With Berkhardt on the sauna floor, the men closed the door and retreated quickly to the stairwell, ran down, and raced to the van.

Once underway, Nick removed the beard, moustache, and hat. "Whew," he cried, "that sauna was hot, man!"

"Yeah," replied Willie with a broad grin, "just right for our recipe. Now, let's ditch this stuff and call the wicked witch of the west!"

7

A presidential re-election campaign staff meeting was an important event, especially when every poll confirmed a week by week deterioration. Bernard Cartwright assumed his place at the end of the table opposite the slide projector. He was characteristically late, his lateness underscoring his importance. Cartwright craved importance, especially self-importance.

Roger Bensalem, Deputy Campaign Manager, was at Cartwright's elbow. Twenty others were in the room, its walls festooned with four-color charts and graphs, all awaiting Cartwright's arrival. Stanley Harwood, in no way prominent, was frequently invited to attend these sessions as one of a group of 'issue experts'.

Bensalem was a professor of mathematics, specifically statistical methods, at Princeton. He had done independent consulting before Cartwright recruited him to join the campaign team full time. That he held a Ph.D. and a tenured professorship was immediately obvious to anyone who had the slightest contact with him. Bensalem had absolutely no understanding of the emotions that drove voters to make choices: love, hate, fear, respect, trust. He did not know how to speak, he knew only how to lecture. A Fine Hall colleague once remarked that "Roger is not even close to the smartest person that ever trod Washington Road, but he is surely the ditziest." And, as another professor observed, "Given the concentration of intellectualism here, to be far from the smartest is hardly an insult. But when you're characterized as the ditziest, now that's something!" At least once, predictably, before each meeting ended, Bensalem would parade and pontificate, thumbs hooked in his braces, "If it can be measured, it can be managed."

Bensalem's detached arrogance made Stanley Harwood want to vomit. Harwood acknowledged that the quantitative approach was a critical part of any campaign. Information was powerful, and to ignore it would be suicidal. But he had seen Bensalem's influence gradually increase, and now the entire campaign was based on printouts of numbers carried to the fourth decimal place.

Cartwright, titular chairman of the meeting, flipped through a four-inch-thick three-ring binder, one of which, embossed with the words "Over The Top", was placed in front of everyone at the meeting. "Over the Top" was the new campaign slogan, concocted by a media consultant who earned $250,000 for the assignment. Everyone sat silently until Cartwright was ready.

"Roger, let's begin with you. Give us an update on where we are."

"Okay, Mr. Cartwright," Bensalem began, "we'll start with the new twelve week post-convention layout. As everyone knows, we've got to make some changes to close the gap by D-day. There's a lot of ground to take, and the bullets are going to be flying."

God, how that man loved military metaphors, Harwood thought . . . a mile wide and an inch deep . . . or, more accurately, an inch wide and an inch deep.

"Our analysis indicates that the President should spend fifty-five percent of his time in the South, thirty-five percent in New England, and ten percent in the Great Lakes States," Bensalem reported. "The numbers tell us that California and most of the Rockies still look good, so we'll ignore them from here on out."

Louis Crawford, the President's Deputy Appointments Secretary, attended for Jim Blunt, his boss. He interrupted, "Does the President know he's not going West again for the balance of the campaign? He's stated publicly that he'd go back out there, and the press will pick up on that for sure. He's on record in California that he'll meet with the Governor for a 'town meeting' in L.A. And, recent polls in the L.A. Times show that Hispanic vote is moving toward Moore."

Bernie Cartwright's impatience and intensity were always near the surface, and today was no exception. "Louis, we've been over this with Jim. First, our analysis shows that it's ridiculous to have the President spend any additional time in his home state. Those electoral votes are in the bag. Plus, this schedule has been thoroughly reviewed by both Bensalem and Pruitt & Associates, our consultants. Obviously, we understand the Hispanic situation in Southern California, but even if we split them, they're not going to have a big enough impact to overcome the President's Bay Area votes. From Half Moon Bay to Yreka, everybody loves Williams."

Then Cartwright added with obvious irritation, "If I'm going to manage this campaign, as my title and responsibility imply, then please, Louis, let's get on board and work as a team."

Get on board and work as a team. Harwood winced. The group, by this point, had heard it too many times. These were Cartwright's code words for "do it my way or else."

Harwood audited the session from his quiet corner, away from the charts and stacks of printouts, trying to be as inconspicuous as possible. The turnover in this campaign had been horrendous, he thought. Half of these people weren't even here eight weeks ago. This campaign has no roadmap, no consistency. Not to mention no vision, or energy. Hollow. The campaign management team is a joke. God, what if Williams saw this charade first-hand? What a disillusionment that would be!

A question from Tony Marpis: "Is O'Malley going to be redirected? I mean, he's been in Boston twice in the last ten days. Do we really need him to keep going back up there? Our folks in Texas are begging for him to get down there, quail hunt, and speak to the Independent Drillers Association convention in Fort Worth on the 18th."

One of Bensalem's assistants, Gretchen Collier, whose full time responsibility, it seemed, was acting as O'Malley's apologist, replied, "We're still reviewing the Vice President's schedule. He's pretty committed already, and the guy is wearing out. I don't know anything about this Texas request, but I don't see how he can do it."

Right, Harwood thought, O'Malley wearing out. The guy is running for Vice President of the world's most powerful nation, and he's wearing out with more than two months to go. He's wearing out all right . . . from too much single-malt from his stock of individually numbered Coleraine. Get O'Malley out to a Texas quail hunt! Great idea . . . O'Malley in field pants. Right! Loaded shotguns and Bushmills make a nice combination. Anyway, to get a 12 gauge into that guy's hands, they'll have to crowbar a highball glass out first.

After much babble over strategy and scheduling, Cartwright suddenly raised his voice to get the attention of the attendees, who had broken down into a number of side conversations. "Alright, listen up, everybody! Roger, Tony, Gretchen . . . see me right after the meeting, and I'll make the decision which way we'll go."

Stanley Harwood was gratified that Cartwright would attempt a decision, probably his first in weeks. But he knew that whatever the decision, it would likely be the wrong one. At this point, Williams' campaign chairman was too ignorant of the day-to-day details of his own campaign debacle, too superior for this group of campaign drones and their mundane, tactical issues. Harwood had seen Cartwright transformed—in fact, debased—from esteemed Wall Street attorney to the blustering, intimidating egotist that was running this meeting.

It was uncomfortable, even tragic. Cartwright came to Washington perhaps already susceptible to the afflictions that this city wreaks upon its so-called political mavens. Perhaps he resisted, perhaps he was helpless. As Harwood watched the meeting, and Cartwright's "leadership" of it, he noted that Cartwright's metamorphosis had been more rapid than most. And now, having emerged from his chrysalis, Cartwright flapped his gaudy wings of power at every chance.

Less with disgust, more with a clinical, arm's-length detachment, Harwood diagnosed Cartwright, considering the inexorable forces that rendered him so overbearing and oblivious to the situation in front of him . . . and his role in it.

I am going to have to move fast, Harwood thought. He quickly condemned himself for not getting something done before the convention. Then he forgave himself, concluding that he'd made every possible effort . . . every possible effort, save one. If I am going to move at all, I'll have to do it now. The situation is desperate.

8

As Stan Harwood sat in a red leather chair, still contemplating the Senator's environment, Rec Calvin opened the library door with a firm hand, stepped into the room, and crossed straight to Harwood who immediately rose and shook the Senator's big and friendly hand.

"Welcome Mr. Harwood. Is this a short meeting or do you have time for a drink?"

"We have time, sir, though I'm not much of a drinker. At least," he added, after a slight pause, "I hope we've got the time."

"Well, fine then, let's do it."

"Sir, before we get started, I want to say thank you for seeing me on such short notice."

Rec Calvin grinned. "Not a problem, Mr. Harwood. You said it was important and seeing people from the White House on important matters is definitely in my job description."

Calvin took four steps to a paneled wall adjacent to a huge unlit fireplace. He pushed a button, a motor subtly whirred and, in a few seconds, a fully equipped bar appeared. He reached out and picked from a set of glasses etched with the rebel mascot of University of Mississippi. "Wild Turkey? Ice?"

"I never argue with Wild Turkey, sir, and ice will be fine." Harwood turned a full circle, reexamining the library. "I love this room, sir. It's got a great feeling."

Senator Calvin spoke as he prepared the drinks. "I love this room, too, Mr. Harwood. My parents were lovers of books, especially my father. He read to me every night when I was growing up. And, if he hadn't stayed up all night, which was not at all unusual, he got up early and read for an hour before going to work. We didn't have a library quite like this, of course, but we had lots and lots of books. My father worshipped books. He bought them whenever he could and lots of folks gave them to him, especially when word got around about how much our family read. My father used to tell me and my brothers and sisters that every secret of the world is contained in books, if you can only find the right ones."

"That man," Calvin continued, "I guess like a lot of fathers, worked long and hard for his family, dawn to dark. It's a lot easier to be successful when you've got models like that. How could I fail with such loving, hard-working parents! That's what's missing today . . . fathers that stay home, work hard, nurture and mold their offspring."

The Senator halted his reminiscence, faced toward a wall of books, and turned his head, seemingly surprised at the magnitude and glory of the mass of leather-bound, gold-embossed volumes on the shelves. He sighed.

Harwood used the moment to second the Senator's sentiments. "Yes sir. A hard-working and loving father creates a great path to walk down."

Senator Calvin held a sterling silver serving spoon, undoubtedly engraved and a gift from some grateful constituent, Harwood thought. He spooned a few ice cubes into a tumbler, the distinctive clink resonating for a moment, then dying in the books, upholstered furniture, and Persian rug.

"Yes," he continued, nostalgic, but nevertheless comfortable with his personal reflections, "my father was a man of great sophistication and grace, but he was one hard worker. And hard as he worked, sometimes, when he should have been deep asleep, I'd get up, a scared little kid in the middle of the night, and I'd leave my room and find him reading by candlelight. Literally, by candlelight! Like Abe Lincoln or somebody. He read the Bible more than anything . . . Lord, how he loved reading the book of Matthew . . . and Greek myths, the dictionary, Thucydides, Paine, Sandburg's biography of Lincoln . . . he read anything and everything. I remember one time asking him if he really knew all those big words in a book he was reading. He grinned at me and said, 'Sure, and if not, I can usually figure them out.' Well sir, when I got scared in the middle of the night, I'd just crawl up into his lap with my blanket, and he'd read softly to me until I fell back asleep. Then he'd take me back and put me to bed, and go back to his reading."

The Senator looked down into his glass, swirled his whiskey, and continued. "This library means a lot more to me than the physical presence of the books here."

He closed his eyes, as if to savor the recollection, then turned toward Harwood with a sudden look of self-consciousness at having shared such a personal moment with a stranger. Harwood did not respond.

Calvin stood for a moment behind a tall leather chair, then walked to Harwood, and handed him one of the crystal tumblers. After his brief foray into the personal, Harwood noticed, it took the Senator a few moments to recover his professional demeanor.

Harwood broke the silence with a comment on the tumbler's Ole Miss seal. "This is an attractive set of glasses, sir. I'm sure you're proud of the University."

"I love these glasses. Home state stuff, I guess. You know, a lot of folks are angry . . . out of sorts about the rebel mascot at Ole Miss, and the Stars and Bars of the Confederacy that the white kids keep waving around. I suppose it's improper in this day and age, but I keep telling them there are more critical issues facing the University. For example, Ole Miss is the only major state university without a Phi Beta Kappa chapter. It's an insult to the school, but it's our own fault, too. That's the kind of stuff we should be focusing our energy on . . . not flags."

Calvin sensed Harwood's uneasiness about not moving on and changed the subject. "Well, Mr. Harwood, what is it this time? Let me guess: China, Israel, the Soviet Union? Damn, why do I always still call it that! It's tough to break old habits, isn't it? Make that Russia. Or maybe it's California? At this time of year, anything's possible . . . if you know what I mean."

"Yes, sir. I know exactly what you mean. It seems as though the closer we get to that Tuesday in November, the more bizarre it gets."

"Well, where's the crisis, not Mississippi, I hope?"

"No sir, not Mississippi. And none of the above, sir," replied Harwood, still deferentially waiting for his host to take an initial sip of his drink.

"What then, at this time of night?"

"First, sir, some ground rules, if you don't mind. The President has asked me to obtain your commitment that nothing disclosed here will be repeated to any party, at any time, for any reason whatsoever without his prior approval. I need your agreement before I can begin. Otherwise, the President has instructed me not to proceed. When I disclose the reason for the meeting, the request for a confidentiality agreement will become apparent."

The Senator's previously casual tone abruptly became formal. He turned slightly and, with his back to the bar, squared his broad shoulders toward his guest. "Mr. Harwood, I work hard, damned hard, at never being disrespectful of anyone, much less the President or one of his emissaries. But, Mr. Harwood, with all due respect, I do not accept 'ground rules'. This Senator from Mississippi has been serving the public interest in this town for quite a long time. Meetings have been held and deals have been made in this room that the American public, bless their hearts, will never hear about. And it would curl their hair, if they ever did. So far, my name, integrity, and reputation for discretion have served me just fine, thank you."

Harwood maintained a deadpan expression, letting the Senator catch his breath.

"You know, where I hail from," the Senator continued, "I'd have never been asked such a question in the first place. Now, if you don't trust me to know the difference between what can be repeated and what can't, you're in the wrong place to begin with. And, I might add, that that's got nothing to do with party." He added, rhetorically, but not scolding, "Is that clear, Mr. Harwood?"

There was no antagonism, no preaching in the Senator's tone. The Senator was matter-of-fact and constructive. Harwood quickly took a mental inventory, re-crunching the Senator's personal data profile through his cerebral mainframe. Reginald Calvin: winner of the Medal of Honor for bravery in the rice paddies of Vietnam, only the fourteenth winner to serve in Congress, only the fourth in Senate history. Harwood was pleased. I wouldn't have expected less from him, he thought.

9

Stanley Harwood was beyond impatience. Indeed, most considered impatience one of his virtues. That he was brilliant, an expert in legislative process, was inarguable. His driving desire to see his country well served, fueled by his own impatience, had driven him to work impossibly hard, trying to complete the first step of his mission: how to get close to the President, to speak with him alone, without causing suspicion. His efforts in vain, at least so far. Two weeks gone since the convention and, all the while, the campaign clock ticked away.

For months, there had been lots of times that Harwood would take a wall seat, sitting mute throughout interminable staff and planning meetings with the President attending, waiting for his opportunity. But before and after, expectedly, someone was always there. The President was Stanley Harwood's Holy Grail. How did one get the President of the United States alone, without Secret Service, family, or staff—ever attentive and officious—present? How had that intern done it, he thought, then grinned, quickly abandoning any ideas about thongs.

The President was always a cordial man, never effusive. He typically remembered and used the names of middle level staff when he encountered them in the office corridors or meetings. More than once Harwood had gotten a "Good morning, Harwood" from Williams when they chanced to encounter each other. But in such cases, despite the awesomeness of this proximity to power, for Harwood's purposes, an inch was a mile . . . or more like a light year. Like nuns and lawyers, the President always seemed to travel in a pack.

The plotting of the President's physical movements, foot by foot and minute by minute throughout the day, was typical of the planning and intensity which Harwood brought to every task he undertook. For most of the summer, Harwood had kept detailed notes of the President's schedule. He knew where the President was, or was going to be, as well as anyone in the White House except for Emily, the President's executive assistant; Charles Whittingham, Williams' Chief of Staff; and Bob Schmidt, White House Counsel and *de facto* Assistant Chief of Staff. To know as much as the inner circle was more than a matter of diligence and dedication, it was a product of passion.

And so, after frustrating months of fruitless design, Stanley Harwood had decided that, if he was going to turn his concept into reality, he would have to have help. He would have to take someone in with him, an ally.

At first, enlisting a partner seemed an impossible task. But the alternative was the frustrating demise of a Presidency, and a President. He considered the list of candidates. It was a short list that began and ended with Tony Battaglia.

10

At the meeting in his library, Senator Calvin would not be antagonistic toward Stanley Harwood. The Senator had learned, often the hard way, to be forthright and direct, without allowing emotion to rule his discourse. He was universally respected on the Hill for his candor and equanimity.

Rec Calvin had earned his moniker "Rec"—short for "wreck"—not because of his initials, although they served as an excellent mnemonic device during his rising political career. Rather, the nickname came from his hard charging style, first as a star football player at West Point, and then as a decorated infantry lieutenant in Vietnam. Calvin's winning touchdown run against Navy sealed his nickname with less than a minute remaining.

With Army down by four points, Calvin took a hand-off and broke through the Navy line. Only twenty yards of green grass separated Army from victory, when Calvin, who could have jogged easily into the end zone, looked to his right to see the Navy safety angling toward him. On his final play as a cadet, he cut back, to the shock of a packed stadium, and ran directly at the stunned Navy player, picking him up as a Czonka-like target. For a second, where a tackle or stumble would have cost Army the game, the fans held their collective breath. Then, the force of the impact sent a gold Navy helmet spinning down the field, Calvin walked into the end zone, and casually flicked the ball to a referee. Then, before the throng of screaming fans, half numb and half ecstatic, he knelt, crossed himself, and etched his memory into the minds of not only football followers, but a nation.

But that was a long time ago. Rec Calvin was today a controlled and patient statesman. With what most political analysts considered the safest seat in the Senate, he could afford to be. In some ways, he personally reflected the traits of the state that he represented: esteemed and easy-going. While his speech was normally toothy and clipped, Calvin often unconsciously reverted to a soft, melodious drawl, affecting speaking style more similar to that of the historical leaders of his home state. And, with his benign face, broad nose, and salt-and-pepper hair, he bore a patrician demeanor—like some folk's genteel image of the state he represented—in other ways, Calvin was fundamentally different: he was progressive, where the state of his birth, the state which he served with dedication and passion, was not.

As the Senator ended his "no rules" mini-speech, Harwood was pleased. Rec Calvin mounted his moral soapbox and when he did, Harwood knew that his plan was right on target. This was the perfect man, he thought. This plan may seem outrageous, but it wasn't. And it was going to come off. Smart people, experts in their fields, with good planning and big dreams, can do anything.

Harwood feigned a troubled expression and stroked the right side of his face nervously a couple of times, like a man checking the closeness of his shave. He knew he could not afford to capitulate too quickly without it appearing that his response was staged.

"Very well, sir," Harwood stuttered at last, "you have asked us to trust you and I will reciprocate. I hope you understand that I'm going out on a limb here, Senator."

The Senator stared at Harwood, singularly unimpressed. "I don't see any saw in my hand," he stated bluntly.

Harwood reached for his inside suit pocket, unfolded a single sheet of paper, and read from a typewritten page. He finished the six sentences in less than twenty seconds, refolded the letter, returning it to his pocket with a deliberate motion.

"That's it, sir. The President will meet with you personally, tonight if you wish, to discuss the details. You have been made a formal offer."

A man like Senator Calvin was not easily shaken, but he was visibly troubled now. He sat, momentarily disbelieving. Harwood was silently gratified that he had accurately predicted the Senator's response. It was identical to that of the President, when Harwood had originally proposed the plan.

Finally, the Senator spoke. "Is this some kind of joke, Mr. Harwood?"

Harwood sat motionless. "No sir."

"It's impossible. I'm a Democrat. Are you sure the President himself authorized you to do this?"

"First things first, sir." Harwood pulled out the letter again. "You may examine the letter, sir. It's White House stationary, bearing the President's signature. Yes, of course, you are a Democrat. The President realizes that from time to time people make poor career choices." He paused only slightly for the sarcasm to take effect. "He asked me to tell you that he's a man of forgiveness and is willing to overlook your past transgressions, specifically the one of joining the 'other' Party."

The Senator's brow furrowed. If he had understood the intended humor, which he had, he did not acknowledge it. "Help me out here Mr. Harwood. I don't know you. Are you serious?"

"I am serious, sir, deadly serious. But I must stress that first, you will have to become a Republican. That's mostly a matter of form over substance, we think. Second, and this is a matter of substance over form, you will not be asked to renounce any personal views. The President recognizes there are differences, some significant, in your respective positions. He'll ask you, when you meet, that for the sake of victory, well, we'll see if you can minimize them. But as for maintaining consistency on issues, and your integrity on matters you've stood for, we will not ask you to do any one-eighties."

The Senator fingered his glass, swirled his ice, and took a long drink. "Not that you would ask me to do so anyway, right?"

"Right," Harwood grinned.

Calvin continued, "Who else knows about this, Mr. Harwood?"

"Absolutely no one, sir. There are only three people on earth who know I am here, sir: you, the President, and me. And four, if you count your housekeeper. If you decline, this conversation will remain confidential. We'll take it to our graves, literally and figuratively. On the other hand, should you wish to move forward, then we'll mutually agree on the process. We've got some of it already planned out, but, obviously, there are lots of details, and precious little time, remaining."

"You mean to tell me that Chief of Staff Whittingham, Vice President O'Malley, and Campaign Chair Cartwright, know nothing of this?"

"Correct."

"You and the President have cooked this up without anyone else's knowledge?"

"I'm not sure if I agree with the implications of 'cooked this up', sir. It's a bit pejorative. I'm here to tell you that this is what the President wishes to do and, he is, of course, the President and the head of the Party. He can and will do it."

The Senator had been taut, coiled, and concentrated. Finally, he stretched his legs and sighed, letting the tension draw from his body.

Harwood continued, "No one knows about this and, for right now, others' consent is moot."

The Senator sought some relief from his shock by changing the subject. "What's your background Harwood? I like to know something about a man. Tell me about yourself."

"What do you have in mind, exactly?"

"School?"

"Yale undergraduate, Phi Beta Kappa. A Masters and Doctorate from Princeton. Religion and Foreign Policy, respectively, although I'm afraid I don't use the foreign policy stuff much anymore. Plus a little fellowship work at Hopkins and a little law."

"Just as I thought. Gold-plated, huh?"

"Lucky is more like it, I think . . . or blessed."

"I find the latter's usually the case," Calvin offered.

"What do you do there on Pennsylvania Avenue, Mr. Harwood?"

"Well, sir, actually I wrote my dissertation on 'Implications of Legislative Changes on Soft Money Regulation,' but that doesn't buy a burger, much less pay the rent. Basically, I coordinate legislative policy between the senior advisors at State, Defense, and the White House with the Hill."

Suddenly Calvin crossed and re-crossed his legs uncomfortably. "Will you leave that paper with me?"

"Respectfully speaking, I don't have authority to do that. Not yet, anyway. You may examine the offer, but you may not retain it, sir."

Harwood reached out, offering the document for examination. Calvin took the paper, unfolded it, and examined it closely, staring at it much longer than it would take to actually read the short paragraph. After a full minute, he refolded it and handed it back to Harwood.

"Mr. Harwood, are you prepared to make this offer to me in a manner which I can legally and formally review?"

"Yes, sir, of course. Senator, we can develop any number of ways to assure us all of a favorable outcome in this endeavor. We understand that you will need comfort, assurances, and maybe even protection."

"Protection?"

"Well, sir, there's bound to be a few folks who are, how shall I put it, disappointed by this."

"More than a few, Mr. Harwood. A lot more!"

"The President is confident," Harwood confirmed, "in fact certain, that he can provide you with everything you'll need. There's a lot to be done, and unfortunately, we don't have a lot of time. I'm sorry I can't leave you anything in writing. And, sir, I don't think you'd want that at this point either. What's more important than this written offer is what this means historically . . . the political and social significance of this."

Harwood paused momentarily for impact, then continued. "Notwithstanding whatever mistakes he's made during his first term, I think you'll agree that the President's integrity, like yours, has never been a matter of doubt."

Stanley Harwood remained professional and straightforward, if somewhat abrupt. But, his demeanor and obvious preparation served to calm the Senator, rather than make him more ill at ease. There was a legitimacy in the approach and a formality in the method that seemed to contradict the obvious absurdity of the situation.

The Senator's shoulders dropped slightly and his jaw relaxed, as he stretched further in his chair. "Yes, Mr. Harwood, I agree so far. Williams' reputation for honesty and fair play is impeccable. And he's a nice guy, to boot . . . maybe too nice to be President."

"Well, sir, it's that same sense of integrity that's brought me here tonight. You wouldn't be offered this opportunity, if not for your own integrity. This meeting is not serendipitous, Senator. To the contrary, sir, it's purposeful and substantive. This is not some political trick. This is the expression of a vision that will change the nation."

"A vision that will change the nation?"

"You don't agree?"

"Well, that's a little heavy for me at this point, I'm afraid." Rec Calvin's rural Southern upbringing taught him—the hard way—the consequences of speaking before thinking. After a long, palpable pause, he spoke, "Well then, Mr. Harwood, I don't need any more time, even if you were prepared to give me any. It's impossible. The answer is an unequivocal 'no' and you can tell that to whoever sent you."

"Yes sir." Harwood noticed a trace of wetness, a nascent bead of sweat on Calvin's forehead, but the room was hot and the Senator's face seemed to shine in the light anyway. "As I told you before, The President sent me here, and I'll tell him that. And you do have some time to think about it, sir. Not a long time, of course, but some time."

Harwood finished his sentence, but remained motionless in his chair. With a barely perceptible wrist movement, he swirled his drink, the remnants of ice generating a gentle, tinkling sound. His eyes remained fixed on Calvin, as if to deny him the momentary comfort occasioned by a glance away. On the table next to him was a small bronze sculpture of a dog. Harwood turned and touched the animal's head, affectionately, as if it were alive and real. "This statue, Senator, it's very attractive. What is it?"

"Do you bird hunt, Mr. Harwood?" Calvin was at once gratified by the change in subject and pleased to have an opportunity to expand on his love of hunting.

"Birds, sir?"

"Quail. Bobwhite. Colinas Virginianus. We call them 'birds' back home. That's a bird dog, to be more exact, it's a Grouse Ridge English Setter, the finest line of bird dogs bred by man. They don't like the Mississippi heat but, unless they're in the field for training, we keep them coddled in the air-conditioning, usually until late October."

"I'm pretty much a city boy, Senator. Is this a specific dog?" Harwood asked.

"Yes, sir! It's Mama's Ridge Buck Baby, on point . . . the best field dog I've ever owned. I keep a kennel of dogs back home, all Setters. Pointers are the big breed in the South, but I prefer Setters. They don't have the stamina, but they're more elegant, more refined, than pointers. Mr. Harwood, I should take you bird hunting sometime. In some folks' minds, it's the essence of the South: walking slow, watching your dogs work a field, getting a rush of adrenaline every time the dogs freeze up and point a covey. You'd love it . . . telling lies on the porch, late in the afternoon, over a beer or a bourbon . . . bragging about how well you shot and how great your dogs performed . . . complaining about Washington and politicians. It's one of the many things I miss about home. Doesn't make a difference if you kill anything, heck, it doesn't matter if you shoot your gun. The anti-gun folks don't believe it, but it really is all about being outside with friends, watching your dogs work, and breathing deep of country air."

Calvin enjoyed sharing the South and its customs. But, suddenly, he stopped and silently measured Harwood, concerned that he had been too personal, even patronizing, with his discourse on quail hunting. He concluded that his excursion into such chatting could only have been possible because he somehow felt comfortable with Harwood. Then he quickly reflected on their conversation of the evening, noting that he had gotten nearly as many "sirs" from Harwood in twenty minutes as he got in two thirteen-month tours in Vietnam. "Anything else, Mr. Harwood?"

"No sir. That's it, sir." Harwood's "it" dragged out to mean that is not all, there is more. He leaned slightly forward, consciously using his body language to enhance the intensity and drama of his well-rehearsed response. He carefully placed his elbows on his knees and intertwined his fingers in front of him. "The President will be very disappointed in you . . . . " Harwood's "you" was carefully, subtly accented. He paused, and then went on, ". . . as an individual, a statesman, and a leader of men. You have an opportunity for greatness which will never be offered in such a way, ever again. This carousel horse won't come around again for another ride, Senator."

Had Stanley Harwood not quickly continued, his words might have resonated as a threat. "Here's a chance for an already great man to achieve a degree of unparalleled greatness in his own time, for all time. Perhaps you owe it to yourself. You certainly owe it to others . . . to the people whom you represent, to give this unique situation the most careful consideration. Please, think not only of yourself, but also about what you can do for the nation as a whole. And, more specifically, for the country's various and diverse constituencies."

Though the phrase was superficially vague, both men well understood Harwood's point. "The various and diverse constituencies . . . ." To the Senator, the message could not have been more manifest than if Harwood had chiseled four-foot high letters on a granite slab and left it in his vestibule. "The various and diverse constituencies . . . the various and diverse constituencies."

Harwood stood, leaving his still-nearly-full glass on the table. He had studied his subject well. His final comments had been a matter of considerable preparation. Nothing was left to chance. A dry fly had been cast with precision, and the line expertly dressed. There would be no slack to enable the hitting fish to spit the hook.

That Harwood's speech had been rehearsed was not lost on the Senator. He was too sophisticated, too long in Washington, to believe that Harwood's words had not been carefully crafted. Calvin knew whom he represented, he knew for whom he stood as a symbol and role model. They were the people of Mississippi, who democratically elected him. But, of course, it was never so simple. The Four Ps, Calvin thought: people, politics, passion, and power. The unspoken message was ever more powerful than the said.

The Senator sat, thinking and staring, as if awed by the imminent promise of his own potential, personal power.

Harwood finally moved deliberately across the room, opened the library door, and with his hand on the polished brass knob, looked back at the still-seated politician, war-hero, Renaissance man. "Thank you very much for listening, Senator Calvin. I can find my way out. The number for my secure line is written on the napkin under my glass. You can leave me a message as 'Mr. Falcon", and I'll get right back to you. Good night, and thank you again, sir, for seeing me on such short notice."

"Good night, Mr. Harwood."

Harwood stepped through the doorway, paused again, turned and retraced his last two or three steps. He looked down at the carpet for a moment and cocked his head to the side. His brow knitted and then, seemingly satisfied that his message was worthy, he lifted his head and said, "One thing more, Senator . . . ."

"Yes, Mr. Harwood."

"Well, sir, you mentioned how your father loved the Book of Matthew."

"Yes, Mr. Harwood, that was certainly his favorite."

"Well, I'm not much of a New Testament scholar, Senator, but I'd like to remind you of something from Matthew. This may not be exact, sir, but I'll come close."

Harwood squinted, as if to remember the passage. "In speaking to his disciples, Jesus said, 'You are a light for the whole world. A city built on a hill cannot be hidden. You must allow your light to shine among people so they can see the good things you are doing and praise your Father in heaven.'"

When Harwood finished the paraphrase, he dropped his head slightly and waited.

The Senator swallowed and closed his eyes. It seemed as if a full minute passed, when Calvin broke the silence.

"If that was not exact, Mr. Harwood, it was pretty darned close. Of course, it's from the Sermon on the Mount, Chapter Five. But don't ask me the verse."

"No, sir, not exact, of course not." Harwood politely responded, with an incipient smile on his lips.

"The way I learned it, by candlelight from my father, was 'Let your light so shine before men that they might see your good works and give glory to the Heavenly Father.' Actually, I'm afraid I've been in enough hotels to know the Gideon version pretty well. It says 'let your light shine among people', but I prefer the King James' 'shine before men.' So, thank you, Mr. Harwood. I was already impressed. Now I am very impressed, and very moved."

"Good night, Senator Calvin, sir."

Harwood closed the library door, and the modest click of the brass lock pounded in the brain of Senator Reginald Edward Calvin all night long.

11

Late summer in Washington is legendary for its steamy weather. When heat and humidity peak, those favored enough to use the outside tennis courts and jogging track abandon them for the air-conditioned fitness center located deep under the West Wing.

The indoor pool, built for Franklin Roosevelt and once popular with the true workout freaks, had long since been covered over to make additional room for the press corps. Sacrificing the pool stood as symbolic evidence that the media had merely grown in proportion to the bureaucracy it struggled so consistently and unsuccessfully to explain. The hydra-headed monster typing stories about the hydra-headed monster.

The White House bowling alleys were not usually occupied, except for the occasional late night, black tie visits of upstairs party-goers who had sampled too much of the fabulous wine collection at 1600 Pennsylvania.

While there had long been gyms in the Old and New Executive Office Buildings, Williams had installed one in the White House basement. In the summer heat, the fitness center was as busy as any snowy day in January. It was the home and haunt of the President's best friend, Tony Battaglia, born to Sicilian emigrant parents in the North Beach section of San Francisco. The Battaglias were among the last of the Italian families to hold onto their North Beach heritage. Astronomical housing prices and the influx of techno-yuppies had long since displaced those from the old country to less expensive neighborhoods.

Tony had been Williams' personal trainer when the President was California Governor. The five-foot-five inch tall Battaglia had shoulders as wide. He had won a weight-lifting gold medal in the 1984 Los Angeles Olympics and, after blowing out a knee and wrecking a shoulder in competition, had settled to manage a small gym near the Statehouse, frequented by sundry legislators, lobbyists and bureaucrats. It was here that Battaglia was to meet the future President.

The first meeting of Williams and Tony Battaglia was serendipitous. Governor Williams had repeatedly complained to his personal physician of headaches and stomach pains. He had convinced himself he had cancer or a brain tumor. Williams had gone three months without a full nights' sleep.

"Governor Williams, I have tested secretions and excretions from every orifice of your body. I have cat-scanned, palpitated, poked, probed, and pricked every square centimeter. I've used every piece of expensive medical diagnostic equipment between here and San Jose, and I can analyze and test no more. We are at an end. Now, Governor, that said, do you want to know what I think is wrong with you?"

"Of course I do, John. That's why I'm here."

"Well, Governor, let me put it to you straight then," Dr. Bock explained. "Plain and simple, like the old doctors used to say, you're just not taking care of yourself. Look in the mirror, Governor. For once in your life, you need to put yourself first. You need to start taking care of the whole person: heart, soul, psyche . . . and body."

"Is that your way of saying I'm working too hard?"

"That's part, but it's the simplest part. For a philosopher, you need to look inward a lot more . . . reflect on yourself."

"I'm not a philosopher, I'm a politician. Remember?"

"Governor, I'm not going to tell you to quit your job. The Bee wouldn't appreciate a physician making that choice for the voters, and I've got enough problems just practicing medicine. But I am saying you need to change the way you're doing things. You need to meditate, find a hobby, relax, train for a marathon . . . something. You can't go on pushing yourself. It's not good for you, for Phyllis, or the kids. And, it's not good for the people of California, either."

"And, may I ask, what do you specifically propose?"

"Well, Governor, I just gave you some ideas. Find something that fits your schedule and something you enjoy doing . . . hopefully with someone else who can support you. Do you have a friend that you can do something with?"

"No . . . nobody."

John Bock chuckled. "Welcome to the world of the male professional . . . a thousand cronies and no good friends. Governor, you've got to turn this around or you're never going to feel better. I think I'm going to call this 'Sacramento Stress Syndrome' for a prestigious article in the Journal of the American Medical Association. SSS. A good Governor never hurt a disease presentation! Seriously, either you're going to get sicker, leave your job . . . or worse."

"Want to tell me what 'or worse' is, Doctor John?"

"Use your imagination, Governor," Bock rejoined.

If the words themselves were not enough to motivate Williams, the stony stare from Dr. Bock was. The next day, with an aide accompanying him and a Stanford gym bag clenched in hand, Williams nervously walked the seven blocks from his Statehouse office to Tony's Gym and Fitness Center.

Tony, alerted by the Governor's office to await Williams' arrival, stood by the door. Who was the more anxious is unknown. But when Williams shook hands with the stumpy Italian-American weightlifter, a deep friendship—founded on mutual admiration and respect—began.

The Governor returned the next day, a return that was to be repeated time and time again. He pumped iron with Tony every day he was in Sacramento, and they both loved it. They worked out and they talked, a pastime that was to be repeated, month after month.

Almost overnight, the oxymoronic image of a lanky weightlifting philosopher/governor became a popular one in California press. And the Governor's improving physique and mood immediately heightened his already popular appeal. Usually depicted as an enigmatic intellectual, Williams' weightlifting helped him shed his professorial reputation. For this unintended benefit, Governor Williams was lastingly grateful first to Doctor John, but mostly to his new friend Tony Battaglia, who made the experience tough, rewarding, and fun.

Tony's father and brothers were house painters in San Francisco, thought of by their wealthy Nob Hill and Pacific Heights customers more as craftsmen than house painters. And craftsmen they were. Tony could not recall any relative who had ever attended college. Ralph Williams could not recall any family member who had not been to college.

Williams' most precious memory was of his father reading to him from deToqueville. Battaglia's most precious memory was the story his grandfather told about meeting Dom, Vince and Joe DiMaggio—together with their older non-baseball playing brother, Tom,—on the same night, when all four had showed up unannounced at a Spaghetti Night fund-raising dinner at St. Theresa's Church out in the Avenues.

Though their root systems were markedly different, the branches of these men intertwined. They looked forward to each day's regular session of cathartic strain. And, over the course of their weightlifting sessions they bonded, not in spite of their differences, but because of them. Through the sweat, Battaglia became Williams' counselor, comforter, and most of all, friend. Williams listened as attentively to Tony's personal advice about the burdens of governing as to his lengthy anecdotes about holiday meals in the basement with the extended Battaglia family, and the seemingly infinite amounts of food that the Italian women prepared throughout the day.

After a time, some reported that the Governor of California had become addicted to the weight room. In reality, Williams had become addicted to the personal peace that flowed from his friendship with a short, dogfaced, muscle-bound Italian-American weightlifting philosopher-trainer.

"You're gonna be in the White House some day, Governor Williams. And not as a visitor either. Ya hear me?" There was never anything gratuitous in Tony's words. If Tony said it, Tony meant it.

"Tony, why don't you try calling me Wally? For the thousandth time, this 'Governor' stuff is getting really old."

"Like I've said a thousand times, Governor, one of the reasons I like you is that you want me to call you Wally. But for the thousandth time, Governor, it won't happen. You're the Governor, duly elected, and you're entitled to be addressed that way. And anyway, it's only a matter of time before I stop calling you Governor, Governor."

"What's that mean, Tony?"

"Like I said, someday it'll be Mr. President."

The future President smiled. Tony had predicted this ultimate result dozens of times before and each time the Governor would reply, "If it ever happens, Tony, you're going to be there with me."

Each was prophetic and, true to his word, one of the first appointments announced by the newly elected President was Tony Battaglia—as White House Physical Fitness Coordinator, the name that the Civil Service Commission's Official Directory of Executive Branch Titles bestowed upon the position.

Once in the White House, the President made sure his fitness program with Tony remained as much spiritual as physical. Under Tony's guidance, Wally Williams continued to exercise and lift weights to the extent that his limited schedule allowed. And the fitness center at the White House became the President's new Peace Place, the only spot where he could find the perfect antidote to Sacramento Stress Syndrome, whenever its contagion spread to Pennsylvania Avenue.

12

The crowd cheered at every prepared pause in his speech, and Connie O'Malley loved it. He looked up from the double-spaced, typewritten page and beamed his old sod smile with a misplaced confidence that could come only from a man who did not read the newspapers, and whose TV consumption was confined to black-and-white sitcom re-runs and sports.

Four years ago, when Williams presented O'Malley as his running mate, the Williams/O'Malley ticket became a reality to the deafening cheers of loyal Party conventioneers. It was considered an unbeatable ticket. Three months later the claims were backed up at the polls. The ticket was typically "balanced", at least in historical terms: the Presidential candidate, once a philosophy professor at Stanford and thereafter Governor of Stanford's home state; his younger running mate, the House Minority Whip, a forty-five year old from Boston's Southie.

While not outright opposites by education, geography, or religion, they were as far apart as a Republican ticket could tolerate. The differences in their respective backgrounds were exacerbated by differences in style and personality, the distinction further lubricated by O'Malley's behavior: his already-affected brogue grew stronger as the campaign matured, as did his affinity for Guinness Stout and Bushmills.

During their first campaign, *The Boston Sun* was the first paper to unequivocally endorse these unlikely running mates. The Sun, of course, could be expected to be a homer and favor the local fair-haired, or in this case redhead, boy born at St. Brigid's Hospital, educated at Francis Xavier High School, and graduated from, if with little distinction, Boston College. To no one's surprise, though he publicly espoused regret over his decision not to become a priest, Connie O'Malley took work as a bartender, eventually becoming president of the union local. The next move was from union politics to elective government politics.

Despite O'Malley's trade union, blue-collar background, he eschewed the crowded Democratic races, ran, and was elected in a district where, as he put it, "Republicans are rarer than rhinos and reindeer."

Though he remarked later that his decision to run as a Republican was always a matter of political philosophy, few doubted that the wiry, ruddy O'Malley was more motivated by the practicalities of election than Party tenets and credos. After moving quickly from state legislator to state senator, he ran for Congress, winning handily. Throughout their first term, *The Sun* had been editorially consistent in support of the Williams Administration, even conveniently ignoring the innuendo of a connection with the IRA that trailed O'Malley, rumors that were reported by every other city newspaper across the nation.

But today, four years later, even *The Sun*—part of the McHugh and Duffy families' publishing empire and still headquartered in the South Side brick warehouse of its 1920 birth—expressed doubts about the incumbents' chances the second time around. While *The Irish People* had held its journalistic tongue, a *Sun* editorial concluded, ". . . whatever Vice President O'Malley has done or failed to do for Bay State constituents, if national polls are remotely accurate this year, the Republicans' ignominious fate appears virtually assured."

Seemingly ignorant of the polls, Connie O'Malley campaigned . . . in his own way. He loved campaigning for campaigning's sake. It was not just *in* his blood, it *was* his blood. And the fact that blood is thicker than water was nowhere more evident than in the South End, where O'Malley was on the soapbox again.

Here, he was at his best, thumping the rostrum, punching the air, all the while preaching to a room jammed with enthusiastic disciples. In front of an audience redolent with "O apostrophes" and "Mcs", the Vice President, safe among his partisans, preached with fervor to those who already had personally embraced The Gospel According to O'Malley.

"You see this Presbyterian minister sneaked out to Suffolk Downs to bet on the ponies," O'Malley told the assembled faithful. "He's betting his congregation's money, and he's losing his ass . . . see, he's starting to panic, when he notices a priest makin' the sign of the cross over a horse at the startin' line and mumblin' a prayer. The Protestant minister watches as the horse wins by five lengths, an' continues to watch as the priest repeats the blessing twice more, each time the horse winning away.

"The minister then sees the priest do this again . . . and he takes every blessed cent of his church's money and bets the horse to win. After the start, the horse runs a quarter of a mile and drops dead. The minister, completely panicked having lost his church's funds, rushes to the priest to tell him what he's done and find out what happened. After exchanging a few words, the priest replies to the minister, 'Well, my brother, next time you'll be more careful about telling the difference between a blessing and last rites'."

And the crowd roared its accustomed roar to an O'Malley yarn. Everybody glowed, and everybody was happy.

There was much less happiness fifteen years earlier in Boston when O'Malley, according to Democratic pols, "stole our seat." But, after continued exposure to O'Malley's relentless charm, the Democratic ward heelers finally got over their wounds and rallied behind their native son to send him, uncontested, to Washington. All was forgiven, and while they couldn't openly endorse a Republican vice president, or even be seen with him at these public rallies, the Democratic pols would nevertheless run a purposefully light campaign. Their "oversights" would help underwrite another rare Republican victory in Boston, and therefore Massachusetts, putting the Williams/O'Malley ticket in the White House.

It had been long accepted political folklore, at least until two Ivy League white boys from neighboring Southern states whacked the hell out of that paradigm: winning the Presidency required "a balanced ticket." But the 'good 'n' evil grits twins' notwithstanding, the folklore was mostly supported by historical results. When he and Williams were elected four years ago, O'Malley understood his role, and he would play it well, or at least as well as he was able. And, in the tradition of Boston-born Irish-American politicians, he would pay his dues. For the vice presidential nomination, he would bite his tongue and play kennel dog for a few months and, if necessary, a few years.

The Vice President was much in the tradition of Fitz, Curley, and

McCormack—and, like them, grew up in Boston, or as they said, "the next parish over from Galway Bay." O'Malley possessed sufficient self-awareness to realize he was no genius. And most people knew why party leadership had sought him out: bring home the Irish and the Roman Catholics' vote; and assure victories in Massachusetts and the other New England states. More truthful was the standing joke that with O'Malley on the ticket, the hops and barley farmers, brewers, and distillers were safely in the Republican fold.

Other than deliver particular constituencies, Connie O'Malley's duties were limited: stay sober in public, avoid any mention of The Troubles, and attend as few White House staff meetings as possible . . . in that order. And, as everyone predicted, O'Malley found it impossible to carry out the first two of these important assignments. At the third, he excelled.

13

Lewis Calendar was a senior options trader, until this summer, the most respected options trader at Amerco Securities and, arguably, the best on the Street. He was the thirty-six year-old "dean" of the industry, and the most highly regarded trader in "the Room." His skill had guaranteed River Club bills and Argentine dove shoots for life. "Williams, Wharton and balls like boulders" was *Institutional Investing and Trading* magazine's description of Calendar. He was not sufficiently rich to retire: twenty million in securities and real estate was a comparative pittance. A few more good years and he would be home. "Home" in this case was fulfilling his desire to fund a chair in arbitrage studies at Columbia Business School.

"The Room" was located at the newly-built Midtown New York head-quarters of Amerco, having migrated north after 9-11with Lehman and the rest of the crowd. Here, five-hundred stock and bond traders sat every day, cheek by jowl, phones glued to their ears, staring at computer terminals whose incessant blink, wink, blink, wink, blink of alphanumeric data changed, in-exorably, as if the Sorcerer's Apprentice abided in each multi-colored monitor. Dollar signs, mark signs, and pound signs . . . head-sets and mind-sets . . . the arcane and mystic code of the security trading clique. Every nanosecond each terminal was loaded, unloaded, and reloaded with that moment's reality of the world's money markets. In front of each trader, an electronic Cyclops reported each financial wheeze and whisper. No financial footstep in the global markets went unseen by this multitude of computer monitors.

The Room was the eye of the Amerco hurricane, and it was the stuff of legends: the largest, most cutthroat, most profitable trading floor in the world. There was, at least literally, no blood on tooth or claw, but figuratively the Room may have well have been painted scarlet. Had he the chance, Darwin assuredly would have chosen to study this place over the Galapagos. An option or bond trader would undoubtedly make a better evolutionary survival subject than a tortoise or finch. It was a high stakes work-game that these men and women played. These were verities in the most literal of senses.

These traders would earn for themselves at least a million dollars this year, most a lot more. Those that earned less would leave Amerco, involuntarily, and go to work for the treasury department of a large multi-national corporation or ply their trade for a commercial bank, for a fraction of the pay garnered by those they left behind in The Room.

The best of The Room's practitioners were arrogant and young. Trading bonds, currencies, or commodity futures is an intense and enervating endeavor and, by its nature, it is a young man's game. On the floor of The Room, where suspenders—or braces as they are called south of Vesey—abound, there was apparently no one over forty years old. By forty, one was expected to be wealthy enough to retire, in which case one was an admired and respected investment banker, belonging to the right club in Locust Valley, Rye, or Greenwich. Or, alternatively, one had burnt out, and made feeble apologies that one's children attended public school instead of Groton or St. Paul's.

The losers, however unfairly, were characterized as mono-dimensional, tapioca-brained, alcohol-addicted, cigar-smoking lightweights, with closets full of custom tailored pinstriped suits and monogrammed Dunhill shirts—and no marketable job or life skills. They knew the shibboleths of the practice, but secretly struggled to pay the next club bill or get in on the next white-winged dove shoot in South America.

This summer, things had unexpectedly turned sour for Lewis Calendar. Another year like this, in which his alcohol and cigar consumption trebled, and Calendar would be flogging long bonds for Suntrust. It had been a tough summer, one in which he had lost tens of millions of Amerco's money. He was within three months of closing the door on his worst year since the day he walked into the exclusive training program for The Room.

Today, on his crowded train ride home to Short Hills, when he usually relaxed by reading Batron's and catching up on internal reports and organizational memos, Calendar instead poured over his trading history and mounds of statistical data, stock supply-and-demand regression analyses, and research reports . . . trying to make sense of a market which always had been his trusted partner, but now had turned on him like a jilted lover.

He fretted during his short drive home from the station and was still absorbed when he usually would have made small talk with Sally about her homeless project, Northwestern alumnae affairs, or whether to rent in St. Vincent or St. Bart this winter.

"It doesn't make sense, Sal," he explained to his wife over their first Chardonnay. "There has never been such a big spread between the six month calls and the spot prices, and the spread at ninety days is huge, too. It's got to correct . . . it can't stay this way."

Sally Calendar did not much enjoy discussing her husband's work with him. It was technical and complex, and every time they talked about it, she ended up feeling defensive, or worse, stupid and inadequate. Number two in her class at Northwestern, with two Masters degrees—Business and Education—she was unequivocally his intellectual peer. What really troubled her was that it all seemed a Gordian knot of both quantitative analysis and intuition.

"Where does thinking stop and feeling start?" she'd often asked Lew. Whenever Lew worried, she nodded thoughtfully in response to his frustrations, "Uh huh," and added without much thought, "Why don't you trade something else, sweetheart? Casino stocks are too scary. Why not gold, silver, or maybe bonds?"

"I trade options on all the hotel, casino, and entertainment stocks, honey. I've got big positions in Hilton, Disney, Carnival Cruise Lines, and I'm doing okay on those. It's just the casino stocks that are killing me. They've wiped out every cent of profit I've made from all the other stocks combined, plus millions on top. Look, darling" he continued, "I really don't give a baboon's butt about casino stocks per se. They're just commodities to me . . . just as simple as any other damn thing and no more risky. Trading an oil position, oil futures . . . it's the same thing. It's just numbers . . . just a game. Plus, the casino market is small, with thin float. There's lots of movement and, for a good trader, that creates the ability to make a lot of money fast."

Sally looked at him impassively. She was, at the same time, totally enthralled with him and not the least bit interested in the subject.

"Honey," he went on, "it's like grits, baked potatoes, white bread, and popcorn. Aren't they all just vehicles to carry butter and salt to your mouth? Otherwise, who the hell cares? Casino stocks, gold . . . I don't care. I just want to be on the side that makes the most money. It could be orange juice or hog bellies, except that I happen to know entertainment and casino options better than anyone else in the world. Heck, I've never been in a casino . . . wouldn't know what the inside of one looked like. But I sure know their securities."

"You said you're struggling. So far you haven't told me why you're struggling."

"Because for the past several months something has been screwy as hell with these markets. Maybe I'm getting too close to this. My first boss, Mike Schectman, used to say the number one rule in trading is 'don't fight the tape'. And I've been fighting the tape because the tape is wrong."

"What's the tape and what's wrong with it?"

"The tape just means the trend, darling . . . whatever the crowd is doing. If everybody is buying and you're selling, maybe they know something you don't. Schectman used to tell me that I was the smartest person he'd ever met. Then he'd add that just because you're smarter than any single one of them out there, doesn't mean you're smarter than all of them put together."

"Where's Schectman now, honey?"

"You tell me . . . Hobe Sound, Beaver Creek, or up in his G-4 somewhere."

"Those places sound pretty good. I'm starting to agree with Schectman." Sally Calendar's laugh broke the tension. "Don't fight the tape."

"Look, Sally, if the market price of a stock is seventeen dollars today, without looking at the screen, I'll give you a pretty tight range of what I can buy it for out six months . . . its future price . . . subject to float, interest rate volatility, and the cost of capital. It's mostly a function of capital cost and volatility, which itself is a measure of risk."

"And that means . . . in English?"

"Okay, say you want to buy a tenderloin for a party on New Year's Eve. It's selling for ten bucks a pound, but it's September. The party's a few months off, and you're worried that at the end of December it'll be fifteen bucks a pound."

"So I buy it now and freeze it," Sally teased.

"Hah! Just my point. See, you can't buy and freeze a stock price. So you go to the butcher and say, 'I'll give you a dollar right now . . . today . . . if you'll guarantee to sell me the tenderloin for ten dollars a pound in December.'"

"And he takes it?"

"Maybe, maybe not. If not, you offer him two bucks . . . and keep raising your payment until either you can't afford it, or he accepts. I simply deal in selling a special kind of insurance . . . insurance that guarantees the price of stocks, instead of tenderloins—either up or down—in December."

"That still doesn't tell me what the problem is."

"A 'call' is the right to buy the stock—you can 'call' it from someone—for a specific period of time at a specific price. Now, say, a stock sells for $20 a share. Then its call should have a price of around $2 to $3, maybe $4—that's what you'd pay for the right to buy that stock from someone at $20 in the future. So, I buy the call for $2, and a couple of months later the stock drops from $20 to $10. I bought the right to buy it at $20, and I lose my money, because I'd never use my call to buy the stock at $20, when it's selling for $10. But I still had my 'insurance policy'. So, if the price of the stock had shot up to $30, my right to buy the stock—my call—is suddenly valuable. I use my call to buy the $30 stock for only $20, and I make $10 . . . less the $2 cost of the call."

"I repeat, Lew, what is the problem?"

"Ah, here we go now. Say, the calls are selling for $1. That means the market isn't paying enough for them. I know they're really worth $2 or more, that's their real intrinsic value. The irrationally low call price would only exist if the market were crazy . . . or someone somehow knew the price was going to fall . . . by a bunch. The problem is that the call price is way too low, compared to the stock price. So, I buy a bunch of calls, expecting that down the road either someone else will buy that call from me at a profit, or the stock price goes up and I can use the call to buy the stock cheap."

Sally smirked. "Perfectly clear, sweetheart."

Lew Calendar ignored her jibe and went on. "I buy the call, thinking it's a great deal. Then, the price of the stock doesn't go up *and* the value of my call disappears when it expires. I lose my money . . . or the firm's money, that is. So I do it again, even more this time, because I'm so convinced of my own infallibility, I guess. Same thing: more and bigger losses. Now, I figure, who in the heck is on the other side? Who is selling so many calls the prices are out of whack? Who's driving down the price of calls? Why doesn't the market adjust? Why does this anomaly continue month after month. I'm stumped . . . and nearly out of the kind of funds that the firm allocates to me for this crazy business. And I'm already out of the patience they allocate me, too!"

"Okay, Lew, what now?"

"I don't know. The problem is that the calls got so underpriced relative to the spot price, I bought them naked . . . that is, no hedge whatsoever. I doubled up like some drunken sailor at the craps table. Then they got way underpriced and I bought some more, still naked . . . totally unhedged. That's what I get paid to do."

"And then?"

"They went down some more and I'm losing my spine, baby. My balls have gone from boulders to BBs. This hasn't happened to me in the fifteen years I've been in this business. My position is huge, I'm naked, the market's totally screwy, and the senior partners are reviewing my position, as we speak."

"Could you be out?"

"'Out' isn't the word for it! Out, gone, done . . . unless this market straightens out. Do you know what Bill Rosen told me the other day? The same thing he said on the day I was hired. I remember sitting down in the training room and him coming over to me and whispering, 'I'll always be on your side, Lew, but you gotta know . . . these guys shoot cripples.' And they do. Rosen was right. I've shot plenty of them myself."

"This is starting to depress me, Lew."

"Wait, honey, I'm right."

"I've got an MBA too, Lew. Harvard, not Wharton, remember?" Sally Calendar asked rhetorically.

They both knew that Lew had a tendency to patronize her, a trait arising more out of his raw intelligence and supreme self-confidence, than any ill opinion of his wife's capabilities. Whenever he paused long enough to think about it, he realized that one of her many great strengths was a Job-like patience with this tendency of his. But, notwithstanding a combination of her adoration for Lew and her great sense of self-esteem, Sally Calendar had her limits.

"What's your point?"

For the first time in the conversation, the Wall Street wunderkind's voice filled with emotion. "I don't know . . . I just I keep getting frigging killed. This is a dangerous business."

"Lew, didn't you once say that sometimes an Arab country comes into the oil market, does something unexpected, screws things up? You've said it yourself . . . there's no such thing as a long-term anomaly. The water eventually finds its level. After all, after the disaster downtown, everything has got to a little wacky."

"This time it's doubtful. The whole industry segment isn't big enough . . . we're talking about fifty or sixty companies whose aggregate value is about the same as a bunch of half-dead dot-coms . . . even after they've 'corrected'. If some mega-investor started playing around, the market would fling wildly out of control in a second. This is more controlled than that. This has been slow, incremental. The whole market has shifted without any spikes. And other players in the options market are guys with an operating need to hedge."

"Like who?"

"Corporate treasurers. They're in the market day in, day out. . . buying and selling. In oil, they're hedging production and supplies between different months and different areas of the world. In orange juice, they hedge the weather. In cattle and hogs, they hedge the cost of feed corn. Everyone of us, Goldman, First Boston, we all handle unbelievable amounts of currencies and options for these guys for a couple of basis points, max. But it's part of the oil companies' and ag companies' operating businesses. The big guys mostly even each other out and even if they get out of balance for a while, a correction follows pretty quick."

"Think about it, darling. The Street says that Lewis Calendar knows the numbers better than anybody. You've always said you could walk across the street to Lehman or Merrill anytime you wanted."

"Not now, honey, those days are over. Everyone on the Street is getting wind of this."

"Lew, you've always maintained that the numbers talk to you. They haven't just stopped talking. Maybe they're using a different language. Maybe this time, instead of English, it's Esperanto."

"Sally, I haven't mentioned this to anyone before, but if I didn't know this business as well as I do, I'd swear that there's some huge buyer out there somewhere trying to manipulate this market. The logical conclusion is that someone's loading up on the short side. Lord, they'd laugh me out of Amerco, if they heard me talking like this, but my gut tells me that someone is selling tons of uncovered calls, improbable as it seems . . . betting on a major downward price move on the whole industry. And because of it, these prices are jumpier than a Jew at the Hadj."

"So, Lew," Sally probed, "you're saying this is logical and improbable at the same time?"

"It sounds stupid, Sal. But the numbers are shouting the kind of imbalance that could only come from somebody piling up on one side."

"Like who?"

"Who knows? Someone who could manage this without having the SEC or CBOE come down on them. And someone with a hell of a lot of money."

"An individual? A company? An investment fund?"

"Maybe 'D', all of the above. But, if it's true, it's been carefully done over a long period, a building process. This isn't some Arab sheik blundering around with a few billion, and it doesn't smell like an industry player. If it were, we'd have heard about it. If I were certain that this group of stocks was going to take a beating for some reason . . . if I was absolutely certain, I'd be dumping calls just like this. If I had a crystal ball, that is. It'd be like selling insurance today knowing no one would ever make a claim on the policy. It's like free money! It's conceivable, but who'd do it? And why? If Iraq bought a couple of billion calls knowing they were going to send troops into Kuwait, the markets would panic, and the price of oil would skyrocket. Voila, I make not millions, but billions. You buy insurance, and then you make the accident happen."

"Wynn maybe?"

"No, Steve's too smart, too much of a businessman, and too damned old and blind now. Maybe thirty years ago, but not now, especially after the Mirage takeover."

"Who else then?"

"Who knows? There's nothing wrong with industry fundamentals. There's no growth boom like there was, but these puppies are cash machines.

This is a mature and very profitable industry. Plus, if there's really something going on, somebody's got to have enough capital to commit."

"How much?"

"Several billion, probably. Depends on how it was structured. And in this volume, he'd have to execute the trades through a variety of traders so no one could catch on!"

"Is this legal?"

"It depends, Sal. So far the government hasn't outlawed either making money or stupidity."

Lew Calendar shrugged. "I'm out of answers. This market is small enough that if a major player committed a few billion to one side of the market, he could wreck havoc, and if the market moves the way he wants, he's going to make an untold sum of money."

Sally opened the refrigerator door, pulled out a new container of Brie, and placed it on the kitchen table with a plateful of bagel crisps.

Calendar watched her move across the kitchen with a gracefulness undiminished by the birth of three children and ten years of marriage to a workaholic options trader. Losing money was a new experience for him, and dumping his fears and insecurities to his mate was equally as new an experience. It surprised him how good it felt . . . a hell of a lot more comforting than nearly two glasses of forty-dollar Chardonnay, he thought.

Sally pressed once again, "Use your left brain. You haven't paid for Telluride and Quogue by being reactive or emotional," she challenged.

Lewis Calendar pondered his wine, paused, bent his head back, and drained the last of his second glass.

"I don't know. I've got no enemies, and the competition on the Street doesn't deal personally anyway. It's too risky, and it's not good business to get your psyche involved in this stuff. You've got to walk away every day, win or lose, and still sleep like a baby."

"Lew, darling, if there was just one thing to attribute this to, what would it be?"

"Someone is manipulating, Sal, and I'm the manipulatee!"

"And?"

"And I'm going to find out what the hell is going on!"

14

Stanley Harwood stared at the glass-encased, gold medal hanging on the wall of Tony Battaglia's office. Each time he went to the fitness center, Harwood stopped at Tony's office to chat, but also to look at the gold medal. Looking at the medal made Harwood feel good: feel good for America, feel good for Tony, feel good, in fact, for himself. In a way, the medal, this particular medal, was an exquisite symbol of what America is all about, Harwood concluded: this little guy making it to the top . . . this Italian-American overcoming the two strikes of social position and small stature with pure, unadulterated hard work. Sometimes nice guys do finish first, he thought.

Harwood had been a regular at the fitness center since moving from the old Executive Office Building to the West Wing, a year ago. Here, Harwood and Battaglia had become friends. Harwood cared about Tony and Tony could feel it. That was all that mattered.

For Harwood, Tony was a welcomed break after a long day of bullshit politics, dealing with the spineless bureaucrats on The Hill—the "Turkish Bazaar" as his department had come to refer to the process of negotiating with Congress. Down in the fitness center, Harwood left behind the surreal world of lobbying Congress. The fitness center was, in Harwood's mind, a lot closer to being with 'real' people, especially, Tony. Often, after a workout, Harwood sat, his feet propped on Tony's desk, and talked to the also-slouching Tony. Tony would recount his old weight lifting stories and Harwood would listen patiently, an atypical activity for him.

Harwood now knew that recruiting Battaglia was his best—indeed his last—hope. This conclusion was no lightning bolt. As his need-for-an-ally thinking emerged, he mentally sifted candidates, considering, and discarding them over a period of weeks. His frustration with the President's situation, and with his own inability to solve the access puzzle, had grown gradually. Just as gradually had grown his idea that Tony was his best chance. Harwood cursed himself for not taking some action before the convention, perhaps long before. Now, this late in the game, the need for action waxed, while the probability of success diminished with each passing day.

While Tony was not ideal, Harwood had exhausted all other angles. In one sense, the concept was appealing. Harwood would not have to concoct an affection for Tony. Battaglia was a real friend, and enlisting him to the cause would be a favor of a friend, a fillip to the relationship. Harwood was, on the other hand, loathe to involve a friend in any scheme, however noble its goals.

By the time the concept had fully crystallized, one night in early September, drenched with post-workout sweat and lounging in Tony's office, Harwood decided that the best tactic was to cast the die.

"Hey, paisan, you know what you and I have in common?"

Tony twisted his face, making his large nose appear even larger, and stared at Harwood.

"Stan, what did you just say? Did you just call me 'paisan'?"

"Yeah, it just kind of came out." Harwood didn't apologize.

"Paisan. You called me paisan."

Harwood quickly reconsidered. "Well, I guess I'm sorry."

"No, it's okay. Nobody around here but the President calls me 'paisan' and you just called me paisan. I like that."

"Thanks Tony. Now, what's the answer? What do you and I have in common?"

"Easy, Stan. We love good Italian wine and beautiful women with long black hair and big noses. We're probably the only two guys in D.C. that order Chianti in a fancy restaurant. Also, we try to stay in good enough shape to enjoy the wine . . . and pretend that if a good looking lady . . . and I mean lady, not woman . . . crossed our path, that we'd really know what to do. That what you meant?"

"Yeah, you pretty much nailed it. Anything else?"

"Paglia y fieno?"

"Yeah, that too. What else?"

"I dunno. What Stan?"

Harwood paused. "We both share profound respect and admiration for the same man."

Tony Battaglia ruminated, but it did not take him long to respond. He knew at once from Harwood's tone that this was not a normal b.s. session.

"Is this a quiz or a joke?"

"This is deadly serious, Tone."

"Wally?"

"You got it, Tony."

"What's going on, Stan?"

"Nothing yet. But if we get our wish, there will be."

Harwood stood up and stripped his sweatshirt from over his head and dropped it at his feet, leaving him standing in Tony's office in a faded Yale crew shirt, soaked and clinging to his torso. He propped himself against the wall of Battaglia's office and began.

It was, of course, a pitch . . . *The* Pitch. A pitch he had practiced a hundred times, if not more. He suffered the pejorative connotations of "pitch", but understood that if it was a pitch with a purpose, surely to influence—yes, to convince Battaglia—but absent exploitation or guile.

"Look, Tony, the election is lost. Come January, Tony Battaglia and Stanley Harwood are out of work."

"That bad, huh?"

"No, Tony it's not that bad, it's worse. It's one thing to lose an election, it's another to be humiliated. And it's still another thing to be humiliated when you're as great a man as he is."

Tony's basset hound-face was blank. "He's my friend, Stan. You know that. In Sacramento, everyone else treated me like the wop gym rat that I am. Like those lobbyists and guys from the legislature who used to come to the club. And when those money-stealing, tell-'em-what-they-want-to-hear hypocrites treated me like, well, you know, like shit, well, the Governor . . . he's the one who treated me like a friend . . . like I was somebody special."

"Tony, you *are* somebody special."

"Thanks, Stan. You're one of the few guys around here with class."

Harwood ignored the compliment. "Tony, the real tragedy is that no one around the President gives a damn. They're all like rats leaving a sinking ship. His Chief of Staff and campaign chairman are already interviewing the top law firms, PR firms, and lobbying firms in Washington and New York. They'll land on their feet with million-dollar-a-year puff jobs, not to mention fifty-grand-a-pop speaking fees. And the President will suffer the worst defeat of any President in history."

"Are you including Bernie Cartwright?"

Harwood frowned. "Cartwright is a big joke, Tony. Rumors are that he's screwing the President's biggest campaign contributor, a multi-millionaire oil executive, and skimming off her contributions at the same time. A hell of a guy he is, our great Wall Street attorney. Worse, he's got no plan for this campaign. He thinks because he was a top dog in the first campaign that everything will be the same. Cartwright somehow thinks that his job is special . . . honorary or something. He's got no concept, no idea of where he's going. He's never in Washington, he doesn't keep the President informed, and he's totally isolated the poor man. I'm telling you Tony, if something radical doesn't happen soon, pack your bags for Sacramento."

"So why has Wal . . . the President let these guys go only so long like this?"

"I wish I understood it, Tony. They were the guys that made things happen for him before, at least most of them. The Party shoved some of the new ones down his throat. Most of all, I think the man is too nice to chop heads the way they need to be chopped around here. We've both seen him make plenty of tough decisions, but this time around—and I mean for the last year or so—it seems like he can't act on stuff. Plus, Moore just looked strong in that last debate. I think people sense that maybe Wally's ideas are now four years old. Moore's offered a lot of new programs, and he campaigns with a huge amount of energy and charisma. What it comes down to right now is that six weeks ago it seemed like the President was trailing slightly. But since then, heck, it's been a steady slip. Each poll is worse than the one before."

Tony Battaglia did not attempt to stay apace of polls or politics. He was surprised by the seriousness of Harwood's message. "I mean, I kinda knew he was behind, but I keep thinking he'll catch up. He's done, huh?"

This man is an Italian Prince, thought Harwood, but without the legendary capacity for artful deceit that many associate with the title. Perhaps he was simple, but, if that was indeed the case, with that simplicity came absolute incorruptibility.

Harwood looked at Tony and realized that in the months that he had known him, Tony's sincerity had led him across thresholds of relationship. First, Harwood reflected, he had moved from liking Tony, to respecting him. But now, now as he sat in the man's office, preparing to beg a favor without recompense, Harwood realized that he admired Tony. And, that admiration was not merely a matter of his integrity, but the grace with which Tony bore his virtue.

Harwood abandoned his brief reverie, returning to the task at hand. "'Done' is an understatement, Tony. Burnt to a crisp is more like it."

"What are we gonna do?"

Stanley Harwood sighed an invisible sigh and smiled an imperceptible smile, a smile forced back deep down inside, noting the "we" in Battaglia's plea. And Harwood took the question—that may have been rhetorical to Tony— literally. There was nothing rhetorical about "What are *we* gonna do?" to Stanley Harwood. He was ready and he knew what to do.

15

Ralph Waldo Emerson Williams had been underestimated throughout the political portion of his career. As a professor, writer, and thinker, he was held in high regard, indeed sometimes envied, by his peers, his students, and university administrators. But as one who could effectively run a campaign and lead in the public sector, he was consistently regarded lightly.

First in his California gubernatorial run, and then in his campaign for the Presidency, there were many reasons why Williams was not taken seriously. Williams genuinely viewed elective politics as a public service . . . something to give to the state, the nation, and the people. He thought of holding office as a form of service to others, a calling. Such a personal philosophy was regarded usually as disingenuous or ignorant—but to Williams, it was the ultimate in personal fulfillment.

His first campaign strategist visibly flinched when Williams, answering a question in a TV interview, said, *"Cui servire, est regnare."* Apart from a handful of Latin teachers and Catholic priests, few would know that the statement meant, "Those who serve, lead." It sounded elitist, detached, and—the worst—professorial.

But it was the voters that the media and professional campaign strategists had most underestimated. They understood Williams, felt his sincerity and believed in him. While the professor often ascended into unabashed intellectualism, the voters understood that this was no affect, but rather the essential Williams. He was an artless politician, and in spite of it—or perhaps because of it—his popularity soared.

Williams' experience—like that of other occupants of the nation's highest office—was one more bit of evidence that just because people love you, doesn't mean they want you as their representative. And, conversely, voters don't need to love you—or even respect you—to believe that you can represent them well. Yes, he was still loved and respected by the American voters, but that didn't mean they wanted him in the Oval Office for another four years.

He was not naïve. Many, perhaps most, who embarked on a similar path, sought to prove something to themselves or others. They saw politics as some sort of grand stage upon which they were destined to play themselves, fully costumed in the garb of self. Time and again, to the continued frustration of his campaign management, Williams spoke what was in his heart. In a televised debate, the soon-to-be governor, challenged by his opponent to reveal his greatest weakness, had replied, "It is very difficult to esteem a man, particularly one who is running for office, as highly as he wishes to be esteemed or esteems himself. My greatest fear, in fact I am petrified by the prospect, is that one day I will find myself giving thanks that my constituents are not unworthy of me."

As the last of these words left Williams' mouth, the screen was filled by a close-up of his opponent, and debate raged for weeks as to his reaction. Editorialists and news reporters across the country had a field day with the image. The opponent's look was variously described as "a dumbstruck australopithecine", "an Amazonian tribesman seeing himself reflected in a mirror for the first time", and "a ten-year old child witnessing a massive train wreck."

Attempting to hone his image, early supporters urged Williams to change his nickname from "Wally" to something more sophisticated and masculine. "'Wally' sends the wrong signal, Wally. It's not a name people will feel comfortable using," explained one of his closest friends, using the nickname with ease and oblivious to the inherent contradiction in his sentence. Sitting around the living room of his Palo Alto home with a group of associates from the University, Professor Williams finally capitulated.

"I've thought a lot about this name thing and I've finally decided that you are correct. I can't possibly win a political office running with a handle like Wally," he grinned. "I'm going for something new, something powerful, something that will send a real message to the voters of California."

"Great!" was the unanimous reply.

Whereupon Williams casually rejoined, "Waldo it is, then!"

"Boo, boo, hiss, hiss!" cried the assembled team of close friends.

"Okay, folks, either it's Waldo, or I stay what I've been since age three, when my sister started calling me Wally."

And stay he did, just as all along he knew he would. The lanky, gentle professor of philosophy remained Wally.

He had been Wally, to everyone but Phyllis, since his growing up days in the Central Valley. Wally Williams' father, a Stanford grad himself, was a philosophy professor at Cal State—Stanislaus, finishing a book on phenomenological psychology. The elder Williams was at home one evening writing a challenge to Husserl's Theory of Intentionality, when his son announced his intent to follow in his dad's footsteps. Abel Williams, rarely at a loss for words, was speechless. Here was a boy declaring his life plan to attend Stanford and become a college philosophy professor. For a few moments he nervously bit his lower lip, a habit which he fervently he denied he had, despite the perpetual callous on the inside of the lip. His only reply was "Well, here we have living proof of the fallacy of the commonly held belief that lightning never strikes twice in the same place." And then Abel Williams cried.

When Wally was a tall and gawky, Galbraith-like freshman at Stanford, Phyllis came right up to him at an orientation meeting and announced "Hi, I'm Phyllis Bolmer from Indianapolis, Indiana. What's your name?"

Though he'd been Wally his entire life, it suddenly occurred to him that now was his chance, perhaps his only chance in life, to change from being a Wally. Now, he could be Bubba, Beauregard, or Brutus. But, not having foreseen the immediacy of the opportunity, he was totally unprepared. He would say later that he wished he'd told her his name was Damon or Xeres.

But he said, instead, "I'm Ralph Williams, from Turlock."

"Turlock . . . that's a funny name. Ralph, you said that kind of slowly . . . are you sure that's your name?" she gurgled.

"Positive."

"What's your full name, Ralph Williams?"

"Uh . . . uh . . . my full name?"

"Yes. Back home, where I come from, that means you tell me your middle name, if you have one . . . plus your first and last names, as your parents gave them to you. Anyway, that's the way we do it in Indiana."

Had she not been so beautiful and so refreshingly sassy, and had she not exuded such a Midwestern 'howdy folks' air, he would have dismissed her and her sarcasm at once. But he played along. He was having fun.

"Ralph Waldo Emerson Williams" he announced.

"Really?" she shot back.

"Really."

From his reply, Phyllis could tell that he was telling the truth. "Waldo!" she shouted. "Waldo, Waldo, Waldo . . . I love that name. I shall call you Waldo."

"Well actually, my friends call me Wally. I don't really go by Ralph. I just made that up . . . I mean, made it up right now. Uh, I mean, I didn't make it up, that it's my name . . . but no one calls me that. Okay?"

"So articulate! But, never mind, it's too late, Waldo Williams, too darned late!" she giggled. And from that day forty-eight years ago she had called him nothing but Waldo.

A singular strength was Williams' profound belief that, while he was personally responsible for making the most of his gifts, the basis for whatever success he enjoyed was attributable to a higher power. He never hid gratitude to God, or his appreciation of the circumstances of his birth, his mentoring parents . . . the opportunities accorded him that he knew were unavailable to millions of others.

His siblings did not share this outlook on life, and that fact caused Williams more pain and more regret than anything else in his life. He bore a scar, internally, inflicted by his brother's and his sister's reactions to their names.

His brother George, a rancher in Fresno County, struggled for decades to get over having been named George Friedrich Wilhelm Hegel Williams, and being referred to variously throughout his life as Georgie, Freddie, and Willie.

And Williams agonized over the death, from cancer at the age of forty, of his older sister, 'Henry'. She had never forgiven her father for naming her for Henrietta David Thoreau Williams and insisting on calling her 'Henry'. She remained bitter and resentful of the youthful torment and merciless teasing her name brought upon her.

In her long days of slow death, Williams believed she had the power to cure and heal herself. He often counseled her to forgive, if not forget, but she was incapable. When, on her deathbed, bald and emaciated, she cursed her parents equally, he read to her from Matthew: "Then Peter came to him and said, 'Lord, how often shall my brother sin against me, and I forgive him? Up to seven times?' Jesus said to him, 'I do not say to you, up to seven times, but up to seventy times seven.'"

"Fuck Peter and fuck Jesus," Henrietta replied.

Williams had always resisted the idea of determinism. But, in his own desperate mission to help both of them comprehend the origin of her pain, Williams talked with her about free will, and quoted from Spinoza: *There is no such thing as free will. The mind is induced to wish this or that by some cause, and that cause is determined by another cause, and so on.*

On her deathbed, with a bony hand, she beckoned him out of his chair, to come close, until his head almost touched hers. Then, barely audible, she hissed, "Fuck Spinoza, too." Those were her last words. Three hours later she was dead. "That name killed her . . . killed her young," her husband said.

Wally Williams, to his great credit, never allowed the virus of his siblings' resentment to infect him. In fact, he was nearly immune to all negative feelings, and in the rare moments of self-reflection, he concluded that his lack of bitterness was just another asset with which he had been blessed.

16

The phone on Chris Weiner's nightstand jolted her awake. She rolled over, groped with one hand for the cellular phone, and rubbed her eyes with the other. "Hello."

"He's down, Ms. Smith."

"God, it's the middle of the night."

The raspy voice still held a vestige of its Brooklyn origins. "Actually it's morning here in D.C. Eight o'clock to be exact."

Chris Weiner tried to blink the sleep from her eyes, and stared at the moiré silk canopy over her bed. "That makes it five a.m. here."

"You said to call when the job was done."

"Alright. I assume 'down' means completely down?"

"Well, we didn't stick around, but he won't make it."

Weiner sat upright in the massive bed, adjusting a huge pillow behind her. "What if he does?"

The man's vitriol gushed into her ear. "Hey, bitch, we've done this before, you know."

"Are you guys using the scrambler I gave you? You'd better be, I don't want anyone tracing or taping these calls."

"Yeah, yeah, calm down."

"*You* calm down. If you're professionals, as you constantly remind me, start acting like it."

"Yes, ma-a-a-'am," the tall killer whined in a falsetto taunt. "now, it's late and we're tired."

"Poisoning a guy is tiring?"

"Hey, we've been planning this job for a month. We're ready for a break."

"Tough. One hit, a half a million bucks split it two ways, and take the rest of the year off."

"This wasn't just a hit. We had a hundred chances to whack this guy and get away easy, but you set pretty tough ground rules."

"Hold on a second . . . ." Weiner pressed an intercom button next to her nightstand, and her live-in housemaid answered immediately.

"Yes ma'am?"

"Rosa, I know it's early, but bring me my regular, okay?"

"Yes, ma'am, right away."

"Okay guys, I'm back."

"Anyway, they probably've found him by now."

Chris Weiner relaxed barely enough to organize her thoughts. "Have you made any other calls with that phone I sent you?"

"Nah," replied the raspy voice.

The voice belonged to Willie, the six-foot-four inch, Brooklyn-born killer who handled all the "client communications," as he called it. He cupped his hand over the phone, looked down at his short partner and hissed, "Nick, you oughta hear this bitch! We gotta find us some better clients."

His partner, the "project planner" as Willie called him, was, like Willie, an uneducated, highly-intelligent hit man. He was wiry, intense, and, if lacking in verbal skills, well-schooled in his primary art: killing people for a fee. Nick stood close by his partner and replied, "Yeah, but the money's awful good."

"Are you there?" Weiner asked.

"Yeah, Ms. Smith, we're here. Just a little static or something." Willie grinned at his partner.

"Listen, guys," Weiner instructed, "I can't afford any screw-ups on this job. Once is a million times too many."

"We *don't* screw up. Just get us the rest of the money, okay."

"Listen, send all the stuff to the address I gave you. And remember to pay cash to FedEx. And you know what to do with the gloves and clothes I sent you, right?"

"They're already in a dumpster off the Southeast Freeway, never to be seen again."

"Good. Now, did he go like you planned? I want to hear exactly what went down."

"Well, he's drunk, okay. Your file said he was a boozer and . . . ."

"A recovered alcoholic."

"Recovered, whatever. They're all the same. They have one and they can't stop, at least your precious target couldn't this time. It went just as we practiced. Nick made an impression of the lock, and cut a new key for the side door to his club. Around three, we unlocked the club door, carried him up the service stairs, stripped him, put him in the sauna, cranked it up, and left. Easy and clean."

"He's dead?"

"Not when we left him, but we don't want him to die right away. Takes a few hours for his body to use up the drugs. That'll leave just the alcohol for the medical examiner to find. We left a half bottle of vodka outside the sauna with his paw prints all over it. The cause of death will be an accident. The guy's a known drinker."

"Former drinker, straight for over a year."

"Yeah, well, this time he fell off the wagon, and next thing you know, he's found at his club, cooked . . . parboiled in the sauna. I can hear the cops now, 'Wow, did you see this guy, he's completely blue.' You know, they turn blue when they cook in a sauna or steam bath. Pink first, then a kind of light gray, and then completely blue."

Weiner could hear Willie's high-pitched abrasive chuckle and, in the background, the deeper chortles of the little Nick. "Hey," Willie joked, "he's becoming a man of color . . . but in this case, the color is blue!"

Weiner cut off this laughter. "Alright, guys, what else?"

"That's it. He dehydrates, his heart stops, he cooks. Put a meat thermometer in his ass and he's at about 140. Most of the alcohol stays in his system. The drugs are gone . . . don't show up in the autopsy. Only thing missing is a nice Italian marinade. It's a tragic accident that took the life of a great man."

"He follow our plan?"

"Like a puppy. He thought he was meeting with some lobbyists representing wealthy donors who need favors . . . to talk about water legislation. We dropped some big names, the ones you gave us, and he bought it completely . . . hook, line, and stinker."

"Malapropism . . . Sheridan."

"Huh?"

Though the men were proven experts, Weiner was nonetheless amused by the contradictory image of two professional and proficient assassins that acted, at the same time, like buffoons. Their combination of brilliance and idiocy appalled her. When it came to planning and consummating a hit, they were creative, if not ingenious. And diligent. But sometimes, the simplest of concepts blew by them like a butterfly in a hurricane. When it came to crossing the street, she thought, it seemed like they needed a Boy Scout escort.

"Never mind," she snarled. "Any record of the meeting?"

"He said no one in his office knew anything. That was supposed to be a requirement of the meeting."

"He could've told his A.A."

"Yeah, that could be administrative assistant or alcoholics anonymous."

"I forgot about his daily meetings. You don't think he'd talk about this there?"

"Nah, I doubt it. We had a guy attend a couple of his meetings. Small group, mostly Southwest Washington bums, with a couple of Congress types wandering in and out of the meeting to take calls on their cell phones. Anyway, he just thought he was meeting with some lobbyists wanting to talk about getting his help. He had a few pops and got carried away."

"Yeah, literally, in this case."

"Huh?"

"Never mind, again. So you did good?"

"There's no alternative in this business. It's pretty easy to attract these kinds of flies . . . just have to know your bait . . . usually, they come equally to shit or sugar."

"Yeah, all the 's' words. Including shekels."

"Huh?"

Weiner grimaced. "No marks?"

"Nah, but our research paid off . . . we're glad we knew he liked grapefruit juice. Our stuff doesn't have much taste anyway, but in grapefruit juice, it's like it's not there. I call it 'Willie's Wonderful Wine.' One drink and the guy is totally gaga . . . like a date-rape cocktail, 'cept this guy didn't get buggered, he just got dead."

"So he just slips away?"

"Well, he's still kind of awake, just enough so he'd just take a drink without knowing what the fuck is up. We followed the first one with another, and then the guy takes about eight shots of vodka . . . pretty good stuff too."

"Shame to waste it on a stiff," Weiner said.

"You know, we like working for you, but you are one tough . . . uh . . . witch. Is it all the money that makes you that way, or were you born that way?"

Chris Weiner basked in the warmth of a comment that she interpreted as a compliment. She blinked and squinted again, and tossed her black hair back on the large, fire-engine-red, silk pillow.

"Both. My father used to say it's in our blood . . . do the best, be the best. To him, that meant the richest. But, don't you guys forget about how our greedy buddy ended up. He was going to make a big score and instead ended up shake 'n' bake."

Willie's patience for family reflections was meager. He looked toward the Capitol and saw the first traces of light, pink and yellow in the sky. "Hey, money makes the world go 'round."

"No," Weiner replied, "just a way of keeping score."

"You ever gonna have enough?"

"Enough is not in my vocabulary . . . it's a word for guys like you. Now, what happened after he's out."

"Okay, our hotel room was next to the elevator, see, so we only had to carry him a few feet, with his arms over our shoulders, like he was drunk, in case we saw anyone. Nick's got the elevator fixed, he jimmied the control box and just held down the button, so it won't stop until it got to the lowest parking level. The van's there by the elevator, a couple more steps, and bingo, he's gone."

"No cameras in the garage?"

"Nah, that's why we picked the place. We even had a buddy come in and check for those little ones, hidden stuff, you know. Nothing."

"Not even at the entrance?"

"Nope. For Washington, it seems crazy, I know. Shit, they should film everything in this fuckin' city."

"There's bank ATM cameras and other videos in all kinds of places."

"We checked 'em out. No problem."

"Could there be any pics of Nick in the guy's car?"

"No way! Nick's a pro, aren't you Nick?" The tall man received a return grin and nod of acknowledgement.

"As soon as he's in the guy's car, he pulls a beard, moustache, and ball cap out of his briefcase, and he's a new guy. If he's on film, they'll be looking for a different guy."

"Okay. Rent the van?"

"Hell no, that's a paper trail. We bought it up near Grant Circle, for cash. It did the job, then caught on fire—accidentally, of course—back over where we bought it. We paid some street kids a hundred bucks to torch it, and stayed just long enough to see the flames. Had to stay . . . we needed these guys to escort us out of the neighborhood! It's scary over there! No cabs in that part of town. So our little firebugs drove us out. That's another hundred. Anyway, the van's a marshmallow . . . nine grand, and we only owned it for eight hours. And a couple of those hours and another grand we spent in a chop shop grinding off VINs."

"VINs?"

"Vehicle identification numbers. They don't burn real well."

"What about the room?"

"Paid for in cash by an out-of-town friend. He flew in, rented the room, met us, handed us the key, and flew out."

"You got a lot of people involved. One to go to the guy's AA meetings, one to check the cameras, another to get the room."

"All top pros, nothing but the best. Plus, they know if anything funny happens, they go down, too. The room's wiped clean . . . but not too clean. There'll be plenty of prints, but none of ours. We left some glasses in the room, so it'd look like he was meeting with someone. We couldn't just wipe our glasses clean and leave 'em, that'd be too obvious. So we stole a half-dozen used glasses off tables in bars around town and left 'em in the room. They'll get prints, but they'll be untraceable."

"Anything else?"

"We left his car on the street, unlocked. It'll get stolen, maybe towed, but we figured on that. Either way, it'll be a couple months before the cops find it. The traffic guys tow these cars, then bury them in one of their garages. And their computers are about six months ahead of smoke signals. The chop shop says the impound lot uses different computers from the cops. I guess it's pretty bad. Anyway, none of the parking guys' computers talk to the computers the regular cops have. They have to check everything by hand."

"And, we left a couple of bottles in the car, just to make it look a little better. Plus we pressed his hands on the bottle to make sure they've got his prints."

"No rough stuff . . . no blood, huh?"

"Naw, totally clean. The medical examiner will look this guy over, and he'll look just fine. Or as good as he can look, under the circumstances. In that sauna," Willie chuckled out loud, "he'll shrink up like a strip of bacon. After four or five hours in there, the coroner will be able to put the guy in his hip pocket."

"Cute guys! Okay, so, I need the cell phone and the new key you made for the club. And his car keys?"

"In his pants pocket outside the sauna room. Like the vodka bottle, we pressed his thumb and index finger on it, so it'll look like he took it out of the ignition himself. Now, how 'bout the money?"

"Same way, guys, I'll call you. And, by the way, if this one goes off like you say, I may have another one coming up."

"Anybody big?"

"You bet. Big ones are the only ones worth taking down. Mice can't hurt you, elephants can. We don't take down mice . . . maybe a rat or two . . . but no mice."

"Rats, no mice. Real funny."

"Bye, guys."

As Willie slipped the cell phone into his shirt pocket, he turned to his short friend and offered his hand. Nick slapped the open palm of his tall friend and growled, "Awright!"

In Beverly Hills, Rosa knocked lightly on the bedroom door, then appeared carrying a silver tray with black coffee, a fresh New York bagel with even fresher lox, and a single, dark red rose.

"Buenas dias. How is everything this morning?"

"Things are just peachy, Rosa. Be careful setting that tray down. Accidents *will* happen, you know," Weiner grinned.

"Yes ma'am."

"I ought to know. I just made one happen."

17

Stan Harwood toweled more sweat from his face and neck, as he stood in Battaglia's office, propositioning his intended ally. "I've got a plan to win the election, Tony. It involves O'Malley, and it'll work."

Tony flinched at the word O'Malley. After three years' experience, some of it first hand, O'Malley disgusted him. "A real idiot" was Tony's abrupt and simple assessment. Too many times, O'Malley had asked Tony about "finding some ladies" for him. Too many times, he had shown up at the fitness center with Killiens or Guinness on his breath, with no notice, bumping lower staff off the fitness machines, or massage tables. Tony Battaglia knew O'Malley and didn't like him. Tony Battaglia was ready to listen.

"What's the plan, Stan?" Tony chuckled at his rhyme.

"Here's the tough part, Tony. I can't tell you everything right now. In time, I can clue you in . . . a month, a week. I'm sorry, please trust me."

Battaglia shrugged the shrug of an experienced shrugger. "It's okay, Stan. Nobody tells Tony shit. I don't mind. But why me? I don't get it. Why don't you take this plan of yours to somebody who can help? What about Cartwright? Or Whittingham?"

"I told you, neither of those guys is doing anything to help the President. What makes you think they'll want to change? All they're doing is setting things up so they avoid the blame. Everybody's suddenly trying to look as uninvolved as possible. And what I've got in mind will really shake them up. So, there's no one I can go to with this plan, except for the big man himself. And I can't get close to him, at least alone. You know how it is. I need to go directly to him, just him and me, one-on-one. Lay it all out for him."

"So why don't you just do it?"

"Because, my man Tony, like I just explained, I can't even get close to him. Staff, cabinet, travel, Camp David, Secret Service. . . it's a joke. I've been trying for weeks and there's no way. And time is running out. If you can't help me, I'm out of ideas. Tony, you're his best friend, someone who's known him since his Sacramento days, someone he trusts."

Battaglia arched an eyebrow and emitted a long, drawn out, "And?"

"And . . . you can get me close to him. Where does he love to come and what does he love to do when he's in the White House?"

"He comes down here to lift weights, get a rubdown from ol' Tony, the best in the business, and bullshit about nothing in particular."

"And who on the face of God's green earth can get me some time alone with the President of the United States?"

"You're not serious, Stan! I don't like where you're headed all of a sudden. You want me, a fitness trainer, to arrange for you to be alone with the President, surrounded night and day by large mean men, wearing loaded guns and trained to use them?"

"Tony, you're the last hope to save this man. Don't think about me, think about him. We'd be doing this for him." The line came out just like Stanley Harwood had rehearsed it.

"Okay, I got the picture. I don't like the smell of this, but tell me, what's the deal?"

"Here's the only way it can work, Tony," and Harwood proceeded to carefully explain exactly what he needed Battaglia to do.

"Let me set up the President so you can corner him alone in the massage room! And what if you shoot him, or stab him, or just tell him some damn dumb shit. I mean, I'm hanging out here, Stan. Something goes wrong, I'm up shit's creek."

Harwood grinned and added "Paddle-less."

"Right, Stan, paddle-less."

"I thought about this a long time before approaching you Tony and here's my only answer. Take a good look around, then stop, and think about what's happening. Look at the people on Wally's team, particularly O'Malley and Cartwright. They're either abject fools or pathological egotists, none of whom give a damn about anything at this point. I realize some of these guys did a good job in the first campaign, but somehow things have changed."

"Great, Stan. What's 'abject' mean and what's 'pathological'?"

"It means they are absolute losers."

"Right. 'Abject'. I'll try and remember that one."

"And who else around here cares about the President more than you and me?"

"Probably nobody."

"If that's true, Tony, and it is, then it all comes down to trust. You've got to trust me, Tony."

"Stan, I've had a plan too, a plan that I've been working on for a couple of months."

Harwood suddenly became worried. He had already gone on record refusing to discuss his scheme with Tony. Now it turned out that Tony had his own plan. Harwood sat down, leaned back in his chair, breathed deeply, and waited for Battaglia to talk.

You see, Stan, I've been worried too. I mean, I give the President advice, and stuff, but, you know, not on government stuff. I don't really understand all these issues and all the polls, but even Tony Battaglia can see something's wrong around here. I can feel it. So I said to myself, this man needs help."

It was Harwood's turn for an attenuated "And?"

"And starting about two months ago, I stopped going directly home from the White House. I started walking over to St. John's Church over on Lafayette Square, you know, across the park there. Can you imagine, me, Tony Battaglia, seventeenth cousin to the Pope—three times removed, of course—going to a wasp Episcopal Church? Hey, Stan, you know that the guy who runs the place is the Reverend Luis Leon? Can't be all that waspy, huh?"

Harwood was silent.

"Well, anyway," Battaglia continued, "I figure it's close by, it's where Wally usually goes to church and, after all, it's the same Mary, same Joseph, and same Jesus, know what I mean? I go over there every night after the gym closes. I walk in that little door on the side. You know there's a plaque of Mary right there by that door, up on the outside wall. You'd think you were going into a Catholic church when you use that door," Tony laughed.

"Well, like I said, I go in there . . . they don't really have those little white candles, like us Catholics, so I bring my own . . . set 'em up on this small altar on the side where they got this nice gold cross, next to this blue and white stained glass window. So I get one of these needlepointed kneeling cushions with St. John stitched into it—Stan, you gotta go over there and see these cushions they got . . . a bunch of them have the names of Presidents stitched into them—and I set up my candles. I light three, one for Wally, one for Mrs. Williams, and one for the campaign."

Harwood was a jumble of shock and renewed respect for Tony. Battaglia had a habit of underselling himself, evidencing a self-effacing vulnerability that was both innate and adaptive. This was unfortunate, Harwood thought, because Tony's ideas were among the most wise and profound of anyone he'd ever met.

"Then," continued Tony, "I say the Rosary and pray to St. Jude for help. To us old-timers, well, St. Jude . . . he's still the one to talk to when things look bad. The prayer is old and kinda out of date, but it's still just as good.

Pray for me, I am so helpless and alone. Make use, I implore you, of that particular privilege given to you, to bring visible and speedy help where help is almost despaired of. Come to my assistance in this great need that I may receive the consolation and help of heaven in all my necessities, tribulations, and sufferings . . . .

"Nobody prays like that anymore, Stan, but when you go to mass every day as a kid, you either learn a prayer or you get your knuckles whacked by a no-nonsense nun. So, I just say 'em like I've always said 'em."

"Tony, I cannot tell you how much it means that you are willing to share this."

"I like you Stan, and I want you to understand how much I care. I stay in that church for an hour or more, almost every night now. I ain't told anybody this. But I pray for something to happen to pull the President out of this thing. And now, after all that hard praying for help, you come along. This ain't accidental, Stan. The Father has a bigger plan than either of us could ever understand and we're both a part of it. Let not our will, but Thine be done. That's what The Book says."

Harwood continued to sit, stunned, overwhelmed by the moment, staring at Tony, and waiting for the denouement.

Tony finished. "So I guess the bottom line is, I'm at your service. I gotta trust you. I got no choice. You didn't come here yourself. You were sent."

Battaglia pushed his chair away from his desk, stood up, and walked around the desk to meet Harwood face to face. He stuck out a meaty hand and said, "Just tell me what you want me to do. I'm your man."

The still sweat-soaked Harwood gave Tony Battaglia the hug of his life and Tony hugged back, his head at Harwood's shoulder.

"Thanks, Tony. It's going to be great. You'll see."

18

His habit was to change into workout clothes in the locker room, then accompanied by Tony at each station, complete a routine of weightlifting and stretching exercises. His physique belied his years. Even in his seventies, the President's body was firm from the discipline of lifting weights and the luxury of having had Tony Battaglia as his personal trainer for eleven years.

After his workout, the President adjourned to the locker room, stripped down, wrapped in a huge towel embroidered with the Presidential logo, and walked down the hallway to Tony's massage table for a rubdown.

Few words passed between the men during the massage session. While Williams enjoyed talking with his old friend, the pure pleasure of the massage, in fact its spirituality, overcame his desire to talk to anyone, even Tony. Reciprocally, Tony respected the peaceful respite that it represented to his friend and mentor.

Of the sixty-eight rooms in the White House, and the eighty-two in the East and West Wings, Tony's office was Williams' favorite. After the massage, feeling simultaneously drained and restored, Williams got dressed, went to Tony's office, and plopped down for their regular dialogue, its length, usually short, determined by the number of meetings still on the Presidential calendar for that day.

The President's arrival in the fitness center was a daily activity, at least each day he was in the Capital, and one of no great note to staff privileged to share the facility. While nothing could afford to be routine to the Secret Service team assigned to protect the President, here in the security of the lower level, they were noticeably more relaxed than in most other places.

When he approached the fitness center, President Williams was preceded by one agent and followed by another. "Good afternoon, Tony," Agent Snowden chirped to Battaglia.

"Hey, Pete, what's happenin'?"

"Anything unusual today? Any non-regulars?"

"Not today, Pete. Just the same ol' lardball desk jockeys looking for some miracle from The Tone Man."

Pete Snowden strolled through the locker room, glanced around as he had done hundreds of times before, and with a professional, if perfunctory, wave motioned his approval to the President to enter. Snowden stood by the door as the President came in, while the other agent checked out the weight room.

After the President changed, they walked him the few steps to the weight room. During his workout, they remained outside the door, lolling and chatting with whoever came down the hall, checking the credentials of any newcomers to the White House whom they may not yet have gotten to know. After Williams' workout, when he was ready for his rubdown, one of the agents stuck his head into the massage room to assure that it was vacant, except for Tony.

Today as usual, when the President lay down on the white sheeted table, Tony draped him with another large white sheet. Williams emitted a small animal sigh as Tony began to work first on his trapezius. "Ooh, that feels good, Tony."

"Mr. President, 'cuse me a second. I gotta get a couple a more towels. You just sit tight, or lay tight, that is, and I'll be right back."

The President no sooner heard Tony repeat himself to the agent and heard the door close, when another voice materialized in the dim massage room. Stan Harwood stepped from behind a screen in the corner.

"Please don't be alarmed, Mr. President, I've got something of the utmost urgency to talk with you about."

The President lying face down on the table, rolled halfway over, securing the sheet with one hand, and lifting his head said, "What the heck are you doing here?"

"Stanley Harwood, Mr. President."

"Yes, I know you . . . Harwood . . . on our staff . . . here . . . the Congressional staff."

"Yes, sir, Mr. President, senior analyst in the Congressional liaison office."

"Stan Harwood? Where's Tony? What the heck is going on here?"

"Tony will be right back. Don't talk too loud or the agent will hear. Please, just give me three minutes, sir."

"For what? What are you doing in here?"

"Mr. President, Tony stuck his neck way out for this. Give me a minute, please."

Harwood sensed he was losing his moment and jumped in. He talked as fast as he could and still be understood.

"Mr. President, you are not going to win the election, and you are not only going to lose it, but lose it by the widest margin of any Presidential election in history. Your chief of staff and your campaign chairman are doing nothing to help you. You ran your first campaign with a firm hand on the tiller. This time, it appears that you tended to the affairs of state, leaving the campaign to be run by Party regulars. They have not done the job. You are being left high and dry and, if you'd take a couple of giant steps backward and look at it, you'd agree. Believe me when I say this, please. You are an expert at what you do, but, with all due respect, I'm no less an expert at this. Trust me. I came here to tell you that I have a plan to guarantee you'll be re-elected . . . not only re-elected, but remembered in history."

The President sat up, clutching the sheet that had covered his prone body. "Are you crazy, young man? Go get Tony."

"Mr. President, Tony is in on this, we're working together. Tony isn't coming back for exactly two minutes. He let me in here, showed me where to hide, and left on purpose to give me a couple of minutes with you."

"Tony is in on this?"

"Yes, sir. He'll give you a wink and a nod when you leave to let you know that everything's okay. But this was really my idea . . . I got him in on it. I have tried for weeks, months really, to find a way to approach you. It's a bit of an understatement to say that you're never alone. Tony was my last shot. You know he trusts me, sir, to stick his neck out like this. Sir, we both care about you and we both want the best for you."

"You guys are totally insane."

"Yes sir, that may well be. But we both know a great man in a deteriorating situation when we see him."

"Okay, what's the story Harwood? Pitch it quick. What's the miracle dust you've got to sprinkle on this, as you would describe it, debacle?"

"Sir, I really can't go into detail here. I can hardly put forth a plan while hiding from the Secret Service in Tony's massage room. Here's what I propose: you call a meeting with your entire campaign staff. Have O'Malley and his staff there, too. Beforehand, tell them you want a comprehensive status report. In particular, you want to know exactly how far behind we are and where. Tell them you want them to present the specifics of how they're going to close the gaps, geographically, gender-wise, ethnically, demographically, whatever. No excuses. No long winded, indirect, rambling answers. No maybes, ifs, or buts. What's the plan . . . what specific action is each individual in the room going to take? Call the meeting immediately, tomorrow if possible. I caution you not to lead the discussion. Just be simple and direct and ask for the specifics of their plan."

"And then Mr. Harwood? What then?"

"Then think about it, analyze it for twenty-four hours. If you're even remotely satisfied that your team is on the right track, committed to seeing you win, willing to do everything possible to succeed . . . then do nothing. Que sera, sera. But, if you have serious doubts, as you can see that Tony and I do, then allow me an hour of your undivided attention. It's not much considering the stakes."

"Who else knows about this, Mr. Harwood?"

"No one, Mr. President. As I said before, only Tony, and all he did was arrange this meeting."

"You're going to take a big chance, Mr. Harwood."

Harwood grinned. "*Have* taken, Mr. President. Past tense, not future."

"We'll see." Williams paused, more than a little confused. "Now, back to your corner, Mr. Harwood."

As Harwood retreated to his niche, Williams grabbed his sheet around him, rose from the table, opened the door, and pushed his way past a surprised Agent Snowden.

"You're not waiting for Tony, Mr. President? He just went down the hall to get some stuff, he ought to be right back."

"No, Pete, I've got some things to do. Tell Tony thanks a lot, but something came up. And, remember to give him a wink and a nod for me, okay? I'm sure he'll understand."

"Yes, Mr. President."

"And, Pete? Make sure to tell Tony that the night people need to do a little better job cleaning up. There's some strange stuff building up in the corners of some of these rooms around here."

The President winked and nodded, and turned into the locker room, leaving the befuddled agent standing in the hall.

19

"Emily, get me the Attorney General, please. Tell her it's important. Thank you."

"Yes, sir."

After all the years, Williams' fundamentally self-effacing nature continued to surprise Emily. If he had ever failed to use "please" and "thank you" with her, she could count the times on one hand. And she couldn't imagine another President adding to his request to tell the person that his call was important. So many people at the White House are full of themselves, she thought. Every peon here acts as if his call to Domino's pizza is a world event. What a contrast: arrogant bureaucrats who order up Air Force One to take them out for nine holes, and a President who never forgets to use his 'magic words'.

A brief buzz preceded Emily's voice, "The Attorney General is on line one, Mr. President."

"Good morning, Julie. Where are you?"

"On my way to Andrews. Remember, I'm flying down to Florida on a combination campaign swing and meeting with gang leaders and ministers in Miami and Tampa. It's on your daily briefing memo. Any problem?"

"No Julie, not at all. Listen, I need a favor. This is confidential. You'll have to use your people, but I want it contained."

"Yes, Mr. President."

"Okay, there's a gentleman named Stanley Harwood on the staff here. I'm not sure of his title . . . Senior Director of Legislative Policy Analysis or some such stuff. Ever heard of him?"

"No, sir, Mr. President. The name maybe is a little familiar, but I've not had direct contact with him."

"I want to know everything about him. Capital E, Everything. Where's he from, what toothpaste he uses, the tread wear on his tires . . . what he thinks, and why he thinks it."

"With him on the staff, there has to be a complete file on him over there, as well as one with our people at Justice. Have you checked your files?"

"No, Julie, and I don't want to do anything from this end. And I can't explain it now, either."

"Yes, sir. Got it. I trust that this isn't going to bite either of us in the butt. Do you want progress reports?"

"No progress reports. Just do it all thoroughly and do it all in forty-eight hours . . . less, if you can. How's that for an assignment?"

"I've had a lot worse. From you, I think."

"Yes, you're probably right. And don't go through Whittingham. If he starts to get involved, call me directly. Okay?"

"Yes, Mr. President."

"Thanks, Julie. Knock 'em dead in Florida."

20

"Yo, Mickey, what's up?"

"I wanna sell some more calls on the casino index."

"Mickey, you're kidding, right?"

"'Fraid not."

"Your money, Mickey . . . it's your money. Want to use the numbered account in Bermuda again, or the Cayman account?"

"Cayman, this time."

"Okay, hold on. Let me check the margin balance in that account."

"I'll wait."

From his fifteenth floor office, the stockbroker stared out over the smog of East Los Angeles and shook his head as he dialed his margin department.

"Margin Department, Rita Samatra speaking."

"Hi, Rita. John Wilson. I need some margin information on an account."

"Hi, John. Shoot."

"Numbered account, Bank of New Hebrides, Trustee. It's a GH account, the number is two, six, nine, dash, three, three, four, eight, seven, dash, five, oh, nine, eight, two."

"Got it. Hold on John."

Wilson waited, longing for the day when he could smoke without a five-minute ride down the elevator. I'm frigging fifty, he thought, too old for this business, too old to fart around with these no-name freaks calling up with their crazy fuckin' trades. All I need is one more SEC suspension. Rita broke his train of thought.

"I'm back."

"Whaddya got?"

"We got in a big wire transfer from a Canadian bank yesterday. That account has buying power of forty-eight million."

"Thanks, Rita."

Wilson returned to his biggest customer, one he had never seen or met. "I'm back, Mickey. My margin clerk says we've got forty-eight million of buying power."

"Good. I want to buy a million out-of-the-money puts each on Global Casinos, Mandalay, and Western Gaming."

"Jesus, man, I don't know how much more of this the market can stand. There's no liquidity in these stocks, and their puts and calls are even thinner. You've already hit the index hard. Either your client is crazy or knows that something is gonna happen to make these stocks drop."

"Johnny, we've been doing business for four months. How many times have I asked for advice?"

"Never."

"And, how much in net commissions has this account generated for you in that time?"

"About a half a million dollars, Mick."

"And, does Wonderink have any better customers than us?"

"Not that I know."

"Then kindly shut the fuck up, would you?"

"You got it, Mickey. Me, I'm three monkeys, all of a sudden. I don't see nothing, I don't hear nothing, and I don't say nothing."

"And, Johnny, all these trades are legal and aboveboard. My client is just a big trader and a big risk taker. So don't go do anything stupid like sitting down with your compliance officer and bringing any special attention to this account. We can move it in a heartbeat, okay?"

"You read my mind, Mickey. Let me read 'em back."

"Screw reading 'em back. Just do 'em and courier the confirms to that law firm."

"Done. Thanks for the order."

"Talk to you soon, Johnny."

When her cell phone gave its distinctive ring, Chris Weiner reached quickly into her purse, simultaneously, saying to her luncheon partner, "Hey, I'm really sorry." She quickly connected to the call, "Hello."

"Uh, this is Mickey Stuckler at Ridgeco Security in New York. Is this Ms. Smith?"

"Yes," answered Weiner, "this is Ms. Smith." She winked and smiled at her friend across the table.

"I'm just reporting the put order was executed through the Cayman account. We'll send duplicate confirms to the trust company in Bermuda, per our standing instructions."

"Okay, thanks. Bye." Weiner returned the phone to her purse, took a sip of water, and returned her attention to her friend. "Did I ever tell you how much I love money? Now, what were we talking about?"

21

"Show her in, Emily."

As Julie Shaer entered the Oval Office, Williams moved from behind his desk to the sitting area across the room and greeted her with a warm handshake.

"How was Florida, Julie?"

"Warm, Mr. President. Very warm."

"Do I sense a double meaning?"

"Yes, sir, it was a tough trip. The Democrats are definitely unfriendly at this time of year and some of our Republican friends down there are sounding a lot like Democrats. But, let me get on to your request."

"Okay, let's have it."

"Well, Mr. President, we're moving as fast as we can. Just so you know, at this pace we could have missed something important, but I wanted to get you what we've got." She opened a large portfolio which she had placed next to her chair and withdrew a five-inch stack of papers.

"If quantity is quality, you're doing excellent work, Julie."

"This is just the important stuff, sir. There's another room full back at my office. I'm not sure exactly where you're headed, but here's the bottom line. In a word, 'wow'. In a few words, this guy's cleaner than Mother Theresa's Our Fathers. And he's smarter than you and me combined, sir. But, before I go on, I'm going to finish this conversation with some direct feedback, Mr. President. The way you brought me this thing, well, I just want to make sure it's kosher."

There were few that Williams heeded as much as the Attorney General. She was tall—nearly six feet—and slim, skinny some say, but with a cherubic—a Washington Post editorial used the term "chubby"—face that belied her lean frame and flat chest. She was plain, not ugly, but not pretty. She was also brilliant. As the crime-fighting, no-nonsense Attorney General of California, she distinguished herself on matters as diverse as illegal immigration, earthquake insurance, anti-smoking initiatives, and old growth logging in Mendocino County. She had served Governor Williams with distinction and forthrightness before their common sojourn East. The President expected no less from Julie Shaer in Washington than he had enjoyed in Sacramento. He was not disappointed.

Julie Shaer became mechanical: "Stanley David Harwood, thirty-seven years old. Father a small-town pediatrician in Connecticut. Mother a professor of history—medieval, European, American, whatever they throw at her—at a local community college. Parents married forty-one years. Looks like they separated a couple of times, but never divorced. Harwood is the youngest of three. Brother, divorced, was a partner, worked in 'syndication'—whatever that is—for Morgan Stanley, an investment banking firm in New York, died at the age of twenty-five, in an automobile accident. Sister is a housewife, lives in suburban Boston, married to a partner with a Boston law firm. Sister, herself, has a law degree from NYU.

"Harwood is a certified academic superstar. High school #1 in everything, including the chess team. Valedictorian. Class president and president of the Spanish club. Yale University, scholarship, Phi Beta Kappa, majored in economics. Junior varsity crew, junior varsity basketball. Sports-wise, this guy is junior varsity everything. Two years of Princeton divinity school heading for a doctorate in the Epistemology of Comparative Religions, I think." Julie Shaer stopped. "Epistemology of Comparative Religions? Does that make any sense, Mr. President?"

"Close enough, Julie. It's a long and not very interesting story. Keep going."

"Yes, sir. Well, after dropping out of the doctoral program at Princeton—earning only his Masters, mind you—he tours Asia and Africa, pretty much on his own. Then, decides he wants a different career and goes for another Master's at Johns Hopkins in International Studies . . . follows that with a doctorate. While he's going to Hopkins, he apparently decides to study law, too, and goes to the University of Baltimore at night for a law degree. This guy is definitely overeducated, Mr. President. Maybe he's really from Calcutta."

"Very funny, Julie."

"Clerks three years for Jaime Perez on the Federal Bench in L.A., focusing mostly on international stuff, but handling some of the regular federal business, as well. Outstanding in every respect. Highly regarded by Judge Perez. Actually becomes recognized for his scholastic and academic contributions to several of the best policy journals in the country. I didn't bring copies of the articles, but we've got everything, including his doctoral thesis, if you want to see it."

"No thanks, I've already got plenty of boring, overwrought, intellectual articles to read, most of them from my own staff. Keep going."

"Harwood spends two years on the Hill as Assistant General Counsel to an *ad hoc* joint committee looking at international energy policy. He's noticed by everyone he meets, including both parties, the GAO, Department of Energy, et cetera. Apparently the guy just stands out everywhere he goes. Brilliant and nice, too. Not thought of as dogmatic, and apparently not an egghead or nerd either, despite his educational background."

"The guy sounds a little like Robert MacNamara and his whiz kid cronies. IQs of a million, and they commit huge, fatal errors anyway. All brains, no sense, and fifty eight thousand end up etched on a black granite wall."

"No signs of that intellectualism cum hubris with this guy."

"Did you check his body for stigmata?"

"What can I say, Mr. President. This is what our people came up with."

"No problem, Julie, it just seems a tad eerie."

"Mr. President, I'm only hitting the highlights. No record of contributions to any causes, political groups, or even the Party. Nothing to charity, churches, synagogues, United Fund . . . anything."

"Sounds like a fun guy."

The Attorney General returned to her dossier.

"Harwood's name comes to the attention of Cameron Acaba, Deputy Director of Legislative Liaison. When Acaba came on board, sir, he was desperate for help. With all due respect sir, he was strong-armed into taking on a lot of campaign workers, party loyalists, and favor seekers. A real bunch of dopes."

"Yes, Julie, and those so-called dopes helped put me in office. That's a handicap that every elected official in history has had to deal with, trading off loyalty and patronage against competency. We didn't invent it. The Caesars had the problem, big time, and so do the Republicans."

"Anyway, while they're taking long lunches and congratulating themselves on the great campaign they'd run, Acaba realized he needed help, and was savvy enough to resist attempts to shove another political hack down his throat for this particular job. He downright refused to use this position to repay another favor."

"I knew there was a reason I liked Acaba . . . other than the fact that his parents waded the Rio Grande at midnight, dodging Border Patrol searchlights, just to work in the fields of Salinas at thirty five cents an hour . . . permanently injuring their backs in the process."

"Okay, so Acaba hears about Harwood and thinks this is the pro he needs. He cold calls him, interviews him, reads his articles, and makes him an offer. Acaba has no inkling about Harwood's politics, he just needs a pro, a policy wonk, so he takes a chance. Harwood accepts and moves down here from the Hill. He spends a year or so in Old EOB, then they move him to the West Wing."

"You've given me nothing personal yet, Julie."

"Yes, sir. Well it's basically a little strange."

"Strange like how?"

"Like Ralph Nader strange. His personal life is clean and straight, but it doesn't seem necessarily *normal.* Nonexistent might be a better word. Lives alone, owns a really nice co-op not too far beyond the Cathedral, paid for most of it in cash, the rest a standard mortgage. We couldn't find the source of the cash, but his tax returns all appear clean as a hound's tooth. He had to come up with close to four hundred thousand, including legal and closing costs."

"That's a lot of money for our man."

"Yes, sir. But he's been working and doesn't spend any real money that we know of. Sorry, I don't know more at this point. Anyway, our people have been through his place as thoroughly as we could without showing any signs of disturbance. Nothing strange or weird there. From the photographs, it's one hell of a lot neater than mine!"

"You've been through his place? Please, tell me it was legal, Julie."

"Yes, sir. We got all the paperwork done before we did anything.'

"Good. Has he got a girlfriend? Boyfriend?"

"No sign of either. He has a baby grand piano in his living room and it's covered with photos. We've identified almost everybody as a relative or a friend, but there's one good-looking female we can't match. About his age with dark hair. Strange, my folks say the picture is computer generated or enhanced. Anyway, it's definitely not an original photo."

"What do you make of it?"

"I don't know, sir. We'll just have to wait and see. We've also shopped Harwood's picture around bars and restaurants in his neighborhood. No recognition there. Plus, his picture isn't recognized in any of the fifty or so gay bars we've checked in Washington, suburban Maryland and Virginia, Princeton, Baltimore, or Los Angeles. We've checked all credit card purchases for the past two years . . . dinners, clothes, ski trips to Winter Park, Colorado. That's it."

"Winter Park?"

"A locals place close to Denver, limited cachet, but great skiing. One informant said he remembered Harwood, and every year he takes a day or two off from the slopes to do volunteer work in a handicapped ski center there."

"This guy's too good to be true."

"There are still a few holes, Mr. President. I mentioned the cash for the co-op. And he makes occasional large cash deposits. No idea where they come from. Also, he spends a lot of money on clothes and books. Those seem to be his passions, if, in fact, he's got passions at all. Custom made suits at three thousand each, hundred dollar Hermes neckties, custom made shirts, John Lobb shoes, and lots of old and rare books . . . antiquarian books is how they're referred to."

"Lobb?"

"They're custom made English shoes, Mr. President. A couple of thousand a pair, I'm told. I never heard of them either."

"So the guy's a clothes horse?"

"Yes, sir. Other than that and some cash that moves around there's no skeletons yet. But we're still hard at it. I might add, sir, no trips to Las Vegas, Tunica, or Atlantic City. No gun permits issued, no hunting or fishing licenses purchased. He plays a lot of racquetball and squash . . . works out like a fiend."

"Great job, Julie. Typical of your work, of course."

"Thank you, sir. Shall I report back when the rest of our information comes in?"

"Only if it's different, then let me know immediately."

"Understood. I do want to emphasize this guy's overall reputation. His professors—Yale, Princeton, Hopkins—all remember him as brilliant, incisive, creative . . . a real thinker. His peers like him, trust him, and respect him. One word we constantly hear is 'expert'."

"Thanks a ton, Julie, great job."

As Julie Shaer stood to leave, she smoothed her skirt, and turned toward Williams. "Mr. President, on O'Malley . . . ." She was rarely tentative, but her words trailed off as she looked for encouragement from the President.

"Yes, Julie?"

"From our standpoint, my department is on good legal grounds with this stuff, sir, but you must tell me if there's anything more to this. I don't think that we'd have much fun with the successor to Cox, Walsh, and Starr. Maybe I'm an old conservative, sir, but I'm looking out for you, you know. That's part of my job. I'd fall on my sword for you, but, all the same, I'd rather not *have to*."

"Now, Julie, how long have you known me?"

"Eight years, Mr. President."

"Have you ever seen me get into a gray area on ethics or law, or not deal with people straight up?"

"No sir, never."

"Well, this is no different. This is an important matter but no matter how lofty our goals, we won't pursue them in an unethically or unlawfully. I'm not about to get either of us in trouble, okay?"

"No offense, sir, but like I said, sounding cautionary notes is part of what you pay me for."

"Julie, the people pay you, I don't. We both have the same boss. Is that all?"

"Well, I'm going to sound like a broken record, but again, as Attorney General and friend, please be careful in matters of intrigue. I say that generally speaking, of course, but also specifically with our Mr. Harwood. Monday morning quarterbacks can make straight arrows look pretty ridiculous . . . even crooked. I'm considering this Harwood thing a routine security investigation, but the deadline and the intensity of the assignment give it a highly unusual flavor. I can do magic, but I can't make things disappear entirely. I'm no Sigfried and Roy."

"Thank God for that, Julie! Listen, we're on solid ground. I think too much of you to let that change."

"Thank you, sir. By the way, we're checking Harwood's phone bills, reviewing all numbers called in the past two years. If anything unusual turns up there, we'll let you know."

"I'll pray it doesn't . . . ."

22

Standing beside the "Gate K1 Restricted Area" sign, Bernard Cartwright curled his fingers anxiously through the Signature Air chain-link fence. As the jet taxied close to the terminal, one of the ground crew, wearing massive ear protectors and waving bright orange signals, backed up slowly as the GV approached. He signaled the plane a few feet further on, then crossed his arms and Weiner Oil's jet abruptly halted.

As he watched for the plane's stairway to descend, Cartwright mentally wandered through the prospects for the meeting. In a few minutes, they'd be face to face. What this time? Alternatively bitch and princess, she could confuse and confound like no other person he knew. A straightforward fundraising meeting? More of her shit on O'Malley and his assignment? The tender kisses of a woman that was hard on the outside, and could barely be herself in an environment of complete privacy and trust? What kinds of mania control this person? Bi-polar? Maybe. Driven? Of course. Shadow syndromes, defying analysis. Would he ever know what drove her?

No less perplexed than usual, Cartwright released his grip on the fence, walked down the short sidewalk, and turned into the building. Crossing the lobby, he absently waved his credentials to the desk attendant, and walked through the double doors to the tarmac, noting the logo on the side of the plane: a block lettered "WO", the W worked intricately into an oil derrick, and the "O" rendered as a huge drop of oil, black and glistening. Corny, he thought, but probably effective as a communications icon. Anyway, the fifty-million dollar jet bearing the logo was sufficient evidence of the company's success. As the engines' whine faded and the stairs dropped down, Cartwright hurried out to the plane.

Though he knew his way, Weiner's assistant showed him back to a small sitting room attached to Chris's bedroom. Not wishing to set himself up for disappointment, Cartwright tried to stifle any rumblings of desire for her. Don't fantasize, he told himself . . . don't obsess. But repressing his libido was too much of an effort, and he mentally wallowed in self-gratifying reminiscences of her strong thighs around him, her mouth on him.

Had he sold his soul for the intense physical pleasure of a woman twenty years younger? Was he returning political favors for sexual ones? *That goddam tax . . . what difference does it make anyway? God, do I really love her? And her me? So fine the line between love and lust! Come to your senses, Cartwright! Weiner . . . ah, physically, things I've never done before. But, the lying, the deceit . . . things I have never done before.*

"Bernie!" she cried as she emerged from the bedroom. "Oh, Bernie, I've missed you so much!"

As usual, when he first saw her after an extended absence, he was speechless. Weiner's black wool skirt was at mid-thigh. She wore a pink oxford cloth shirt, well oversized, so that it appeared to be a man's, but discreetly bore her monogram. Cartwright's eyes feasted on Chris Weiner's chest, covered only partially by the shirt, unbuttoned to just below her breasts. The too-large shirt admitted a view of her white lace bra at almost every angle.

Finally, Cartwright's eyes lifted. "Hi, Chrissie. God, I've missed you too. I have to admit, when I saw your plane taxi up, well, my heart literally started pounding. Not good for an old fart like me."

"Bernie, Bernie," Weiner cautioned, as she shook her head, pursed her lips, and placed an index finger to his mouth. "None of that talk now. You know you please me in every way possible. You're a young colt . . . or maybe stud horse would be better as far as I'm concerned."

Cartwright and Weiner hugged a long time. Usually their hugs were perfunctory preliminaries to the frenetic fumbling with zippers, buttons, and hooks that would follow immediately. But, this time, the hug was long, neither seeming to want to break first.

Still holding her tight, the Republican campaign chairman leaned away, tilting his head back so he could look Weiner in the eyes. This close, he was taken aback. "Chris, your eyes are red and kind of puffy. What's wrong?"

"I'm just feeling a little weepy. I guess my period's coming on, I don't know."

Cartwright's voice was low and comforting. He lifted a hand from behind her back and stroked her hair, slowly. "This is not good, Chrissie. What can I do?"

"Nothing, Bernie, I'm just a little tired. Too much on my mind . . . too much going on."

"Damn, Chris, why don't you go down to the Palm Desert house and relax a while . . . or out to Aspen? I'll join you if I can."

"Thanks, Bernie, but I have too much to do."

There was a long pause, as if the billionaire oil baroness wanted to say more, but the words could not escape her. Finally, she said, "Bernie, what's the point of it all?"

"Of all what?"

"I don't know . . . us . . . the tax legislation."

"Are you okay, Chris?"

Chris Weiner unlocked her arms from Cartwright and gently pushed herself away. "Yeah, Bernie, I'm fine. Come on, let's go lie down."

She took his hand and led him into the bedroom, closing and locking the door behind her. Cartwright methodically closed each of the curtains, not before looking out the cabin windows and noting the incongruity of being in her bedroom in a luxurious jet, looking out on the Reagan Airport ground traffic. He plopped himself on the bed, and clasped his hands behind his head.

Pacing the floor at the end of the bed, Weiner asked, "How're we coming, Bernie?"

"It's coming, Chris."

Weiner frowned. "That's not what I hear, Bernie."

"You're a worrier, Chris, at least when you're not bouncing off the walls, ecstatic about your most recent oil deal." Bernard Cartwright rarely ventured a critical comment under such circumstances, afraid he might insult her, losing his opportunity for sex. His lust usually kept him careful and quiet. This time, the mood was different . . . Weiner was different.

"What's with you, anyway, Chris?"

"What do you mean, Bernie?" Cartwright sat up slightly, outstretching his arms, and Weiner lay down next to him. Weiner squeezed her eyes tight, as if focusing on a distant memory, or stoically suppressing a pang of pain.

"Bernie, I wish you'd met my father. He was something."

"I've read so much about him, I feel like I knew him. But, Chris, you've done more in fifteen years, than he did in fifty."

"No, he didn't have the opportunities I've had."

"That's not right, Chris. Your father gave you a great education, but you were the one who was first in your class, learned the business from the bottom up, and leveraged the company into a big time player."

"Bernie, when I was a little girl my father used to ask, 'Darling, do you know why money is green?' I'd always answer, 'No Daddy, why is it green?' And he'd say, 'That's because us Weiners pick it off the trees before it gets ripe!' Then he'd laugh and laugh. But he was serious . . . money to him was serious business. After I'd heard it a hundred times, I obviously knew the answer. But he'd ask me the question over and over, and I'd always say, 'No Daddy, why is it green?' Just a little girl, trying desperately to please her daddy. He named me Chris 'cause it was a boy's name. I'm not Christine or Kristin, just Chris. It couldn't be Jennifer, Jessica, or Courtney, like the rest of the world, it had to be a boy's name. Anyway, I could never deprive him of the pleasure of repeating that line about picking money before it's ripe."

Weiner pushed an arm under Cartwright's head and swung a leg across him, her already diminutive skirt climbing up over her thighs, and bunching at her waist.

Cartwright kissed her hair gently, then looked down, and saw tears welling in her eyes.

"You had to know him, Bernie. Look up persistence in the dictionary, and there's his picture. Old country values . . . came from nothing. God, he was relentless on himself and everyone else."

"And your mother?"

"Jesus, Bernie, leave my mother out of this. He didn't kill her, she killed herself. She held the gun, and she pulled the trigger, he didn't."

"But he pushed you hard . . . really hard?"

"Sure, and I thank him for it every day. Daddy was everything in my life. He challenged me to do things other people didn't think were possible."

A look of concern crossed Cartwright's face. "And did you satisfy him, Chris? Did you please him?"

"Huh?"

"I mean, was he ever satisfied with you? Did he ever say, 'Great job, Chrissie. I'm really proud of you?' Did he ever say, 'Wow, number one in your class at Harvard. Way to go!'?"

"He wasn't that way."

"You mean you could never satisfy him . . . that's what you mean."

"Bernie, when our phone rang, as a little girl it was my job to answer it, preferably on the first ring, but never after the second. It could be the Secretary of Energy, a Saudi prince, or the Chairman of Arco. I answered professionally, took good messages . . . the person, the time, the content of the message . . . and impressed people. He told me that was my job, and I did it well. I used to go to the fields, deep water rigs, too. If anyone complained about a little girl being there, my father would laugh and say, 'You'd better look out, because you're going to be working for her pretty soon!' He loved me, he cared about me."

"As you were . . . or as he wanted you to be? It's one thing not to be verbal with praise . . . not to laud out loud. It's another thing just not being satisfied, wanting perfection out of yourself and everyone else. He wanted you to be everything he couldn't be . . . or wasn't, didn't he? He wanted you to be perfect."

"Don't get psychological on me, Bernie. And, what about you? You were the big shot lawyer in New York . . . sitting on important boards . . . raising tons of money for charities . . . managing *pro bono* suits against the school system on behalf of ghetto parents whose kids' teachers couldn't spell 'dog' and 'cat'. Now you're fucking the top Republican donor . . . about half your age . . . taking a little cash on the side, from what I hear, and running . . . if that's the word . . . a disaster of a campaign."

"I'll land on my feet, Chrissie."

"You'd better, Bernie, for both of our sakes."

"Chris, is this tax some kind of obsession?"

Weiner giggled softly. "I warned you Bernie, no psycho-babble, no head stuff, okay? If there's going to be any head stuff around here, it's going to be me giving it to you."

Despite her girlish giggle, Cartwright knew he'd pushed too far. He had forced a key into a rusty lock, and was afraid to turn it . . . afraid of every consequence . . . both that the door might open and that it might stay locked. He backtracked instead. "Well, Chrissie, whatever, you turned out great."

Weiner suddenly rolled off the bed, stood, and methodically unbuttoned her shirt, dropping it to the floor, unveiling a white lace demi-bra, her nipples, small pink crescents, just peeking over the top. Reaching behind her back, she unhooked her skirt, pulled down the zipper, and allowed it to fall to her ankles.

"Bernie," she whispered, "I really need those tax hearings to happen . . . I need that legislation."

Cartwright was catatonic. "Uh, yeah, it'll happen . . . no problem."

Weiner stepped out of her skirt, returned to the bed, kneeling next to him, her hands moving with precision to his belt buckle, unfastening it, then moving to his zipper. Slowly, teasingly, she pulled on the zipper, then placed a hand inside the elastic band at the top of his boxers. "Ooh," she feigned surprise, "what do we have here?" Grasping the top of his boxers with both hands, she pulled them, together with his pants, down to his knees. Cartwright raised his head, then dropped it back to the pillow, stared briefly at the ceiling, and closed his eyes.

Her hand moved down to hold him, rhythmically stroking. Her mouth, starting at his navel, moved slowly, side to side, lightly licking, kissing, and sucking his fleshy belly. Her head dropped down and, her mouth consumed him. Her head bobbed slowly, deliberately, producing small, wet sounds.

Cartwright let out subtle cries, soft whines, sounding remotely like a small wounded animal, his labored pants increasing in intensity.

Weiner looked up at him and whispered, "Don't come too fast, darling. I want to make this last for you."

The only response was the groan of pleasure that rose, unconscious and guttural, from somewhere deep in Cartwright's throat. As her mouth and hands moved in precise unison, his animal cries grew closer together, increasing in volume. His legs twitched and, suddenly, his entire body jerked and writhed in the cathartic paroxysms of a man who had been a very long time since being pleased like this. Then, the injured, whining animal in his throat emitted its death cry, a final, gasping shriek, followed by short labored breaths.

Weiner took him from her mouth, wiped her mouth on the sheet, and laid her head on his belly. "That was nice, Bernie . . . that was really nice."

Cartwright's chest and belly heaved, small myoclonic twitches breaking out across his body. No words came from him, just the panting of a man who had spent himself.

"Bernie," she whispered, "we've got to get that casino legislation going."

His belly and chest heaves grew deeper, and further apart. Another primordial groan came out through his partly open mouth. "Uhh, uhhh, huh . . . ." His panting now progressed to a deep breathing that rattled the flesh in the back of his throat.

After a minute of silence, broken only by Cartwright's noises, she spoke again. "Bernie? There's something else I want to tell you about my father. This is important. You see, I really don't think you understand about him . . . ."

Chris Weiner lifted her head slightly, and looked up at Cartwright, his mouth gaped open, emitting post-ejaculation wheezes. She listened as they migrated into a muffled snorting, then the groaning snore of sleep. Every few moments, his body twitched, each successive spasm further apart, and smaller than the preceding.

Studying his face, she watched his lips puff and purse with each breath. She laid her head back down, then took him, now soft and wet, into her mouth again, and slowly sucked. The tears ran down her cheeks, between his legs, and wet the silk sheet under them.

23

Two days after her first meeting with the President to discuss the Harwood investigation, Julie Shaer returned to the Oval Office. Having covered an abbreviated agenda of other matters, the President turned to the subject of Harwood. "From your bullet-point summary, it sounds like you've gotten a lot done in forty-eight hours, Julie."

"We've been hard at it, sir. I'm just worried how he's going to react. Any thoughts before we begin?"

"I think we just go for it. One way or the other, we've got to move on."

"That sounds like the Wally Williams I used to know," chirped Shaer, typically upbeat. "This Harwood situation has you more energized than I've seen in months."

"He's got a lot on the ball, and right now, I'm feeling pretty much 'no harm, no foul'. I mean, what's the downside to listening?"

"Part of the downside is this individual approaching you in the massage room. I'm still shaking my head over that one." Before Williams could respond, Shaer continued, "And more downside is going around your campaign chairman and chief of staff. You may be the President, however you do have obligations to others."

"Well, Julie, my friend, I can't say I'm not anxious. But he was right-on about what I'd hear at that campaign pow-wow. He said there'd be no plan and that Cartwright would bully and bluff, and he was totally correct."

President Williams could not hide from Shaer's persistence. "Mr. President, I could have told you that. Any cab driver in town could have told you that! You're eleven points behind, if you believe this morning's Post! Moore's decided the worst thing he can do right now is campaign. He's become a cigar store Indian: no talk, no walk, no nothing. My husband's greatest peeve is seeing a quarterback who's up by three touchdowns, kneel down for four straight plays. Drives him crazy. And that's what Moore's doing, kneeling on every down, waiting for the clock to run out."

"You really know how to burst a guy's bubble don't you, Julie?"

"Well, Mr. President, almost by definition, there can't be much of a plan. And Cartwright, even if he is smart, rich, and powerful, is just a card-carrying member of BBA, Bullies and Bullshitters of America. Mr. Harwood didn't need Jeanne Dixon for that one."

"Darn, Julie, don't they call that piling on? Or unnecessary roughness?"

"It's just that his arrogance . . . his taking you down with him, it all makes me sick."

Before the President could engage a debate, Emily knocked lightly and entered without waiting for a reply. "Mr. Harwood is here, Mr. President."

"Please, bring him on, Emily . . . and thanks."

When Harwood walked in, he stopped for a moment just inside the doorway, visibly surprised to see Julie Shaer in the room.

To Julie Shaer, Stanley Harwood looked just like the dozens of photos of him she'd sifted through. She regarded him carefully, more with professional dispassion, than distrust.

"Mr. Harwood, I don't believe you've ever met Attorney General Shaer. Madame Attorney General, this is Stanley Harwood."

The Attorney General stood, offering a long arm toward Harwood, who responded, with a slight stutter, "How do you do, ma'am? Uh, this is a genuine honor."

Williams motioned his guests to specific chairs, pulling his own chair close to form a tight triangle.

"Mr. Harwood, Julie and I want to cover a few things with you. Go ahead, Julie. You've got the floor."

Shaer's long, lean form did not compliment the furniture, or perhaps it did not compliment her. She was the kind of woman who looked better standing. Despite her tall and narrow figure, her round, cheek-dominated face and tight blond curls imparted an unfortunate over-aged Shirley Temple look. Had she not been the nation's top lawyer and universally esteemed by opponents and supporters alike, she might have been thought to have a slightly dissipated look. Though attractive, her face had a flushed and veiny appearance, as if she might have gone a step or two beyond being an oenophile. She was, Harwood thought, a living contradiction: a tall, lean form, topped off by an inconsistently chubby face. Her physical appearance wholly belied her intellect, intense determination, and stony professionalism. Shaer always wore black dresses, today being no exception, and Harwood noticed the unfashionable antique brooch that closed her collar at the neck. He did not, however, allow his analysis of her curious aspect diminish his respect for her.

"Mr. Harwood, the President has told me that you requested a private meeting with him. He asked me to check you out before he proceeds."

Harwood said nothing, merely looked at the Attorney General, listening intently for her next words.

"The results of our investigation are impressive," she continued, "academically and personally. There are only a couple of things we'd like to clear up."

"Madame Attorney General, before I could get this assignment, I had to undergo the most comprehensive of security checks."

"We've reviewed that work and it looks great. Specifically, what I want to know is, when you clerked for Judge Perez in L.A., where did you live?"

"I lived in West L.A . . . near Hollywood, at least most of the time I did."

"Where specifically?"

"Well, I lived with several different people. It's more than a tad expensive there, and I moved from friend to friend. All I had were a few suits and shirts and about a million law books. My clothes filled the back seat of my car and my books filled the trunk," he laughed. "It was the perfect size."

"Can you give us specifics?"

Harwood rapidly moved his eyes from the President to the Attorney General and back, apparently looking for relief. There was no relief forthcoming. "Madame Attorney General, that was a long time ago. As I'm sure my associates from that period will tell you, I mostly lived in my office. I slept there more than any place else. I must've pulled an all-nighter at least twice a week. Somebody should tell the taxpayers about how hard some government employees work. We're not all slouches."

"Amen to that, Mr. Harwood," Shaer replied. "And I agree with your assessment of your dedication, at least as far as we've been able to determine. But we still want to know who you lived with and where."

"I lived quite a while with another clerk I met at the court's cafeteria, a guy named William Blunt. Anyway, I'll gladly get together all of the addresses I had then, even if I stayed with someone for a week. Anything else?"

"Yes, could you tell us the source of the money you put down on your co-op."

"That one's easy, my rich uncle."

"Seriously?"

"Seriously, my mother's oldest brother. He's from Hungary. My mother was the only kid in the family born here. Uncle Larry's as rich as Croesus! Inventions, computers, that kind of stuff. You know Andrew Grove, the multi-billionaire from Intel? He and my uncle are buddies. George Soros, the investment guy . . . him, too. Grove got him into Intel early on. As you can imagine, the rest is history."

"He gives you money?"

Harwood chuckled. "He gives everyone money! He'd give money to Grove, if Grove would take it! And he usually gives cash. Still old world, this guy. Still talks with a heavy accent. Hates banks. He gave me cash to put down on the co-op, and I've never been so scared in my life. I open up a package and it's full of cash! He still sends me cash all the time. I return it, and he sends it back again. It's a kind of game we play."

"Sounds pretty unusual, Mr. Harwood."

"It's downright wacky! The man is a joy . . . creative, crazy, and disgustingly rich."

The Attorney General tried to hide her astonishment. Harwood had already surprised her, and the surprises seemed to never cease.

"What's his name and where does he live?"

"Well, his name now is Larry Sabo, but you can't find him in the phone book that way. He lists himself as Lazlo Szabo, his birth name. You can understand why he changed it! A lot worse than Grove's original name, Andras Grof, don't you think? Anyway, check the Scarsdale, New York phone book. But, I'll warn you, get ready to hear a kooky voice message."

"Okay, we'll check it out." The Attorney General reached into her briefcase and extracted a white envelope, from which she removed a black-and-white faded photo, a copy of the photo from the piano in his living room. "Recognize this individual, Mr. Harwood?"

The FBI lab had reproduced the photograph, reduced it in size, then crinkled and aged it, so it appeared old from use, as if carried in a wallet or a hip pocket for a long time. Shaer extended the photograph to Harwood.

Harwood studied the photo closely. "Yes," he replied with hesitation.

The President and the Attorney General waited for him to resume. Uncomfortable with the long pause, Julie Shaer asked, "And?"

"This photo is personal. I guarantee you that there are no skeletons in my closet. There's too much at stake here . . . I'd tell you if there was something you needed to know."

Shaer glanced at the President, and he took over. "Mr. Harwood, if we're to move on, it's essential that we have complete, honest information. I'm sorry, but that's the only way this is going to work."

"Yes, sir. Well, for starters, to my knowledge, the only copy of this photo is in my living room, a much larger version, that is. You must have gotten access to my apartment to enable you to make a copy. So by now, you probably know the color of my underwear, right?"

The rising tone in Stanley Harwood's voice and his steady eye contact with the Attorney General, told her that his question was not rhetorical, and that he was waiting for an answer.

"Your boxers or your briefs, Mr. Harwood?" she casually replied. "Now, who's the woman?"

"This is extremely embarrassing, but I suppose I'm at the point where I have to tell someone."

"Mr. Harwood," offered the President, "unless you are going to tell us about a crime, or something like that, I promise you that nothing you say will leave this room. You've asked me for a one-on-one meeting, in a highly unconventional manner, to say the least. I've asked the Attorney General to do a complete background check on you, and, so far, everything is great. Now, this picture came up in the course of the investigation. The Attorney General is just closing the only open items."

"That's fine, sir," Harwood relented, and turning to Shaer said, "That woman is my sister."

"Our investigation indicates that you had two sisters, one who died in an automobile accident, at the age of twelve or so, and the other living in Boston. Nothing I've seen so far says anything about another sister. The sister in Boston is much older than this, and this doesn't look anything like her, either. We do know about the sister who died at a young age, with your older brother driving."

"Madame Attorney General, it appears as though your research hasn't gone back quite far enough. Let me explain . . . . I had another sister, yes, in the past tense. We were born only twelve months apart. Irish twins, they call them. And we were like twins, like identical twins, closer if possible. We weren't joined at the hip, but we might as well have been. More than siblings, we thought we really shared the same soul. We talked about that . . . about how we'd always live together and how no one would ever separate us.

"Kate—that was her name—well, Kate and I not only felt as though we were one, but we thought that we were our own way out of the pain, out of the hurt of growing up the way we did: the ever-present alcohol, the random discipline, the parents screaming at us and at each other, the chaos, the spankings—always a little too hard—for being thirty seconds late to the dinner table. There were lots of times when Kate and I were not sure if we'd make it to adulthood.

"You may think there's lots of kids like us, but there're not. This was different. Together, we had the key to life. Separately, we had no real existence, no place for peace or security. Or sanity.

"As little kids, we'd talk about how we were the only normal ones in the family, how we'd been transported by some terrible accident into this horrible family, with its continual shouting, thrown bottles, hitting, cursing. I'm surprised this didn't come out in your background check, but, it was a long time ago, and our teachers . . . our neighbors . . . never suspected what it was like in our house.

"Kate and I used to stay up late at night talking about my parents, and how we were trapped. We were both strangely adult, strangely mature about it. In some bizarre way, we were able to detach ourselves from our environment, to see the situation as an outside observer might. Even when we were little, as far back as we could remember, our minds worked like adults' minds. Together we were rational—almost supra-rational—analytical, and logical.

"We knew we were inextricably woven, tightly, into this grim tapestry, yet all the time, we could look over the weaver's shoulder and see how each thread was worked in. Including the threads that were us.

"It was scary. We thought that this insight, whatever it was that we were blessed and cursed with, was somehow a product of our being together, a sort of synergy that, absent one of us, would send the other spiraling into the abyss of alcohol, accusation, and self-disgust that surrounded us. More than the pain, was the absurdity. Kate and I . . . well, it was less about our physical and psychological pain, and more about what we regarded as a crazy situation, absolutely insane, a situation over which we had no control . . . no influence.

"My older brother and older sister never quite figured it out. They always thought that either they were the cause of the problems, or that the kind of family we had was, well, like everybody else's . . . that we were actually normal."

Julie Shaer maintained her professional detachment and suspicion. She eyed Harwood carefully, looking for some non-verbal sign, and she was ready to catch a twitch, a failure to make eye contact, a hand covering the mouth . . . any sign of duplicity. But Harwood maintained his composure, completely. And, despite her initial skepticism, Shaer was somehow pleased that he had not fulfilled her fears.

"My father is a pediatrician, and my mother a college professor. That's the headline, but to fully understand, you've got to read the entire story, you've got to turn to Section C, page 5, and finish reading to the end.

"My parents were both brilliant students, top of the class, all that stuff. But both had demons, demons that nearly destroyed all of us. My father could have done anything in medicine he wanted, but today, he wipes kids' snotty noses, gives 'em some Tylenol, does pre-school physicals, prescribes Ritalin, pats mommies' hands, and sends 'em to a specialist if anything is a little complicated.

"My mother should be the president of an Ivy League university, Secretary of Education, or writing for prestigious academic journals. Instead, she's teaching uninspired forty-year-olds at a community college. Three times a week she teaches night classes.

"Though neither of them has had a drink in over twenty years, they both suffered through years of alcoholism, years of numbness. And we kids suffered, of course. Today, it would be 'a highly dysfunctional family unit, accompanied by substance-addictive parental behavior suggesting the need for institutional intervention in an abusive and potentially harmful situation'. Kate and I had our own word for it. We called it hell.

"I'm sorry, Mr. President, Ms. Shaer, but I'm afraid I'm rambling."

The President's voice was supportive, comforting. "To the contrary, Mr. Harwood, that's why we're here."

Harwood noted the Attorney General slowly nodding her agreement, and he proceeded.

"When Kate was twelve, my older brother picked her up from a party at her girlfriend's house. It was eight o'clock at night, and he was already drunk. He drove off the road, Kate was thrown out and killed. He walked away without a scratch. I did not speak another word to my brother. Ever. Several years later, he died in a single car accident, drunk, of course . . . plowed into a bridge abutment. Maybe it was guilt that killed him, maybe alcohol. Probably both. I didn't care and I still don't."

Throughout Harwood's cathartic disclosure, Williams and Shaer sat speechless. They had not wanted to talk, and had they wanted, there was nothing for them to say. Nor did Harwood ever indicate that he was prepared to be interrupted. Although he paused frequently, his presentation had a measured tone and pace that demanded that it continue without outside words of inquiry or condolence.

"Suddenly, life was sucked out of me, like I had died too. I wondered how it would feel to be an amputee, to have your arm or leg cut off. I'd see people without limbs—on the street or at the airport—and feel like them. I was an amputee, but not a physical amputee. I was a spiritual and psychological amputee. I'd have traded anything to have been without a leg or an arm, rather than feel the way I felt. My heart and my spirit had been cut out, discarded with the rest of the medical waste . . . severed limbs, replaced hips, the remains of a thousand biopsies . . . thrown out together, taken from the hospital loading dock by a pick-up service, carted off, and burned to dust, my soul with them."

Harwood swallowed and looked to a side table where there stood a pitcher of ice water. He poured a glass, and took a long drink. Neither Williams nor Shaer took their eyes off him, nor said a word. The diffuse hum of air moving through the White House air conditioning system was the only sound in the room.

"Until college, I just took up space. I inhaled oxygen, consumed food, and manufactured enough energy to ambulate from place to place. I did not live my life, I just sustained it. I got good grades, and yeah, I did all the crap that everyone does in high school, student government, sports, that stuff. The academic stuff was easy. But I was living a lie. I hated my family, my life, and most of all myself.

"I went off to Yale and, to the outside world, seemed to be fine. But I was dead inside. I drank my way through freshman year, skipped classes, and, though invariably semi-comatose, sobered up enough to cram all night for a paper or exam. I did nearly nothing academically, and still managed a B average. Just like they say, the hard part is getting in."

Stanley Harwood had been a robotic narrator. Now, for the first time, he altered his facial expression, as a slight smile crossed his mouth. Then, as quickly as it had come, the smile faded and his stony visage returned.

"The first or second week of my sophomore year, I was drinking with some buddies. One of them went to the bar for another round, and one headed off to the john. As I sat there alone, I looked over and there was a wall mirror next to our table. One of those like you see in fitness centers, covering the whole wall, except this one had little gold squiggles going through it, like somebody's idea of interior decoration.

"Anyway, I saw this guy reflected in the mirror and I didn't like him. He was slumped, elbows on the table propping up his head. He wore a dirty work shirt with one button missing. He hadn't shaved, his hair was dirty, he had black circles under his eyes, and he was drunk. It was, of course, me.

"It was a shock. I was becoming one of them. The pain of losing my sister had long since transformed itself into a behavior that was without purpose, incapable of love, much less self-awareness.

"For a long time, I just stared into the mirror at this guy. He disgusted me.

"I finished my beer, left, and, to put it short and sweet, turned my life around. I got help from the University counseling center, started meditating and praying, and came to understand that my sister wasn't ever going to be there again. Wherever she was, she did not have me to lean on, and I did not have her. I would have to construct a whole person out of what had been half a person.

"I stopped drinking, changed roommates, changed everything, in fact. I stopped hating everything around me, except for that person that I'd allowed myself to become. I say 'allowed', because from then on, I took responsibility for what I'd been and what I could become.

"Meanwhile, I'd barely communicated with my parents. They'd gone through therapy, separated, got back together and, after many attempts, stopped drinking. I still rarely talk to them. I know I don't love them, but I know I don't hate them, either.

"Who killed my sister and almost killed me? My parents? I don't know. Still to this day, I wonder about that.

"I say 'wonder', because it's not an obsession. Don't get me wrong, I miss her every day. I don't regret the hard years. I'm not rationalizing, I've just gotten to a place where I don't look back. Or if I peek, I want it to be with curiosity, not rancor or resentment."

The President watched Harwood blink and saw the tears run down his cheeks, parallel, as if competing in a race for his jawline. It was a tie, and Harwood had not raised hand or hankie to stop the race. For a few moments, the tear trails remained, glistening just enough to allow Williams and Shaer to remember the wetness that had just passed.

But for the silent tears, Harwood remained impassive, even stoic. He folded his arms and leaned back, signaling that he was ready for questions or comments. When neither Williams nor Shaer ventured to break the ice, Harwood grinned slightly, "You got more than you bargained for, huh?" After a short pause, he added, "So did I!"

The Attorney General struggled to link Harwood's tale to the practical purpose of the meeting. "I'm sorry, Mr. Harwood, but am I to take it that the photograph on your piano is your sister?"

"Exactly," he replied.

The President felt Harwood's agony, noting the film of perspiration across his own forehead. He knew the account, indeed the purging, should continue—for everyone's sake. But, at this point, he was determined to minimize the anxiety that filled the room. Abruptly, he stood, and moved toward the door of his office.

"Let's take a short break, eh? I have a few things I need to check on with Emily. Use the restroom or stretch your legs, I'll be right back."

Shaer's familiarity with Williams' style told her immediately that this was a calculated break, intended to make the process easier for Harwood. She respected Williams' intuition and natural sense of timing, and she used to opportunity to excuse herself for a couple of minutes. As she strode toward the door, she glanced back to see Harwood vigorously rubbing his eyes, then folding his arms and leaning back deeply into his chair.

24

When the Attorney General returned to the room a couple of minutes later, she faced Harwood and tried to reassure him, as she knew the President would want her to do.

"I appreciate your honesty, Mr. Harwood. It's necessary, but I know that doesn't make it any less difficult.

Harwood forced a half-smile. "In fact, while you were gone, I thought that whatever comes of this—I should have done this a long time ago. It's me that should be thanking you."

The President reappeared bubbling, "Okay, where were we?"

"We were discussing the picture on the piano, Mr. Harwood's sister."

"Of course. Mr. Harwood, why don't you pick up where you left off?"

"Uh, yes, sir. My sister . . . ." began Harwood, verbally groping for continuity.

"She was twelve when she died?" Shaer asked, attempting to help him position his thoughts. "I'm confused about that."

"Yes, ma'am, she was twelve, but let me explain. Although, I eventually got my act together, Kate never stopped being a, rather *the* defining force in my life. I stopped wallowing in a quagmire of self-pity, but she never left my mind.

"That year at Yale, I finally realized how far that little twelve year-old girl was from the young man in New Haven, struggling to cope. So, I had this inspiration, I guess you'd call it. I needed to have Kate there with me, while, of course, recognizing that was impossible. Meanwhile, I was always fearful that my memory of her would fade.

"I wondered, what Kate would look like, if she were alive? Strangely, I knew what she'd *be* like . . . creative, caring, and brilliant . . . but I didn't know what she'd *look* like." For the first time Harwood seemed self-conscious, cracking a knuckle, squirming in his chair, and taking another long drink of water.

"Well, after lots of research, I found a photo lab, run by a retired police guy, that takes a photo of a kid and creates an image of what she might look like today. He specializes in re-creations for police investigators . . . for abductions, missing children, that sort of stuff. Computer enhanced aging. That was that. I mailed him a set of photos of my sister, as a baby, as an infant, up to the last one taken only a few days before she was kil . . . she died. He sent me back a computer-generated photo of what she would have looked like at age twenty.

"A few years later, I got him to produce another photo, and later, still another. My sister, through a computer picture, is growing old with me. Like a beneficent Dorian Gray, I guess.

"Madame Attorney General, I can see you starting to gnaw on your lower lip . . . I can guess what's going through your head right now: 'This guy is absolutely whacko. Beam me out of here, Scotty, we've got a nut case here.'

"But indulge me this one peccadillo. Everyone has a 'dark side', a skeleton in the closet. Well, now you know mine. I don't drink, except to touch a glass to my lips now and then. I rarely swear. I don't smoke or chew, I go to church on Sundays. Hey, I was a Boy Scout . . . pretty much still am.

"There are things people think or do when no one else is around. What's that one thing you don't share with even your therapist, much less your spouse or best friend? As a friend used to say, 'Stan, there are some frogs that just don't need dissecting.' Now, I've dissected my frog for you. Is mine much worse than everybody else's?

"I don't constantly rub a lucky clover, like our Vice President. No blow-up doll at home. I don't look at naked pictures of little kids, or visit the wrong side of town to pick up someone. I've chosen that the love of my life, my anchor, that singular person who enabled me to survive a childhood of whisky and whippings, be with me, to support and comfort me. I want to remember her. It's my way of honoring her.

"Maybe I'm weird, maybe idealizing. Maybe I'll outgrow it, like I outgrew my years of stupor. I hope not. If it's a crime, it certainly has no victim. It's the opposite, it has a beneficiary . . . me."

Silence, neither stifling nor uncomfortable, followed Harwood's 'confession'. Like a rubber band pulled taut, with the whole of its energy focused on returning to its original state, when released or broken, it enjoys a new, subtle solace. It was not purgative for Harwood only. Williams and Shaer were similarly released.

The President finally spoke, "I assume that's it, Julie?"

"I do have another question, but it's not as objective as the rest. Mr. Harwood, what do you get for this? Why are you doing this?"

"What you're asking is 'What does Stanley Harwood want for himself?'"

"Okay," Shaer replied matter-of-factly, "have it your way."

"I just sat in my office thinking about how messed up this situation is. To be honest, I thought I could do it better . . . fix it. I just want to put things right. I'm not on some power trip, if that's what you think, ma'am."

Shaer did not respond.

"That it?" the President asked.

Harwood thought for a second. "I really admire President Williams. I hate to be too self-analytical, but . . . "

Harwood looked at the President and dropped his head a little sheepishly. "Well, I wondered the other night if the President wasn't somehow a figure that I wished I'd had in my early life. I don't know . . . I'm not looking for anything other than to make a difference."

As his voiced trailed off, it was apparent that Harwood was both pained and embarrassed by the admission. Williams broke in to terminate the session.

"Mr. Harwood," he continued, "you may go now. Thanks for your time . . . and your honesty. It was not, of course, our intention to make you uncomfortable, but this had to be done."

"Like I said, sir, if this is the price of moving forward, it's a small one."

"Well," the President said, "you said that you sometimes allow yourself a peek back. Perhaps it'll help to take a good, long look now." He walked to his desk, buzzed Emily, and turned back to Harwood and Shaer.

"Mr. Harwood, if we need anything further, we'll be in touch."

As Harwood left the Oval Office, President Williams motioned to Shaer to return to her seat. "Well, Julie, what do you think?"

"I'm not sure what to make of it. We'll need a little time to confirm everything he said."

"Forget the facts . . . what about the man?"

"I'm no psychologist, sir."

"But you are a human being?"

"That I am, Mr. President. I'm just accustomed to speaking to you as a lawyer and administrator."

"There's a line from a Star Trek episode that goes like 'one of the great virtues in being captain is being able to ask for advice and not having to take it.' I need your feedback, Julie."

Shaer did not relish the land of the subjective. Along with her great intellect, her innate gravitation to the logical and the rational had been the strength from which she'd forged her professional success.

After long contemplation, she offered, "As a human being, I'm impressed, and I admit that I didn't want to be. Part of it is the factual stuff I knew before I came in here. 'The main problem with the world is that it's full of fools and fanatics that are certain of themselves, while the wise are in doubt.' See there, Mr. President, you quote Shatner, and I quote Bertrand Russell."

"Okay," he continued, "what about this guy?"

"I believed him. Not only that, I liked him. He's professional, comes across as honest. I don't know, something just feels right about him."

"Well, for what it's worth, I agree, Julie. Give me a follow up as soon as possible, please."

When the Attorney General left the Oval Office, President Williams stretched his arms to the ceiling, and stood on his toes with his head back and his fingers widespread, his eyes shut tight. He wasn't sure if this was a physical reaction to the long, intense session or some subconscious manifestation of joy. He also didn't care.

25

Chris Weiner liked the O'Hare Hilton. It was convenient, almost a landmark, an icon to the business traveler. As she crossed from the airport to the hotel, she ruminated about O.J. Incredible, she thought, with admiration for his charm and skill. How he, all so mysteriously, ditched a bag in the airport, came and checked in, went to his room, and cut his hand on that darned glass. She grinned at the absurdity of it all.

Weiner cherished the anonymity that the Hilton afforded, with its bustle and crush of corporate trainers, stranded travelers, mid-level sales managers, conventioneers, and recruiters. And if you speak only Tagalog, or want a Kosher meal or an H.P. laser printer delivered to your room, this is the place.

She checked in, as usual, under her alternate identity, Ms. Mary Smith, paying cash, all ten-dollar bills, for the room. Seeing herself to the non-smoking room, she quickly placed a brown leather briefcase next to the phone table, hung an insubstantial garment bag in the closet, and began dialing her gaggle of lawyers, agents, trust officers, and stockbrokers, getting up-to-the-minute data on the markets, particularly a group of "casino entertainment" stocks.

After twenty minutes, three brief quick taps followed by a pause, then a final single tap, told her the men had arrived. She peered through the peephole and opened the door, admitting two men, one tall, and one short, to the room. With a mumbled grunt, Weiner directed one to sit on the edge of the bed and the other in an unoccupied chair. Taking the other chair, she quickly complimented the men on their recent effort.

"So far, it looks like an unfortunate tragedy took the precious life of Speaker Berkhardt, loyal public servant."

The tall man spoke. "For sure, Ms. Smith. Now, how about the money?"

"Right here, Willie" nodding to the briefcase sitting at her feet.

"You're sure there's no evidence, no nothing? Completely clean?"

"You don't know the half of it, lady," Willie said. He turned to his partner, laughing as they shared an inside joke.

"What's the deal, guys? What's so funny?"

"Well, let's get us the money in our hot little hands first. Then we'll share our secret."

With her foot, Weiner pushed the briefcase halfway over to Willie's chair. He reached out, taking it carefully by the handle, and placed it on his lap. Popping the latches, he opened the lid and examined the contents.

"Nicely aged bills," he remarked, re-latching the briefcase and placing it behind his chair.

"Okay, lady, we don't need to brag, but you oughta know what a good team you got. But, we own the rights to this, okay?"

Weiner grew impatient. "Alright, what's up?"

Willie took a deep breath, as if to charge his lungs with enough oxygen for a long monologue. "Well, you know how I told you how we drugged the guy. Well, that's not all of it. You see, the drugs get used up, but they don't really go away, because there's no way for them to get out."

Willie described the drug, provided by "a friendly chemist", as a "hybrid of GBL and GBH, some kind of gamma-hydro-butyl-something-or-other, but, something different from the stuff you can get commercially."

"Okay, so where do the drugs go?"

"Trouble is, even though the body processes the stuff pretty fast, it still leaves traces, stuff that's left over after the liver does its work, breaking the stuff down. And, while there's nothing left of this stuff in the blood, they can find it in the guy's pee. So, we needed to come up with a way to get it out of the dead man's urine. Well, if that ol' mountain won't come to Mohammed, then Mohammed will just have to go to the mountain, huh? What could any coroner find, if there's not any urine left in the bladder? But an empty bladder after a night of drinking would look pretty suspicious, huh?"

As the tall man recounted details of the Speaker's murder, Weiner slowly inched forward on the edge of her chair, mesmerized. This was her kind of stuff, and she realized that despite their rough edges, these hit men were real pros, creative and productive . . . the kind that got things done, the kind that you could admire.

She sat, incredulous. "And the coroner's not going to be able to find the drugs?"

Willie stretched out his tall frame, looked at his sawed off partner again, patted the briefcase behind him, and puffed out his chest. "Not only that, but he's gonna find what should be there. Right, Nick?"

"What the hell does that mean?" Weiner asked.

"Well, one of our 'friends' got to know a staff flunky in the Speaker's office. Followed him to a bar after work, and met him there a couple of times for drinks. She finds out Berkhardt was taking a high blood pressure medication, Zocor, it's called, and another drug called Xanax. Made no secrets about it in the office, though it wasn't known outside. So, to close the holes in the chain of evidence . . . that's what Nick calls it, the chain of evidence . . . well, Nick here began taking this Zocor stuff and Xanax. When the M.E. found these drugs in the Congressman's pee, he probably called the Speaker's doctor and found out that Berkhardt was taking these medications. No reason for the medical examiner to check any further. No sleepy-time cocktail in his urine, and it's got the high-blood pressure stuff and the Xanax, pre-mixed! Perfect crime."

"You guys absolutely ought to franchise," Weiner squealed.

26

Agent Pete Snowden arrived at Harwood's office at three o'clock in the afternoon. "I've been asked to get you for a meeting, Mr. Harwood."

"A meeting?"

"Well, actually I was told to say 'the' meeting."

"Now? Really?"

"You got it. Let's go."

Harwood smiled, jumped up, and pulled his coat from the back of his chair. He took a massive set of keys from his pocket, examined them, and selected one. Unlocking a desk drawer, he withdrew a thick file and almost ran for the door, balancing the file while stuffing an arm into his coat sleeve.

"Calm down, Harwood. It's just the President of the United States, the most powerful man on earth."

"Pete," Harwood replied, as they strode quickly down the hall, "are you the same guy that coaches his kid's Little League team and tells his ten-year-old-star who's batting with the bases loaded in the ninth, 'Don't blow it, kid!'"

"I'm the guy!"

"Big help you are."

Pete Snowden laughed and threw an affectionate, if unprofessional, arm around Harwood's shoulder. "You know, Harwood, sometimes the kid hits a home run."

The President was anxious about a private, in fact secret, meeting. Nonetheless, he recognized that some undefined need drove him to accept Harwood's invitation, on Harwood's terms, no less. Anyway, at this point, Williams thought, he had nothing to lose.

Williams could play devil's advocate with the best. After all, that was his professional training. But he also knew when to listen, and when to learn. Besides, Harwood had passed the smell tests of the Attorney General and the FBI. The puzzling piano picture was strange, but it did not smack of the more serious kinds of character weaknesses that have afflicted other White House staff.

Also, Harwood's direct approach made the President feel comfortable. There were not many folks these days who made him feel comfortable. Despite Harwood's often nearly stifling professionalism, he conveyed an easy air.

And, unlike so many others in Washington, thought Williams, Harwood's personal achievement was not built at the expense of others. His success was by all accounts, fairly derived.

Most important, the President reasoned, Harwood's relationship with Tony spoke volumes. Tony did not suffer sycophants and snobs. Yes, Tony was the acid test. Tony could not be taken in. His tough Sicilian genes wouldn't permit it.

Snowden and Harwood continued their brisk walk.

On the ground floor, they cut through a wide arched corridor from which Harwood could see the back side of the gleaming white and stainless steel kitchens from which state dinners for up to five thousand guests were prepared. Proceeding to an elevator, they rose to the second floor, exited the cab, and walked down a small hallway. To the right were double doors, outside of which sat an alert Secret Service agent. "This entire house is the President's house," Snowden noted, "but that's really where the family lives, there in that apartment."

Harwood barely had time to see, as Snowden turned left down another hall.

"This is the Lincoln Bedroom, that there is the Rose Room, and there's the Empire Room."

"Never heard of the Rose or Empire Rooms," Harwood replied earnestly.

"Yeah, the Lincoln Bedroom's pretty famous, especially as put to use by some occupants here . . . either for selling or for sleeping, I'm not sure which." They quickly arrived at a large carved door which stood ajar by a few inches. "This is it." Snowden knocked on the door, pushed it open slightly and stuck his head in. "We're here, Mr. President."

Harwood could hear the friendly reply, "Great, come in, come in."

Snowden ushered Harwood in and stepped back away, touching Harwood's shoulder lightly. "Good luck," he whispered.

Stanley Harwood stood stiffly at the doorway, as the President, setting aside a stack of briefing papers that had been piled in his lap, waved him to a vacant chair. "Come on in, Mr. Harwood. Sit down right here."

The President noticed his guest surveying the room, as he offered his hand. "This is as pretty big room for a two man meeting, but then everything around here is pretty big. I trust you've never been here before?" Williams inquired casually.

"No, sir. It's quite an experience."

"Well, this is the Treaty Room. There're various treaties from the Nineteenth Century displayed in here. I use it for small meetings, when I want to escape the West Wing. It's awfully darned formal, but Mrs. Williams has added some personal touches, like this little family corner for me over here."

Harwood glanced at the corner, then took in the large crystal chandelier that dominated the center of the room, the huge gilt mirror, and the emerald carpet. "It's a beautiful room, but I guess I agree about its formality." Harwood was loath to make small talk, allowing the President to set the pace for their discussions.

"This has been a bedroom, study, sitting room . . . all kinds of uses, including press conferences for Eleanor Roosevelt, and a map room for Churchill during the war. Lincoln held his war strategy sessions here. He actually signed the Emancipation Proclamation in what's now called the Lincoln Bedroom, next door. Sometimes, I like to sit here quietly, and imagine what it must have been like then."

Williams remarked, as if to no one in particular, "I feel honored to be in this house, but the feeling is strongest when I'm on the second floor." Gesturing to portraits on the walls, he remarked, "That's Grant there, and that over there is McKinley signing the treaty with Spain."

Few people on the White House staff visited above the first floor. Stanley Harwood accepted the meeting venue as the honor it was.

The President had forgone a suit and tie for the meeting, substituting an open collar shirt with a blue blazer, Timberland walking shoes with rag socks completing the casual image. It was 'casual Friday' at the White House anyway, a practice which Williams brought from the Sacramento Governor's mansion. The Haas family, close San Francisco friends and major campaign contributors, had encouraged Williams to "go casual." As owners of Levi-Strauss, and with a multi-billion dollar investment in casual dress, their support may have been driven by more than their interest in Williams' personal comfort.

"Well, enough history. Let's have a seat, Mr. Harwood."

He moved with the President to sit in one of a pair of matching chintz wing chairs. Harwood, as it turned out unnecessarily, feared that Williams would further break the ice by photograph chat. His inherent professionalism and his natural focus on outcomes, rather than process, made him the type who felt that, if one could not direct or improve a situation, then there was little need to discuss it. And he had always loathed conversations about the weather, in particular, regarding any energy spent on the subject as wasted. The weather was a subject for small minds.

Harwood did not wait. "Mr. President, as you know I wasn't invited to the campaign review meeting on Wednesday, but everyone is talking about it. How do you feel it went?"

"Pretty well, Mr. Harwood. We've obviously got some serious problems, but Cartwright has some interesting ideas about how we're going to turn this thing around. It's going to require everyone's dedication, but I think the meeting had an upbeat tone. There's reason to be encouraged."

Baloney, thought Harwood. He's feeling me out . . . that's okay. It's probably unfair to expect him to sit here and admit his campaign is out of control . . . just weeks before Election Day.

Harwood heard the reports: the meeting was a disaster of predictably major proportions, replete with the backbiting and obligatory assignment of blame that were hallmarks of the Cartwright-chaired campaign

"What do you think, Mr. Harwood? You said everyone's talking about the meeting."

"I'll be honest, Mr. President. After all, that's why I'm here. All I ask is that you don't shoot the bearer of bad news."

"I shall holster my pistol, Mr. Harwood. Let 'er rip."

"Rearranging deck chairs on the Titanic, from what I hear, is as close as one can come to capturing the essence of the meeting, Mr. President." Harwood waited for the response of the most powerful man in the world when he had been told his election campaign was a farce.

"Is that so, Mr. Harwood? A disaster, huh? Well, there are differences: the Titanic was an accident . . . that's one place your analogy falls apart. This campaign is self-inflicted. Another difference, as the old joke goes, is that the Titanic had a band. I'm sorry, no, embarrassed really, that you had the intestinal fortitude to be more honest than I."

Harwood was shocked, "Sir?"

"I'm sorry you weren't there, because it was a doozy. O'Malley was all the way across the room, but from fifty feet away, he smelled like expensive booze and cheap cigars, with a nice dollop of drugstore perfume thrown in. And I'm sure he picked up the fragrance by proxy, if you know what I mean."

"Yes, sir. I've even seen her . . . Miss Proxy, that is."

"Whittingham was like a cigar store Indian, though rather less dignified and probably more stoic. He didn't say a word in two hours. And Cartwright . . . you should have seen him. He was Robin Williams doing Carmen in Urdu . . . unintelligible histrionics, if that's not redundant . . . finger pointing, excuses, apologies, promises, meaningless statistics supposedly supporting conclusions which were really like Edna St. Vincent Millay's shining palaces built on sand . . . and all of it absolutely, and purposefully, incomprehensible. I swear, it was like an Old Testament tale: Tower of Babel meets Noah's Ark in business suits . . . ."

Stanley Harwood had come to the meeting expecting a positive attitude from Williams. After all the President had consented to meet without knowing the full nature of the meeting. That alone demonstrated that Williams was ready to consider change, ready to listen to someone or something new.

Williams' catharsis exceeded Harwood's wildest expectations. In an instant, hope began to yield to reality. Where there had been a dim-yellow-sunrise gleam of light, now there was the heat and glare of an equatorial noonday sun. Harwood was nothing less than ecstatic, though professionally ecstatic, to be sure.

The President sat silently, as if to communicate to Harwood that it was his turn. Harwood, was silent, as well. His plan was at once simple and complex, he thought. Though he had struggled to consider all of the ramifications, he wondered if anyone could predict its impact. Certainly, no one else could anticipate the profound shock the nation would experience . . . assuredly for many decades to come. The plan would work, work well, for everyone. The nation, the President, and Calvin's people will be well served, he thought.

Williams breathed deeply, and folded his hands behind his head. He closed his eyes and leaned his head back. After nearly a minute in this position, savoring his emotional emetic, he returned his hands to his lap and opened his eyes.

He faced Harwood, and continued to muse, silently. *Deck chairs on the Titanic . . . good metaphor . . . exactly . . . deck chairs on the Luisitania is more like it. I mean, after all, didn't the Titanic have survivors? The Luisitania is better. No accident that. The result of a well placed enemy torpedo. This campaign has been a charade . . . like the Emperor's New Clothes. And Harwood knows it better than anyone.*

Finally Williams spoke, "Mr. Harwood, it looks like you've gotten your shot. Where would you like to begin?"

Harwood unhesitatingly picked up a file folder and placed it in his lap. He leafed through some handwritten notes, looked up, and took a deep breath. "Mr. President, the Republicans will have spent a hundred and twenty-three million dollars on your campaign by Election Day. That money is going down the drain, a lost investment. After the election, you'll retire to California, make speechs and have your photograph taken with sales managers who'll prop their photos pretentiously behind their desks, and expound on how they 'know' the President."

"Former President, according to you," Williams remarked.

Harwood was more anxious than he expected. "Uh, I'm not trying to offend. I just think there's an opportunity before you . . . ."

"If you don't get going, Mr. Harwood, you'll never offend anyone. You'll just run out of time, like you did in the massage room." Williams gave Harwood a warm smile adding, "Why don't you just relax and tell me what you've got in mind. You've gotten this far, you may as well just continue in your own rather direct style, don't you think?"

"Yes, sir . . . so we know you can't win the election the way you're going. Next step, the Williams Presidential Library. So what can you do to win? Can you change advertising or the media approach? No. In fact, the Party has twenty-four million budgeted for TV and radio between now and Election Day, which is just throwing good money after bad. They might as well spend it for increased teacher salaries, or vaccinations for poor children. At least somebody would be getting something out of it."

"Go on," the President said, "with a little less opinionated digression, if possible."

"Can you introduce new programs? Tax cuts, job bills, strengthen defense? No . . . you'd have no credibility this late, and Moore would turn it around on you easily, 'Why didn't he propose that last year?' he'd say. 'Or three months ago?' And he'd be right. It'd be the move of a desperate man."

"Mr. Harwood, is this something like Nixon's 'secret plan' to end the war in Vietnam?"

"No way, sir."

"How about a Willie Horton ad or something in that vein?"

"Nope, that won't work against Moore/Jenkins. This year, the Democrats have you covered on crime. Their platform is as tough as ours. They look like Rockefeller Republicans, or rather Clinton Democrats."

So," Harwood continued, "would replacing Cartwright accomplish anything? No, though it might make you feel a lot better. Can you find something on Moore or Jenkins to assail their integrity or ethics? Alcohol, drugs, milk fund money, Abscam, Jennifer, Monica?"

The President quickly interrupted. "You know that's not the way I play ball, Mr. Harwood."

"Yes, sir. If you won't let people excavate, they're not going to find any treasure. And, if something came in over the transom, you probably wouldn't use it. Anyway, I've talked to some folks about what's in the National Committee's files on Moore and Jenkins and there's nothing on these guys. Nothing." Harwood took a break from his monologue and re-examined his notes, giving the President a chance to take the floor.

"Mr. Harwood, how about a drink?"

"Your call, Mr. President. But I'm not much of a drinker."

"I know," smiled the President. "It was in Ms. Shaer's report."

President Williams picked up the phone and pushed a button. "Emily, would you please ask John to please bring us some wine. What? Sure, that would be great. And two glasses, please, Emily. Yes. Thank you, Emily." Williams turned to Harwood, "Now, please proceed with your analysis."

"Well, sir, looking at the traditional approaches, even the most radical ones, if something can be radical and traditional at the same time, to winning an election, there are no alternatives."

"Except the one you're about to tell me about."

"Yes, sir."

"I'm waiting . . . ."

Harwood did not pause for dramatic effect. "Dump O'Malley, pick a new running mate who's so strong that together you turn the tide and take back the election." Harwood leaned back, closed his folder, and waited for Williams' response.

"Drop O'Malley off the ticket? That's it? Drop O'Malley?"

"Yes, sir. It's profound and simple. Also, it's the only way to secure reelection."

"Is re-election that important?"

"Is O'Malley worth your even asking that question? But whatever the answer, if the question is about the value of status quo versus change, well, I'm afraid that's your call, and only yours, Mr. President."

"And, if I don't get rid of O'Malley, I am sure to lose?"

"That is a certainty at this point. We both know that."

"And might I have the audacity to ask what ever happened to loyalty to one's running mate?" Williams asked. "After all, I wouldn't be here, if it weren't for O'Malley being on the ticket four years ago."

"I realize that, sir. I'm not saying that loyalty isn't important. It may be more important than being re-elected. But, if you decide to keep O'Malley, then you must acknowledge, at least to yourself, that you've made the decision of loyalty over victory. That's a matter of intellectual honesty. And I'm not going to render a judgment on that one."

Williams' voice rose. "You already have, Mr. Harwood. Your very presence here and the nature of this conversation is *prima facie* evidence that you've already rendered your judgment."

Harwood paused and thought a moment about the President's contention and the new intensity in his tone.

"Yes, sir, I agree. Stanley Harwood has already made up his mind. He chooses victory for the Republican Party and for you over loyalty to Cornelius McGillicuddy Xavier Joseph O'Malley. If you don't dump O'Malley, you'd be saying that getting crushed with O'Malley on the ticket is more important than the Republicans staying in the White House."

"It's that simple?"

"Mr. President, I hate to use the word, but O'Malley is expendable. And before you go scolding me, hear me out. My issue is not whether or not he's expendable, because in politics, everybody is. The question is what's he expendable for?"

"That sounds awfully raw, Mr. Harwood."

"Sir, your reputation for fairness and integrity is legendary. One of your great strengths is that you don't abandon your friends or associates when they err. One of the reasons the press corps loves following Moore is that when one of his team missteps, he disavows not only the mistake, but the man, as well. The press eats it up."

"And what about O'Malley? Let's get back to him."

"Of course. Well, first of all, if you dump O'Malley, no one will see it as exploitation for political expediency. More important is what are you dropping him for? If there is a higher purpose . . . call it a vision . . . some reason that doesn't serve just you, but serves the people . . . then that's not only defensible, it's laudable."

"That depends on your point of view," offered the President.

"It's not a matter of point of view, Mr. President. This isn't appearances, it's reality. To put it in philosophical terms, sir, this isn't Plato's shadow and cave . . . there's nothing epistemological about it. On-line, real-time politics, that's what it is. You beat them or they beat you. The results in a presidential election box score are always one to nothing, always a shutout."

Harwood suddenly realized how cynical he sounded. His tone and words, his sarcastic reference to philosophy . . . clearly resounded as a personal attack, one which could not have been missed. "I'm sorry, sir. I'm out of line."

A knock at the door broke the tension. The President rose and walked slowly to the door. He disappeared for a moment, reappearing carrying a silver tray, placing it on a coffee table between them.

"Well, Mr. Harwood, our wine is here. Good time for a break, wouldn't you say?" Williams smiled and winked at Harwood.

Harwood returned the President's smile, relieved at the older man's indulgence.

"Yes, sir, Mr. President, and again, I'm really sorry."

Williams carefully opened the wine and poured two glasses, handing one to Harwood and said, "Here's to the rest of our session. May the Lord use His wisdom and power to transform average philosophers into great presidents, if that be His will." Then the President added, "And may the Lord forgive Stanley Harwood for the way he talks to presidents, for I certainly do.

"Okay, Mr. Harwood, back to your analysis. With nine weeks to go until the election, the aging President is dumping his Vice President, Connie O'Malley."

Harwood laughed out loud. "You see, sir, O'Malley was an asset four years ago, but things aren't the same now. Today he's a liability. The public is no longer amused by O'Malley stories . . . they're tired of him. Now he's an anchor, or maybe a hole below the waterline. Need I add that he's put on thirty pounds in four years? He looks terrible . . . bloated, veiny, and dissipated. That's not lost on the public, for sure. The Tulsa Times called him 'Rudolph, the Red Nosed Vice President.' A paper in Lyme, Connecticut, of all places, referred to him as a 'bloated, reddish tick.'"

"Okay, okay, I've got the picture. He probably can't spell potato. Now, Mr. Harwood, you're not suggesting that I run alone?"

"No sir. You need a new running mate to assure victory. That's the key."

"We've been over that a million times. Even if I could convince the Party, the truth is, despite O'Malley's failings, no one's any better. Williams and O'Malley may lose, but they'll still get more voters than Williams and anybody else."

"I respectfully disagree, Mr. President."

"Okay Mr. Harwood, let me list the choices: Stanton, Bergstrom, Bellafusco, and Crandell. That's it."

"I agree so far."

The President continued, "Okay, first, David 'Rantin' Stanton from Colorado . . ticket would be unbalanced with two Westerners. He's too cowboyish, and no help on the major issues. Plus, he says exactly what he thinks, bad habit these days, especially with me already on the ticket. His affairs don't help, either. Next, Bergstrom, Minnesota… too old, tired, intellectual, and liberal . . . like a Republican Hubert Humphrey who stayed out in the sun too long. And one ex-college professor on the ticket may be too many—two certainly is. Then there's Bellafusco from New York, arguably the best choice, now that he's reversed a career of pandering to ethnic and religious minorities. Italian-American, married to a wealthy Wall Street heiress, a beautiful and down-to-earth Jewess, I might add. The kids' names are Saul, Sarah, Isaac, and Herman Bellafusco. Go figure. One small problem: his ex-father-in-law, is a 'made' mobster in trucking, cement, and trash hauling, and his own father is tainted, too. The Democrats undoubtedly have a complete file on his dad, a corpulent capo known to everyone in Bayside, Queens as 'Belly' Bellafusco. Apparently, Belly's cash flow didn't match his tax returns for several years, when he built net worth to finance his son's political aspirations."

"Yes, sir. That's well been documented."

"Last, Kathy Crandell from New Jersey: a woman, but a total maverick who won't stand by the platform . . . her views on abortion, capital punishment, immigration, and about nine other things maker her an impossible choice. She's weak under pressure, our voter surveys say we'd get a huge male backlash against her. Not an iota of team player in her. Bitch, if you'll excuse me, is the most common feedback. So then, what's your conclusion, Mr. Harwood? "

"It's obvious, sir. You'd lose with the present candidate and your backup choices are not choices at all. Plus, how could you switch to people you passed on at the convention?"

The President sipped his wine, licked his lips lightly, and set forth the predicament: "Everything we know tells us that a Williams/O'Malley ticket fares better than any other conceivable combination. We're boxed."

"Paradigms!" Harwood responded.

"What?"

"What the heck does 'conceivable' mean, anyway? You're in a prison of your own construction and you can't get out. Your own prejudices are holding you in."

"Explain." The President's single word was somewhere between a request and a demand.

"First of all, sir, about polls. The American Association for Public Opinion Research polls are no better than what you ask them. Even Harvard's vaunted 'Vanishing Voter" poll doesn't do justice to voter fickleness. More important, your thinking is totally predictable. I know what you're going to say before you say it. Not just you, but everybody. People are just physical matter, a big lump of activated flesh and bone. Then they're subjected to, in your case, seventy-four years of observations and experiences. We're all just the cumulative aggregation of all the data ever downloaded to us."

Williams, despite his proclivity to reason in abstract terms, grew impatient. Though his life's training had been mental gymnastics, Harwood's metaphorical approach made him uncomfortable.

"Okay, Mr. Harwood, the universe is my Skinner Box. Now, when do I hear what you've got in mind?"

"Okay, everyone you listed is a Republican. Second, they're all white. Third, they're all Christians. Only one is a woman. None are handicapped or physically disabled, though we dare not approach the area of the mental limitations."

"Okay, I'm getting your drift" said the President.

Harwood resumed the litany, "They're all elected government officials, all American citizens, all born in the U.S.. None are under five foot six—including Crandell—nor over six foot two. Pretty easily, I can define the pool from which they came. That's the prison of the paradigm."

"Okay, I've got the picture. We need to expand our thinking, break the mold, use the right side of our brain. I've got all the clichés, Mr. Harwood."

"Yes, sir. Think non-traditionally . . . go crazy."

"I said that I *have* it . . . Buckminster Fuller, Linus Pauling . . . that kind of thing, right?"

"You're catching on pretty fast for an old Republican!"

Williams grinned. "Okay. I get Democrats, instead of Republicans; blacks, Asians and Hispanics, instead of whites; Shintos, Hindus, Jews, Muslims and animists instead of Episcopalians; gays instead of straights; dwarfs and giants instead of the vertically gifted . . . co-opt a rainbow coalition. Then my Party disembowels me, puts my head on a pike in Lafayette Square, and burns the remains, certainly figuratively, and maybe literally."

"Exactly, sir. At least there're no ravens to pluck out your eyes, like at the Tower of London."

"Okay, whatever your secret weapon is, it won't go down easy with traditionalists. And they still give money and want to sleep in the Lincoln bedroom."

"Mr. President, wouldn't you rather be uncomfortable and win the White House, than comfortable and lose it?"

"Truthfully, I'm not sure yet. Things are so dire, that I almost look forward to Ojai, picking avocados, and planning a library, maybe even teaching a course at Thacher. History books are full of people who stood on principle even when they were sure to lose. That's where martyrs come from."

"You want to be a martyr?"

"That's not exactly what I meant. Did Joan of Arc compromise her faith, even when the English toasted her as a witch? St. Paul? For his beliefs, he lost his head, so to speak, putting his missionary work to an abrupt end."

"Mr. President, don't those comparisons seem a little, uh, aggressive?"

"Right. Their deaths were literal and mine will be figurative," the President laughed.

"Retiring to a thousand acre ranch in Ojai is a tad different than burning and beheading."

"But, there are lots of folks who'd help me draft a new gospel of St. Wally's Epistle to the Washingtonians. Straight from the dungeon or pyre."

"And if you don't compromise the Party's tenets? Out in that Machiavellian universe of compromise is the running mate who'll keep you in office."

"Fairy dust, Harwood."

"Don't forget, Mr. President, that St. Joan recanted when burning at the stake was imminent."

Williams took great pride in his knowledge of history. He was surprised. "She recanted?"

"And when she did, the English commuted her sentence to life in prison, only to change their minds and burn her anyway. She must've been scared and confused. But she did indeed recant. I think she was a practical nineteen-year-old girl, who wanted to live. Maybe she thought God's work could be better done if she were alive."

"You think I'm on a heavenly mission, do you Mr. Harwood? Is running for president doing God's work?"

Harwood realized he risked debating philosophy with a Stanford professor, a dangerous undertaking. Nonetheless, there was no turning back. He was awed by the magnitude of the situation he had created, but he was not daunted by it.

"Mr. President, God gives us gifts, by His grace, and His grace alone. We don't deserve them, we just get them. He creates this world, puts us in it, and gives us another gift called free will. We exercise that free will, either in respect of Him by using our gifts, or not. Using our undeserved gifts is not always the easiest course. Sometimes it's the most difficult."

Stanley Harwood paused long enough to gauge the President's level of interest in his monologue. Williams was fixed on him, canted forward in his chair.

Harwood continued, "I didn't mean to get off on a spiritual tangent, sir."

"It's okay, Mr. Harwood," the President responded. "I put you in that trajectory."

"Well then, Mr. President," Harwood said, "is getting re-elected 'God's work'? You've stated publicly that you pray. Pray about this, ask God if this is His work. I think He'll answer."

The President grinned. "What do you think He'll say?'

Harwood took a tiny sip of wine and stretched his legs in front of him. "You're asking me to speak for God? I think I'll just speak for myself, at this point, sir," Harwood laughed. "I'm here because I think the American people need you and I think you deserve a second term. And the only way that's going to happen is with a new V.P. candidate."

"So, for this new Vice President," the President said, "we're looking for a miracle worker, but ladled out of the cauldron of American politics. You obviously have a specific suggestion as to who might be this Miracle Superhero politician and public leader."

Stanley Harwood smiled broadly and tilted his head slightly to the side in a manner that betokened more self-assurance than arrogance.

"Absolutely. The man is Senator Reginald Calvin, sir."

Stanley Harwood and the leader of the world's most powerful nation sat silently, staring at each other. The President broke the silence with a short, grunt-like laugh, followed by more silence. Finally, as the mutual silence built to an untenable level of discomfort, the President spoke, the timbre of his voice resonating equal measures of humor and gravity.

"Mr. Harwood, you cannot be serious! I'd get *shot . . .* by *somebody . . .* or *he* would!"

"I hope not, sir. That's not a part of my plan."

"Well thanks for that. I'd not like to get shot. But there're plenty of folks who'd like to do it, and putting the senior Senator from Mississippi on the ticket will certainly lengthen that list by a lot."

"Mr. President, it's the right thing to do!"

"Whoa, hold on now. This has been an interesting talk, but it's impossible."

"Mr. President, this man is . . . is . . . is a man of *noble simplicity*. He's *earned it!*"

"The man is a life-long Democrat, not to mention the rest, *Stan*."

Williams and Harwood savored their respective epiphanies. For President Williams, it would be about *the rest . . .* the rest . . . of course, isn't that what it's always about . . . not the *said*, but th*e unsaid . . .* not the obvious, but the subtle, the inferred.

Harwood's epiphany was deeper, more meaningful. Outside 1600 Pennsylvania Avenue, while other men rushed to fulfill their own destinies, the afternoon warmth had not yet abated. Inside, two men from different times and different places sat quietly, sharing their visions.

Perhaps as the mind of man evolved, it developed devices to help keep events in order—to allow us to file, sort, and retrieve data, absent overload, with a minimum of gibberish. Many people measure their lives by chronological landmarks: Where were you when Kennedy was shot? When Neil Armstrong walked on the moon? When King was killed? When Nixon resigned? The Berlin Wall fell? The hijacked jets hit the twin towers? Events inexorably etch, like notches on a gun handle, the heart and mind. Memorable occasions: a new car, new school, new job. Marriage, birth, death—each inscribing the gradual continuum of human life.

Thus, events are a series of small personal epiphanies, like chisels that shape the granite of the brain. And it is nature's way to wield her chisel more powerfully with some events than others, carving more deeply into the stone.

The President had said "*Stan.*" Unconsciously and viscerally, he said Stan. Not "Harwood" or "Mr. Harwood," but "Stan." "*This has been an interesting talk, STAN, but it's impossible.*" The President of the United States has called Stanley R. Harwood "*Stan.*"

27

When Stanley Harwood returned from his typically brief lunch, he checked his message log to find the expected pack of calls from overanxious, underpaid Capitol Hill aides. Among the messages was a call from Mr. Falcon. "Call ASAP", it read.

"President Williams' office."

"Hi, Emily. It's Stanley Harwood."

"Yes, Mr. Harwood, thanks for calling me back. The President wants to know if you can come over right now. He'll send Agent Snowden."

"Yes ma'am, absolutely. I'll wait for Snowden. Thank you."

This time, Snowden accompanied Harwood directly to the Oval Office. The agent passed Emily's desk with a mere nod, and tapped lightly on the Oval office door. The President stood and waved them in, "Come on in. Thanks, Agent Snowden. Come in, Mr. Harwood, have a seat."

Harwood sat, as directed, in a chair directly across a small coffee table from the President.

Williams began, "I've thought about your ideas quite a bit over the last twenty-four hours. I'm still more than a little confused, so I figured I might as well hear the rest."

The President's mood was different today. He initiated no small talk, and waited for Harwood to make the most of the opportunity.

Harwood cleared his throat to buy a few seconds to organize his thoughts. "First, Mr. President, I want you to know that I have studied this and studied this hard. I have very little in writing. I thought it would be better if I just talked, rather than present a memo."

"Stan, the idea seemed ludicrous yesterday. But, you know Mark Twain's observation about the sixteen-year-old who considered his father the dumbest man in the world. But when he was twenty-one, he was surprised how much the old man had learned in five years. So, let's just see where this road takes us."

Harwood, relieved, proceeded. "Well, Calvin is the perfect answer. With him, Republicans are guaranteed to win. What could be better than that?"

"That's still debatable,'" the President countered.

"You're familiar with the PRI?" Harwood asked.

"Mexico. Dominant political party, at least for most of the Twentieth Century . . . Partido Revolucionario Institucional," the President answered.

"Exactly. They have a long history of co-opting their adversaries. In fact, until very recently, they never lost a major election. They compromise with their enemies, by bringing them into the power structure. If your adversary joins you, then there's no adversary. Give a little, get a lot. You give your enemy one of your jerseys, and say, hey, you join the winning team. The Republicans have had the PRI opportunity open to them plenty of times, but they're too darned doctrinaire. At least they looked that way until Clinton ran as a Democrat and governed as a Republican."

"And they called Nixon 'tricky'," the President chimed in.

"Despite all their rhetoric, the Democrats have never succeeded at the 'party of inclusion' gambit, sir," Harwood said. "They keep leaking at the edges . . . an amoeba with a weak cell wall, oozing valuable plasma . . . in this case ideals. This year, the Republicans can capitalize on co-opting the enemy. Mr. President, everyone, even a good President, needs a wake-up call once in a while. I'd love to be the one who helps you see the forest *and* its trees."

Williams loosened up a little and said, "Let's go on and hope they don't end up stumps."

Harwood's excitement grew. "By putting Calvin on the ticket, Democrats will cross over in droves, First, he's from Mississippi and those electoral votes will be in the bag."

"And the backlash?" the President asked.

"Unfortunately, there's no empirical way to measure it. He's a distinguished southern senator. We could get a lot more of the South than you think. Also, Northern liberals will come over big time. Right now, we're good for less than twenty percent of the Jewish vote, about typical for a Republican.

If that rises to forty percent, which it easily should with Calvin in place, even New York will come our way."

"Calvin has a strong record in support of Israel, a lot stronger than mine." the President noted.

"Exactly! Next, you've got to consider Calvin's resolute position on 'family values." And his own family, think about that. For God's sake, the man is one of eleven children."

Harwood pulled a binder from his stack of reports, laying it open on his lap, and read:

Raised in a three-room shack. Father worked the fields, literally chopped and picked cotton. He stressed education and making the most out of oneself. Eight of the eleven went to college. An article from Newsweek, written when he was first elected, says his parents still hold hands in public. His siblings include a nurse, a doctor, a millionaire Burger King franchisee, two teachers, and an Air Force flight maintenance tech. Married for thirty-one years, with no whiff of infidelity. Two kids, the older a boy, like himself a West Point graduate, and a daughter who works for a law firm, Baker Tuggle, in Memphis. Neither child is married.

"We'll kill the Democrats on family values," Harwood added rhetorically.

When he was in the eighth grade, his parents decided that the one-room schools in their Mississippi Delta town weren't good enough. They'd already sent a couple of others to school in Memphis, so they pack him off to stay with an aunt there. His father writes a passionate letter, a supplication really, to the Catholic schools for help. They respond favorably, and allow Rec to enroll. He graduates from Catholic High with honors, captain of the football team, All-state, to boot. He's president of the senior class and, get this, captain of the chess team. The chess team finishes fifth in the state his senior year.

The President interrupted Harwood's catalogue of Calvin's achievements. "How do you know so much about this man? This has an air of obsession about it."

"Actually, Mr. President, that may be a legitimate concern. This is an idea for its time, so sure, I'm consumed. The closer we get, the more it makes sense, and the more intensely I feel about it."

"Just so you know where you stop and Rec Calvin starts," the President observed. "Don't start letting this blur the edges of self."

"Perhaps there's such a thing as constructive compulsion," Harwood said.

The President grinned. "Like 'practical idealism' and 'compassionate conservatism'? You know, I'm a pretty abstract thinker. It's fine when writing a book or teaching, but in politics philosophy is a contagion that contaminates process. Maybe it's as simple as the eternal struggle between thought and action. Point is, Stan, philosophy is the diametric opposite of progress. Philosophers spend their time thinking about what's been and what is, not about the future. I have come to realize that philosophy is inaction incarnate."

Harwood felt uneasy with this introspective digression. He was determined to stifle it, if he could. "I've got a different view: the relationships you create and the character you project *are* action. You decided to run for governor against all political logic, and virtually unknown outside the Stanford philosophy department. You were disgusted by the Governor, the Speaker, the Mayors of L.A. and San Francisco, and someone said, 'Hell, why don't you *do* something about it?' You actually did, to everyone's shock, and you won. Then, you got sick. You went to see your doctor, and he instructed you to begin working out to improve your attitude and reduce stress. You packed your own gym bag and walked over to Tony's place and put yourself in his hands, literally and figuratively. You made a radical turnaround, and every paper in the country ran at least one picture of you, wearing a 'Tony's Gym' T-shirt, bench pressing two hundred pounds. With Tony's help, you changed the direction of your life. You had enough self-esteem and energy to run the nation's most difficult state with confidence and equanimity. Then, you successfully ran for President, a job that's never easy, but probably a lot easier if you're not encumbered with silly things like I.Q.

"So, now you 're in a tough spot. But there's a way out. The opportunity to capitalize on Calvin won't be here in weeks, perhaps not days. And that opportunity wouldn't exist, if you hadn't taken all the actions precedent to it . . . and, if you hadn't had a special relationship with Tony. We wouldn't be here but for your ability to form lasting and trusting relationships. Maybe philosophy isn't action, but, sir, relationships *are* action."

"But, Stan, I've got to be careful," the President interrupted. "Your approach is both weird and incredible. I've got to continue to poke at you."

"Yes, sir, I respect that. This is new for me, too." Harwood continued, "So as I was saying

Calvin's parents send him to Catholic schools because they want not only education, but structure and discipline. They get more than they bargain for: Calvin converts. Until then, he's spent every Sunday going to a little white clapboard church on a red dirt road, a church like thousands in the South: a raised-up baptism tank behind the altar, covered by an old faded curtain, no air-conditioning, no stained glass windows, no telephone, people parking on a driveway that long ago needed a new load of gravel, or parking on the lawn. Here he is praying with the AMEs and the Church of Godders, and he converts to Catholicism. O'Malley, a Catholic, is out, and Calvin, a Catholic is in. An even trade on religion. Calvin graduates from Catholic High and gets an appointment to West Point. He graduates near the top. Captain of the football team that beats Navy 31-28 in his senior year. The team has the best record in twenty years. He makes third team All-American, not quite good enough for the NFL. Has a few tryouts, but can't quite cut it in the pros.

Calvin's famous for his ferocious, all out style of play. He plays both ways, running back on offense, and middle linebacker on defense. Anyway, his aggressive play, gets him the nicknames "wrecker" and "wreck" which, coincidentally, happen to be his initials, "R-E-C." The nickname sticks.

"You do know this man pretty well. Does he drink Irish whiskey?" the President asked."

"I'll find out, Mr. President," Harwood laughed.

So, after West Point, it's on to Bragg and Benning for Green Beret, Ranger and jump schools. He's off to Vietnam, two tours, and he's a genuine war hero, Medal of Honor winner, loved by his men. He decides to stay in the Army, is promoted faster than an intercontinental ballistic missile, and ends up one of the youngest generals in the Army . . . ever.

"Let me describe the Medal of Honor story," said Harwood, consulting his notes. "First, no Medal of Honor winner has ever been elected President. There've been only three governors, ten Congressman, and two Senators, not including Kerrey and Calvin."

"Sure, Bob… Nha Trang."

"Yes, sir. And neither his nor Calvin's Congressional bios say anything but 'Served in Vietnam . . . awarded Medal of Honor.' By the way, Calvin's son is named Adelbert Ames Calvin, named after a former Union Army General and Mississippi Governor who also won the Medal . . . Battle of Bull Run . . . 1861."

"And Inouye?"

"Oops, I forgot. Of course, a shattered arm in Italy . . . just before the end of the war. Sorry"

"Don't apologize to me, apologize to Dan."

Okay, so it's summer 1967. Calvin crosses a rice paddy under furious VC fire, and drags these wounded guys two hundred yards to safety, despite being shot himself. . . twice. And the names of two of those guys? Roberto Martinez and Edgar Morales, a Cuban and a Tex-Mex. Martinez is from Miami, his father came over on one of the last boats and spent weeks demonstrating outside Elian's cousin's house. Juan Fitzgerald Kennedy Morales is from Alice, Texas, where they stare at Anglos on the street and you'd better speak Spanish if you want to order a beer. His great-grandfather crossed the border, who knows when, to work on the King Ranch. His father sells for a used car dealer. Martinez and Morales! Calvin is still an idol in every Hispanic community in the country. With the Senator on the ticket, we'll get every single Hispanic vote. Put Arizona, New Mexico, Texas, and Florida in the bag. Plus, he delivers Southern California for you.

"It's quite a story, Stan, but you're painting with a pretty broad brush."

"I guess, but . . . . "

"Taking blacks, Jews, Hispanics and other groups and consolidating them as a voting group . . . well, it's dangerous to assume too much."

"If you mean there are no absolutes, then, sir, I agree with that. But facts are sometimes counterintuitive. Mr. President, do you know what percentage of blacks were registered to vote back in 1972? Sixty-six percent. And how about in 1996? Sixty-three percent! In 1972, nearly forty percent of registered Hispanics turned out to vote . . . in 1996, a little over twenty-five percent.

"These groups are driven by issues. Nevertheless, ethnic, religious, and racial groups vote in blocks. It makes sense that their problems, things they care about . . . well, they're darned similar, if not identical. Take Catholics, for example. Even though there's a lot of 'cafeteria' Catholics out there, picking and choosing which parts of that belief system they want to support, when it comes to birthright and anti-abortion, they line up. Senator Calvin, I might add, has really struggled with this issue. He's a social liberal, but his Catholic upbringing weighs heavily in how he approaches pro-choice."

Stanley Harwood looked up from his binder and took a deep breath, allowing the President a chance to reflect. Williams scratched his nose and looked at the floor, as if to stretch his neck and shoulders. He interlocked his long fingers, wiggled them a bit, and put his hands behind his head. "You have studiously avoided the biggie, haven't you Stan?"

"Maybe it's saving the best for last, or not wanting to state the obvious at the outset."

"Well, it is the main issue, isn't it? Or are we kidding ourselves?"

"Before we discuss that, Mr. President, may I cover a little of Calvin's voting record?"

"Sure, go ahead."

Harwood continued,

Where he differs from us, well, he doesn't differ much. After all, he is a Southerner. He's a moderate on defense, against funding some big technology expenditures the Pentagon wants, but generally supportive, particularly on base closures. He'd let the military do what it danged well pleased in eliminating bases.

"We can spend a lot of time on policy digressions, Stan. We have to get to the point," the President scolded.

"One more point, sir, if you will. Listen to this, verbatim, from the Republican platform: . . . .*secure jobs . . . personal security . . . education . . . a balanced federal budget . . . foster opportunity for those unable to care for themselves . . . welfare reform . . . tough law enforcement . . . rights of the family . . . emphasis upon basics of learning . . . protecting Medicare and Social Security . . . equality of all people before the law . . . individuals judged by ability rather than race, creed, or disability.*"

"Stan, I know our platform pretty well."

"Okay, now, this from the Democratic platform:
welfare reform that will strengthen families, reduce child poverty, and promote responsible fatherhood . . .

"Even Gore said he wanted to, quote, 'crack down on deadbeat fathers,'" Williams noted.

*. . . increase charter schools . . . expand parental choice in schools . . .
aggressively improve teacher accountability . . . strengthen Medicare . . . secure
Social Security for future generations . . . assure a balanced budget . . . reclaim
public spaces so our streets and neighborhoods are safe again . . . crime prosecution
faster and firmer . . . strengthen crime victims' rights . . . tough penalties for violent
crime, including the Federal death penalty . . . eliminate government inefficiency,
making it cost less and work better . . . make government smaller . . . strong support
for faith-based organizations . . . fiscal discipline, open markets . . . greater freedom
around the world, supported by strong national defense that supports American
interests globally.*

"Interesting juxtaposition . . . ." the President mused.

"Now, you tell me, sir, who are the Republicans and who are the Democrats? Sure, I left out some subtleties, but except for the fact that the Democrats don't speak directly to affirmative action and individual responsibility and the whole area of women's issues and abortion . . . well, it looks on paper like Tweedledeedee and Tweedledeedum."

"Kind of scary, isn't it," the President grinned.

"You bet."

"So," Williams poked, "we just go to Mr. O'Malley and say, 'By the way, would you mind terribly if we asked you to step aside?'"

"Well, sir, once the convention has nominated him, it's kind of out of your hands. You could go to the National Committee now, but what we really need is for him to formally resign . . . just from the ticket . . . he'd actually stay the Vice President until January. McGovern got Eagleton's resignation, allowing Shriver on the ticket."

"Okay, Eagleton resigned . . . but he wasn't an incumbent Vice President. That makes it a lot tougher from our standpoint. So, we drop the incumbent, a man who won't go away quietly, replacing him with a damned Democrat. How do you propose I pull this off . . . or haven't you gotten that far."

"Oh, I've gotten that far, sir, but that doesn't mean you'll like my answers. Basically, the best way out is through."

"That means?"

"It's an old Robert Frost saying . . . you've got to tackle things head-on."

"Yes, and Mark Twain said that all one needs for success is ignorance and confidence. Where we're heading, we might suffer plenty of the former."

"Once you know in your heart this is right, you won't have any difficulty *telling* the Committee what we're going to do, not asking them. Sir, it isn't courage unless you're scared half to death. We get O'Malley's resignation, Calvin's commitment, and tell everyone how it's going to be."

"And, presumably, *why* it's going to be, too."

"Of course. Striking out with boldness doesn't mean that we don't have to *sell*."

"And if the Committee objects?"

"They can do one of three things, sir: approve Calvin; shoot you down and put a different candidate—not Calvin or O'Malley—in as your running mate; or stonewall."

The President hesitated, "Some football coach said he liked to run, because when he passed, three things could happen . . . and two of them were bad. Sounds similar to your plan. Now, how about timing?"

"Every week, until Election Day, various states close out, that is certify, their ballots. A few have already passed. That means that when you change O'Malley for Calvin, that O'Malley will remain on that state's ballot."

"You mean 'if'."

"No, sir . . . I mean *when.*"

Williams was impressed by Harwood's self-confidence and preparation, but remained silent.

"But, regardless of whose name is on the ticket as your running mate—resigned or not, dead or alive . . . the Electoral College casts the only votes that count. If we win the majority of the electors and those electors are loyal, we get whatever vice president we want. Any time prior to their December vote, we can substitute a new candidate, even after Election Day, and try to prevail on them to accept that person. It could be messy but, if you're willing to ht the good fight, it can be done."

The President stood up and paced for a moment, finally saying, "He'd be the first in history."

"Precisely," Harwood answered.

The President, clasped his hands behind his back and rocked back and forth. "That's this entire plan, isn't it?"

After a brief silence, Williams added, "Not that I'm demeaning that as a valid reason to put him on the ticket . . . ."

"It's critical," said Harwood, "but it's not everything. The man is too special. Like you, he's done a lot for his state and his nation. For neither of you has it ever been a matter of what you look like."

"Come on, Stan. Catholic, Southern, and war hero aside, aren't we skirting the real reason he can bring the ticket home?"

Harwood did not reply.

Williams continued, "Your plan is simply this: place Senator Reginald Calvin on the ticket because of his color. America gets its first black VP. And, if he succeeds me, he'll become the first black president."

What at first appeared to be a grimace, slowly turned into a broad grin, spreading across Stanley Harwood's face.

"Uh, Mr. President, that "if" is something else I want to talk with you about."

28

"You can't do this to me!" he bellowed. The "can't" came out as a South Boston "cahn't." Stan Harwood winced, as the Vice President pounded his fist on the President's desk and his orange locks flared as much as his temper. His heritage, his greatest personal pride and political strength, was his ace in the hole, and he knew how and when to play it.

Cornelius McGillicuddy Xavier Joseph O'Malley, descended from the finest people of Connacht County, Rosecommon, was named for Connie Mack. Perhaps this was why O'Malley had always been an inveterate Red Sox fan and why he too became a 'Connie'. His parents had high expectations for their children, and the children did not disappoint. An older brother breezed through Duke Medical School. A younger sister held a Ph.D. in education. A younger brother, a Georgetown-educated lawyer, working on his third book, practiced maritime law with the bluest-blooded firm in Boston.

Connie O'Malley's greatest asset was that he knew his strengths. He knew he was not smart, but he was plenty smart enough to know when to pull a trump card casually from his hand. And he knew when to lay it down, and when to slam it on the table. His vocabulary was limited, but it was forceful and wholly functional. His words came from the same limited lexicon, whether he was smiling and kissing babies, spitting hate, or spewing anger.

President Williams had heard some version of it a thousand times before. "My family goes to Mass every day. Every day! My sainted grandmothers scrubbed white marble steps on Beacon Hill, until their knees bled. My fatha's fatha drove a beer wagon. The poor soul lost a leg, trampled stopping a runaway team from killing a little girl whose name just happened to be Peabody. Did they care? My fatha still drives a cab, to this day. Six trips a day, minimum, to Logan. His lungs have been destroyed by tunnel fumes."

The President had not heard "fatha" in a couple of years, but he knew how the Gaelic accent could thicken and deepen when it suited the Vice President's cause.

"He gets up at 3:30 every day. Works thirteen hours a day, six days a week! And the Republican Brahmins, our damn Party loyalists, still screw him on tips."

After repeating this litany, he reverted to his generic bellowing, "You cahn't do this to me!"

"We're doing it Mr. Vice President, " Williams replied stoically.

"It's the right thing," added Harwood.

"And who the hell are you to tell me anything, Stanley Fucking Harwood?"

"Mr. Vice President, you're not helping the ticket. You've missed half of your commitments over the last three weeks. I'm sorry, but you're off the ticket."

"The American people won't stand for this! You cahn't do this!"

"We've explained to you now several times the reasons for this," the President insisted. In the twenty minutes since the meeting began, it was the first time that the President had even slightly raised his voice.

"Yeah, and I don't give a rat's ass what you or Harwood here have to say about anything. His great grandparents are probably the ones that wouldn't let my people—starving and diseased—off the ships in Boston Harbor. We died on those ships, by the thousands, because of you." His reticence diminishing as the argument continued, Connie O'Malley grew increasingly agitated and volatile.

"This ticket is in trouble." the President continued. "We've got to do everything possible to keep the Party in office. Stan has explained that we'll take care of you."

"Fuck you both."

The President went on, "Ambassadorships, boards of directors of major companies, chairing Presidential review commissions, special projects. And, I might add, you'll make a lot more money than a Vice President. A Cabinet appointment's not out of the question, and we even want to consider your brother for the next Supreme Court opening."

"You pricks have underestimated me. Do you know how much money I've raised for this campaign?"

The President knew exactly. He also knew of hundreds of times the campaign staff, in a noble effort to assure that all fundraising was legal, had to return O'Malley-raised funds because of the questionable source. Guns, booze, and military contractors seemed to be O'Malley's specialties. God, Williams thought, O'Malley's donors make the Democrats' Hollywood and labor money look good. And worse, the rumors of the O'Malley connection with the IRA never abated. Whether the diverted campaign funds went to the Vice President personally or to some arm of the IRA was a matter of continued speculation among administration and campaign staff.

"Yes, of course we do, Connie. We know exactly what you've raised," Williams answered. "And we want you to continue that good work."

The Vice President would not be distracted. "Continue be damned. You want my ass off the ticket! You don't understand the friends I have. You don't know what I can do."

Harwood rose and spoke, "Mr. Vice President, several things are certain. First, you're not pulling your weight like you did four years ago. You and the President were a good ticket then, good enough to win. But, not now. Something's got to change, and that something is you being replaced."

Harwood paused to see O'Malley's face turning from ruddy to a frighteningly surreal scarlet. He continued, "You have received a good faith commitment from the President. He's an honorable man, and he's just given his word that he will look after you in every way possible. But you must cooperate fully."

O'Malley, apoplectic, vaulted to his feet. He screamed, his spittle flying into Harwood's face, "Continue that good work . . . if you cooperate . . . ," he sputtered, but his words devolved into an invective-filled stream of hissing epithets and teeth-baring, eye-bulging blasphemy.

Williams thought he had seen his Vice President's emotional extremes, but this reaction was beyond appalling. He was thankful for the desk that physically separated him from the enraged figure standing only a few feet in front of him.

Harwood vainly persevered. "Mr. Vice President, you're doing a great service, one which will not soon be forgotten."

Harwood's words merely heightened O'Malley's fury.

"You chicken shit cocksuckers!" O'Malley raged. "You won't even tell me who's replacing me on the ticket. What if it's a Jew, or a chink, or a nigger! How about that stupid fuck from Illinois, or Wally's wop Mafioso buddy?"

Harwood smirked, "The man you're referring to is from Indiana, not Illinois and, as far as I recall, being Italian-American never condemned one to a life of permanent disrepute."

"Same thing: corn growers, pig fuckers, and greasy-haired green-grocers, all of them."

Now, the President's own long-simmering ire began to peak. He pushed himself away from his desk, stood straight up, and said in a low, stern voice, "O'Malley this meeting is ended."

Then, the Vice President leapt from his chair, lunged at the President, grabbed him by the lapels, and shook him violently. As he screamed, globules of spit and sweat spouted into the President's face. "Your mother's ass this meeting is over! This meeting ain't just begun!"

Anticipating such a possibility, Harwood had posted Secret Service agents immediately outside the Oval Office, and upon hearing the rising voices and O'Malley's increasing use of the F-word, they stepped just inside the doorway. Harwood turned to the door and shouted "Clauson! Snowden!"

Suddenly the two agents rushed into the office, grabbing O'Malley, and bullying him toward the door. Struggling to wrench free, Connie O'Malley, purple-faced with pencil-sized veins protruding from both sides of his neck, shouted over his shoulder, "We'll get you for this! Don't forget my words!"

William Clauson, the agent-in-charge, stood stolidly in the middle of the Oval Office, bewildered. "What now, sir?", he asked.

The President answered matter-of-factly. "Take him to his residence at the Naval Observatory. Here is a copy of an Executive Order, revoking his security privileges and denying him access to any secure areas. For the next forty-eight hours, keep him at the Observatory. No calls, no nothing. Make sure he doesn't hurt anyone, especially himself. Get a doctor in to examine him, someone we can trust. I don't need an alcoholic coma, DTs, or an attack on one of your men right now."

Agent Clauson looked up, cocking his head slightly to hear O'Malley's invective still booming down the hallways. Looking back, he offered his standard, "Yes, sir."

"Right now, he's barred from the Executive Offices and White House. We'll work out the details later. For now, just get the man on ice."

"Yes, sir, Mr. President. Clear. And his wife, Mr. President?"

"She's at the Cape this week and, if she leaves there at all, it'll be on a scheduled campaign tour with Mrs. Williams. I don't think she'll be a problem."

The President's brow furrowed. "Listen, about Mrs. O'Malley . . . I don't think we ought to ignore her. She's a fine lady, caught in a tough situation. She shouldn't have to hear this from anyone else. I'll give her a call."

"Anything more, Clauson?" the President asked.

"I'll prepare a statement, if you need one. I can attest to what I regard as a physical attack."

"Thanks, Bill. Go ahead and give us a statement, and give signed copies to Emily and Harwood in the morning. Oh, and Clauson . . . ."

"Sir?"

"Keep him within arm's reach of some good Scotch, unless the doctor objects. It may make things a lot easier."

"We'll handle it, sir. And I happen to know that the residence is already fully stocked with the best." Clauson hurried out, leaving Harwood and the President in the Oval Office together.

"Worse than I expected, Stan, much worse," the President sighed.

"There was no good way."

"Yes, I know, but as volatile as that man is, we should have considered his reaction as a possible outcome. In retrospect, it looks awfully predictable."

"Yes, sir. And I'm responsible. I should have thought out that part better."

"I have to say, I'm shaken. I just hope he'll calm down and go through a reflective period. Connie's really not so bad at heart. He's just been through something that none of us would ever want to go through ourselves. I suppose that if that's the worst thing we run into, we'll be doing pretty well."

"But that 'I'll get you, we'll get you' stuff . . . from some folks that might be considered a hollow threat," Harwood offered. "But from O'Malley, it gives me the chills. He may be dangerous."

"Crazy might be a better word," answered Williams.

Harwood continued, "But, I suspect he'll realize that he's only going to damage himself with a lot of loud protest. He's still a consummate politician, and his political head ultimately will overrule his Gaelic temperament. He'll do what's best for himself, politically. He's been around long enough to know that people don't like sore losers. He's got a lot more of Tip O'Neill than Bob Dole in him."

"Easy to say now, Stan. How about when we announce his replacement?"

"We'll see, Mr. President. Whatever happens, I think we'll rest pretty easy knowing that we're doing the right thing. Somehow, ultimately, right does seem to make might."

The corner of Harwood's mouth turned up into a slight smile and the President reciprocated, albeit half-heartedly, still troubled by the recent vitriol and threat. "I guess the Rubicon has been crossed, Stan."

"Yes, sir. Caesar and his men are definitely on the other side."

29

Harwood left Senator Reginald Calvin's home, having presented the President's offer. He turned the corner, his feet moving quickly over the brick sidewalks of Georgetown. He crossed M Street, turning into Mr. Smith's. It was, as he anticipated, dark. The music was loud, but the pay phone, which Harwood had checked on the previous day, stood behind the bar, at the top of the stairs down to the restrooms, and it afforded sufficient quiet to call. He took an open seat at the bar and turned toward the door to see if anyone had come in behind him. He was still staring at the bar door when the bartender interrupted his concentration.

"Hey, I said 'what'll it be?'"

Harwood turned. "A Budweiser and a clean glass."

The bartender briefly considered if Harwood had made a request or an insult.

"Uh, we've got frozen mugs . . . that okay?"

"Yeah, great, thanks."

Harwood stared at his beer, waiting for the foam to settle, then put the glass to his mouth and washed his lips with the cool beer without drinking. He surveyed the bar, studied the bright light from the dining area, took a final glance at the door, then spun his stool from the bar, and walked to the unoccupied pay phone, dialed, and waited. After several clicks and a second tone, he took a small piece of paper from his shirt pocket, and quickly punched five digits. After another tone, he retrieved from his pocket a small plastic cube with three buttons. Holding the device to the phone's mouthpiece, he pushed a green button. A whistle-like tone sounded, and he punched a four-digit code. After a single ring, a voice answered.

"Hello."

"Mr. President, it's Stan Harwood."

"Well, I see you managed to do it. Usually people get lost with all those numbers and tones. I'm glad you're Phi Beta Kappa. Well, how did it go?", the President asked.

"As expected sir: shock, followed by dismay, then disbelief and denial."

"Am I to take it that he said no?"

"Yes, sir. He was pretty abrupt. He reminded me that he was a Democrat and it would be impossible for him to accept. I told him you were ready to meet with him at any time."

"You think he'll come back to us?"

"Definitely. I'll bet he's really stewing right now, confused as hell. This man is not going to get a good night's sleep tonight."

"What now?"

"Now, we wait and pray. I'm feeling pretty good about this. He's a man of tremendous self-control and self-confidence, but he was awfully quiet and introspective when I left."

"Let's not count our crows before they caw, Stan."

"I agree, Mr. President. Let me know when you hear something, and I'll do the same."

"You said 'when', Stan, not 'if'."

"It's 'when', sir. There's no 'iffing' here."

"Okay. I hope you can remember those codes. I'm a little uncomfortable having you walking around with them.

The Secret Service boys just hate when that stuff gets out."

"Yes, sir, I'll be careful."

"Don't get hit by a bus."

"I'll do my best to get the numbers committed to memory. And I'll stay out of bus lanes, sir."

30

In a modern, undistinguished glass-faced office building on Connecticut Avenue, a few paces from K Street, an emergency meeting was about to get underway. A telephone speaker sat in the middle of the large conference room table, surrounded by a dozen Democratic campaign leaders and aides, awaiting a call. A box of sandwiches and chips, a cooler of soft drinks, and just-brewed pots of coffee sat on a mahogany credenza, ignored.

Frank Moore, the Democratic Presidential candidate, rushed to another conference room at the Chicago law offices of Pines, Winston, Feldman. Moore, in Chicago to finalize negotiations for endorsements from the Chicago Police and Firefighters, began his mad dash after being struck by political lightning, whispered to him by an aide in the middle of his meeting.

Proffering the obligatory excuses, Moore immediately abandoned his meeting with the ward heelers and union leaders, and hurried to join the conference call. Whether from the speed of his trip in the unseasonably warm fall Chicago morning or from the nascent anxiety caused by uncertainty, Moore was sweating when he opened the conference room door. He nodded acknowledgment to the assembled team, and moved the vacant seat at the head of the polished oval table.

Moore had expected his team to be well-organized and attentive. Instead, the crisis nature of the situation had created an air of anarchic cacophony. No one seemed to be in control of either the meeting or themselves. The Democratic candidate tried to get the team's attention, but sidebar conversations abounded.

"Hey, okay, ladies and gentlemen," Moore finally shouted, "let's get an update. What's going on?"

Speakers from Washington and Chicago began simultaneous narratives, each apparently trying to impress the candidate with how current and factual his information was. Moore silently audited the exchange, until he found his bearings.

Finally, he spoke. "Dammit," he started, "I want answers from you guys. This is absolutely outrageous. Will somebody, *one person*, tell me what the hell is going on?"

In Washington, the deputy campaign chairman, Bill Miller, took up the challenge.

"Frank, this is Bill. Let me read the press release. 'The Republican National Committee and the President of the United States announce jointly that Connie M.X.J. O'Malley has resigned as the Republican candidate for the Vice Presidency. Vice President O'Malley will remain the Vice President until his term expires in January. He will conduct the normal and customary duties of the Office until that time. We regret the Vice President's decision and thank him for his loyal service and great dedication during his years of service. The Party will immediately seek a replacement for Vice President O'Malley and will make an announcement as soon as a new candidate is selected.' That's it."

Moore jumped in, "That's it? That is fucking it? That's the stupidest damned press release I have ever heard, and I have heard a million. What the hell is this, 'I've Got a Secret?' Tell me, guys, please tell me there's more."

Ken Kravitz, a senior aide who had accompanied Moore to Chicago, spoke, "I'm afraid that is it, Frank. We've tried to contact O'Malley, but no luck. As you can imagine, the Press is going bonkers. This will drive them absolutely berserk, and it'll certainly explode in Williams' face. The Press is already down on him, and this will infuriate them."

"You mean there's nothing else. Nothing?" Moore queried, again incredulous.

"The phones are ringing off the hook all over the country. Our switchboards in New York, Chicago, and Washington are melting down. I can get you Rather, Brokaw, Jennings, Walters, anybody you want in less than a minute. They all want to talk to you, and none of them knows anything more than we do."

"Jesus," Moore spurted, as he buried his face in his hands.

Kravitz offered his opinion. "They have really screwed up big time on this one, eh, sir?"

Frank Moore lifted his head and stared at Kravitz with contempt. Then, finally moving from Kravitz, he stared at each individual around the table in silence, slowly shaking his head as if to say, "You guys really don't have a clue, do you?"

31

It was early morning and Stanley Harwood had hardly touched his first cup of coffee. He was thinking about what Rec Calvin must be thinking, when the phone rang. Harwood flinched from his contemplation, and answered on the first ring with a perfunctory "Stanley Harwood."

"Mr. Stanley Harwood?"

Harwood recognized Rec Calvin's voice immediately.

"Good to hear from you, sir. How're we doing?"

Fine, fine, Mr. Harwood. This line is secure isn't it?

"Yes, sir. Absolutely."

"Did you guys fire O'Malley without an answer from me?"

"Yes, sir."

"You and Williams are among the smartest pair of operators I've ever met, and I mean 'operators' in the most complimentary sense. So I can only conclude that you are certifiably insane and need to be institutionalized immediately. Who's your backup?"

"No backup, no subs on the bench."

"And if I say 'no'?" the Senator asked.

"Well, sir, I guess we'll figure that out then. In the meantime, we're sticking with the right, and in my mind, the only choice. You."

"You guys are playing mumblety-peg with cruise missiles."

"Mumblety-peg?"

"It's a kid's game we used to play back home. Maybe it's a Southern thing, I don't know. Anyway, a couple of boys stand across from each other and throw jackknives into the ground close to, presumably without hitting, the other guy, trying to get your opponent to spread his feet wider and wider. As it happens, plenty of throws miss their mark . . . I've still got the scars on my feet

. . . symbols of a veteran player. Of course, that was before adolescents toted Uzis and Kalashnikovs."

"Senator, we're not playing mumblety-peg, or juggling hand-grenades, or whatever the analogy. The polls show we're going to lose this election by the widest margin in history. It will be a rout, an embarrassment. We've got darned little downside. If you say 'no', we'll get someone else. We don't want to, but we can and will. But, we just can't believe that you'd turn down this opportunity."

"Have you made this offer to anyone else, or discussed a replacement with anyone?"

"No way. Until you say 'yes', everything is locked down."

"Or, 'no'," Senator Calvin added sternly.

"Yes, sir," Harwood laughed. "I learned that from a tape called Successful Selling. It's called the 'presumptive close'."

"Okay, Mr. Salesman, your customer wants to talk to the President . . . personally."

"Yes, sir. We'll arrange that immediately. Do you have something in particular to report or do you want to continue the discussions?"

"As you already know, I'm not a man to beat around the bush, Mr. Harwood. That's got to be part of the reason you contacted me on this project in the first place."

"Certainly, sir."

"It's a long shot, but I'd like to talk to Williams directly, just to, I guess, just to say that I didn't pass this up without meeting with him personally. To be fair, if you asked me for a decision right now, it would be no. But I still want to meet with the President."

"That's great!"

"Well, I think it's only a toe in the water, but maybe it's one foot on a banana peel, and the other in a grave."

"No way, Senator. This is birth and re-birth, not death," Harwood encouraged.

"Mr. Harwood, if this ever comes off, a lot of people are going to be gunning for the President. And probably me, too."

"Well, Senator, I'm sure you mean that figuratively, not literally."

"This move, again if it happens, is going to rattle so many cages that I hope it's just figurative."

"A lot of folks are going to come to the President's defense, folks that certainly aren't defenders now."

"I guess you're right. It seems like a big piece of political life is deciding not whether or not you want enemies, but which ones you want."

"Sir, if you're really concerned about physical safety, we'll make sure the Secret Service doubles or triples its coverage."

"And how about Lincoln, Garfield, McKinley, the Kennedys, King, Wallace?"

Harwood gulped audibly.

"And how about Reagan, Jim Brady . . . and three Gandhis, and a bunch of Anthrax. What assurances do you suppose they got?"

"Well, Senator, when you list like that, it does raise concerns. But, we will do everything we can to make sure everyone gets through this safe and sound."

Harwood, more than slightly disturbed by the implications of gunning and rattled cages, changed direction, "How do you want to proceed from here, sir?"

"I've got a bunch of questions. Basically, I guess I want to hear the offer directly from him. One-on-one."

The Senator's rich and distinctive regional accent, no doubt part military, and part Washington, yet unrelentingly suffused with the Mississippi Delta of his youth, suddenly struck Stanley Harwood. While bearing the thick-tongued traces of his youth, the Senator's voice was nonetheless crisp and articulate.

Harwood replied, "No problem, sir. When do you want to do it and where?"

"Hold on, I'm not through. I want to hear the battle plan in specific detail. I'm a strong believer in process. As you can imagine, I got that from the military education and field duty, not my Congressional experience!"

"That's about ninety-five percent done now, sir, and we can lock up the rest immediately. I think you'll be satisfied."

"And I want to hear from Williams' lips how he feels about this. What's in his heart, not in his head."

"Yes, sir. That will suit him fine, just fine."

Harwood was now convinced that the Senator was going through some written notes as he talked. That's okay, he thought. It showed that Rec Calvin was taking this seriously enough to have worked on it.

Calvin went on, "I think that it's best that I just come over to the White House. I'm sure the President doesn't want to leave and there aren't a lot of good places anyway, at least without stirring up the press or his staff."

"I agree, sir."

"Good. And the offer that you read to me?"

"Yes, sir?"

"I want a copy in writing to keep . . . signed by the President."

"Fine. That's part of our deal. Two signed originals, no copies. You both each keep one. You are bound and committed."

"Now, if I'm still a 'no' when I leave. I'll just walk away empty handed, okay? This evening at seven."

"Okay. Can you hold on?"

"Take your time."

Harwood's heart raced as he punched the hold button, got onto a new line, and dialed up Emily.

"Emily, this is Stanley Harwood."

"Yes, sir, Mr. Harwood. How can I help you?"

"Would you please let the President know that Mr. Falcon will be here at seven tonight. This is confidential, Emily. Only he is to know. Also, would you ask the President where he wants to meet?"

After sixteen years in government service, working for some of the most powerful men in the world and never having thought about repeating a confidence shared with her, Emily still was amazed at the unconscious condescension that comprised her everyday world. She wore it well, as did her peers, and that was their greatest asset.

"Yes, Mr. Harwood. I'll make sure and give him the message, and I'll be sure that it stays totally confidential. I'll get back to you as soon as I know something."

"Great. Thanks, Emily."

"Yes, sir. Good-bye."

Harwood quickly punched the blinking orange button on his telephone console to return to the waiting Senator.

"I'm back. Assume we're on unless you hear from me to the contrary. Where can you be reached?"

"I'm in my office on the Hill. I've already told my staff that if you or President Williams call, I'm to be interrupted wherever I am. And one more thing, Mr. Harwood."

"Sir?"

"Thanks."

Harwood's mind did not immediately calculate the magnitude or meaning of the Senator's word, and he repeated, "Sir?"

"I said thanks. I'm grateful for the opportunity, whatever the outcome."

"Yes, sir, Senator. Opportunities for greatness are a gift from God and He wants us to use His gifts."

"Mr. Harwood, somehow the process is the same . . . over and over. Every four years, somebody moves a little to the right, somebody moves a little to the left. Think about it, Clinton republicanized the Democratic Party, and they didn't even mind. Most of them, I'm afraid, didn't even notice. He told organized labor to stuff it about ten times—particularly on NAFTA and China trade. And, if a Republican signed the kind of welfare reform that Clinton did, he'd have been characterized as something only a little short of a baby-killer. If Reagan or Bush had been caught in immoral acts with women half their age, the Democrats and women's groups would have their genitals in a Mason jar on a pedestal in the Rotunda. Those women's groups that defended Clinton, or remained silent, they're not interested in *truth*, they're interested in standing behind meaningless symbols."

Harwood could not resist. "If those guys had affairs with women half their age, the women would've been so old there might not have been a problem."

"Right," Calvin laughed. "Elder Bush bombs Baghdad, Clinton bombs Kosovo, young Bush bombs Kabul. Sometimes it's like the Emperor's New Clothes. Now, who'd ever think of putting a Democrat on a Republican ticket . . . even if it was the best thing for the country? Why have I never been seriously considered as a Presidential or Vice Presidential candidate by my own Party?"

"Those aren't rhetorical questions," Harwood noted.

"Not at all. You know, something about this heretical approach appeals to me. I'm way off the record here, but a man like me still doesn't get this far in life without giving people what they want and telling them what they want to hear. It may be ugly, but it's a fact."

"Senator, everyone plays roles in life. It's called survival. Who's immune to wanting to be popular? Plus, if people went around doing and saying exactly what they wanted, this world would be out of control."

"Well," Calvin sighed, "there's enough reason for me not to do this, but plenty of reason to give it serious consideration. It's just hard to make the opportunity align with reality."

"There're may be a hell of a lot of broken eggs by the time this omelet is done. But it'll be worth it."

As the Senator replied, Harwood heard his voice tremble with palpable emotion, "Worth it, I hope, for the American people, looking for government leadership that'll give them opportunities for comfort, productivity, and security . . . delivered by honest people in an honest way."

"Your acceptance will take us a long way in the right direction, Mr. Senator. It really will."

Calvin's voice was still tremulous, "Let's get this straight, before we close. I'm still a 'no', and will remain that way until convinced otherwise. See you at seven, and again, thanks a lot."

"Yes, sir. Seven o'clock."

32

Calvin's driver arrived at the gates of 1600 Pennsylvania Avenue just after dark. The Secret Service log showed a meeting with Stan Harwood in the West Wing. The purpose: to review proposed policy changes on United Nations funding. That the Senator would come to the White House on such a mission was preposterous but, as for that, good excuses were not abundant. Now, eight weeks before the first Tuesday in November, all of the President's legislative initiatives were stone cold dead on the Hill.

Secret Service Agent Snowden greeted the car at the public visitors' entrance on the opposite end from the West Wing. The arrival point had been cleared through security and the paperwork was complete; that was all that mattered. The guards remembered Clinton trying to manipulate the logs and memories of White House security in a vain attempt to alter the picture of specific visitors. The White House security staff, proved that it had integrity to manage its processes correctly, even under pressure from the highest levels.

Snowden escorted Calvin to the Blue Room, stationing an agent outside the door. He hurried to pick up Harwood and led him to the meeting, along the way staying several steps ahead to make sure Harwood was not seen. Snowden considered the absurdity of his assignment. Peeking around corners, he thought, was the stuff of grade-B spy movies. But, any iota of intrigue gave his normally mechanical job some interest for once. Grade B or otherwise, he was enjoying it. He ushered Harwood into the Blue Room, and closed the door.

"Good evening, Senator Calvin. Great to see you here."

"Thank you, Mr. Harwood, I appreciate having had a little time to think. I'm still doubtful, more than doubtful, I guess, but maybe we'll see if you're a better salesman than you give yourself credit for."

"Ninety-nine percent of great sales is having a great product, Senator Calvin."

"That's a gracious way of putting it. Thanks."

It was a full fifteen minutes before the President entered the room. Harwood and Calvin immediately rose to their feet. William's long strides quickly closed the distance to the waiting men. With a broad smile, he offered, "Senator, great to see you."

"Good evening, Mr. President. Thanks for seeing me on such short notice," the Senator said.

"Senator Calvin, I'm the one who should thank you . . . for being here . . . to change history, I hope. What could I have to do that could be more important than meeting with you and discussing our potential partnership?"

Calvin was deferential. "Thanks, I appreciate it."

"You should know, before we start, that I have great regard for you, Senator . . . despite the fact that you currently wear the wrong color jersey."

"But then, you're trying hard to change that, aren't you, Mr. President?"

"I certainly hope you can be persuaded to work with us on a, how shall I put it, change in direction. Even at this point in your life, Senator, I suspect you're not totally uneducable."

Calvin smiled. "Thanks for the compliment. You know, I'm twenty years younger than you, sir. But somehow I imagine you're trainable too."

Stanley Harwood was relieved to see the casual banter between these men. His confidence, high but guarded, began to soar. Nonetheless, though not superstitious, he furtively crossed the index and middle finger of his left hand.

"Where would you like to start, Senator?" Harwood asked.

Senator Calvin began without further small talk. "Gentlemen, I'll have to admit it, I'm struggling. Quite honestly, I don't mean to sound egotistical, but I really don't struggle a lot. I don't know if it's a matter of *que sera, sera*—or that I'm really at peace with my Lord. I hope, and I think, it's the latter."

"You wouldn't be quite human, if you didn't struggle with this . . . don't you think?"

"Sure, I suppose so. Listen, Mr. President, I think it's only fair to tell you that… well, if I had to answer right now, I'd have to turn you down. As the situation exists, I just don't see any way I can accept your offer."

"Okay," Williams replied calmly, "that seems reasonable to me."

"But, of course," Calvin replied, "given the seriousness of this, well, this offer, I couldn't really say no . . . in good conscience . . . without meeting with you . . . seeing you face to face."

The President continued to approach the Senator's words with equanimity "Well, Senator, I'd be deeply disappointed if I couldn't find a way to demonstrate to you that this is the right thing for you to do. Certainly, I want to hear you articulate the reasons why you feel this way. I know you've thought it through enough to have some clear reasons . . . you're not the kind of guy who's thought of as a vacillating type. And, regretfully," the President added, "using euphemisms is something I've become accustomed to here in Washington."

"I've got your point, sir," Calvin offered with a grin. "Mr. President, first of all, what's the situation with the Vice President?"

"There are some things I don't know, and others that I can't share. As to the most important point, we have his formal resignation from the ticket, signed, witnessed, and notarized."

"Was he *compos mentis*?"

"Apparently he was *compos mentis* enough for Mr. Harwood and the Secret Service agent who secured his resignation."

"He was fine, sir. He understood and was quite helpful," Harwood added. "In fact, it was a lot less difficult than we initially thought it would be. Mind you, he merely resigned from the ticket. He's still legally the Vice President."

"Okay. Now, in truth, I have barely slept since Mr. Harwood visited me the other night. I've gone from an unequivocal 'no', to an enthusiastic 'yes', and back full circle again. And, like I said I just can't see how I can do it. There're a million reasons, but you can probably guess nine hundred and ninety-nine thousand of them."

"And why don't you think that this opportunity is better than the status quo?"

The speed of Calvin's response left no doubt that he had thought deeply about his answer. "Several reasons. First, although I don't have any skeletons in my closet, accepting this position would put me under a type of scrutiny to which I've never been subjected. Just the intensity of the glare, if you will, is not appealing to me. I know how it works, and it's not pretty, even if you're clean."

"Point well taken, Senator. I agree that there is a substantial discomfort factor . . . another of my grand euphemisms. Somebody once suggested that if Mother Theresa and Mahatma Gandhi ran together, the press would tear them apart."

"Yes, sir. Quite honestly, I don't really need that at this point in my life. I'm also thinking about my family. I'm not sure if I want to put them through this either."

"Remember," the President cautioned, "that everything in life is relative. What you're saying is that the prospect of being Vice President of the United States is not sufficiently attractive to you to undergo whatever pain you'd have to suffer to achieve that goal."

"Okay, yes sir, if you put it that way. But that brings me to another point, also a relative one, I suppose."

"And . . . ?"

"Well, if I knew that we'd be elected, well that might . . . I mean, it would . . . change the amount of pain—as you put it—that I'd be willing to undergo. On the other hand, if I knew that our election would be impossible, well then, that would also bear on how much crap I'd be willing to take from the press and the Democratic Party."

"And the answer, of course, is somewhere in between," the President observed.

"Precisely."

The President pondered for a moment, shifted in his chair, and, after a long pause, renewed the conversation. "I have perhaps a different take on this, Senator. Let me propose that you should take my offer, even if you knew one-hundred percent certain that we'd lose."

"That's an interesting philosophical conclusion."

"Ah ha!" the President exclaimed. "You see, it's not *philosophical* at all . . . it's totally practical. Let me explain. First, you would reposition yourself *vis a vis* the entire nation, in fact, the world. You'd be thought of differently . . .

better, that is, by Democrats, Republicans, Independents, everyone. You could be either Party's nominee for president next time around. More important, we would really demonstrate—with our actions rather than our words—that there are some great black men and women left behind by the political process. Contrary to your view, I think there's every reason to move ahead, even knowing you'd lose. But, I don't think we'll lose. While there are few certainties in life, I think we'd win, and win handily. With everything you bring to the ticket, I think we'll bury the Democrats. If you put our chances of winning up against the agony of a hard public campaign . . . well, I'd say it's an easy choice. What else makes you want to turn this down?"

"Well, sir, loyalty is a big one. This would cause me to turn my back on some long time good friends, people that have supported me, and helped me get to where I am."

"You think you owe a lot to other folks . . . those people who 'got you to where you are', as you say? Balderdash, I say."

Calvin was taken aback at the President's position, more frank and open than he had expected.

"You got it, you earned it," the President continued. "I don't think you owe them a darned thing. The Mississippi Democratic Party would be nothing, were it not for you. And why haven't they made you their choice for Vice President . . . or even President! You're a natural for either position. Com'on, think about it, Rec."

"Either I don't know, or I'm afraid to speculate. Why don't you tell me, Mr. President," Calvin shot back.

"Maybe it's because you're black."

"When African-Americans needed help, historically and today, Mr. President, it hasn't been the Republicans who were there with programs and policies to help them. You're on thin ice, here, sir."

Harwood said, "So, the Democrats have a legacy of social liberalism. You don't think the Republicans have a tradition of being color-blind?"

"How do you mean that?"

"Just what I said. Speaking for myself and millions of Republicans, our legislative initiatives, indeed our very core tenets are based upon treating people according to their abilities, not their color or ancestry."

"We're going to get nowhere with this. This has been battled out over more than a century and we're not going to fix it here."

"Okay, okay, I agree. But, grant me this: Is the Democrats' philosophical *raison d'etre* going to continue to hold together as Asians and Hispanics grow in numbers and influence? Can the Democrats continue to serve the interests of unions, gays, racial and ethnic minorities, women, environmentalists, the aged, and so on and so forth? Isn't it a house built on the sand?"

"Equal treatment and looking out for the downtrodden somehow seem never to go out of style, Mr. Harwood. Seems to me that they're safe on solid rock."

"Are unions downtrodden?" the President queried. "Are gays downtrodden? Are women downtrodden?"

"Is the Democratic Party exploitive? Is that your point? Are we Machiavellian? Is that your point? Are the Democrats without character, without honor, without values? Is that your point? What have *you* got? J.C. Watts? You're not getting anywhere with this, sir."

"Okay, I agree. I'm exaggerating to make a point."

"And that point is . . . .?"

"Senator Calvin, we're all racist, certainly if you define racist as 'race conscious', rather than 'race hating.'"

"This isn't a college philosophy class, Mr. President." Calvin did not intend the comment as a personal insult, nor did Williams take it that way, although he realized that it was, by its nature, defensive.

Williams continued, "Rec, I once asked my class, about twenty of them . . . black, white, Asian, maybe an Egyptian or Pakistani . . . ."

"Sounds like you were teaching across the Bay, Mr. President."

"Right, or as we used to say in Palo Alto, I'm sure it was Stanford, because the kids were bright *and* we had good sports teams, too. So, I asked how many of them considered themselves racists. The answer was, of course, none. No hand went into the air. So then I asked them to close their eyes and listen to this story. Now, Senator, imagine it's a blustery, stormy night, lightning and thunder, and you live way out in the country. No neighbors. It's midnight, you've been in bed for nearly an hour, and there's suddenly a terrific pounding on the front door. You scramble out of bed and go to the door, and

189

standing there is a kid . . . a teenager . . . he's white, maybe eighteen, nineteen, blond, good looking, short hair, wearing a T-shirt, windbreaker, blue jeans, and running shoes. Okay, got it?"

"Yup, got it."

"Okay, same situation. You go to the front door, responding to this furious pounding, and there's this black kid . . . Afro hair . . . eighteen or nineteen, T-shirt, windbreaker, jeans, and running shoes. Identical situation . . . different face . . . different skin color."

The President paused a moment for the Senator to reflect. "So, do you react differently? What's the immediate and truthful reaction to those two incidents."

The Senator did not respond, and the President continued, "Every one of my Asian and white students said that their reaction to the white kid was maybe a little concern, but mostly, 'what the heck is going on?' Their reaction to the black kid was, in one short word, fear. They were afraid!"

"Mr. President, you are explaining something that I have lived my entire life. You, sir, have never walked through a mall parking lot and heard the sound of white people pressing down their automatic locks as you walk by. I live it, my father lived it, my children live it. It's a cute example, but it's real life for me, painfully so. Now, Mr. President, am I supposed to join the ticket on the basis that you're enlightened enough to recognize racism when you see it?"

"Not hardly, Senator," Harwood interrupted. "What it boils down to is that you don't owe the Party anything. Look, they're lucky to have you and, if they had any damn sense, they'd see that. For God's sake, don't go leaving here thinking you should be loyal to the Democrats for what they've done for you or black people. If you don't accept our offer, that's fine. But, please don't do it on that basis."

"Well, I can't argue that American society . . . the whole world really . . . is inherently racist. Plus, blacks are no less racist than whites," Calvin admitted. "I've never believed that color equals identity, or that blacks are for some reason as at least as much African as they are American. I see my blackness as a physical characteristic, not some empowering identity. I suppose I've just never seen myself as a victim. Sure, I have rage inside me, sir, I have anger. But, it's a rage I've tried to focus on solutions. For me, self-esteem is not the same as defiance. I've never felt like I had to defy people to feel like a man. I think of myself as a man, an American, and a black . . . in that order. I love being black, but I don't think I glory in it any more than you glory in being white. Can we leave it at that, then?"

"We're way beyond where I intended this to go already. What are your other objections?"

"My last one is . . . well, it's my personal safety, and that of my family. I'm concerned about what might happen."

"Senator, that's not a rational fear, these days."

"Who blew up the Murragh Building and the World Trade Center? For God's sake, who hijacked three planes and killed over five-thousand people on Wall Street in a matter of an hour or so?"

"Some separatist locos or Middle East conspirators are going to try something?" asked the President.

"No, of course not. But, if somebody can fly a couple of fuel-filled jets into a icon skyscraper or blow up a major building, they can get to the Vice President, if they want badly enough."

"Horsefeathers! If you join the team, I'll double . . . triple . . . quadruple security. For you and your family. You all can move in with me . . . here . . . at the White House."

"Is that reassuring? Who knows where those other bin Laden planes were going?"

"Well, think of it this way, Rec . . . that way, if anyone goes, we all go together!"

"How comforting, sir," Calvin replied with a big laugh.

"So," the President thought for a moment before he recapped, "an aversion to the pounding that you'll inevitably take from the press, a loyalty to your Party, and concern about your family and your personal safety. Anything else?"

"Well, there's always that pesky matter of things like beliefs, values, and so forth," the Senator replied with a large dose of sarcasm. "And, it's not like Jews always vote for Democrats, blacks follow blacks, Minnesotans vote for Lutherans . . . don't you think it's a little more complicated than that?"

"A little more complicated, but not a lot," Williams responded. "In fact, seventy percent of Jews have voted Democrat for the past half a century. People vote in what they perceive as their own self-interest. The fundamental point is that we've taken your voting history and your positions on major issues and compared them with ours. We don't see any major discontinuities."

"Education?" the Senator submitted.

Harwood jumped in, "The only issue, repeat the only issue, on education is a money one. We agree wholeheartedly with your personal mission on pre-school care and education. It's just expensive, that's all. Nobody can argue that it's not something we shouldn't do, it's only a matter of 'can we afford it?'"

"Look, Rec," added the President, "gays in the military, national defense, the environment . . . we're pretty close on all of those."

"The environment? I'm not so sure."

"As we see it, the basic difference is how tough to be on corporate America. We agree that on any new pollution, stuff that's happened in the last twenty years or so, we have to be tough . . . really tough. On national parks, wetlands, auto emissions, nuclear waste . . . well, we're not very far apart. We do believe that the burden of conservation efforts should be accepted more by the private sector, you know, Ducks Unlimited, Nature Conservancy. And we're willing to discuss the tax incentives needed to push that along."

"I think you're making your point, Mr. President."

"Take a look at this." Stan Harwood handed Calvin a folder containing a few typewritten sheets. "It's simple. I've set out, issue by issue, each of our positions, trying to quantify the variance. I gave each one a rating, a 'ten' if we're completely aligned, and a 'one', if we're way far apart. I'll admit, it's subjective, but the average comes out at over eight. President Williams would like to have that ranking with our Party on the Hill."

"Well, as one of my old colleagues used to say, I don't want to beat a dead horse to death," the President said, "but my conclusion is that when your positions are put down on paper in an organized fashion, a black, Mississippi, family-values war hero looks a lot more like a Republican than a Democrat."

"I'll have a look at your analysis, and try to see if I'm really a Republican in Democrat's clothing."

"Can I move on to making a formal offer ?"

"Yes, sir, of course. That's the reason that I came here. This is so significant, maybe momentous is a better word, that I didn't want to give my 'no' over the phone."

"Well, let's get it on the record, shall we? I formally offer you the position of vice presidential candidate on the Republican ticket. I will announce it publicly as soon as we reach final agreement on the details. How's that?"

"Of course, it sounds wonderful to my ears . . . but I'm still 'no.'"

"Okay, I think I understand. Now, Senator, I have a draft release that I'd like you to approve."

"Nice touch, Mr. President. I continue to be flattered. But, let me ask you, when—I mean if—this is announced, don't you think your Party will riot?"

"Sure, some of them will. Nothing like this has ever been done. But I'm still the President and I'm still the Party leader. I may not have acted like it much for several months, but I'm not without a heck of a lot of power and authority. I'm going to move on this . . . I want this, and I *will* get it done. And that's all there is to it."

The President reached into his inside left suit pocket and pulled out a single sheet which he unfolded, reaching far forward from his seat to hand it to Calvin. Calvin read aloud.

Washington, D.C. The White House

Embargoed until 1:00 p.m. Eastern Standard Time.

President Williams announced today that Senator Reginald E. Calvin, senior Senator from Mississippi, is the new Republican candidate for the Vice Presidency.

Senator Calvin's long record of distinguished service to the people of Mississippi and the United States is well known. The President remarked, 'This is a great day for the citizens of the United States of America. We're honored to have on our ticket a man of Senator Calvin's courage, experience, and leadership. He is an individual of impeccable reputation and as Vice President will serve his country with distinction.

I want to personally thank Vice President O'Malley for his years of loyal service and great dedication. He will continue to make important contributions for the balance of the campaign and after the election. Senator Calvin and I look forward to working with Vice President O'Malley and the campaign staff to assure a smooth transition. We also look forward to serving the nation, from the White House, for another four years.

When he finished, Calvin paused and re-read the release, silently. He nodded slowly and unconsciously as he read. Then he took the letter, refolded it, and placed it on the table in front of him.

"Pretty short and simple."

"That's the best way, we think."

Calvin nodded toward Harwood. "'We' means you and Mr. Harwood? You place a lot of trust in this man, don't you Mr. President?"

"Senator, Stan has a great mind, and cares about seeing things done right. We wouldn't be sitting here, were it not for him. And, we've checked him out thoroughly, including his underwear drawer. And I mean that quite literally."

"As a matter of fact, I think my own underwear drawer looked a little disarranged the other day," the Senator said.

Williams laughed. "You've been in the public sector too long. I'm sure all of your skeletons are out of the closet. But if they're not, you'd better make this easy on both of us and tell me right now. Cash funds, girlfriends, boyfriends, manic depression, whatever. Let's not be cute or coy at this point."

"You won't get any surprises from me, Mr. President. I guarantee it."

"Good."

"Mr. President, Stan represented you well the other night. He even quoted a little Bible to me. Some Matthew, eh Stan?"

"And what was that, Senator?"

The decorated war-hero Senator from Mississippi allowed a broad smile to cross his face. "Chapter Five, Mr. President, verse sixteen. I looked it up after Harwood left. 'Let your light so shine before men that they may see your good works and give glory to the heavenly Father.'"

"That passage is perfect for this situation, Senator. Why don't you let your light shine, shine brightly for everyone?"

"I just don't see how I can do it, sir."

"Then, why don't you consider another piece of scripture. I've got to admit that John is probably my favorite, but I like the Old Testament, too. 'Where there is no vision, a people perish.' Proverbs 29:18."

"That quote is greatly misunderstood. The translations vary, but from the Hebrew the original context is more like, 'Where there is no revelation, the people are . . . how does it go? . . . out of control.'"

"I guess I prefer it my way," said Williams, smiling.

"No doubt, sir, but it might work both ways. I was up last night, couldn't sleep—again—and started pondering your name. I'd never really given it much thought. Anyway, I found some Emerson and was up reading 'til dawn. When I saw the faint glow outside, I had this eerie feeling. I told Mr. Harwood about how my father used to stay up all night, reading by candlelight in our little house . . . a shanty, really. It was special, staying up all night, reading, and seeing the dawn. Except, instead of going into the cotton fields, like my dad, I went to the office, wearing a necktie, for a bunch of meetings where I sat on my butt. My father got up, put on a pair of denim overalls, and worked with his hands."

"I'm glad you were able to experience that moment. How was the Emerson?"

Senator Calvin reached into his inside suit coat pocket and withdrew a piece of paper. "I wrote down a couple of things that moved me. They'll surely be 'old hat' to you, but do you mind if I read them?"

"I never get tired of hearing Emerson."

Rec Calvin reached into his pocket, pulled out a pair of glasses, put them on, and began to read . . .

They conquer who believe they can.

He has not learned the first lesson in life who does not surmount a fear.

Whatever course you decide upon, there is always someone to tell you that you are wrong. There are always difficulties arising that tempt you to believe your critics are right. To map out a course of action and follow it to the end requires the some of the same sort of courage that a soldier needs. Peace has its victories, but it takes brave men and women to win them.

What lies behind us and what lies before us are tiny matters compared to what lies within us.

After having read the Emerson quotations, Calvin slowly removed his glasses, laid them carefully in his lap, re-folded his hand-written notes, and returned them to his pocket.

The President better understood the enormity of the struggle raging within the Senator. Although his lips had said 'no', the Senator's head and his heart had not fallen into line with the spoken words.

"Senator, if I'm not mistaken, aren't you making our case for us? You are saying 'no', but acting 'yes'."

"President Williams, I just can't see how I can put everything aside and jump this, just like that. I'm sorry, sir. Please try to see it from my standpoint."

"Well, I can see it's killing you, Senator. I respect your position . . . it's not, of course, my intention to cause you any anguish . . . at least any more than is necessary to get the job done!" the President joked.

"And, in all honesty, Mr. President, isn't my physical appearance ultimately, what this is all about?"

"Senator Calvin, I was raised by a philosophy professor and became one myself. I loved every minute of it, in part because it taught me not to take anything for granted, and how to think logically. It also gave me a foundation of intellectual integrity that I'm loath to sacrifice on the altar of political expediency. Of course, your appearance is in part responsible for your shot at the vice presidency. However, there are several million other folks who look a lot like you, and none of them are sitting here."

"Listen, sir, one of the things I'm sorry about is that you're in such a pickle. You won election the first time by bringing a combination of ideas and integrity to a nation that hasn't seen that in quite a while."

"And then what happened, Rec?"

Calvin paused. He was confused by the President's question. "Sir?"

"What happened to me? What's your assessment?"

"Well, sir, you can just read the Post's editorial. For two, maybe three years, your image . . . not just image, because that implies superficiality . . . your fundamental honesty and integrity were captivating. A breath of fresh air! But, you struggled with your own Party, and your programs weren't strong enough to carry you. Sad to say, but maybe America would rather have someone telling them what they want to hear, whether that person means it or not. And maybe the people get what they deserve sometimes."

"I hope that's not accurate . . . I mean, I accept responsibility for my own situation, but I'd not want to ever find myself believing that people don't deserve worthy leadership."

"Another factor is Moore and Jenkins. They understand you well, and they've slammed you where you're weakest. These guys are not Johnny-come-latelys to the political scene, and they're well funded and well advised."

"And I'm not?"

"You were well advised the first time around, Mr. President. But, this time, some members of the original team aren't around, and those that are have gotten self-important and lazy."

"You forgot to add that I've sat back and watched this happen without stepping in and making the changes necessary to turn it around."

"For what it's worth, you shouldn't be too hard on yourself. I mean, after all, isn't that what you're doing right now, by offering me a place on the ticket?"

"Only with Mr. Harwood's ideas and prodding."

"It doesn't matter how you get there, it's the results that are important."

The President noticed Calvin's voice taking on a low, gravelly tone, one filled with emotion.

"Really, sir, I'd never imagined I'd be the subject of this kind of discussion. I'd resigned myself to continuing to serve that state that I love so much. Sure, my name was bandied about a little as a possibility for the Democrat's second spot, but I was never considered seriously. Then, out of the blue, you and Mr. Harwood come along."

"This is not a gimmick, Rec. It's the right thing to do . . . from *everyone's* standpoint: ours, yours, the Party's . . . most of all the American people's. It's that simple."

"Mr. President, I have to ask again about my color. Isn't this all about me being black?"

"In all honesty, when Stan first brought me the idea, that seemed a critical element of the package. But, the more I thought about it, I realized that here is a guy who should have gotten this opportunity anyway. I think it's all about your capability to lead the nation . . . something about which I have absolutely no doubt."

"But you're concerned aren't you, Senator?" asked Harwood.

"Well, I've never held myself out to be a spokesman for the civil rights movement . . . I've resisted the temptation. In that way, I'm what some people call a Ralph Ellison black, though hopefully not as intellectual, and not as thickly constructed. Ellison said, 'I'll know I'm free, when I know who I am.' Well, I know who I am. I am a man . . . and I am a man who's a symbol not because of the color of his skin, but because of the content of his character."

The President interrupted, "By the way, Senator, do you know Ralph Ellison's full name?"

"No, sir, I sure don't."

"Ralph *Waldo* Ellison."

"Small world," Calvin quipped. "Anyway, I don't see myself as representing the disenfranchised or marginalized in particular. Some people seek to represent specific individuals or classes of individuals at all cost, even at the expense of stressing otherwise effective and valuable institutions to the breaking point."

"Didn't Jefferson do that?"

"Yes, but his objective was democracy and his enemy was tyranny."

"And aren't the George Wallaces, James Earl Rays, and David Dukes tyrannical?" Williams asked.

"Sure, and we've dealt effectively with them without changing our core beliefs and our two-centuries-old institutions. Sometimes it's taken a lot longer than we'd like, but our institutions prevail. Mr. President, I'm an American before I'm a black man, and that just isn't going to work for some people."

"Backlash?"

"And more! Look, lots of black Americans put on a dashiki and go to Africa, and the first thing the Africans think is 'Hey, there's an American.' Not an African-American, not an African, but an American. That's a problem for some folks. Plus, I'm a lot less interested in what's been than what is and what's going to be. Unlike some of my colleagues, I try to look more than five minutes ahead, thinking that we must get everything for everyone from the government."

"What you've just said is already on the record, Senator," Harwood noted.

"Sure, but if I join you, they're going to have a field day with me . . . and you. We're not in doubt about our beliefs . . . that's one thing in our favor. We agree that power without love is reckless and abusive . . . and love without power is sentimental and anemic."

"It sounds more and more like we're on the same page, Senator."

"Mr. President, I think, at this point, it's best we part friends."

The President turned to Harwood. "I'm afraid we have misjudged the Senator."

"Well, gentlemen," Harwood responded with an air of confidence, "I am not accustomed to quoting professional baseball players, but all I have to say is 'It ain't over 'til it's over.'"

Though Harwood's statement was one of perseverance and optimism, Reginald Calvin readjusted himself uncomfortably in his chair.

33

Mr. and Mrs. Bernard L. Cartwright sat in the kitchen of their expansive Spring Valley home when the private line rang. Bernie had just fixed drinks for them. The level in his glass was about three times that of his wife's. Suzy Cartwright, as always, noticed the disparity and, as always, made no comment. Neither did Suzy say anything about Bernie's history of extracurricular sexual activities. She never had.

The campaign debacle was as prominent as a huge festering sore on Cartwright's face, but it was not a matter for discussion. Sex, drugs, legal or illegal, and politics were off limits in the Cartwright household. See the evil, hear the evil, but never speak the evil. Such ground rules had left this Washington couple, married nearly forty years, very little to talk about.

The line had a distinctive rattling buzz, different from the household phone's normal ring. Without looking, Bernie Cartwright knew it was the official line ringing, and he knew he had to take the call. This line could not be left to an answering machine, even tonight, when he wanted to avoid the world.

The President's announcement was only hours old. It had not only shocked him, it had brutalized him. His bones and his muscles ached.

He reached the phone, picking up the receiver on the fifth ring. "Bernie Cartwright" he answered. It was not a 'hello' kind of line.

A traumatized voice screeched into his ear. "Bernie, tell me I'm in a dream. Tell me I'm doing LSD like the old days. Tell me it's posttraumatic shock, or post drug shock, or some fucking post something syndrome. Tell me I'm hallucinating. Tell me you haven't screwed up. Tell me something, Dead Meat Bernie."

The Republican campaign chairman turned to his wife and calmly said, "Darling, it's the White House. Things are really in a turmoil over this

O'Malley thing. I'm going to have to take this in my study." She nodded, out of habit, not out of any trust in his words.

Stabbing at the hold button, Cartwright left the kitchen, not before retrieving his drink and pouring another two inches. He walked to his study, sat down at the desk, and took a long drink.

Here, in his study, Cartwright was surrounded by the symbols of a lifetime of achievement. Yale degrees hung in matching cherry frames, just over his head; shelves adorned with dozens of memorable photographs, among them autographed pictures of the Cartwrights with the Nixons, the Fords, the Reagans, and both Bushs. The photographs bore not just the famous Republicans' signatures, but personalized inscriptions of warm appreciation and friendship. A football signed by the partners of his blueblood law firm, "To our leader, captain and coach: Good luck in Washington." 'Punt', 'fumble' and 'sack' were words that came to Cartwright's mind.

He looked down at the red blinking hold button. It terrorized him. The warm perspiration that had suddenly appeared in his armpits had already wet his shirt, leaving large stains under his arms. He picked up the phone, half covering the mouthpiece with a cupped hand. "I thought I told you to use this line only if it was an absolute emergency."

A disembodied voice attacked his ear, "You don't call this an emergency? We are screwed and you are the reason!" If Chris Weiner was not hysterical, she was as close as a human could get. "You'd better start talking and talk fast, Mr. Campaign Chairman. Your nuts are on the line. That fucking tax proposal is going nowhere fast and I am in deep financially . . . do you hear me?"

Cartwright was numb from the losing campaign battle, from the President's announcement, from the wailing bitch at the other end of the phone . . . and blissfully numb from the alcohol.

"Where are you, Chris? L.A. ? Let me give you a call back in the morning. Now's not a good time to talk."

"Where am I? I'll tell you where I am, Bernie! I'm up your ass, that's where I am! I want answers, and fast. Where do you stand . . . are you out? Where the hell is O'Malley? And what about our deal?"

"Look, Chris, you know as much about this as I do. The President called me in just minutes before the press conference and told me. We were quarantined with Secret Service agents babysitting us until after the press conference. I heard the press people had to raise their hands to go to the bathroom, and a Secret Service agent walked them in and stood there while they took a piss. I'm telling you it was tighter than a tick's ass. I couldn't get to you or anyone else."

"More excuses, Bernie. Now, what's going on?"

"All I know is the O'Malley resignation was forced. Don't worry, they can't move forward on anything without getting me involved."

"You're not involved now, Bernie! You're completely out of the loop . . . maybe expendable is a better word."

"No, Chris, I'm still running this show. I have calls into Williams now . . . he'll be bringing me in to lead this effort."

"Bernie, this is Chris Weiner you're talking to, not some dumb-ass campaign staffer who just fell off the turnip truck! You're not running shit!"

"Don't worry, Chris. Give it a little time. It's gonna come apart . . . wait . . . you'll see. I don't even know if this is legal. I don't think he can do this."

"He's the President, Bernie and, I repeat myself, you don't know shit. Get this thing fixed or I will."

"Chris, we've got nothing to discuss until I can find out more about this."

"Nothing to fucking discuss! Let's discuss this! Remember that redhead in Chicago, the one with the big tits, you thought was a campaign volunteer? You thought, hey, here's a nice little girl from Northwestern, majoring in political science, trying to learn about the political process. And you were so willing to help her out! Do you have any idea how much I was paying her? She was really expensive, Bernie. I hope you appreciated her. Would you like to see those videos? Don't you remember how she said she liked to do it with the lights on? And you were so excited to please that sweet thing. That light gave us some good film. You must've thought you'd died and gone to heaven when you got a look at those firm, upright tits. A lot bigger than the old lady's, huh, Bernie? You'll particularly like your profile shots with 'little Bernie' sticking straight out. And I do mean little."

"Don't do this to me, Chris, please, I'm begging you."

"Who do you think would like to see my production efforts first? Maybe you'd like a personal preview of the first release from Weiner Videos Limited? Yeah, we oughta let the star get first look at his own work . . . get a chance to comment on the editing."

"Please, Chris . . . ."

"Jesus, Bernie, it's just a sham marriage anyway. I mean, after all, how can I fuck up a marriage where there's no marriage? Oh, I forgot . . . you *are* a guy who's got to keep up appearances. Hey, maybe a videotape should show up in the mailbox someday while you're at work. Suzy really ought to see them before the Washington Post does, don't you think? It's only fair, huh? Maybe she'll see a couple of moves she's hasn't seen from you before. Or at least maybe not with *her* in the last twenty years."

"Chris, I'll get this thing fixed" Cartwright blurted. "Don't worry."

"Oh, I don't have any reason to worry. I'm not in the movies, Bernie. I'm not a big movie star like you are . . . I'm not some important Wall Street lawyer, drafted into loyal service for the good of The Party. I'm not two-faced like Bernie Cartwright. Or should I say ten-faced or twenty-faced? I don't have to impress everybody like you do. You know, the lab did a wonderful job. Just a firm, hardbody with an old man on top . . . and on the bottom . . . just about everywhere, huh Bernie? How'd you like those orgasms she faked? Want to hear it again? Uh, uh uh, uhh, ah . . . maybe she's the one who should be getting the Oscar, not you."

"Chris, I can't talk anymore. I've got to get off."

Chris Weiner howled. "You already got off, Bernie! It's on the video! You got off and then fell asleep! Shit, my little actress had to wake your ass up to finish the shoot! I think those little white lines helped. That's on the videos, too, Bernie. The Drug Czar will love those scenes. God, I wish Katherine and Ben were still at the Post!"

"Chris, stop it!"

"Stop it, shit, Bernie. I've told you a hundred times, you'd better deliver, but you just don't seem to fucking get it. Unfortunately, I stuck with you too long and now it's too late to find someone else who can deliver. You still don't understand what I'm capable of. And it isn't my money that gets things done, either. It's my love for the chase. And you're in on the chase this time, but now you're the game, not the hunter. So my next call better'd be the one where I congratulate you for your fantastic recovery work."

"Listen, Chris, you've got to back off and let me . . . ."

Bernie Cartwright's sentence trailed into electronic oblivion, as only a hollow click and dial tone answered his words. Stunned, he frantically cracked his knuckles. Sweat streamed down his forehead and temples, some concentrating in little dots on his upper lip which he dispatched with a reptilian flick of his tongue. Still holding the phone with the dial tone blaring into his ear, his elbows on the desk, he wiped the sweat off his forehead with the back of his left hand. After a full minute, he finally dropped the phone into its cradle, reached under the desk for the wastebasket, and threw up. He pulled a monogrammed handkerchief from his back pocket, wiped his mouth, and dropped the cloth into the basket. The stench of his vomit filled the room. Then he dragged himself and his now empty scotch glass back into the kitchen.

"How are things at the White House, darling?" said Suzy.

"Not so good, dear . . . not so good tonight."

34

When he returned from the floor, his assistant reported that a "Mr. Falcon" had left an urgent message. While not accustomed to looking back, in the less than twenty-four hours that had passed, he'd thought of nothing else. Senator Calvin's head was spinning.

Can one be too much of a straight-arrow? What good is it to die on the altar of beliefs, and fail to live another day to serve those beliefs? What about Moore, Jenkins, and the rest? Deliver Mississippi, deliver the South, deliver the veterans and, of course, deliver African-Americans . . . but you can't actually be on the ticket! Never said, of course, but always looming—not a suspicion—but a truth. What do I care about the Democrats? Aren't Republicans and Democrats like Ford and Chevrolet . . . Time and Newsweek? All of it labels, brands, marketing, image . . . . Debate me . . . shake my hand on it . . . Washington bunker . . . voodoo economics . . . you, sir, are no John Kennedy . . . no controlling legal authority . . . What have I passed up . . . for myself . . . for my people . . . for America? Once-in-a-lifetime opportunities are just that, aren't they? Do they want me to change my mind? The wind blows the same strength, from the same direction . . . under those conditions you don't tack.

Calvin took his phone messages, all of them on white slips, except the 'Falcon' message on shocking pink paper. Retreating to his office, he set the others on the corner of his huge, paper-strewn desk, sat down, and read the 'URGENT AND IMPORTANT' legend emblazoned across the message. He ruminated over the message, then grabbed the phone, and nervously punched the seven digits. "Stanley Harwood," came the response.

"This is Calvin . . . Senator Calvin."

"Senator, the President wants to meet with you again. Can you come over this afternoon?"

"Mr. Harwood, this is a brutally hectic time of year. And, as my father would put it, I really don't want to work my mules back over plowed ground."

"This ground isn't plowed, Senator . . . no mule has trod it, and no plow has worked it."

"So, let me hear what you've got."

"Sorry, can't do it that way, Senator. However, let me say that since you've turned down our initial offer, the President wants to propose something further."

Calvin was shocked. The word "initial" brayed in his ears.

Initial? Are they holding something back? Is this some Turkish trading bazaar where the loser's the one who gives in first? What can they offer beyond the Vice Presidency of the United States of America?

35

He had been waiting in the Oval Office for several minutes. Some mixture of anxiety and eagerness made him pace, and the pacing stimulated his mind.

It is so close . . . but the press will chop me up. Uncle Tom . . . Uncle Rec. Plowing over plowed ground . . . Lord, how I remember that team. Daddy, grinning, used to wink at me and say, "They aren't the two strongest mules on earth, but they're the two smartest!"

What the heck do Harwood or Williams know about mules . . . or about the kind of men who work mules? Their bodies, arms and legs aching numb, after a day in the fields . . . their shoulders arthritic from holding the plow, working it to keep it steady, so that after twenty years, a man can't lift his arms over his head. And the knees, how they lose the range of bending and swell, gnarled from bone spurs, grinding and crepitant from walking to the moon and back a dozen times.

This kind of farming was a race between the knees, the shoulders, and the bank: Will the knees fail first? Or will the shoulders surrender to the fieldwork before the knees? Or will the bank come, while the body is still strong and able, and take the land.

The days are wet or dry. Too wet to plow, you must still get into the field. Then, mud cakes thick on worn boots, sticking in massive globs, so that the mud itself weighs more than the boot and foot. Each muddy row beckons the foot to stay in and abide a while, that request—a demand really—overcome only by sheer physical effort of foot, ankle, leg, and back, pulling hard, together, to overcome the sucking black Delta mud's resistance.

And the dry days, when the dust clogs the nose of man and mule alike, and the clods behind the mule stay big, like boulders. Where each step risks a sprained knee or ankle.

And the paradox of the dry days when you must walk carefully, deliber-
ately, else stumble and fall on the huge dirt clods, but you cannot do that—you
cannot walk carefully and deliberately—you must go fast or you will never finish a
row. So you go fast, and stumble, punishing knee and ankle . . . a hundred times a
day, maybe a thousand . . . certainly a million times before you go to sit on the
porch, for good . . . not too tired to work, but too worn.

To men like Harwood and Williams, it's a quaint postcard from the South.
Earthen rows churning up from behind the plow blade . . . my father in worn
coveralls, behind the mules, stumbling . . . year after year, begging, coaxing, threat-
ening, and loving those mules over mile upon mile of cotton and bean fields.

Those darned mules . . . how he loved those mules that he described to a
little six-year-old boy as 'brilliant'. And then he would chuckle.

How ironic . . . a black mule and a white mule, Billie and Sammie, the
only pair of black and white mules in the county. No one saw any meaning—or
humor—in it at the time. Today it would be full of meaning . . . dichromatic
symbol of the inseparability of dark and the light. Black and white bound together
in the traces, eyes ahead, ignorant of the color of their respective coats, focused on the
task . . . all this expressed, incongruously, in the archaic vocabulary of the Deep
South.

The Senator, still alone, still walking back and forth in the President's
own office, laughed aloud.

Those white cotton buyers . . . they'd ask Daddy why he called his mules
Billie and Sammie, and he'd answer, impassively, 'cuz that's their names', without
any of the smart-ass tone or intention that would come with that response today . . .
though I recall, once in a long while, he'd allow himself a laugh when the mules—
and he himself—were safely back in the shed that we kids called the barn . . . the
'barn', next to the free-standing wooden building that we called the bathroom.

Those white cotton buyers that used to offer to buy Daddy's cotton—at
prices half what they offered the white farmer down the road – and when they
couldn't get it cheap, finally finding a reason to come up to market price.

And how he didn't care . . . or at least never let it show he cared . . . politely
responding, over and over again, 'that sounds a little low' . . . all the while standing
at the edge of the field, shifting his weight from foot to foot, stroking Billie and
Sammie softly on the nose, cradling their large heads in his hands, nuzzling their

faces with his cheek and chin . . . and whispering secrets, close into their ears, in sort of lilting speech-song . . . secrets intended for him and the mules . . . only them . . . co-workers . . . the trio sharing thoughts and ideas shared only by best friends who have been bonded, literally and figuratively, who have shared the excruciating pain and exhilarating joy of working a plow.

And how, after ten years, or was it twenty, or thirty, the buyers, finally came straight to their best price, the market price, the fair price, the same price offered to the white farmers across the road, across the county. How that little victory, that ultimate demonstration of equality—equality earned, not given—was destined to be unnoticed, a minor footnote- no, a miniscule footnote—in a huge tome of progress. Maybe unnoticed is how it should have been . . . .

Reginald Calvin stopped pacing, closed his eyes, and dropped his head, hands clasped in front of him.

Those mules . . . and those books. "Praise the Lord for good mules and great books," *Daddy would say. Great fathers know how to get the best out of each.*

His eyes still closed, still motionless, Calvin smiled.

Lord, if those mules could have read, they would have stayed in the house and shared the bed with us.

"Thanks for agreeing to come back over, Senator."

Rec Calvin, musing on his legacy, flinched at Harwood's words. He spun, mentally grasping for relevance.

As his mind adjusted to the present circumstances, he responded, "Well, I've come a long way on trust and a short way down Pennsylvania Avenue. Neither trip seems too far, under the circumstances. You've been open and fair with me, so I suppose I don't mind. I'm assuming, of course, that my mules won't balk at having to pull my old plow through the same acres, Mr. Harwood."

Harwood tilted his head and offered an enigmatic smile. "No sir, like I said, no danger there."

Suddenly, the President burst through the door, smiling. "Welcome, sit down, gentlemen," he said, as he quickly filled the closest chair.

Calvin silently noted the absence of papers, notebooks, briefcases, writing pads. This was going to be a very short meeting, he thought, or a very long one.

"So, Mr. Harwood," the President began, "shall we give Senator Calvin the whole picture? I'd hate to think he made his decision without the benefit of all our thinking on this matter."

The benefit of all of our thinking.

"Of course, sir."

"Then, I'll just read him the little corollary to our offer? But first, some preparatory comments."

Corollary?

Harwood and President Williams beamed, like schoolboys who'd caught a teacher in a particularly embarrassing moment. Calvin was not much amused, uncomfortable with the men's breezy air.

The Senator's impatience overcame him. "Let's get to it, gentlemen."

"Senator, you're well aware that our original concept worked only because of who you are, what you've done, and what you stand for. Well, not long after you left," Harwood continued, "I proposed to the President a slightly different arrangement."

Calvin frowned, and Harwood determined to pick up the pace. "We have an enormous historical opportunity before us, a way to return a highly qualified professional and a wonderful human to office . . . and, at the same time, create an opportunity for the nation, and for you, personally, Senator, unachievable in any other way. We have an expanded vision, to put the country's best qualified individual in the country's highest office, possibly breaking the race barrier forever."

Calvin's mind raced. Consternation overcame confusion.

The three men sat, silently, motionless for a moment. Then Harwood unfolded a single page, and read:

The President agrees that, in the event he is re-elected, he will resign from office on or before the second anniversary of his second inauguration. Upon his resignation, the Senator will automatically become President. The President intends to do this because of the Senator's skills, experiences, and leadership. He believes the Senator will be a great President, and will provide great leadership for the nation. If the President fails to so resign, Senator Calvin may make this letter public, without any prior notice or agreement. Otherwise, Senator Calvin shall never reveal the existence of this letter.

Harwood set down the paper, looked at the Senator, and said, "That's it. I've got two places for your signatures. Here's your copy, Senator."

Senator Calvin numbly, almost reluctantly, extended his hand to take the copy from Harwood. He grasped the page lightly, as if it were toxic, and drew it toward him so slowly that his motion appeared at first to mock the very proposal. His face began to glisten, his skin becoming a dark shining brown. Folding his hands gently in his lap, he bowed his head, and closed his eyes. For fifteen seconds, he did not move.

Calvin resumed an upright, almost military posture, looked first at Harwood, then at the President and said, "Let me get this straight: I join the ticket, the tide turns, President Williams is re-elected, the President resigns, I become President?"

"Precisely," Williams responded.

Calvin was stern. "I'm still confused about whether you are manipulating me, or are sincere. You're certainly going to drastic means to get yourself re-elected, Mr. President."

Harwood challenged, "I don't think that selecting a brilliant and respected legislator, decorated soldier, and servant of the American people is a drastic step."

"Mr. President, Mr. Harwood, what do you know about mules?"

The men were taken aback at the incongruity of question. The President looked briefly at Harwood and answered, "Nothing, I guess. Why?"

"It's just that my father worked a team of mules, and it seems like such a long time ago . . . such an anachronism. I told Mr. Harwood that I didn't want to walk plowed ground here today, and I was just wondering if you had ever seen a mule team working. It's just symbol, perhaps, of how far apart some people are culturally, chronologically . . . you know, the distance between men."

The President was at the same time confused and clear about the Senator's message. He asked, solemnly and evenly, though naively, "Rec, are you familiar with *Letter from a Birmingham Jail?*"

Calvin considered briefly whether to scold the President, concluding quickly that William's honest intent was more important than his naiveté.

"Yes, sir, I'm familiar with it." Calvin stifled the "of course" that should have accompanied his response, also repressing that he had visited Birmingham as a youth, and many times since. He had walked the streets of Dynamite

Hill, met the families of Johnny Robinson and Virgil Ware, seen the sole remaining stained glass window in the 16th Street Baptist Church, a representation of Christ leading a group of little children with Christ's face blown out by the blast. He had gone to see what King saw and, if possible, feel what King felt on that September Day of Sorrow and Shame.

"What we are doing here . . . I mean you, me, and Stan, if I may embrace your expression 'teamed together' . . . is extremist. Extremist was King's word. He didn't like the word, but eventually became comfortable with it. He wrote that Jesus, Paul, Jefferson, Lincoln,—and he cited Martin Luther, too—were all extremists . . . extremists for conscience, truth, and freedom."

"Mr. President," Calvin responded, "I have great respect and admiration for you, but when you start comparing the three of us here to Jesus, Lincoln, and Jefferson . . . well, that's more than a slight exaggeration?"

"I'd like to think not, at least as it applies to you, anyway. Now, the circumstances are perfect for you to make your move . . . to capitalize on the opportunity."

"But, Mr. President, the most extremist thing is that you would never have done this, were you not losing an election . . . in fact, desperate. "

"Senator," the President responded, "I once had a lengthy debate with a student about whether great men—generals, inventors, Presidents, business executives—were somehow accidents of history, or rather themselves responsible for their fame and greatness. My student claimed that if Churchill had not come forth to give the English hope and tenacity in the face of World War II, that another would have. The need was there and someone, if not Churchill, would have filled it. We'll never know who it would have been, but, he insisted, somebody would have stepped forward. He claimed the situation demanded it, and the English people were emotionally and culturally prepared for it.

"Similarly, he maintained that if Fulton hadn't made the steamboat commercially feasible, if Fleming hadn't developed penicillin, if Edison hadn't invented the electric light, if the Manhattan Project team hadn't developed the atom bomb . . . all of this . . . everything . . . would have been done at or around the same time by someone else. While I had fun discussing the question, I still don't know if we'd still be reading by candle light had Edison not been born, or if we'd have gotten nuclear bombs, if Fermi and Oppenheimer hadn't been born.

"Truly, I don't know, and will never know, if there's pre-destiny, if things happen because the time is right, or if great men themselves manufacture history because of their individual power and vision. "But, I do know this: what Stan and I are trying to accomplish . . . well, it's the right thing to do."

Stanley Harwood put in his pitch. "What else do you get, Senator? Immortality, that's all. You've earned this offer, deserve to be recognized and remembered for what you're doing here tonight. You're changing the face, shape, and color of a nation, I hope for good. And, by that, I mean 'for good' both ways . . . permanently, and for the good of the country. The name of Reginald 'Rec' Calvin might stand up there with names like Lincoln and Kennedy . . . and King."

"Sure," Williams added, "you turn my campaign from dirt to diamonds. But, I was already resigned to defeat. I was taking no new vision into my second term. I was burnt out, subconsciously looking forward to Ojai. But now I'm restored, renewed . . . because of this opportunity that only you can make possible . . . just by being you, a great leader, personally and politically."

"Senator Calvin," Harwood said, "you get the chance to make history by becoming the first African-American President. Maybe it seems like a gimmick, but I believe *you're* worth it."

Suddenly, Harwood jumped to his feet, as if to underscore the magnitude of the moment. "Had you not been born black, Senator, given what you've done in your life, you – instead of Ralph Waldo Emerson Williams—you would be in this office already!"

Calvin turned quickly to assess the President's response.

"Are you expecting me to contradict, Senator? Stan and I have examined this over and over. That's our conclusion. In fact, Stan's original concept was to offer you the Presidency at the outset, and I resisted. It was just too much for me then. Maybe I lacked the kind of vision that Stan has, taking me a while to see the rightness of it, the elegance of it. Rec, I'll not patronize you, nor would you permit me to do so. But, I believe that the Lord has blessed me. He has given me riches beyond belief. I am, in a very real sense, in a state of grace. I can't take personal credit for what I've done or accomplished. In one

sense, I don't give a damn whether or not I'm re-elected. I have no other expla-
nation for why I allowed myself to get so far down, to continue to suffer that
buffoon Cartwright and his bevy of bootlickers. I guess I wasn't happy doing
this job, and my inertia was just my way of getting out. Now, this has moved
way beyond any desire of mine to spend four more years in Washington. Now,
this is all about hope, about fulfilling dreams. It's all about a black man, raised
in a tarpaper shack in the Mississippi Delta, whom we believe has a greater
purpose in life.

"We quoted Emerson yesterday. Well, Emerson said that every revolution was first a thought in a man's mind. This 'revolution' started as an idea, a
thought, in Stan's mind, but now it's a full-fledged revolution, that is, if you'll
find the courage and faith to allow it to be."

President Williams was nearly out of breath. The glistening sweat on
the Senator's face had dried and faded as he relaxed, focusing on Williams'
words.

Calvin realized that the President's speech came from the heart, not
the head. The rapid pace of his delivery, without notes, made it obvious that it
was not a contrived plea.

After a long silence, the Senator broke the tension with a nervous laugh.
"Mr. President, when Stan visited me with your offer, I was in a state of shock.
I didn't believe it was real, much less practical. I didn't come here to negotiate.
I'm beginning to recognize this is an historical opportunity that neither of us
can really afford to pass up. I believe that you guys think I'm good enough for
the job," Calvin replied. After a brief pause, he added, "And so do I. I thought
about how distant you two are from me, my background, my youth . . . how I
grew up in and, in many ways, the kind of person I am."

Calvin swallowed, and spoke again, his voice deep with emotion. "I
thought, perhaps allowing myself some unaccustomed bitterness, what the hell
do these men know about my father, how he slaved—literally and figuratively,
I suppose—to scrape a living out of some acreage he'd managed to put together . . . then come home and read great books, and do his damnedest to
create opportunities for us kids, always encouraging us to use our gifts to create
opportunities for others after us?"

Again, Calvin paused to compose himself. Then, he smiled and said,

"Just now I realized that you guys are honestly trying to create an opportunity for me . . . so that I can create opportunities for others after me."

The Senator's smile broadened, "I also thought, hey, what do a couple of career politicians like Moore and Jenkins—from Idaho and Wisconsin—know about working mules in the black, rich soil of the delta?"

President Williams turned to Stanley Harwood, as if to find some key, some interpretation to Calvin's enigmatic discourse, quickly turning back when Calvin continued.

"A few minutes ago, Mr. President, you asked if I knew *Letter from a Birmingham Jail*. Similarly, with no offense intended, I ask if you recall a gentleman named Barry Goldwater."

"Of course . . . *Conscience of a Conservative*."

"And his famous campaign slogan when he ran against Johnson?"

President Williams thought for a moment and smiled. "You're a rascal, Rec. *Extremism in the Pursuit of Liberty is No Vice*."

"Well, two thousand years ago, everyone thought Jesus was a dangerous extremist. George III certainly thought Jefferson was a dangerous extremist. More than half the country considered Goldwater a dangerous extremist who'd get us into war or change welfare, kicking tens, perhaps hundreds of thousands of poor off welfare."

"Surely, you're not a Goldwater fan?"

"Oh no. He's one of six Republicans to vote against Johnson's civil rights bill. Plus, there's a place for federalism, maybe as a rifle and not a shotgun, but it's society's job to step in and help those that can't help themselves. I *do* admire Goldwater's honor, and commitment to ideals. And then, three decades later a liberal Democrat from Arkansas changes welfare, kicking hundreds of thousands of poor folks off welfare. Now, tell me, who's the extremist, and who's the real visionary?"

"Rec, I know you can be a great beacon of hope for this nation, Rec."

"I don't know about a beacon, Mr. President, but I think I can let my little light shine." A broad smile flashed across the Mississippi Senator's face. You guys can toss that document. I've just become an extremist . . . and I'm about to become a Republican!"

36

"'President R.W.E. Williams announced today that his running mate is Senator Reginald Calvin of Mississippi. The President and Senator Calvin will hold a joint press conference today at 6:00 p.m. Eastern. Inquiries should be directed to the Press Office of the Republican National Committee.' That's it, sir."

Democratic Presidential candidate Frank Moore was ashen. "Can they do this? Is this legal?" he demanded from his limousine in North Carolina.

"They don't seem to care, sir."

"Damn it, what kind of answer is that?"

"We've got some people researching it now. O'Malley hasn't resigned as Vice President, just as Williams' running mate. What we don't know is how you resign as a candidate, and we don't know how they're going to put Calvin on the ticket. He wasn't nominated by the convention, and he's not on the printed ballots in any state. Seems to me like this won't work. Anyway, it's the move of a desperate man. We'll bury them now."

"Well then," Moore broke in, "you're one dumb shit. This isn't desperation, this is brilliant. You guys just don't get it. Has anyone found Calvin . . . talked to him?"

"Yes, sir, we've tried, at least. We've been to his homes and offices both here and in Jackson . . . there's no trace of him. He's got a home on the Gulf beach . . . it's locked tight, no sign of life. His office has no comment. Off the record, they're as shocked we are. They've got no idea what's going on. His home line has a tape recorded message. Nobody's seen him since the day before yesterday. I've got people staking out his homes, twenty-four seven, until further notice. The press is completely frustrated. They've got a hundred times the resources, and they can't find him either."

"Have you checked the Naval Observatory?" Moore barked. "Maybe he's already moved in!"

"We're doing the best we can, Governor."

"Well, it's not good enough, dammit. Look, I'll stay here in Charlotte for a couple of hours. Check in with me every half-hour, and let me know what's going on. By the way, has anybody talked to the Republican National Committee headquarters . . . Bernie Cartwright or any of his staff?"

"No, sir. We haven't tried them."

"Well, get in contact with Cartwright, see what he says. My guess is he's as confused as we are."

37

To have arranged a private meeting proved an almost-impossible task. The press was everywhere, staking out their offices, regular haunts, and homes. Various evasive devices were employed, the most successful being simply circuitous routes, dummy limos, and an illogical meeting spot.

Each arrived from a different direction, separately, by cab rather than by government car or limousine. Each arrived, as carefully planned, ten minutes apart, so that they would not be observed entering. Getting out would not be a concern. By the time they had met, they would have picked each others' brains, and determined the "true facts", as McBride redundantly said. And, perhaps, they might leave a bit relaxed and restored, but more likely the session would do more to feed their respective anxieties, than mollify them. Conjecture was always part of the Capital landscape, but it suddenly had assumed monstrous proportions.

Upon entering, none waited to be escorted upstairs, rather they quickly passed the large portraits, turned right, ascending the stairs without hesitation.

Foundering Campaign Chairman Bernard Cartwright arrived first, hurrying up the steps, head down, and seating himself in the Presidential Room. Two bottles of Far Niente were on the table, 'one for drinking and one for breathing', as Cartwright ordered. He finished a full glass before Whittingham arrived. Charles Whittingham similarly crossed the tiled vestibule, passing the Occidental's maitre d' rostrum with a perfunctory nod, and scurrying upstairs. He was disconcerted by the photographs that festooned the walls, particularly put off by Robert Kennedy, who stared from his framed black-and-white permanence, taking personal measure of Whittingham's character.

Bill McBride, former Special Domestic Affairs Advisor, who had been transferred full time to the campaign staff, arrived last, completing the trio.

Quickly closing the door behind him, McBride stiffly exchanged pleasantries before breaking the ice, with one of his typically profound observations. "Well, gentlemen, here we are."

Cartwright, his anger already fueled by wine, commenced. "What a stupid thing to do! I am a hard man to shock and I am in shock. This is crazy."

"The rumor is that a guy named Stanley Harwood put the whole thing together. Jesus, no one can even get close to the President," said McBride.

"The American people are going to demand some answers," Cartwright blustered.

"I just can't believe this," added McBride. "How could we not have known about this? Did either of you know what was going on? Williams has blown it big, this time. I think he's had a breakdown."

Whittingham, typically a man who thought carefully before speaking, sought to assess the dimensions of the situation and his dinner-mates' initial critiques. As Cartwright began to vigorously nod his approval of McBride's analysis, Whittingham spoke in a near whisper.

"Listen, you guys don't know what you're talking about. Lots of people—most people, in fact—will argue that this is a wholly logical conclusion. This campaign has been jammed in neutral, or maybe reverse, for six months. Mostly because of the folks sitting at this table, I might add."

Cartwright broke in. "What the fuck are you talking about? Suddenly we're the problem? Bullshit."

"Lower your damned voice, Bernie. And, yes, we *are* the problem! You running around humping the oil heiress, having Bensalem produce reams of papers that don't mean a damned thing . . . making promise after promise . . . none of which come true. Nobody will level with Williams . . . tell him, straight up, that the wheels have come off the campaign wagon. We're not being honest with him, or ourselves. And, Bernie, you know better than anyone that we're all scrambling for a safe perch for January. You're not even subtle about your interviewing. You're the bullshitter, and the person you're bullshitting the most is yourself."

Whittingham went on, "Look, Williams came here as a prototype outsider, almost a Jimmy Carter. He did fine with his own people, then suddenly the Party started helping him. Guys like us started telling how it should *really* be done. We almost cooked him, but now he may have found a way out of the box. This is the most brilliant political career enhancing move since Lincoln got shot in the temple, except Williams and Calvin don't have to die to assure their respective sainthoods."

"I didn't know Lincoln was Jewish," McBride deadpanned.

Cartwright didn't get it. Whittingham got it and was not amused. "Very funny, Bill. Look, this is like the Williams of old times."

Whittingham looked across the table. Cartwright's glass tilted up to his lips. It seemed to have been fixed to his mouth since they had sat down. "You'd better lighten up on the Cab, Bernie."

"You're the one who ought to lighten up, Charlie," Cartwright fumed with sarcasm and frustration. "'Cause you're talking out your ass."

Whittingham, still in a near whisper, turned to Cartwright and said, "You know what, Bernie, you're a pompous charlatan . . . have been since about ten minutes after arriving in Washington. You came here with all the talent in the world, and pissed it down the drain. If I'd told you that two years ago, we might not be in this situation."

"And you're a complete asshole, Charlie . . . I ever tell you that?"

Charles Whittingham grinned. "Follow this one closely, kindergarten class. Calvin is a lifelong Democrat, thus a split ticket, and Democrats come over in droves to the Republican side."

"And Republicans move to the other side, too."

Whittingham understood the political dynamic. "Maybe some, of course. But, with Moore and Jenkins, where do they go? You think any mainstream Republican would desert the President over this? And go to Moore? They're trapped."

"Half the registered voters in the country don't vote," Cartwright pointed out. "So, why don't you tell me, who's going to vote, and who're they going to vote for now?"

"Third party!," McBride exclaimed, proud of an original thought. "A la Anderson, Perot, Buchanan."

"Crazy! Who could mount a fundraising campaign and get media attention this late? Not to mention the little problem of getting on state ballots."

"Hey, there's still fifteen million of unspent matching funds that the Feds would love to give away."

"An independent movement in eight weeks? No way. Now, Calvin's from Mississippi, which except for the dubious exception of Arkansas, is the poorest, most downtrodden, third world state in the Union . . . and one of the blackest. Southern strategy redux."

Bob Kreppe, their waiter, stood discreetly outside the door, judiciously balancing privacy and service, refreshing Whittingham's and McBride's Cabernet, and delivering, with appropriate timing, their orders of roasted rockfish, seared venison, and crabcakes. Kreppe conveniently ignored Cartwright's slurred words and untouched venison, and poured the campaign chairman more water.

Cartwright, without waiting for the server to leave, stabbed his index finger in the air, as if to make a point of order. Indeed, he knew his statistics, even drunk.

"Correction, counselor, Mississippi is poorer than Arkansas . . . lower per capita income, and twenty-five percent of the people below the poverty line. Apparently, the casinos haven't helped that much. There's a million blacks there just waiting to vote for Calvin . . . and two million whites down there waiting to shoot him. Wait 'til we see the backlash. It'll make Chernobyl look like a backyard wienie roast. Southerners will leave Williams like rats from Hamlin."

Whittingham ignored Cartwright and continued, unperturbed. "He's one of a swarm of kids . . . nurtured and supported by their parents. Father chopped cotton . . . mother took in laundry, worked in a sewing factory. And they thought they were blessed . . . taught their son to think he was blessed . . . thought life had bestowed great gifts upon them and they were God's special children. Never complained, and he never complains. His whole life story is a text book statement on family values.

"Then, his parents send him to Memphis to be educated at a Catholic school. He converts to Catholicism . . . there's the Catholic vote; notwithstanding the presence of Baptists on this earth, there *are* Catholics . . . nearly sixty million in the U.S. Plus, as much as Calvin poses as a liberal, dancing around that ol' Catholic upbringing, it's still's a part of him . . . he's pretty straight out on Right to Life. Social liberal, conservative on religion, defense. That gives them all the Baptists and more than half of the South . . . the entire religious right. They'll understand Calvin on abortion, and those that already weren't Republicans will become ones pretty damned fast."

"We had those people already," said McBride. "And maybe Calvin's got a granite reputation for fairness, but Baptists are white and bigoted. Where's the gain, huh?"

"Well, we got Baptists and Catholics in *spades* now," sputtered Cartwright, "so to speak. And, how about dumping O'Malley? Like the Irish really love the blacks. Check out Boston. It's worse than Montgomery, Alabama, and no Democrat wants to admit it. Talk about two-faced."

"Screw the Irish, anyway," said McBride. "We don't care how it plays in Peoria . . . there's no Irish in Peoria."

"Yeah. Caterpillar replaced them all!" chimed Cartwright.

A thorough round of right-wing guffaws followed what McBride and Cartwright perceived as humorous. They swigged more wine as Whittingham picked up his analysis.

"Now, our man goes to West Point . . . then off to Vietnam, saves three guys, dragging them, one by one, across a rice paddy under enemy fire. One's from a small town near where Calvin grew up . . . a place called Rich, Mississippi... go figure *that* one. Anyway, here's a white guy lying legless in a rice paddy, telling Calvin 'don't save me, 'cuz I don't want no help from no nigger.' Calvin, apparently taking the double . . . or triple. . . . negative literally", Whittingham laughed, "saves him—Audie Murphy kind of stuff—drags him a hundred yards to safety, taking a couple of slugs himself along the way. Now, the guy goes to Washington once a year in his wheelchair and takes Calvin and his family out to dinner to thank him. The two other guys he saved are named Morales and Martinez... they call 'em the M and Ms."

"Yeah, both brown ones," said Cartwright sullenly.

"Don't tell me we got an Hispanic connection?", asked McBride.

"Bingo! Morales is Tex-Mex and Martinez is a Cubano, a strong anti-Castro leader. There's not a Spic in the nation that won't go Republican with Calvin on the ticket. He's a legend . . . 'Si es Rec, tiene que ser bueno' . . . that's what they say over their domino games on the streets of little Havana. If it's

Rec, it's gotta be good!. We got thirty-two million Hispanics, twenty million of them born in the U.S. Three-quarters of them Mexicans and Cubans, and the Cubans are rich as hell."

"Hey, I still say it'll never work," complained Cartwright.

Whittingham, undeterred, plodded on, "Okay, so he goes to Ole Miss law school, returns to the military, a string of quick promotions, then, surprises everyone, returns to Mississippi to fill a Congressional seat."

"You haven't mentioned the clincher, Charles."

"Oh, wow, did I forget." In a grand gesture of sarcasm, Whittingham struck his forehead with the heel of his hand.

"Silly me." His cynicism dripped slowly, as from a maple tap on a warm Vermont day. "Did I forget to mention the fact that Reginald Edward Calvin just happens to be . . . ."

McBride shouted holding his wineglass aloft. "Black!"

Cartwright scowled, adding under his breath, "African-American, if you don't mind."

"Yes, our new number two man is black, or whatever they want to be called these days. Calvin guarantees a turn-around, giving the President four more years. Then he runs four years from now, and is the first black President."

"He might make a perfect Republican," added McBride. "He's about the only one in the Black Caucus who'll tell the others to fuck off. Lined up with any Republican candidates, he'd could have been chosen as the running mate anyway . . . if he weren't black, that is."

"Yeah, they call him 'Chocolate Trent' down there. I'm afraid he's bulletproof. Strange, he'd never be the Democrat's choice, and now he's ours," Whittingham sighed.

"They tried a woman, didn't they?"

"Yeah, well 'try' is too strong a word. Ferraro! Man, are all woman politicians today strident? Whatever happened to the Margaret Chase Smiths of the world?"

"You're showing your age, Charlie. Anyway, Williams *has* co-opted the left . . . by going around us and pissing on the Party."

"And a lot of big donors aren't going to like this," Cartwright bitched. "They won't appreciate being pre-empted like this."

"Wally's calling the shots, and that's the way it should be," continued Whittingham. "This is crazy, but good. I'm ready to get on board, and you two should decide whether you want to win or whine. Let's lead, follow, or get the hell out of the way, guys."

McBride experienced another of his regular epiphanies. "Wait, wait," he said urgently. "The liberals would never attack one of their own!"

Cartwright temporarily rose from his stupor. "Nice try, Bill, but now, Calvin's fair game. The liberals won't just throw dirt on Calvin, they'll murder him. I can hear it now, 'He hasn't done enough for his own people . . . he's an Uncle Tom . . . the President picked him just because of his race . . . dee, dah, dee dah.' The liberal press will fill him full of holes like he never thought possible."

"Very impassioned, Bernie, but wrong, wrong, wrong. How're they going to attack a guy that was a Democrat just this morning? A West Point-trained, Catholic, black war hero?"

Cartwright shot back, "Yeah, everyone was so nice to Clarence Thomas. It's okay to be black, but don't have a conservative or capitalist thought in your head. If you're Jackson or Sharpton, you're on the front of the Times. If you're Keyes or Hamblin, you're ignored. More likely vilified. We'll get another high tech lynching here, just watch."

"I agree with Bernie, Charles," McBride said. "Keyes was smart and articulate. His positions were stereotypically Republican, down the line, and nobody noticed him, much less voted for him. And African-Americans are quite capable, even renowned, for eating their own."

"Well, if voters don't pay any attention to Keyes, the press isn't going to. And a VP nomination isn't quite the same as the Supreme Court," Whittingham said. "Plus, you're not going to find a pubic hair on a soda can here. It's over, guys. Williams is as good as re-elected, and we'll have the first black vice president in history. And after that . . ." Cartwright and McBride hung on the silence. ". . . . who knows?"

Cartwright frowned. "What happens if someone pulls a Martin Luther King or a Bobby Kennedy?"

"What's that mean, Bernie?" asked Whittingham.

"You know exactly what it means. What if somebody shoots Calvin?"

McBride, as usual a full step behind the others, turned to Cartwright, "Who'd shoot him?"

"Who wouldn't! There's a million people who'd shoot him!" Still glowering, his wineglass clutched firmly in his hand, Cartwright had an inspiration. "Hey, let's each throw a couple of hundred bucks into a pool."

"On what?"

"Oh, I've got a couple of fun ideas. First, let's bet who gets shot first, Calvin or Williams. It's probably a fifty-fifty. All the whites will go for Calvin, and the blacks will be gunning for Williams. What black guy wouldn't love to put a bullet through Williams' head . . . voila, instant Negro President . . . just add water or, in this case, lead."

"You're sick, Bernie," said Whittingham.

"I guess it's like Clinton and Gore," McBride recalled, "Bill needed Al as vice president to make sure no one would assassinate him."

"How about we set up another pool for who does it," Cartwright asked. "You know, KKK, black guy acting alone, O'Malley's Irish buddies, white supremacist, pissed off Democrat . . . all kinds of categories."

"Let it go, Bernie," Whittingham said. "You're drunk, again—and you're injured by being on the outs with Williams. Just let it go."

Cartwright, slurring his speech so that his audience had to concentrate on his words, was undeterred. "How 'bout a pool on how it's done. We'd need some odds, of course. A bullet is the most likely way to take one of them out. We could make separate sub-categories for pistols and rifles. Odds should be pretty favorable on a bomb, especially with O'Malley in the hunt, so to speak. I'd guess there'd be long odds on poison and knifing."

McBride chimed in, "Charlie, there are lots of folks who wouldn't like to see Calvin as Vice President . . . starting with all the white supremacy groups on remote ranches in Montana and Idaho, looking for a cause. Then, the Christian Right loonies, and a dozen various hate groups. Or, just any ol' redneck with a black velvet painting of Elvis in his twenty thousand dollar trailer, a freezer full of venison, and a closet full of high-powered rifles, some with night scopes."

Whittingham continued the role of mediator and moral disciplinarian. "You're both out of bounds, guys! Hell, I'm the damned chief-of-staff. I've got as much reason to be pissed as anybody, but for God's sake, I'm trying to understand the reality of the situation. This is good for Williams and Calvin . . . and probably a damn good thing for the country, too."

Cartwright dropped his voice—a voice more of threat than point of view—below that of Whittingham, his frown gradually deepening to a glower. "It's not over, not over by any means. You guys watch, a lot could happen. Maybe Senator Reginald Calvin just *won't* be our next vice president."

"The way you said that, Bernie, a chill just ran down my spine," Whittingham said.

"We'll see, Charlie, we'll see . . . ." Bernard Cartwright, arguably, with only Mary Matalin in the running, the worst Republican campaign strategist in history, gulped more expensive Cabernet, twitched, and pondered.

38

Patrick Sternberg, the managing partner of Amerco Securities, over-saw risk positions in equity-based investments. He had been one of the many Lew Calendar fans, a boss at times, but more often mentor and friend. But one of Sternberg's strengths, in fact a strength of every top manager on Wall Street, was that business always came before friendship. Always.

Sternberg had scrutinized Calendar's trades and positions, and watched with dismay as the ace trader dug himself deeper and deeper into a financial hole that seemed to have no bottom. The Sternberg-Calendar shared family trips—skiing at Telluride and chartered yacht cruises out of Tortola—were distant history when business intruded. Calendar was summoned to Sternberg's office for a "consultation."

"Lew, what the heck is going on?"

"The numbers speak for themselves, Pat."

"What the hell kind of answer is that? I know what the numbers say. The numbers say you're down ninety million in three months. Your position makes it look like you're trying to imitate what that Jett guy did at Kidder."

"My trades all make sense . . . the markets are screwy."

"It's a poor workman who blames his tools. Losses are losses, Lew. Is everything alright at home? Kids okay? Sally okay?"

"Yeah, yeah. This is pure business. Give me some time. This portfolio will be dynamite. Look at these fuckin' short positions. The shorts have to cover, Pat."

"In 1986, Citi was a god, and the arbs and shorts banged it so hard that John Reed's toenails turned black and blue and he traded in his wife – in that order, I think. Most of 'em covered between nine and thirteen and made millions . . . excuse me, billions."

"This isn't like that," Calendar replied. "No Arab princes here. These stocks are in great shape. No real growth, but steady, with good cash flow."

"Lew, you're bleeding. I might agree theoretically, but we're not talking theory. You're a trader, not a frigging light-bulb-head analyst. We're talking real money . . . the partners' money."

"For Chrissakes, Pat, I *am* a partner. And I've made more money for this firm than any other man here. Look at my numbers."

"Look at Ty Cobb's numbers! Look at Babe Ruth's numbers! But Ty can't hit the fast ball anymore. And George Herman can't hit the long ball. Lew, did you ever see short rates higher than long rates?"

"Don't patronize me, Pat, because I won't stand for it! Everybody that's been in this business for more than a few years has seen an inverted yield curve. For God's sake, Pat, in 1981 T-bonds were over fourteen percent and bills were over twenty percent. Just a couple of years ago, the 30-year bond was yielding less than both the seven and ten-year notes. What's your point?"

"Maybe that's what's happening here . . . an anomalous situation. Remember derivatives? Proctor & Gamble and their 'buddies' at Bankers Trust?"

"Rates always correct, Pat. Markets always correct. Long term is always riskier than short term, right? Risk 101. Remember a little book we all had to memorize called the 'Inside the Yield Book'?" And just because the NASDAQ went 5,000 doesn't mean that somebody repealed the law of gravity. Eventually, Newton still gets hit on the head by the apple."

"Right, exactly, Lew. In the meantime, while apples are floating around in space, a lot of people get killed, go broke before they correct. Even Keynes said in the long run we're all dead. I just want our investors to be around when markets finally 'correct.'"

"Okay, so you wouldn't lend someone money for a long time at a lower rate than you'd lend it to them for a short time. But it happens anyway, Pat. Financial markets are queer sometimes. I don't need to know why. All I need to do is make money off it. Things adjust, Pat. Eventually the market corrects."

Pat Sternberg reached into his upper left-hand desk drawer and pulled out a dark leather folder bearing the embossed logo of Amerco. "Lew, let me share with you a story about LTCM. Remember those guys? Long-Term Capital Management had these economics gurus, Nobel Prize winners in fact, managing, owning, or somehow associated with a firm that had trillions, not billions, of risk exposure. Two of them, Scholes and Merton, guys from MIT, Chicago, Harvard . . . who the hell knows. Big fuckin' deal is what I say. Here's what these guys said when they lost eighty billion of investors' money. First Merton: 'It was for us a broadening experience about the multi-dimensional aspects of setting up a new financial entity.' Lew, as Dave Barry would say, I am not making this shit up. Now Scholes: 'I have achieved a better understanding of the evolution of financial institutions and markets, and the forces shaping this evolution on a global basis.' Have you ever heard such hypocritical, mealy-mouthed, weasel-worded bullshit in your life! It makes me want to puke! Eighty billion dollars! What a pair of assholes!"

"What can I say? They fucked up bigtime, Pat."

"Right. And I pull this out and read it once and a while, just to remind me of a position I never want to be in, and remember the type of person I never want to be, and the excuses I never want to have to make. I'm not going to let you or anybody else jeopardize the partners' money, my money, or our investors' money like that. We take risk, a lot of risk sometimes, but we make money commensurate with that risk. Not like some air-headed, crap-spewing professors! Real investors, real people lost that money . . . real money, Lew. This firm creates value for its clients. We didn't have to apologize to our clients for having them in Cisco at 82, Lucent at 85, or Nortel at 85, because we got out of them when they became helium-filled."

Lew Calendar had heard enough soapbox preaching for one day. "Is that it, Pat?"

"That's it, Lew. Just watch that position. Pets.com is Pets-dot-fucking-dead. And they're turning Silicon Valley office space into bowling alleys and storage facilities for about a hundred tons of overpriced office furniture sat in for ten minutes by a Stanford MBA who thinks "Graham & Dodd" is an intellectual property software consulting firm. Those casino stocks might be squirrelly, but it's still your job to make money. Without excuses. You've done a great job here, but we can't stand these kind of losses anymore."

"I'll watch it, Pat. But I'm right."

Without another word between them, Lew Calendar stood up, turned his back on his friend, and walked out the door, leaving it wide open behind him.

39

"The Attorney General is here to see you , sir."

Julie Shaer stepped quickly into the Oval Office, and energetically pumped the President's hand. "Mr. President, I'm sorry but I had to see you right away, face-to-face."

"Okay, Julie, you can stop shaking my hand now and take a seat."

President Williams freed his hand. He had known the Attorney General for a long time and could discern the difference between an anxious and an eager state. She was more anxious than eager.

"Mr. President, we've come up with something important. Unfortunately it's kind of embarrassing. I don't mind being personally embarrassed, but professional embarrassment, departmental embarrassment, well, that's a different thing."

"Enough self-flagellation, Julie, let's get to it."

"Mr. President, when Speaker Berkhardt died in that sauna, the Capital police with some Bureau support, checked out everything, and concluded it was a horrible accident."

"I don't like the sound of this, Julie. "

"Sir, we've got our doubts, now. Serious doubts. One of Bureau's top investigators took the case files home, studied them, did some independent investigation, and with a fresh eye, got a different conclusion."

"And that would be?"

The Attorney General was stone-faced. "Murder, Mr. President."

Williams rubbed his forehead in an unconscious act of frustration and disbelief. "Murder! You're telling me the Speaker was murdered!"

Shaer took a deep breath. "Sir, there are too many things that don't add up."

"Damn, Julie, I'm sorry, but how does this stuff happen? Didn't the coroner examine the body? Don't they cut it up, dissect every little bit, check out all the organs?"

"Of course, Mr. President, and the autopsy didn't reveal anything suspicious. The unusual thing was that he got terribly drunk."

Shaer lifted the top page of a sheaf of papers, read quietly for a moment, and looked up. "This is a very troubling picture. I can give you an executive overview, or go into detail, depending on how much time you have and how much you want to hear."

"I think I'd better hear as much detail as you know."

"Then, let me review some of the inconsistencies."

Shaer returned to her notes and, without looking up, began to speak. "First, we can't figure out how Speaker Berkhardt got into his club that morning. No one let him in. The doors were all locked, although they don't have an alarm system, so we can't prove that. His personal key was still in his desk drawer. The club accounts for all its keys, and the Speaker had been issued only one.

"Next, we carefully examined all the locks at the club for marks of illegal entry, and there seemed to be nothing remarkable about any of them. Later our analyst suggested we physically take out all the locks and send them to the lab. We did, and came up with minute traces of metal filings, like dust, in the lock of the side door. We now think the door was opened with a new key, a key that had just been cut. There were also microscopic traces of a putty-like substance in the lock, like someone tried to make an impression of it.

"In reviewing the death scene photos, our analyst thought Congressman Berkhardt's clothes didn't make sense. They were neatly piled on the floor just outside of the now-infamous sauna. But, when someone gets undressed, he takes off his shoes first, then his socks. I'm also told that however drunk or tired a man gets, he sets his necktie aside, usually hanging it over something, putting it over a chair, a lamp, anything, maybe even laying it neatly on the floor. The Speaker's necktie was folded . . . men never fold their ties . . . and it was laying directly on the floor with the rest of his clothes piled on top. His socks were on top of the pile, with the shoes on top of them. That doesn't make sense to us now. You take off your shoes first, then set them down, and then

231

take off your socks. Whatever happened, his socks should be tucked into or put on top of his shoes, or at least lying aside. But not lying underneath the shoes. The shoes should be on the bottom of the pile. And, for a man that consumed that much alcohol, the clothes were just too carefully folded and piled up."

"Aren't there other plausible explanations?" the President asked.

"Probably. We're just talking about things that don't add up. He could've re-piled his clothes, but it's not a normal thing for a drunk man to do."

"I guess I agree," Williams said. "What else?"

"Next, the Speaker's keys were in his right-hand front pocket. Now, all cars have the ignition on the right hand side of the steering column, but the Speaker was left-handed. In the past couple of days, we've observed dozens of left-handed and right-handed men getting out of their cars. Ninety-five percent of right-handed men put their keys in their right trouser pocket, and about twenty-five percent of left-handed men do the same thing. But our analyst recommended we go back and see what pocket the Speaker *actually* kept his keys in. No one seemed to know, including his wife, so some agents examined all of the pants in his closet, plus the ones he wore before he died. All of his pants' pockets showed considerable wear on the left pocket, much more than the right. The tops of his left pockets were all slightly frayed, and the pockets themselves, inside, were more worn on the left, consistent with his having put his keys in his left pocket and carried them there all day. This man clearly kept his keys in his left front pocket, but his keys were found in his right pocket. If someone killed him and wanted to make it look like an accident, he made a mistake by putting Berkhardt's keys in his right pocket."

"This analyst, what's-his-name, is pretty good, huh?"

"*Her* name is Krautchik, sir, Maria Krautchik. And, yes indeed, she's very experienced . . . absolutely outstanding."

"Sorry Julie," President Williams explained. "Is there more?"

"I'm afraid so. The hotel room. We haven't figured out who the Speaker was meeting with, or why. It's not on his appointment calendar, and he didn't say anything to anyone."

"That supposedly wasn't unusual for Berkhardt," Williams noted.

"That's correct, sir. He had a habit of keeping appointments in his head, which drove his staff crazy. That itself might not be cause for suspicion, sir, but there were several drink glasses around the room, in addition to Speaker Berkhardt's. Funny thing, Krautchik pointed out, none of the glasses matched. They're all what they call 'commodity' glasses, sold both direct and by distributors all over the country to bars, restaurants, and hotels. But every glass was different, only the Speaker's was actually a hotel glass. Now, there were three more of the Grant Hotel glasses there, each of them still wrapped in paper, unused. Did someone bring their glasses with them? Seems an odd thing to do, and the hotel swears that they take all 'alien' items, as they call them, out of the rooms when they're cleaned. Alien glassware is taken to the basement and stored, used in the employees lounge, given away, or destroyed."

"This does not sound good at all."

The Attorney General shook her head, and the President noted how it took a moment for her blond curls to follow the movement of her head, as if her hair were in slow motion.

"Another thing on the key. The Speaker's ignition key wasn't one of those that are symmetrical, that you can insert either way. It had a top that was flat and smooth and a bottom with little teeth."

"Sure, Julie, like the old GM cars. My Jimmy truck out at the ranch has a key like that."

"Okay, so when you start it, your thumb has to be on a particular side of the key, and the pad of your index finger on the other side. Well, Krautchik checked the prints and found out that the thumb and index fingerprints were on the wrong sides, opposite where they should have been. The Bureau did examine the key for the correct prints, but never considered the fact that the prints were actually backward."

"How did Krautchik come up with this one?"

"I don't know. As she explained it to me, think about trying to start that Jimmy truck of yours with your thumb on the side of the key away from you. It's conceivable, but barely possible . . . you'd have to turn your wrist completely around."

"And ?"

"The only conclusion is that somebody, the killer, took the Speaker's hand and pressed his fingers onto the key to make sure his prints were there, nice and clear. But our killer didn't get it quite right. He forgot to account for the asymmetrical key and that a specific print would be on a specific side of the key."

"Unbelievable."

"At this point, we're looking at everything again, taking the most negative view of things, and we have another piece of information that pretty much proves our conclusion."

"You've got a smoking gun?"

"Maybe guns, plural, sir. The only bottles in the room were quarts of vodka. The other glasses had a little beer in them, but there were no beer bottles or cans in the room. Did a killer take them? Why? Anyway, the lab re-tested everything, and found traces of other whiskey in with the beer. One had a tiny bit, just a residual amount, of scotch in it. Another had minute traces of bourbon and what we guess is ginger ale. A third glass had traces of sugar, lemon, and tequila, like it was some sort of umbrella drink. Probably a margarita."

"What's your conclusion, Julie?"

"We think these glasses were accumulated from off hotel premises, and either empty or emptied out, then filled with beer. Nobody puts a beer into a whiskey glass on purpose."

"There must have been prints on the glasses?"

"Yeah, lots of prints, but none that help us. The Bureau hasn't finished running them against all their databases, and we've got some matches. But people we've tracked down are completely clean, and apparently totally random. They had been drinking in bars around town, but can't identify the specific glasses. Some prints are unidentifiable, meaning that whoever held these glasses has never been arrested, been in the military, or never applied for a high-security government or defense position. Anyway, we now think the glasses were picked up somewhere else, and transported to the hotel room."

President Williams was shocked and frustrated at Shaer's revelations. "Is that the list?" he asked as more of a demand than an inquiry.

Shaer shook her head. "The Speaker's route to the Club. If he'd driven out of the hotel parking garage to go directly to his club, he'd have taken a right when he came to the street. There's an automatic teller machine next door to

234

the hotel, with a twenty-four hour security camera. The camera's field of view picks up the traffic lane turning right out of the parking lot. There's also another camera at an ATM a couple of blocks down the street. That camera picks up part of an intersection, including the lane that Berkhardt would have driven in on his way to the Club. His car doesn't appear—at any time during the night—in either video tape," Shaer explained.

"That's significant?"

"Absolutely. To avoid being seen by either camera, he'd have to take a series of left turns, turns that would be initially *away* from the Club. Where was he going? Did he, or someone else, make left turns on purpose to avoid being picked up by the cameras? Did he stop somewhere between the hotel and the club? It's fishy, sir."

Williams sighed, "Is that it?"

"No, sir, I've saved the best for last."

"I can hardly wait, Julie." There was no humor in Williams' voice.

Shaer sighed deeply. "The Walter Reed doctors and District coroner's office went over the Speaker's body with a fine-toothed comb, including testing all bodily fluids, especially urine and blood. They found nothing unusual, except for the high BAC. However, with no other signs on the body, Krautchik was suspicious, and urged re-test."

"And?"

"And, they were still negative. The only things that showed up in his urine were a couple of prescription drugs, or rather metabolites, which are the remains after the body processes the drugs. The autopsy had already revealed this."

Shaer pulled a pink typewritten sheet from her papers, glanced at it, and looked up. "One was what's generically called simvastatin, a cholesterol medicine made by a company called Merck, and sold under the brand name Zocor. The other drug was an anti-anxiety drug called Xanax. It's very popular now for calming nerves and reducing worry. I don't have the chemical name, but it's marketed under the brand name of Xanax." Shaer spelled the word, "X-a-n-a-x."

President Williams commiserated, "God knows with his job, it's a wonder he didn't go through a truckload of that stuff a week."

"Yes, sir. I ordered a truckload for myself! Anyway, there were no traces of any other drugs, illegal ones, that is. But Krautchik is now a cross between a bloodhound and pit bull. Reviewing the files, she noticed one of Speaker Berkhardt's office clericals said that Berkhardt had complained about a headache all day, the day he was killed, that is."

"Or," the President broke in, "the day he killed himself with too much booze."

"Not likely. Berkhardt's office person pointed out to Krautchik how badly the Speaker was feeling, a brutal migraine, apparently. As he's on his way out, presumably to the infamous meeting, she suggests he take something for his headache. He says, 'I probably ought to', returns to his office, coming out a little later with a bottle of aspirin. She keeps a pitcher of water on her desk, and he grabs a clean coffee cup off a nearby credenza and proceeds to take what she claims were six or seven aspirin, a handful anyway. She remembers because she told him he'd better get something to eat right away, or that much aspirin would really eat up his stomach. Then, Speaker Berkhardt mutters a 'thanks' and walks out the door."

"That's it? What am I missing here?"

"Mr. President, the Speaker had no aspirin in his urine. He would've had either the aspirin itself, or some by-product of it, these metabolites, in his urine. Our forensics people swear that six aspirin would have shown up. But nothing."

President Williams was still befuddled. "What does all this mean?"

"First let me give you another tidbit, really more like a feast. After we failed to find the aspirin in Berkhardt's urine, the forensics team from Walter Reed looked at his pee again. This time, they find two, literally two, white blood cells. They tell me that except for some occasional biological material, like these random white cells, urine is totally clean. Anyway, they test these white blood cells, and guess what?"

"He has AIDS?"

"Not close, sir. The white cells aren't his cells!"

"Somebody got their white blood cells in his urine?"

Julie Shaer giggled nervously. "No sir, get this: the urine in the Speaker's bladder was not the Speaker's urine!" she cried. "It's somebody else's!"

"Okay, Julie, laugh at me all you want, but please tell me how someone's else's urine got in there, would you?"

"Somebody put it there."

The President's skepticism, which had turned to astonishment a few minutes before, became utter bewilderment.

The Attorney General went on, "The killer had to have drawn the urine out of Berkhardt's bladder, and replaced it with different urine."

"You're kidding! Just to confuse us, to make it look like an accident?"

"Precisely. And they almost got away with it, but Krautchik figured it out. Seems she was a nationally-ranked gymnast, just missed the Olympic team. She remembered one of the guys trying out for the Olympics talked about how he'd stuck a catheter up his . . . uh . . . how he catheterized himself to pass the drug screen."

"You mean a kid replaced his urine with someone's else's, in order to trick the system?"

"Yup," answered Shaer.

"Will people do anything to win?"

"Apparently. Now, it's not only true in sports, but politics, too."

"How'd they do it, the cholesterol medicine, Xanax, and all? You're sure about this?"

"Absolutely, and, knowing how it's done, it sounds pretty easy. They had to have put a catheter up his penis, drained the urine, left the catheter in, and pumped different urine in."

Williams, raising his eyebrows as far as they could arch, was incredulous. "With the right drugs already in it?"

"Exactly! With the right drugs in the alien urine. This donor had to have been taking the identical medicines, just to throw us off the track. This was planned carefully, and well in advance."

"Someone could do this?"

"Well, Mr. President, we've got the final proof. The original autopsy team swabbed the tip of Berkhardt's penis as a routine procedure, at least when the Speaker of the House of Representatives dies. All the materials and instruments used in the autopsy were marked and stored. The forensics guys went back and analyzed the swab for any residuals that might be left. Sure enough, there were traces of some drugstore-type lubricant used to help get the catheter up his penis and into the bladder."

Williams just shook his head.

Shaer hurriedly consulted her notes. "The entry to the club; the weird way the clothes were piled up; car keys in the wrong pocket; the finger and thumb prints on the wrong sides of the key; alien glasses with mixed liquor in them; aspirin missing from his urine; white cells that aren't a DNA match; the car turning the wrong way out of the hotel parking lot; lubricant on the tip of the Speaker's penis. That's it."

"Isn't that enough!"

"Oh, and we still haven't located whoever rented the room. It was rented in the Speaker's name, paid for in cash, but the registration card isn't in the Speaker's handwriting. The check-in clerk has no memory at all, except that it wasn't Berkhardt. In short, there's plenty to reverse the coroner's accidental death conclusion. This was murder, by some pretty slick operators, too."

"Not slick enough for Ms. Krautchik. Are you going to request permission to disinter him?"

"No, not now. We'll let him sleep peacefully for the moment and, I hope, for a long time. Just in case, we've got a full-time guard on the grave. We're not taking any chances."

"Fine, Julie. I feel terribly for his family, but I'm glad you've gotten this far. I'll have Whittingham contact your office, and draft statements for you and me. God, I dread talking to his family and making this statement."

Shaer winced. "I'm not crazy about it either, sir."

"Julie, you know I'm not a legal-type, but I have been trained in philosophy, an important part of which is logic."

"Yes, sir," Shaer acknowledged tentatively. She knew what was coming next.

"If, indeed, the Speaker was . . . ."

Shaer finished the President's question, ". . . murdered. Yes, he *was* murdered, but why? Yesterday, I established a special 'motive team' to consider possibilities. They're starting with a long list, and they've only been at it a short time, but the best guess is it's professional, probably in the legislative arena, possibly someone who wanted legislation passed, or wanted something blocked.

"On the personal side, Berkhardt didn't make enemies, and we can't find any grudges or disputes. No girlfriends, no boyfriends, no debts, no arguments, no enemies, so far. His staff, both in Washington and Phoenix, have been grilled. We've interviewed his family, and his neighbors in Potomac loved the guy. Our finance people are combing bank records, but there's nothing unusual so far. He *did* like to fund-raise, and loved being entertained by lobbyists."

"He's in pretty good company on that score . . . that could apply to several hundred up on the Hill. On the legislative side," Williams speculated, "why don't you give me the short list."

"Well," Shaer began, "water rights have been contentious in the West for years, and there're several bills bouncing around different committees."

"Right, Henry had been on the side of the ranchers and farmers for a long time."

"Also at the top of the list are Indian reparations and casino taxation. In each case, the sides have staked out their respective territories, and Speaker Berkhardt was right in the middle of it. He was pretty clearly pro-Indian. As to casinos, he was, at least on the record, undecided, but his staff says he opposed tax legislation, and was going to bottle it up in committee forever, while professing, at least publicly, a neutral stance. They claim he was a private ally of the gambling industry, and had been sitting on various legislative drafts for some time. A lot of folks were angry because he wouldn't schedule hearings. His legislative affairs assistant says he got a lot of pressure from the Christian Right—they want that tax passed. To get the thing off his back, he'd drafted a press release saying he was formally against considering the tax in the next session. That would have killed it through next fall."

"What's at stake, Julie?"

"Plenty! I've got someone waiting outside, if you want to hear it now. She knows a lot about this, and I'd like you to meet her anyway."

"Fine, bring her in."

The Attorney General went to the door of the Oval Office, reappearing a few moments later, accompanied by an attractive, petite blond with narrow eyes and bangs covering a broad forehead. Williams discerned a lightly Slavic face, and even he found her full chest difficult to ignore. The philosopher in him emerged. Gestalt, he thought: her individual features were not particularly attractive, in and of themselves. In fact, separately, they might well be considered unattractive. But together, they formed an attractive young face, a physiognomic synergy of beauty and professionalism. The woman, he thought, could be twenty or forty . . . one of those faces.

Julie Shaer approached the President, a hand firmly on the woman's shoulder, apparently as much to comfort her as to direct her across the room. "President Williams, I'd like you to meet Maria Krautchik, the one responsible for cracking this case."

In response to the President's outstretched hand, Maria Krautchik offered her own, though, unlike the President's, it was visibly trembling.

"How do you do, young lady? You've made a real difference on this case, and I truly appreciate it. Take a seat and tell me what you know."

The young analyst glanced around.

"That's fine, right there." The President gestured toward a nearby chair. "Okay, you've got the floor."

Krautchik looked at Julie Shaer who extended an encouraging nod. "Well, as I understand it, Mr. President, the anti-casino people, including some powerful Christian and Family groups, have tried for years to stop casinos, but it hasn't worked. While no states have approved legalized gambling in the past several years, in a very short period, Colorado, Illinois, Indiana, Detroit, Mississippi, Louisiana . . . I'm missing someone . . . oh, yeah, Missouri, and also Iowa, all legalized some form of casinos during the past decade."

President Williams added, "And the card clubs are big business back in my home state of California."

As she spoke, Maria Krautchik's voice grew in volume and lost its initial tremulous quality. "Yes, sir", she quickly replied. "Add to that a bunch of so-called gray-market gambling—the Seminoles in Florida do a half-billion a year with video slot machines—and all the other legal Indian casinos around, and you've got a huge business nationwide. It's one, I might add, that was confined to just Nevada and New Jersey, just a decade ago. Anyway, the anti-casino folks have given up on trying to turn the tide of legalization. They'd basically lost the battle anyway. Their new tactic is to pass an onerous tax bill, federal taxes on all casino revenue. Something like five percent off the top."

President Williams listened intently. "I don't know much about this. It's one of the few dogfights I've been able to stay out of in the last four years."

"Well, naturally, sir, casino lobbyists claim a federal tax would be unfair, that it's a state matter, and that it would kill their business, and all the little businesses that depend on them. If the tax passed, their choices would be to either change the odds, that is, take more of the customers' money, thus driving away business to lotteries, illegal gambling, or forcing people away altogether . . . or try to keep the player's chances of winning close to where they are now, in which case their profits plummet, because they have to pay a big additional tax out of the same level of earnings. If that's the case, then their stock prices plummet. A Federal casino tax is a complete lose/lose, and the gambling people are petrified that it will get up a head of steam on the Hill."

Williams glanced over at Shaer. "I don't get it, Julie, five percent doesn't sound like a lot of tax."

Shaer turned in her chair, nodding deferentially to Krautchik, who continued her narrative.

"I didn't think so at first either. But, the five percent is off of revenues, Mr. President, not income. 'Off the top' is how they describe it. Corporate income taxes are levied only on profits. A typical company might pay thirty to forty percent of its income in taxes. But that might be only two or three percent of revenues. One of the largest casino businesses is Harrah's, and it does about three billion of annual revenue."

"I know Harrah's. Anyone who's lived in Northern California knows Harrah's, at least by name."

"So, this Harrah's makes about two hundred million of profit, before regular income taxes, on their two billion of revenue. The anti-casino lobby's proposed five-percent tax on revenues comes to a hundred million. When you call it five percent, it doesn't sound like much, but, it's actually half of their income. It's like an additional income tax of fifty percent, on top of the state and Federal income taxes they already pay."

"Sounds like you know your stuff, Ms. Krautchik. We've got quite a few experts around here, though everyone in Washington thinks they're an expert."

Krautchik ignored the President's digression with a professional detachment that belied her years, taking up her economics lesson with increased confidence. "The stock of Harrah's sells for around twenty-five dollars a share and the 'market cap', that's the stock market value—what the entire thing is worth—is about two-point-five billion. A five-percent tax could wipe out two-thirds or more of the firm's value, Maybe two billion dollars of shareholder value, driving the stock down to, say, ten dollars a share, maybe lower. This legislation, or anything remotely like it, is a complete disaster for the entire gambling industry, thus their shareholders, of course."

"The tax hits everybody?"

"Not exactly," replied the young analyst. "The biggest companies are publicly owned: Park Place, Mandalay Resorts, MGM Grand, Harrah's, plus some smaller ones. The proposed tax hits them, but exempts state lotteries, church bingo, Indian casinos, charities, and, of course, illegal betting."

"Indians, churches, charities, and State governments. A pretty hefty bunch, with some of the best lobbyists money can buy," Williams observed.

Julie Shaer broke into the exchange. "There's a long list of folks who'd benefit from the tax. Those parties that Ms. Krautchik cited, none of whom would be subject to the tax, well, it would be highly in their favor to see the others taxed and not themselves. Plus, if any of the anti-casino people knew the Speaker was coming out against the tax, they might want him out of the way."

"Would those people really kill the Speaker of the House of Representatives?" the President asked.

"There are zealots in every group, sir, however virtuous they appear on the surface. Psychopathic zealots, at that. Look what's happened at abortion clinics. Why wouldn't some Christian Rights guy take on a big figure like Berkhardt? All it takes is a bad attitude and a good deer rifle." Julie Shaer was matter-of-fact, adding, "And there are plenty of those to go around these days."

"Maybe, but if you're correct, this was a well planned operation. Even though they made some stupid mistakes, this doesn't look like the work of some lunatic who hides in the bushes outside an abortion clinic, pulls the trigger and races off in a rusty pick-up."

"Mr. President," Krautchik offered, "I think Speaker Berkhardt's death is related to this casino legislation. We know it wasn't an accident, and there's nothing else that makes any sense. His staff says the tax has been a contentious and volatile situation, and there are reports that unknown callers had been making vague statements that his staff interpreted as threats. Plus, the water rights people, however belligerent and hard-headed they are on both sides, are well known . . . the Bureau's files fill an entire room. Not only that, but they seem sane enough to confine their antagonism to litigation and fence cutting. I really doubt if they'd resort to this kind of thing."

"You smell a rat, don't you, Ms. Krautchik?"

The FBI analyst unclasped her hands, dropped her shoulders, and crossed her arms on her lap. She leaned back in her chair, breathed deeply, looked to the ceiling, and exhaled. The Oval Office was filled with silence for a few seconds before she returned her gaze to the President, saying in a low, stern voice, "I sure do smell a rat, sir. And I think the head rat has a big stake in the outcome of that casino tax legislation."

40

Reginald Calvin reviewed his notes and turned uneasily in the back of the limousine. His companion ignored his own stack of papers, staring and watching the scenery speed by.

Finally, Stanley Harwood spoke, "It's going better than we'd expected, sir?"

Calvin could not tell if Harwood had asked a question, rhetorical or not, but he was relieved to break from editing his next speech. "Sure is. I'm walking on eggs, though. A fifteen point turnaround in two weeks seems to be too good to be true."

"Maybe we should hunker down," Harwood wondered, "avoid tough issues from here on in. Taking this kind of lead into the fourth quarter, maybe we should run up the middle, and kill the clock."

"Stan, you've seen my hit on that poor Navy safety?"

"Only about a hundred times . . . and that's in the last two weeks."

"An older and wiser man would conclude that was an idiotic move. If he'd tackled me, I'd be in the College Football Hall of Shame, instead of the Hall of Fame."

"So you agree about trying to kill the clock on Moore?"

"Nah, I'm just pulling your leg. I'm a lot older, but I'm not sure if I'm a lot wiser," Calvin grinned. "Even if the press would let us get away with it, we can't take the safe route now. We have to keep running over one hundred and seventy-five pound backs every time we get the chance."

Harwood laughed. To see the Senator teasing, laughing, relaxed . . . well, it was not a Calvin he'd shared much time with. Yet, Harwood thought, Calvin's relaxed mood seemed transient. The Senator wasn't a 'serious' man. Although he bore a solemnity deep inside, he still joked with the best of them.

Yet, despite his grace and humor, Harwood sensed the weight of the campaign—and more importantly, the weight of the 'situation'—on Calvin. And who could expect him not to bear burdens? The Democrats and the Press rendered his newest burden, changing parties, all the heavier. 'Benedict Calvin', one headline trumpeted, a double insult because of Arnold's plan to betray West Point, his own Army command. Thank God, the President's plan to resign remained among the three. If the press was having a field day now—accusing Calvin of crass opportunism, and disloyalty to race and party—how they would dismember him, if the 'covenant' were revealed.

Calvin turned in his seat, extended his arm, placing a comfortable hand on Harwood's shoulder. "Stan, I want to say how much I appreciate your traveling with me. I can feel the resentment of the campaign staff—at least what's left of them. And when it's not outright resentment, it's a sort of disunity that's really unsettling. Anyway, you've been a fine counselor during these few days."

"First of all, Senator, the campaign team is coming together. With each poll showing us widening our lead, they better understand what we're trying to do. As to working with you, I genuinely enjoy it. I'm just sorry that I have to fly back to Washington tonight."

"I'd like you to be there with me tomorrow. You know, I've got a special place in my heart for Birmingham. It's a fine city, despite the momentous events that occurred there. Plus, I like being in the South. With all the furor over this thing, it seems a comfortable place to be. They won't take me apart in Birmingham, at least."

They sat quietly, each keeping his own counsel, when Calvin spoke again. "Will you permit me a little philosophical introspection, Stan?"

"Not only permit, but insist."

"Well, I don't want to sound negative, but you don't think we've created a Faustian bargain, do you? I was just thinking, I'd hate for this to be some sort of contract with the devil. You know, I hock my soul to be President, and it all implodes. Are we overstepping the boundaries of our own humanity, driven by our ambition?"

"Faust was an alchemist, Senator, and alchemists are by nature devious, using arcane tricks to fool people, to get something—gold—for nothing. He was hardly a man of honor."

"But he was a proud philosopher, too."

"Are you referring to the President?" Harwood asked.

"No, he's hardly proud. That's not what I meant."

"Faust described himself as a philosopher, but, he was mostly a magician and fortuneteller. He wanted it all, too much, too fast, to serve himself, not others."

"The press says that's what I'm doing," Calvin said.

"Screw the press! If they can put a negative spin on this, they will."

"Yeah, but Sunday morning television is pretty depressing."

"It's *always* depressing, Senator. Talking heads trotting out other talking heads to disagree with the next round of talking heads. Listen, anytime the press gets you down, remember the close up of that gold Navy helmet. I love that shot. I could look at the replays all day. You walk into the end zone, and pandemonium breaks out. Then, right smack dab in the middle of all the jubilation, some video director—who should be remembered for all time—cuts from the end zone scene. He doesn't show screaming fans, plebes throwing hats in the air, the defeated Navy sideline. He doesn't even show the chaos on Army's bench, or the Navy safety laid out on the turf. A guy in some control trailer outside the stadium, staring at a wall of a hundred camera shots, God bless him, he cuts to that gold helmet, lying all alone on the field. A slow close up, zooming in slowly, closer and closer, and then, that still shot. There's the helmet sitting on the green turf, nothing else but the din of the crowd. Sticking with that helmet for, heck I don't know, an eternity. Or a TV eternity anyway. Must've been twenty or thirty seconds. And the announcers, how they got it, for one time, they understood, and shut up, letting the picture and the background noise say it all. Damn, there it was, that helmet, simple symbol of everything. Army, Navy, winning, losing, risk, reward. Senator, when I saw that clip from the archives, it absolutely brought tears to my eyes. It was reality, but it was art at the same time."

The men turned toward each other. Calvin was speechless. "You are the best, Senator. There's no one who's earned this opportunity, who's more deserving than you. Don't let the turkeys get you down."

Stanley Harwood rubbed his eyes with the backs of his hands. "When you're down, think about that helmet, sir. Close your eyes and picture that long, slow camera shot of that gold helmet."

"Thanks, Stan. Sometimes to comprehend how truly blessed I am, I think about the fact that sixteen members of the Army football team never returned from World War Two. Out of how many? Forty? A full third of them killed, and I slogged through a rice patty with Viet Cong bullets ripping into the water and mud and I lived through it. The reason I never talk about it is that I don't think of it as my achievement. His hand was holding me . . . I know it as surely as I sit here. His hand holds me still, and it will continue hold me until He uses that mighty Hand to take me to him."

As the limousine pulled to the curb, the accustomed throng of reporters pressed forward, randomly shouting questions, as if believing they could be heard over the others' shouting, or that, if heard, the Senator would choose their inquiry from the others. As Calvin climbed from the limo and hurried into the nursing home, he could not distinguish among the cackling horde, neither did he stop. In fact, he could not have stopped anyway, as the next biggest crowd was that of Secret Service agents enveloping him and hustling him, like a steer in the middle of a stampeding herd, into the building.

As the Senator warmly greeted those elderly who could recognize him, Harwood stood in back of the crowd. He sighed and breathed deeply, intensely gratified at the Senator's humanity.

Calvin touched the old people's hands, signed autographs, and patiently listening to rambling, disconnected questions, never failing to offer comfort, hope, and kindness with his answers. Indeed, the Senator 'worked the crowd', but here, as everywhere, it was a connected, empathetic 'working'.

Having checked the set-up in the retirement home's auditorium for the forthcoming press conference, Harwood rejoined Calvin's entourage as it entered the Alzheimer's and senile dementia ward. Damn, he thought, who scheduled the candidate to visit this area? How can he possibly look good here. But, as always, Calvin transcended. Dim eyes and hollow faces somehow lit up as they took in his dark, handsome face and broad, sincere smile. Harwood watched in amazement as Calvin's touch almost seemed to heal. Here, the Senator put an arm around this patient. There, he hugged that one. And then, sitting before an old woman, her eyes closed, rocking to and fro, he comfortingly, took her hands and whispered to her, then softly stroked her hair, before moving on.

At one point, the Senator walked down the hall, glanced to the side, and noticed an old man sitting alone in his room, talking to himself under his breath. He was drooling, strings of spittle oozing from his mouth, running down his chin, and falling on his chest, oblivious to the drool, or the remains of the midday snack that clung to his mouth and cheeks. The Senator quickly entered the room, and pulling a linen handkerchief from his pocket, gently wiped the drool from the man's mouth and chin, then went into the bathroom, dampened the handkerchief, and cleaned the crumbs and crust from the old man's mouth.

Harwood surveyed the group around Calvin. No reporters were in a position to see this small, incidental act of kindness. Then, he thought, of course, that is the way Calvin preferred it.

Hurrying to the auditorium, an aide handed the Senator his notes for the short address he was to deliver on increased funding for home health care and support of the elderly growing old and dying in dignity with their families attending them at home. Calvin secretly wished that the press conference questions would be confined to health care issues of the aged, but he was hardly so ingenuous as to expect this outcome.

As he concluded his talk, the Senator looked up, and took a moment to survey the swarm of reporters, hands vertical and waving. He regarded the press crowd with some anxiety, but without fear.

Calvin pointed into the audience, selecting the first questioner.

The reporter stood, identified himself and his paper, and asked, "Senator, do you see yourself as an icon of African-American success?"

Calvin winced, as much at the fact that he had been asked it a thousand times, as at the question itself. "I try not to . . . next question."

"Senator Calvin, I'd like to explore a little more about the decision making process. Would you share with us how this all came about? Did the President approach you, or did you go to him? What did you talk about?"

Calvin repressed another wince, and shifted his weight from foot to foot. "President Williams and I have already answered that question, and dozens of similar ones, many times already. First of all, he approached me. Second, you and the American people, I think, would be better served by focusing your attention on the result, not how President Williams and I got there. Next, you there."

"Did you discuss your situation with Governor Moore before you made your decision. And, if not, why not?"

"No, I did not. I've a great deal of respect for the Governor, of course. We are old friends. But, as I've said before, I was not in a position to seek his advice or approval relative to this decision."

Calvin recognized another questioner. "Yes, Sam."

"But why not discuss it with him, Senator? He's the leader of your party, he had already received your endorsement, and he was only a few weeks short of being the President himself."

"Sam, he received my endorsement before I was on the Republican ticket. Now, the Republicans are the people's best choice, so, I'm endorsing myself and Williams. And now, Mr. Moore's only a few weeks short of going back to being the Governor of Idaho. I hold the Governor in high regard, and I hold the people of Idaho in even higher regard. I would like to see them continue to have good leadership in their statehouse. That is my mission . . . Idahoans deserve no less from me."

Laughter—rather a polite, respectful giggle—spread through the host of reporters, some confused by the obliqueness of the response.

"Next question. Yes, Shirley."

"Sir, is it not true that the Republicans needed to pull a rabbit out of the hat, and you were their answer?"

"Shirley, aren't those magicians' rabbits usually those snow-white kind, with a terrified looks on their little faces, as the magician holds them by the nape of their neck? Next. Yes, you over there."

"Senator, William Brosatt, Washington Post columnist, wrote yesterday, and I quote, 'Undeniably, the Senator was bought. The Republicans got Reginald Calvin to compromise his position and his values, and join the ticket, solely out of crass political expediency.' Do you have any comment on Mr. Brosatt's observations?"

"I was not bought . . . I was not, and I am not, nor have I ever been, for sale. My great grandfather . . . now, *there's* a man who was bought . . . and he *was* for sale, literally, I might add. The only thing that's been compromised here is the Democrat's chances of winning." Calvin grinned broadly this time, leaving no doubt to the assembled mass that laughter was appropriate.

"Next question. Yes, Erica?"

"Senator Calvin, some observers say that you have not been clear with some of your answers on affirmative action, and the concept of redressing historical wrongs against African-Americans as a race. What is your position on that?"

"Well, Erica, that question has no easy answer. Read Arthur Ashe's letter to his daughter, that sums up a lot of what I stand for. But there's more. One of my most conservative colleagues, a man who's voted against Head Start, funding money for inner city schools, and every social program I can think of, well, I put it to him this way. If I took some inner city African-American child—he moment it was born—and handed it to you and your wife to raise as your own child, to adulthood, do you think that child would be different as an adult, than if raised by its uneducated, drug-using, impoverished mother in the inner city? 'Yes, of course,' was his answer. He added, 'The child would have top-notch medical care and go to the best schools. And we would establish expectations for that child . . . we would expect the most.' Ladies and gentleman, I think my colleague did not realize that he was endorsing us doing everything within our power to help each inner city child. Furthermore, I question individuals in the majority who represent themselves as victims of affirmative action, assuming for themselves the same moral high ground as those who the programs were intended to benefit. Don't get me wrong, I'm not some quota hound. But is it reasonable for one group to go around claiming for itself special privileges and denying them to others, on the basis of race . . . and then when the privilege situation is reversed, claim that there should be no privilege for either group? We must continue to use every reasonable tool we possess to continue the long march to full equality of opportunity for each newborn American. The good Lord knows that I, of all people, believe in just reward for hard work and merit. But, I had special opportunities afforded to me by my parents, by the Catholic Church and its schools, and by a government military college. Let's not use 'hard work' and 'individual effort' as code words for deterring or, indeed, obstructing us from making every effort to help that African-American newborn in the ghetto . . . a life, an individual that holds such great promise."

As the Senator expounded, the room was still, but for the nearly silent whir of handheld tape recorders, and the movement of pen and pencil across paper. When he had finished his short discourse, a couple of reporters hurried from the room. The rest waited patiently for the next question.

The Senator pointed to a young woman in the second row. "Yes, ma'am?"

"Senator Calvin, do you think that you're following in the footsteps of Martin Luther King or Malcolm X?"

"Neither. For one thing, both their fathers were ministers, and they were both preachers. My father was a farmer, and I am a politician. And their influence was greater—and, I might add, purer—because it derived from a commitment to ideals, not from some government position."

"But, sir," the questioner, still standing, continued, "how does your political philosophy relate to those of Dr. King and Malcolm X?"

Calvin sighed, again wishing that someone would do him the favor of asking a question about health care for the aged.

"Well, I'm basically a social liberal, if that's what you're talking about. Philosophically, I guess you could describe me as a New Testament kind of guy. In that way, I'm a lot like King and, I am quite pleased to say, not at all like Malcolm X. I believe in conducting one's struggles on the high plain of dignity and discipline. I believe in loving your enemies and forgiving . . . not seven times, but seventy times seven. Dr. King taught us not to flaunt the central teachings of Jesus: brotherly love and the golden rule. He was, at heart, a man of hope, and I'd like to think that I'm a man of hope, too. Dr. King said that one-day man would kneel before God and be crowned triumphant over war and bloodshed. I think he intended to include hate in the expression 'war and bloodshed', a triumph, by the way, to be achieved through nonviolent redemptive goodwill."

As the conference progressed, the press became more and more comfortable, more and more confident, in asking questions that were increasingly probing, indeed provocative. Calvin did not shirk nor equivocate, but offered straightforward, honest answers, as he had been accustomed to doing for a lifetime. After only a week on the campaign trail, he was disappointed by the press, but not surprised.

President Williams had called the Senator every night to find out how he was feeling and how his day had gone. Calvin drew heart from Harwood and Williams' caring and support. And, however slowly, the GOP old guard was becoming less and less tepid. With a solid lead building in the polls, Calvin was increasingly gratified by his decision. He was not counting weeks or days, but hours, to Election Day.

"Senator, as you know, Colin Powell has enthusiastically endorsed your candidacy. Can you tell us what you've discussed?"

Rec Calvin stroked his chin, then moved from behind the lectern, a high-tech sea urchin bristling with microphones, to the front of the stage. "Yes, I can. First, he encouraged me not to hide behind transparent arguments of states' rights and property rights, not turn my back on hard-won civil rights. And I will not. Second, he advised me not to pander to the black voters, not to descend into Hortonism, and never to play a race card. And I will not. Next, he reminded me that although my father, and to a certain extent me personally, had pulled ourselves up by the bootstraps, there are some folks out there without bootstraps. And, finally, he told me never to forget to always treat every individual with dignity and respect. And I will never forget to do so."

"That was it?"

"Well, there was a little more . . . I'd intended to leave that out. But since you asked, when Colin reminded me to treat everyone with dignity and respect, he added that goes for the members of the press, too."

Senator Calvin walked slowly back to the rostrum and, beaming a broad smile, recognized the next questioner.

"Senator Calvin, in response to an earlier question, you gave us an insight into your philosophies on race, religion, and life. That question asked you to use Dr. King and Malcolm X as benchmarks for yourself. I'd like to know, since both of those men were assassinated, do you yourself fear that outcome?"

"You guys don't give up do you?" Calvin asked acidly. He was not amused.

After a long silence, he spoke, clearly and calmly. "Who knows what will happen? We've got some difficult days ahead. But it doesn't matter with me now. Like anybody, I'd like to live a long life. Longevity has its place, but I'm not concerned about that now. I'm happy, and I'm not worried about anything. I'm not fearing any man."

Calvin had considered referring to the mountaintop, but out of respect for the original, he elected to use a shortened paraphrase. "Okay, they tell me I've only got time for a couple of more questions."

"Yes, you over there . . . Bill," said the Senator, pointing to a middle-aged reporter halfway back in the auditorium.

"Senator, do you think O.J. Simpson was guilty?"

"That's an interesting question, Bill . . . or inflammatory might be a better word than interesting. Does that question have any bearing on my qualifications for the office of Vice President; or on the issues that the American people are interested in?"

"We in the African-American community are interested in the answer, yes, Senator. You must have some feeling about it."

"Okay, ladies and gentlemen, despite the fact that I know you are baiting me, and against my better judgment, let me answer it this way . . . ."

Calvin looked up and noticed Stan Harwood wildly shaking his head, vainly trying to appear subtle, frantically waving his arms in the back corner of the room. He ignored his friend, and went on.

"Abner Louima is brutally violated by Justin Volpe . . . a guy named Berry down in Texas somewhere drags a black man named James Byrd to his death behind a pickup truck . . . for three miles . . . a gay college student is beaten, tied to a fence, and left to die . . . as a retired general, I especially loathe hearing about crimes perpetrated by soldiers . . . but, in Kentucky, a solider kills another soldier with a baseball bat, because he thinks the other man is gay . . . ."

No pencil moved, no ink flowed. The reporters sat, hushed and frozen, as Calvin recited his litany of front-page assaults.

". . . in San Diego, a bunch of crazy white soldiers paralyzed a black man, beat him . . . just because he's black. There's a lot of old against young, white against black, gay against straight . . . and a lot of just plain crime out there. Now, a friend, having just read about some horrible crime, once said to me, 'Rec, it's an awful world we live in, full of evil and dangerous people.' Well folks, my friend was totally wrong. First, it's not an awful world, it's a wonderful world . . . full of honest, caring, hard-working people . . . law-abiding people. Second, it's not full of evil and dangerous people. There are evil and dangerous people in our world, sure. And, yes, they occupy the front pages because of their own form of evil. But ninety-nine-point-nine-nine percent of people out there are just great, loving people . . . living out their lives, and for the most part, helping and loving others. I guess what it comes down to is that I'd like to see folks judged by the content of their character, not by the color of their skin. Now, as to these criminals . . . these Volpes, and Berrys, and the rest of that bunch, well, they probably deserve the death penalty, but at the very least, they need to be locked up for life, preferably in the same cell. And, as to content of character, Mr. Simpson should be in there too, glove or no glove. People who intentionally and viciously attack, maim, and kill other people should not walk away, whatever their race, religion, or age, when the preponderance of evidence indicates they are guilty. Does that answer your question, Bill?"

For a couple of seconds, the room was filled with stunned silence. Then, as if a straining river levee had burst, reporters flooded out the back of the room. The press conference, for all intents and purposes, was over. The press had gotten what it wanted . . . what it needed.

41

"We've been sitting here for nearly two hours," noted the pilot from the front right seat, turning around to address his passengers. "You're sure your client is coming? Clearance is going to be getting back to us and, they really don't like this kind of sitting around."

"He's coming."

The answer came in a heavy brogue from the tall man, the one with a long, sallow face. Willie had barely moved his face from the window since they landed. The young helicopter pilot wondered where these two men were from.

Their heavy tweed overcoats and heavy woolen suits in the late September South, gave them a strangely out of place look. He flew businessmen for a living, thousands of them a year, and these guys did not look to be the businessmen they claimed to be. More like uptight tourists, he thought, from a cold climate, who hadn't checked the weather and hadn't packed properly for the trip.

"What kind of accent is that?" the pilot innocently inquired.

"It's Irish."

"Well, I'm not much on accents. I mean I know them when I hear them, but I really don't know where they're from, you know. It doesn't sound too Irish."

"What the hell do you know?"

"Sorry, just making small talk. Any particular kind of Irish accent? Are there different kinds?"

"Yeah, it's called a brogue."

"A brogue?"

"Right, a brogue", the tall man answered, continuing to fix his stare out of the sliding side window of the Bell LongRanger, twisting his head every few seconds to get a full view of the field.

After a few minutes, the pilot queried again. "You're sure he's going to be here? Maybe he didn't get through security. That black guy, Senator Calvin, the new VP candidate, is supposed to be making a speech here this morning and they say he's flying out of here at some point. That's two calls we've gotten from the tower wanting to know when we're leaving. Security is going to get really tight for a while."

"Not too tight, I hope," said Nick, the shorter of the two men, and the right corner of his mouth turned up as he finished the sentence.

"He'll be here" said the raspy-voiced Willie.

"Well, at a thousand bucks an hour, I guess I don't need to be complaining. You know, we could save you some money by shutting down the engines."

"You've said that . . . six times."

"Just a suggestion," the pilot recoiled.

They sat silently for fifteen minutes more. Still trying vainly and uncomfortably to make small talk, the bored and anxious pilot started again. "Can you see what's going on? Maybe we'll see him. Boy, can you believe what they did with that guy? I think the President has totally lost his marbles going for that guy. Kicking out O'Malley for a black Democrat . . . from Mississippi, no less. Crazy. That's what everybody down here thinks. Maybe crazy like a fox. What do you guys think?"

There was no reply. After a couple of minutes, the pilot continued his attempts at sociability. "Yeah, that Senator Calvin could come right through here. Have you seen the paper today? I guess I said it was crazy, but the polls have them in a fifteen point turnaround . . . say if things don't change, the Republicans will waltz right into office."

"Waltz. Right. We'll see what kind of dance they do," suggested the tall killer sarcastically.

The two customers sat silently in the seats behind the pilot. "Hey, what did you say you guys do . . . oil?"

"Yeah, we're oil drillers."

"Where?"

"North Sea, mostly. We're waiting for a client who's going to look at some property nearby."

"You got oil property near Birmingham?" the pilot asked incredulously.

Suddenly the craft's radio screeched. "Nancy eight six nine alpha charlie, Birmingham Ground Control."

The pilot quickly grabbed a set of earphones from his lap, put them on, reached out and flipped a switch on the dial-covered dashboard. "Birmingham Ground Control, this is Nancy eight six nine alpha charlie, go ahead."

"Nine alpha charlie, Ground Control, what are your intentions?"

"Ground Control, Nine alpha charlie. We're looking for northwest . . . any altitude is okay . . . three thousand would be fine."

After a short pause, the craft was filled with sound again. "Nine alpha charlie, Ground Control, you're re-cleared out of class bravo to northwest at one two four point eight at three thousand. Good for one hour only."

The pilot scribbled onto a lined sheet held to a clipboard by a large rubber band, then read from his notes, "Ground Control, Nine alpha charlie, re-cleared for one hour, northwest at one two four point eight at three thousand. You got a squawk code? "

"Nine alpha charlie, Ground Control, squawk code is five two seven four. Repeat, five two seven four."

Turning a dial on the dash to set his squawk code, the pilot recited back, "Ground, northwest at one two four point eight. Code five two seven four. Good one hour only, Nine alpha charlie."

"That is correct, Nine alpha charlie. Contact when ready to depart. Tower will give you instructions when in position and ready for take-off."

"Ground, will contact when ready to depart. Thanks. Nine alpha charlie."

The tall, raspy-voiced man with the heavy "brogue" asked gruffly, "We okay? What's going on?"

"Yeah, we're fine. We're filed under VFR, and Ground Control needs to make sure they know what's going on."

"VFR?"

"Visual Flight Rules. No biggie. But, we need to get your man and get out of here, though."

"We'll get him. Don't worry."

The three men sat in mutually uncomfortable silence for another twenty minutes, the smaller client occasionally turning around in his chair and pushing back the curtain that separated the passenger compartment from the pilot. The man at the controls grew increasingly uneasy with his pair of passengers.

Suddenly, the radio blared again. "Nancy eight six nine alpha charlie, Ground Control."

"Ground Control, Nancy eight six nine alpha charlie."

"Nine alpha charlie, Ground, security says we are on high alert . . . repeat we are on high alert, over."

"Ground, Nine alpha charlie, we are on high alert. Should I continue to hold or clear out? Please advise."

The pilot turned his head slightly toward the back seat, so he could be heard. "I think we're going to have to clear out and come back, guys. Sorry, but the tower and security are going to be in control of this."

"Nine alpha charlie, Ground, hold on . . . ."

After a half-minute wait, the controller returned to the radio. "Nine alpha charlie, Ground, Secret Service and airport security are going to come over to your craft. You are instructed to hold, as is. Confirm back, over."

"Ground, Nine alpha charlie, got it . . . hold here for security."

"What's going on?"

"We were supposed to be out of here an hour ago, and the tower, they don't talk with that tone unless they're pissed. They may make us take off and come back in a little while. It has to be that Senator Calvin . . . Ground Control says Secret Service is coming over . . . to check us out, I guess."

Nick, sitting directly behind the pilot, snapped open a briefcase on his lap. The pilot started to speak again, but before he could form any coherent statement, in a blur of motion, a gleaming Glock 30 pistol came out of the briefcase. Nick spun in his chair, and pressed the Glock's barrel to the back of the pilot's skull.

"Don't move an inch or your children will be orphans."

He called the pilot's children by name. "You wouldn't want little Stevie and little Jessica to see their daddy's brains all over the windshield, now would you?"

The helicopter pilot froze, stammering, "Where the hell did you guys get the names of my kids? What the hell is going on?"

"Just shut up and you've got an okay chance of getting out of this alive . . . Daddy."

"Nine alpha charlie, Ground Control."

The pilot was paralyzed.

The controller repeated himself. "Nine alpha charlie, Ground Control."

"You'd better answer, Mister Pilotman," the small man demanded. "And leave it on the speaker."

The pilot's arm shot out to flip a switch again. "Yes, Ground Control, Nine alpha charlie."

"Nine alpha charlie, Ground, we are under ground stop. Ground hold. Confirm Nine alpha charlie."

"What the fuck is going on?" the tall man whispered. The pilot switched his microphone off, and whimpered,

"I don't know, they got everything on hold. I have to get back to them."

"Alright, be careful," he warned. "Very careful."

"Ground, Nine alpha charlie, we are on ground stop. Repeat, ground hold."

"That is correct, Nine alpha charlie."

"Okay, Ground, thanks. Nine alpha charlie." The pilot did not turn around, but slumped in his seat. "Look guys, whatever you want, you got it!" he stammered. His mouth tightened and twisted. He winced, his eyes filled, and then he began to sob out loud, his chest heaving and his body twitching. "The tower . . . they're going to be calling me right back."

Willie, still speaking in a brogue, without turning his head barked to his partner, "We're getting real close. Tell that fucker to calm down, quick!"

"Listen, Pilotman, get your shit together, quick. Now, if that tower calls you back, I want to hear a nice, calm voice. No whimpering, no shenanigans. Got it?"

"Yeah, yeah," came the reply amid stifled sobs. "I got it."

The big man hunched and stared out across the field past the milling Secret Service agents two hundred yards away. Dark colored cars randomly pulled up and pulled away, picking up agents, and dropping them off, repositioning them. Two pair of men in dark suits hustled into black sedans.

Quickly, Willie opened a satchel, pulled out a pair of high-powered Zeiss, and began to survey the scene even more intently. He spat in a low voice, "Jesus, looks like they're headed over here. Com'on baby, get here."

An eighth of a mile across the tarmac, Willie could clearly see a couple of Secret Service agents pointing toward the helicopter.

The pilot turned uneasily in his seat, dropped his head slightly, and squinted to look across the airport. "Looks like a lot of activity going on over there. Jesus, you guys aren't going to try to . . . ."

The smaller man poked the pilot's head with his pistol barrel. "Shut the fuck up."

Willie pushed open a small window, then reached down on the floor and picked up a long telescoping antenna-like device. He pushed it through the opening, extended it to its full length, and consulted a digital reading on the handle. He spoke out loud to himself as he read the data.

"Humidity, seventy-eight percent. Temperature, sixty-nine degrees. Wind, six miles per hour from the southwest." He reached into his pocket, withdrawing a small spiral notebook into which he jotted the data, then retrieved the device from the window, folded it, and placed it on the floor in front of him. Picking up the binoculars again, he returned his gaze to the window. After a minute of intense staring, he dropped the binoculars down, calmly stating, "Our client is here."

Then, his hands moving quickly and efficiently amid the sounds of clicks, Brogueman opened a leather case he'd carried on. Reaching for his personally modified .308 bolt-action rifle, he removed the stock first, surveyed it briefly, then reached for the barrel, which he rapidly snapped into place. More quickly, a scope snapped on. With a small Allen wrench he secured and tightened the connections, then reached into a satchel and pulled out a small sandbag that he rested on the window ledge. He made three light karate-type chops on the bag creating a depression into which he laid the rifle barrel.

Quickly consulting his notes, he entered his wind, temperature, and humidity data into a small calculator to figure his offsets, then closely inspected his scope, making final adjustments to its settings. Reaching again into his case, he withdrew two pair of ear protectors, tossing one quickly to the small man. With the ear protectors in place, he slowly leaned back, so that only the last few inches of the barrel protruded from the window and in a continuous motion dropped his head down and to the side.

Within a minute of reaching for the gun case, the rifle had been fully assembled, the calculations and adjustments made, and Brogueman was taking aim. Through his scope, he saw two black sedans inching toward the helicopter. "Here they come," he muttered bitterly to himself.

With Willie leaning back against him, short Nick continued to hold the pistol to the side of the pilot's head. The pilot, barely moving, glanced to the side enough to catch sight of the taller man, his head tilted, his eye pressed to the scope. "Jesus, you guys are nuts . . . you can't get away with this!"

"I told you to shut up or you're dead."

Willie breathed deeply and exhaled slowly and completely. When he reached the bottom of his exhale, his trigger finger moved, only slightly, sending the semi-automatic into its roaring purpose.

The first shot hit Senator Calvin when he was halfway between the door of the terminal and the bottom of the jet's stairs, stairs which, within a few more seconds, he would have safely ascended. The shot spun the Senator around, leaving him staggering in little circles on the red carpet strip which had been carefully laid out for his walk to the waiting Lear. The jet had thrust to near full power in anticipation of the Senator's approach and the whine of its engines obscured the crack of the shot, so that for a few seconds the Senator's movements from the impact of the bullet seemed to be an anomalous, impromptu little dance. As he spun, his legs flailed in a vain, purely autonomic reaction to stay standing, his arms remaining strangely at his side. It was a step dance of death, a Lord of the Death Dance.

When it became obvious that he had been shot, his entourage instinctively dropped to the ground, so that the scene became macabre and ironic surreal theatre. The Senator was still standing, dancing away the last seconds of his life, while his associates lay on the ground around him, like loyal subjects prostrating themselves to their wounded, dancing emperor.

Secret Service agents drew their weapons in an instant and searched frantically and fruitlessly for the source of the shot, vainly shouting to each other to be heard over the engine's din. The pair of black cars, their occupants oblivious to the scene behind them, rolled deliberately toward the helicopter.

A special, flattening, hollow-nosed bullet had hit Calvin's left clavicle, pulverizing the bone and ripping away most of his shoulder. A few strands of tendon and skin, and the cloth of his shirt and suit were all that held his arm on. Small pieces of bloody flesh spewed onto the face of an aide standing next to the candidate, making him look like an acne sufferer whose face had been splattered by a large sausage pizza.

As he began to fall, another shot hit Reginald Calvin squarely in the chest, loudly splitting his sternum and, for a moment, the force of the bullet smashing into his chest again lifted him to a strangely-standing position, his arms spasmodically flailing the air. More death dancing. One agent, describing the scene later in his deposition, compared Calvin's movements to Joe Cocker's in films the agent had seen of the Woodstock concert over thirty years before. *She Came in Through the Bathroom Window.*

An agent rushed to the wounded man and tried to shield him from further shots, a second, an eternity, too late. Calvin's legs buckled and he slumped, one arm still spasmodically flailing. *I Get By With a Little Help From My Friends.*

Willie aimed his third shot at mid-thigh level and as the Senator fell, the bullet caught him in the gut passing through and partially disemboweling an agent holding him from behind, killing him instantly.

Another agent grasped the Senator from behind around the waist in a sort of futile Heimlich grip, eased him to the ground, and spread himself carefully atop the Senator in a pathetically vain attempt to protect him from further harm.

The Senator's legs twitched for five or six seconds and his eyes, wide open, rolled back in his head, so that only the white showed. Eyes from the *Village of the Damned.*

Then, Rec Calvin lay motionless in a spreading pool of his own blood which quickly turned from scarlet to maroon brown as it surrounded him on the tarmac, becoming dark and viscous in the warm sun of October in Alabama.

The black sedans rolled toward them, while other agents on foot sped from the death scene in every direction, ostensibly like spokes from a wheel, but with a confusion which looked more like an anthill disturbed by a stick-wielding boy. One Secret Service agent, sprinting behind the black sedan, drew his gun and fired a wild shot toward the helicopter whose rotors were already spinning rapidly.

With a popping roar, the helicopter lifted and quickly chopped away as the approaching sedans stopped, still a hundred yards away. Agents jumped out, cleared their holsters and began firing randomly at the escaping craft. Within a few seconds the helicopter was out of range, and only seconds later, was out of sight beyond a nearby tree line, which it cleared by only a few feet.

42

"Okay, Stan, what the hell happened?"

"Mr. President, everything is preliminary at this point. We're still getting reports, really by the minute, so I'm going to give you what we've got now, but it could change at any time . . . ."

The atmosphere in the Oval Office was already tense when Williams cut Harwood off in mid sentence, furious and impatient, both uncharacteristic demeanors for him.

"Please, get with it, Stan. For God's sake, the man was killed three hours ago. Just give us an update."

Harwood, unaccustomed to being addressed in such a manner, particularly by the always-polite President, paused and cleared his throat.

"Senator Calvin was shot in Birmingham, Alabama at approximately one-thirty-six this afternoon. Security precautions appear to have been normal. I talked with the agent-in-charge of the detail myself and apparently everything was according to department procedure. All agents on the detail have been relieved of duty, and each is being detained, under guard, in separate locations. A special team of interservice professionals will depose them all today. Although Treasury has line responsibility for Secret Service, I've talked to them about the combined approach, and they're cooperating fully with the FBI. All statements will be on videotape."

"How could this happen with the security we had on this man?" the President demanded."

"How the hell did Kennedy and King get killed, Reagan get shot? How did Columbine happen? How did bin Laden bring the stock market to a complete standstill?" Harwood shot back.

While Williams did not sulk, he remained silent, waiting for the rest of the report. Harwood paused to consult some handwritten notes to either refresh his memory or continue to compose himself.

"Two days ago, a man chartered a commercial helicopter from a local executive aircraft company. The charter was for one full day, secured with a cash payment of five thousand dollars. Treasury is already in touch with the bank where the money was deposited. They were a mix of hundreds, fifties, and twenties, and were deposited in a Birmingham bank on the same day. To the best of our knowledge, the helicopter landed at ten-thirty this morning at a place called the Birmingham Corporate Office Center, one of the few helipads in the area. It's about four miles from the airport as the crow flies. The helicopter picked up two men in business suits with light luggage, a few hand pieces . . . and returned to the airport mid-morning, we think about eleven . . . it's only a couple of minute flight, just across the airport. It's not required to file a flight plan for this sort of thing, the pilot just needs to notify flight control. There should have been a log of passengers on the craft, it's standard procedure, but no log has been found. I'm going to let George Stapes proceed from here. George is a senior FBI crime scene investigator and re-enactment specialist . . . thirty years in this stuff."

"Thanks, Stan. Well, anyway, from what we can piece together the helicopter positioned itself at the edge of the field, over by some private jets. If the persons who chartered the plane were armed, they'd have been able to avoid security this way. It's technically a FAA breach, but not an uncommon practice at a number of airports to let private aircraft, particularly ones known to the tower, have a little leeway with positioning and discharging passengers.

"Anyway, they informed the tower they were waiting for an important customer who was running late, but was expected at any moment. According to flight control, they sat there for a couple of hours. Senator Calvin's departure time was left open, basically for all afternoon. There were some discussions about him traveling by limo to Atlanta and making some stops along the way, or even staying in Birmingham for the evening, and security didn't want to shut the airport down for the entire day. Actually, it wasn't until after the speech at the high school, the campaign team decided to fly directly out. They called the airport about an hour before Calvin's newly scheduled departure and advised them—and the Secret Service team on the ground there—of the departure plan. Secret Service knew the helicopter was there. They'd even checked IDs, and advised the plane that they would be required to leave immediately when notified. They made checks on the status of the entire airport regularly through the tower. I guess the helicopter just fell through the cracks."

Charles Whittingham could not control his sarcasm. "Big cracks, but at least we know who the 'important customer' was."

Stapes continued without acknowledging the barb.

"Anyway, Senator Calvin spoke at a Birmingham-area school, of all things, Kennedy High School, had a sandwich with the kids in the cafeteria and, at about twelve-thirty, motored to the airport which, like the school and the route to the airport, were under strict security."

Whittingham again could not resist. "Apparently not quite strict enough."

Harwood attacked back, using Whittingham's sword of sarcasm. "Look, Charles, if you're going to go on like this, we can all just head back to our offices and wait for a written hardbound autographed copy of *The President's Special Commission on the Assassination of the Republican Candidate for the Vice Presidency of the United States of America*, thirty-nine dollars and ninety-five cents, due soon at local booksellers near you!"

President Williams glared first at Whittingham and then around the room in general. "Everyone let Mr. Harwood and Mr. Stapes here finish their entire report without further comment, please. And, Charles, I want pure professionalism from you. Do you understand? A man has died here. I expect cooperation, not criticism. Plus, a little dignity would be nice."

Stapes continued, "Calvin was shot at least twice . . . we don't know how many total shots were fired at him . . . two, three, maybe more . . . walking from the door of the airport terminal out to his jet. It's reported that he was dead either when he was hit, or immediately thereafter. When he was shot, he did some sort of macabre little dance on the walkway to the plane. The medical and forensics people think that the first shot probably hit his shoulder, and shards of bone or bullet hit his cerebellum—that's part of the brain at the top of the spine—causing him to react that way. Either that, or the first bullet itself actually clipped the cerebellum directly. When this cerebellum is damaged you go 'ataxic', as they call it, kind of spastic. Not that it makes a difference, I guess, except that it really freaked out the people who were there and saw it."

Harwood cautioned Stapes to move along, without digression.

"Okay," he continued, "though we can't prove it right now, our hypothesis is that the shots came from the helicopter. There are no grassy knoll reports, no other kind of security breaches, no other suspects or suspect activity of any kind. We've got a team looking at videotape and stills now. The networks and local stations had cameras galore. I guarantee you that we'll see this more than the Rodney King beating, O.J. chase scene, Zapruder film, and the WTC airplanes combined."

"Maybe the helicopter was a diversion," remarked Fred Collins, the President's Appointments Secretary. "I mean, could a shooter have reached . . . how far?"

"First, Fred, the diversion is an interesting thought, and the FBI folks have already been working on it. Ultimately, from the photos and film, we'll be able to prove the path of the bullets from the way the Senator turns and falls. Right now, it's wait and see. Our reconstructionists are waiting at Reagan for the original film, right now. Anyway, some agents shot at the helicopter as it lifted off, apparently hitting it with a couple of shots, but not slowing it down any. It was pretty far away when they shot. It flew only about a mile away which must have taken around a minute and landed smack-dab in the parking lot of a Hampton Inn on the north side of the airport. Two men got out and walked slowly to a waiting car, a dark sedan, maybe a Taurus, which drove off. One witness says two other cars drove off at the same time, both dark Tauruses, too. They're possibly decoys. We think the Taurus we want went onto the Interstate, but right now nobody is exactly sure what direction it went."

"And what about the ability to shoot him from a distance. And how close could these people have gotten?"

"Well, Mr. President, I'll answer your second question first. Where you are at the airport depends on whether you're traveling commercial or private. At some airports, general aviation terminals are nowhere near commercial traffic. Other places, like even Dulles, the commercial jets roll right past you as you sit in a private plane."

"And here?"

"I'm not familiar with Birmingham, Mr. President, but based on reports I've heard so far, the Senator was flying the campaign's Lear 25D. It was apparently at the older part of the airport, over on the east side. Senator Calvin was flying out of the private air terminal there, called Raytheon. And that's where the helicopter must have been waiting."

"Okay, how about the shot?"

"Well, I'm sorry, sir, but that's kind of one of those 'depends', too. My background is ballistics, plus I'm a deer hunter myself and load my own shells, so I'm pretty familiar with this area. Also, my assistant has already talked with FBI ballistics, plus a bunch of self-appointed experts that are jamming our phone lines. The short answer is, based on what we now know, the shot doesn't appear that difficult . . . at least, for an expert. Current estimates put the helicopter at less than three hundred yards from Calvin."

"What's that, a quarter of a mile?" the President asked.

"Actually less than a fifth of a mile, sir, but still reasonable for an expert. It depends on the various parameters of caliber, bullet type, and load you've got. At that kind of distance, it's a matter of aligning your line of sight, that is, the bullet's line of departure from the barrel, and the trajectory . . . that's really a measure of how far and how fast the bullet will fall due to the pull of gravity. With a typical high-powered rifle caliber, maybe a three hundred, and with a magnum load—a hundred-and-fifty to a hundred-and-eighty grains, that's the bullet weight—well, the drop at that distance might be as little as five to ten inches. That means that, if the guy is scoped in for a straight-line shot, he'd only have to shoot that much over the target to allow for the drop of the bullet. He'd have to figure his MOA on the ground and make adjustments there, but it could be done fairly easily."

"MOA?"

"Minute of angle, sir, techno-speak for making the adjustment to compensate for distance."

"Now, I'm sorry, Mr. Stapes, but I'm totally ignorant of this stuff. Does the bullet still travel fast that far out?"

"You bet, sir. You'd pick the weapon, type of bullet, and the powder charge for the particular circumstances, but if you did it right, you could get a muzzle velocity—actual speed of the bullet when it leaves the barrel—of nearly three thousand feet per second, which, if I remember right, is about two thousand miles an hour. At three or four hundred yards, it'd still be traveling at over two thousand feet per second. That's still well over a thousand miles an hour. Plus, there's one other measurement, which is basically the impact. It's usually related to bullet speed, but it can vary. The situation we're talking about, well, out there at that distance, it's probably around fifteen-hundred, maybe two-thousand—that's in foot pounds of energy. Believe me, that's plenty enough to tear a deer . . . or a man . . . apart. In short, this is not a terribly difficult shot for a practiced expert. While it's highly unusual, I've seen a deer killed at over five-hundred yards. And by the way, although President Kennedy was shot at a distance of a little less than a hundred yards, the velocity of the bullet was probably around two-thousand feet per second . . . and that was out of an ancient Mannlicher-Carcano Italian rifle."

"Okay, let's assume for now that it's the helicopter," the President said. "Let's go on."

"Well, unfortunately, when the Birmingham police got to the helicopter, they found the pilot still strapped in his seat with his brains blown all over the inside of the windshield. He was thirty two years old with a family, including two kids, five and seven." Stapes paused to allow the pain of the loss settle for a few seconds before proceeding.

"The helicopter is secure and we're building a canopy now to protect it from any weather. It's supposed to rain tonight. We may move it tomorrow. There's a crew from Washington headed there now. They'll go over it, inch by inch, as soon as they get to Birmingham. The locals started dusting it for fingerprints and moving stuff around inside before our people could control them. We had some turf arguments about whose evidence it is and whose case it is, but we've explained to them how it works."

Whittingham, his sarcasm gone, turned to Harwood. "Let me know if you need any help in that area," he offered. "We know the Alabama governor well, and he'll jump at the chance to help."

Harwood readily accepted the olive branch. "Thanks, Charlie. What's critical right now are the perpetrators themselves. By the way, we've got roadblocks everywhere and the Alabama Highway Patrol and the Birmingham police have been fantastic. On the assailants, or alleged assailants, we don't think . . . it's not logical to think that they have an office in the Corporate Park where they were picked up by the helicopter. A couple of people we interviewed said they saw two guys hanging around the lobby area for about a half-hour before the helicopter arrived. According to their flight records, the helicopter arrived precisely at the time requested. So that means these guys got there early. If they'd had an office, why wouldn't they wait there . . . stay up in their office until the helicopter arrived, so as to remain unnoticed? Also, they wore heavy suits and overcoats, which seemed strange for a pretty warm October day."

Pausing to review his yellow sheets of hand written notes, Harwood continued, "A bunch of smokers, ostracized by the office anti-smoking policy, were huddled outside the entrance to the building and got a pretty good look at them. We're bringing photo books down from Washington for all of the witnesses to look at. One of our witnesses says he chatted with one of the men, and he swears that the guy had an accent."

"What kind of accent?" the President interrupted.

"He says Irish or Scottish, maybe even English . . . but definitely not Australian."

"What Alabamian could tell the difference?" Whittingham chimed in.

"Good point. Maybe this time you're right, Charlie. Maybe he's seen some Crocodile Dundee movies, I don't know," the Harwood added, "or eaten at the Outback."

"Keep going, Stan, we've got a press release to get out and we've got to get a press conference planned," said the President.

"Yes, sir. The helicopter dispatcher also confirms that the man who came in had an accent. He swears it was Irish. And the dispatcher's name is Paul Ryan, if that's worth anything."

"Where's the Senator now?" asked the President. Harwood cleared his throat.

"The body went by ambulance to a local hospital. He was, of course, dead when he arrived. The body was cleared for transport back here to Washington, but will stay in Birmingham overnight, until we can get some Walter Reed people down there. They'll accompany him back tomorrow. We've got Army and independent pathologists who'll work on it. Everything is being videotaped, including the preparation and packing of the body and its transport. We're making sure there'll be no conspiracy theories for our successors to deal with. Two video cams will follow the body everywhere . . . and stay with it until he's on the ground . . . and *in* the ground, I might add . . . there'll be no claims that any of the evidence was tampered with. By the way, Cheryl Thomas and her team have responsibility for the funeral arrangements and that stuff. She's already talked to the director at Arlington and they're underway over there. The Senator's family is being assembled and brought to Washington at government expense. He was, of course, a U.S. Senator with no official position in the Administration, so we're being a little careful about who does what here."

"Don't be too careful" the President chided. "This man was going to be the Vice President of the United States . . . ."

Williams looked at Harwood, wondering if, or when, it would ever be appropriate to tell people the entire tale.

" . . . and perhaps a lot more," the President added. "We are around nine points ahead in every poll. A record turnaround. And he did it."

"Yes, sir. Understood. A press briefing has been arranged for five o'clock. It's now four-thirty-four. Everyone is clamoring for more information, as you might expect. That's it, sir."

The President assumed control of the meeting. "Okay, nothing gets out that might compromise the integrity of the investigation, or our chance of catching these guys. Short of that, and I recognize that's a lot, I want full disclosure and full cooperation with the press. I don't want it to look like we're hiding anything. First, we're not. And second, they've got the right to know what's going on."

All heads nodded in agreement.

"Also, no one, with the exception of the people from Justice, is to leave the White House without Mr. Harwood's or my permission. I want all of you here for the rest of the day, at least. I also want to create a complete SWAT-type team here, on premises, full-time. Stan and I will decide on the composition of the team. Make sure Emily knows where you are. And no leaks, please. Anticipate sleeping over tonight, so if you need anything, speak to Emily or one of her assistants. She's ordered the third floor to be ready. Anybody got anything else? No? Well then, meeting adjourned."

The twelve people in the room began to stand, arrange papers, chat, and migrate toward the door, eventually leaving the President alone in his office. Stanley Harwood, took slightly longer to arrange his papers than the others, making him the last to leave. With an uncharacteristically blank face, he looked back from the doorway at the President across the room and said, "I'm sorry, sir."

The President rubbed his face hard with both palms, as if first waking up, and answered in a low voice, "There is evil in this world, Stan. And I'm afraid that it is the human sufferings which derive from that evil that distinguish us from the gods."

Silently, Harwood turned and walked out the door when the President added to the vacant doorway, "Stan, stop back tonight. I know I'm going to need to talk."

Harwood's head reappeared in the doorway. "Yes, sir, I'd like that." He paused for a moment, stepped inside, adding, "I had a passion before . . . to see that you got re-elected, and by so doing, to position a deserving African-American for the Presidency . . . ."

As Harwood paused, the President broke in, "And now?"

"Mr. President, this man was going to be President. How do we ever explain *that* to people?"

"I don't know. I think I'm going to have to think about it . . . or pray for direction." President Williams offered a strained smile. "When struggling for answers, I usually find that the truth is a good alternative."

43

"Mr. Harwood, Agent Snowden is on line two."

"Thanks, Tamara. Put him through, and hold my calls."

Snowden went straight into the reason for his call. Harwood could tell he was excited. "Mr. Harwood, we've got some results back from the lab."

He answered slowly and deliberately to put Snowden at ease and return him to a more measured pace. "Agent Snowden, I have a suggestion. Let's drop the Mr. stuff. I realize it's respectful, but how about 'Stan' . . . that would be fine?"

The President, at Harwood's request, had assigned Pete Snowden, to the Calvin assassination investigation team. Snowden was charged up by his new responsibility, and he found comfort in Harwood's candor and keen analytical bent.

"Yes, sir. Well, er, Stan, the lab came up with some fabulous stuff last night. This could be a big time breakthrough. Two actually."

"Go."

"Well, the locals, climbed all over the helicopter and messed up a lot of the evidence. Anyway, we had footprints with mud left on the floor of the back of the helicopter. We've been running that down every way from Sunday."

"And?"

"And, get this. The mud is not even domestic! We have a chromotographical comparative analysis with about thirty types of soil and guess what?"

"No idea, Pete . . . what?"

"We've got a perfect match with mud samples taken from the parking lot at the Shannon airport. You should see the computer printout. Perfect. Ninety-nine percent confidence level, according to the computer."

"You mean the mud in the helicopter might have come from the parking lot at the Shannon airport?"

"Not might . . . did. Near perfect match, like I said."

"No other possibility?"

"The lab tells me it's a 'three sigma' probability. That's their mathematical lingo for, like, ninety nine point nine, nine, percent."

"Unbelievable. How did we get to this point in the first place? "

"One of the team followed up on the lead about the accents. He got the Interpol, and they contacted authorities in Australia, New Zealand, Scotland, Ireland, and England. Each of them sent us overnight about ten soil samples each. The Bureau ran them through a series of chemical analyses and finally this chromo thing, and one of the Ireland samples gave us a perfect match."

"Nice work, Snowden. I'm not one to leap to conclusions, but this leads us in a specific direction. We've got to put every effort into finding O'Malley and working our connections in the IRA."

"Yes, sir, we're deploying additional resources in that direction now."

"We find O'Malley, and we find Calvin's killer. What else?"

"Well, the field team took fiber samples from inside the helicopter. Actually, these guys were not only muddy, but they were shedding like a Samoyed in August. There were fibers all over the copter. And guess what? We've got another match. According to the statistical guys, it's nearly as good as the mud."

"Keep going, Snowden."

"Well, we sent fiber samples to places where you'd hear a kind of English accent. We've got a match back on the fibers and the dyes. First the fibers. They're all wool, known as long loop. It's a trade term for a high quality wool used only in the best fabrics. The lab thought this might be from older suits. There are some new processing techniques designed to keep wool from wrinkling and these methods change the fiber, give it a lot more 'memory'. Nowadays, when wool gets wrinkled, it tries to go back to its original shape. These fibers are not like that. They're apparently from older processing methods. According to the type of wool, the length of the fiber, and the processing method, the lab says that the fiber could have come from only two places in the world, Australia or, get this, Ireland."

"We're getting a theme here, Snowden."

"Wait'll I tell you about the dyes. There were several different dyes in the fibers. Our guys are guessing that one of the suits was one of those kind of mottled jobs . . . brownish with little tiny greenish and reddish fibers woven into the cloth. Tweed, basically. The other suit was gray. These are both older dyes, too. I won't go into all the chemistry, but the colors match perfectly with what witnesses our suspects were wearing. Also, we're still running down some leads and checking some old manufacturers records on dye types and dye lots. But here's where we are right now: the dyes are almost certainly from Kaelin and Sons, dyemakers in, guess where? A little town called Ardara, County Donegal, Ireland. In business since 1878, and they have all of their records, and I mean all, in old ledgers. The Interpol guys have looked through them, and by the end of the day tomorrow, we'll probably know the names of the firms the dyes were sold to and when and where the wool was processed. We may be able to get the names of the suit makers, too. The stores that sold the suits are a little more difficult. There're apparently no good records at that level."

"When will you have the names of the sheep?"

"Sir?"

"The sheep that gave the wool. We'll need to know if one is named Dolly. The President might ask. We'll have to be prepared."

Snowden was a quick study. He replied, "We'll have last names in a couple of days. First names take a little longer."

Harwood laughed, "Great work, Snowden. Pass on my compliments to the team."

"By the way, we're checking all travel to and from Ireland for every Eastern U.S. city for the two weeks immediately preceding the shooting. There's a lot of post-summer discount travel going on, so we've got dozens of people just checking private and commercial flights."

"Good, I'll wait for your call."

"Another thing, sir. It's pretty well known among the investigative team that O'Malley has been missing since before the shootings. Plus, the press has been all over my office with phone calls . . . cameras . . . everything. Reporters are set up outside our offices twenty-four hours a day."

"I know. Take the heat you're feeling and crank it up exponentially. Then you'll know how the President and I feel. When we get our thumb on him, things will undoubtedly change."

"Yes, sir."

"It's not everyday that a sitting Vice President disappears for two weeks. But mysteries like this don't hold together too long. Just keep plugging, and we'll get him. And one more thing, Agent Snowden."

"Yes, sir?"

"Go home and get some sleep. You sound exhausted."

Urging Snowden to get some rest was ironic. Harwood was legendary for his compulsive perseverance in the face of a crisis, and he'd not slept in two days, himself. Since the "incident at Birmingham," as it now was familiarly referred to at the White House, Harwood had experienced the gamut of emotions . . . hollow and insensate at first, then angry and bitter. As his rage ebbed, he found himself wistful and contemplative. For hours, he did nothing but read Matthew. As his mentor, the President, steeled himself, paradoxically Harwood turned philosophical, reading and re-reading . . . *blessed are the meek . . . blessed are the merciful . . . blessed are the peacemakers . . . blessed are those who mourn, for they shall be comforted.*

Then, inexplicably, his introspection spent itself, metamorphosing into a singular dedication to see the sitting Vice President apprehended, and see his plan and Williams redeemed. This renewed passion, though intense, manifested itself constructively, never descending into a vengeful or retributive spirit.

Someone had placed Senator Calvin in the crosshairs of a scope... literally. Now, Stanley Harwood had O'Malley in his own crosshairs, determined to resolve the disappearance and the assassination, and bring him to justice. They would find him. *Stanley Harwood* would find him . . . and, when he found him, he knew that he'd have his killers soon after.

44

The President stood when the three men walked into the room.

"Welcome, Stan. Mr. Milbury, Mr. Snowden, glad you are here. Well then, where are we? Any progress?"

Harwood began. "Yes, sir, I think we're getting somewhere. The O'Malley situation is either becoming more clear or more cloudy, depending on where you sit and when. First, we're still looking at the commercials in and out of the country. At the same time, we checked most all of the privates out of the country in the week before and following Senator Calvin's assassination. We got a huge number of flights, of course, and so we narrowed them to Ireland, Scotland, and England, focusing on Ireland. Then we went back and checked the passenger logs. Then we either had local police or our people visit the pilots."

"And?"

"And we found a private pilot who got scared and told us, off the record, that he had a 'unique' passenger on board who was reported as a different person to the customs authorities. Then we . . . . ."

"I'm sorry, Stan, but can you pickup the pace a little? Is this whole thing going to be about O'Malley?"

"Yes sir, I'm sorry. Yes, it's basically about O'Malley's whereabouts. If we can pin him down, answers about Senator's Calvin's death will come pretty quick."

"Okay, that's logical. But don't take everything for granted. We don't want to let other trails go cold at the expense of chasing O'Malley."

"We agree, sir. O'Malley's our primary focus, but not our exclusive focus."

Harwood continued, "Mr. President, sir, it appears he's had a little help. Perhaps a lot of help."

The President was uncharacteristically critical. "He better have had. The Secret Service keeps making excuses about not being able to trail him, for God's sake, even through downtown Boston. And we're talking about the Vice President of the United States. He's a fairly recognizable individual, wouldn't you say?"

"Yes, sir. Look, the Secret Service and the Bureau are both appropriately embarrassed about it. It's not been a pretty picture for either of them. Okay, so working on the tip from the pilot, we sent agents to interview a Mr. Roger Houle. Houle is Chairman of the Board of American Technologies Enterprises. The company's headquartered in suburban Boston and they have two electronic assembly plants in Ireland. Basically, sir, he admitted to us that he has made several trips to Ireland on his company plane with the Vice President aboard. He's admitted assisting the Vice President in traveling undetected, or rather under another name, through immigration and customs on both sides of the border. In one case, he even had the Vice President in the bathroom of his plane when officers came on board for a quick document check. He seems to be cooperating fully. He's been told he'll be charged, possibly with complicity or more serious consequences, but, at this point, he says he just wants to help, and he'll take what comes. So far, he has rigorously denied involvement in the killings. He's also denied giving assistance, financial or otherwise, to the IRA. His contention about the killing is believable. As far as the IRA is concerned, he's in our files as a suspected IRA money source, but he claims he's a respected businessman, and not one to get this messy."

"So what does all this tell us?" Williams asked.

"We're not sure yet, sir. Bill has been coordinating information on the ground work in Ireland."

"What do you have, Agent Snowden?"

"According to Houle, after he lands, O'Malley is just left at the FBO, or private aircraft terminal. Houle says he doesn't know what happens to him after that. He, O'Malley that is, wears disguises sometimes, sometimes not. A driver picks up Houle, and he goes to his plants, or off to meet with business associates. Sometimes he gets a call from O'Malley saying he wants a ride back. Sometimes O'Malley calls Houle when he's back in the States, wanting Houle to go over and pick him up."

"Does he do it?"

"Yes, sir. He sends his plane."

"You mean to tell me that the Vice President has been traveling in and out of the U.S. with false documentation on a transcontinental private jet?"

"I'm afraid so, sir," Harwood answered. "It's apparently not that hard to do. Customs and immigration folks know Houle pretty well. They apparently come on board, collect passports, give them a cursory review, and that's it."

"Even after the World Trade Center catastrophe?"

"There are still going to be cracks in the system, sir."

"This is a little more than a crack, for God's sake. So what's the conclusion . . . are we saying that O'Malley arranged Calvin's death?"

"Despite the circumstantial evidence, sir, it's really too early to speculate," Harwood replied. "We've got motive, opportunity, and a bunch of circumstantial stuff . . . taken together, it's creates a pretty foul odor. It looks bad, but we're just going to plow ahead. You never know where it'll lead."

"Is that the update, Stan?"

"One more thing, Mr. President," Harwood added.

"We've divided everyone up into special teams to follow other leads and suspects. It's tough, because we're trying to coordinate the activities of several agencies, here and abroad, and get the optimal outcome. Right now, I'd call O'Malley our best bet, but we've got some very good leads on some Klan-type groups. We're also looking seriously at a couple of black groups that have been fulminating, with some thinly veiled threats of physical violence, since Senator Calvin's appointment. In short, sir, we've got all kinds of other roads we're going down, too."

"Alright, thanks. Get back to me with anything else substantive like this. By the way, do we have any idea where our Vice President is now?"

The three men looked at each other with rapid glances.

"We have no idea, Mr. President."

"Then I guess I'd better keep my Secret Service detachment close by, don't you think? And continue to wear this lovely bulletproof vest that you all gave me?"

"Yes, sir, by all means . . . I'm afraid that'll be the case for a while longer."

45

Chris Weiner disembarked in front of the Signature air terminal at Reagan. Carrying a hanging bag and a large brown leather case, she hurried to the wall of spacious glass-front phone booths across from the waiting area. She was forty-five minutes early for her meeting with Cartwright.

Finding an unused phone, she closed the door and began a series of calls to Grand Cayman, Toronto, New York, and Los Angeles. On the Cayman call, she identified herself with a code number and the name she used when trading through this account.

"This is Ms. Smith. Account A, two, two, three, nine, one, dash, ex, dash, bee, edward, bee, nine, two."

"Yes, Ms. Smith, I'll put you right through."

After a brief pause, her account officer answered, "Hello, Ms. Smith."

"What's going on, Antonio?"

"Well, it doesn't look so good right now. We got off those trades you ordered yesterday, but as I've said before, we have nearly a three hundred million-dollar position, totally on one side in these securities. I realize we're your agent for execution only, but I must repeat that these positions have no hedge or risk management in place through our trust company. You're totally undiversified, and, this entire portfolio is bet on the assumption that casino stocks are going down. If they go up, or even if they stay at current levels, you'll lose your entire investment."

"You sound like a broken record."

"Madame, I'm indemnified. You are close to being out of the money on a lot of these positions. You've sold calls, bought puts, and shorted stocks, and meanwhile, the whole industry has stayed strong."

"Double yesterday's order," Weiner ordered.

"I will do it, Ms. Smith, of course. When can we expect the funds?"

"I'll wire you a hundred million this afternoon."

"Fine, Ms. Smith. As usual, please confirm the trades in writing by five p.m. today. And please use your account and security code numbers on all correspondence."

Weiner hung up and dialed a New York number. A secretary answered, "Offshore Enterprises."

"Give me Rusty."

Chris Weiner waited for Rusty Billings to come on the phone. "Rusty, this is Ms. Smith. How are we looking?"

"Good afternoon. I haven't heard from you in a few days."

"I've been busy. How are we looking?"

"Not good. The whole sector's not showing any weakness. My rough numbers show you're down about two hundred million. I hope you don't have any other accounts like this one, because, if you do, you're Wallenda on a silk thread. Of course, if something makes these stocks drop, you not only recover, but make several billion."

"I'm quite aware of what I'm doing, Rusty," Weiner rebuked. "Sell short another hundred million in the stock account and leave the option account alone. Short the top three again, in pro rata amounts."

"Will I be getting funds today?"

"You'll get a wire credit from the Bermuda bank, just as before. When the funds hit, execute the trades at the market."

"Yes ma'am. Will I be able to able to get in contact with you?"

"Nothing has changed, Rusty. I'll call you, if I decide I want to talk with you. That's it." Weiner slammed down the phone. "Shit, shit, shit," she said out loud to herself. "God damn it! Cartwright and O'Malley have really screwed this up big time."

Weiner stomped from the booth, grabbed a Styrofoam cup of coffee from the small beverage station in the waiting area, set her cup on a low glass-top table decorated with fresh flowers, and took a seat. From her sleek, black leather chair, she fidgeted through the back section of the Wall Street Journal.

Bernard Cartwright swung his car away from the main commercial terminal at Reagan, and followed the "General Aviation" signs past a set of out-of-place Georgian style buildings. He parked his car haphazardly at Signature Air's passenger entrance, ignoring the "Area 10 Permits Only" signs.

He found Weiner in the waiting area. They exchanged a brief greeting, and proceeded to the conference room Weiner reserved for the meeting. As they walked by a set of stairs, the stainless steel doors of an elevator, and a watercolor of Mt. Vernon, Cartwright acted like a scolded schoolboy, shoulders drooped, head hung low, avoiding eye contact.

Once in the conference room, Chris Weiner closed the thin-slat Venetian blinds, and took a seat opposite Cartwright at the long polished wood table. Then, Weiner let loose. "Well, Bernie. This is really screwed up. Big time."

"Chris, you didn't need to fly out here just to tell me it's screwed up. I know that. It'll get fixed, I promise you."

"One more time, Bernie, so your little brain can comprehend what's going on here. You and I strike a deal. You promise to deliver O'Malley. O'Malley promises he'll deliver enough people to get the casino tax passed, including getting Speaker Berkhardt on the team. I'm easy . . . I not making a lot of outrageous demands . . . I say I don't even need it passed, just holding hearings, have O'Malley make a speech, that'll be fine. So, I keep on investing . . . I double down, when I'm already under water... based on your half-assed assurances. I'm in so deep now, I can't get out. Now, I'm not asking for a lot. I just need somebody to stir the waters a little, just some public hearings. Simple shit. Get somebody with some influence to say something favorable, in public, about the casino tax, and these stocks go whamo down the friggin' drain. Just get three or four measly senators and an equal number from the House to hold a press conference. I'm not asking a lot, Bernie goddamnit. Not for the kind of money I've spent."

"It'll happen, Chris."

"Happen? You can't even deliver a Podunk congressman, and they've got to be pretty cheap. Now our precious Connie O'Malley is off the ticket and has done a Judge Crater on us. And, while he's hanging out with Amelia Earhart and Jimmy Hoffa, you're on the outs with Williams. Jesus, Bernie, first, you didn't even know he was kicking O'Malley off the ticket. And for this straight-arrow Calvin guy, no less! And you're the fucking campaign chairman . . . or alleged campaign chairman."

"I've made all the contacts on the Hill that O'Malley was working on. Our key targets say they're going to do it at just the right time. A couple of days."

"Bernie, look at these." Weiner flicked a sealed brown envelope across the table. Cartwright fumbled, then tore open the end and pulled out the photographs. He looked at a few in stony silence, returned them to the envelope, and set them on the table between them.

"Well, Bernie?"

"Well what, Chris?"

"Well, how do you like my photographic work? Nice, huh? Check 'em out, Bernie. I've got the eating, the blowing, the fucking, the coke. I got it all. You're quite a subject, you and my hired girl. Hey, if you want to hear the tape, I can play a little. How about the part where you're begging to go in the rear-end, huh? That was real cute, Bernie. I don't know who'd rather have this, Suzy, the Democrats, or the Republicans?"

"Chris. I beg you not to use these. It'll destroy both of us. And maybe others."

"I *am* destroyed, Bernie. You knew I was shorting these casino stocks, right? What you didn't know was that I bet it all," Weiner screamed. "I've taken every cent I own and leveraged it . . . hell, ten-to-one . . . twenty-to-one . . . who knows by now? I have billions invested, and most of it is borrowed! Bernie, I've moved my entire net worth into four investment accounts set up through foreign companies. I'm using banks, and brokers, and numbered accounts all over the damned place. I'm in for three billion, cash money, American! Add the money I've borrowed, most of it through kiting and double pledging my equity. Shit, I am doing deals on margin, then using that stock to borrow more . . . all based on your half-assed promises. Now along comes this Mr. Harwood, the one the Times refers to as the 'campaign genius', together with your incredible incompetence . . . add to that a large dose of O'Malley, and I am out of business... bankrupt."

Cartwright was petrified. He stammered, "You . . . you never told me about this. You never told me you were going in this deep."

Chris Weiner adopted a serious, almost consultative, tone. "Should it make a difference? You either go all the way, or you don't. That's the way we do things. Bernie, if these stocks drop even ten percent, my entire investment, including the borrowed money, goes up five or ten times! I'll have a hundred billion! And, Bernie, there's plenty of room for you to take out enough so you'll never have to worry about anything again. You could have that nice Chicago girl full time, huh? Wouldn't that be fun?"

"Chris, when is 'enough' enough? My God, you've constructed this complicated financial scheme to turn your three billion into what . . . a hundred billion? So what? Right now, without making another cent, you could spend a million dollars a day for twenty years . . . and still have money left over! You're already regarded as one of the most brilliant financiers in the world. Where does this game end?"

Weiner was stunned. How could anyone, particularly a man like Cartwright, not understand, not get it? She spit the words, "Jesus, Bernie, I am on the verge . . . just a press conference away . . . just a Senate or House hearing away... from being one of the wealthiest people, not women, *people* in the world. I will be up there with Buffet, those goddamn little oil emirates, Bill Gates, Waltons, if . . . I mean when . . . this happens."

Her voice began to rise when she considered the low-hanging fruit, still just out of reach. "Game? This is not a game, Bernie! This is real life, not some Wall Street chessboard, like one of your stupid merger ceremonies, where two plus two equals three and a half. And now, thanks to you, I have absolutely nothing to lose . . . and everything to lose. If these stocks don't drop, drop a lot and soon, I not only won't be in the Forbes 400, I won't be in the Forbes Four Million! I am desperate!"

Suddenly, at the word "desperate" Chris Weiner's voice crescendoed. She screamed, apoplectic. "I am desperate, Bernie! These people cannot do this to me. *You* cannot do this to me. I don't give a shit whether I destroy you with pictures or any other way. Or anyone else for that matter. You saw what happened to the Speaker, didn't you? I mean, I'm doing my part, aren't I?"

Cartwright was speechless. He pushed his chair from his table as much in fear as in shock. "Oh, my God! You had the Speaker killed for bottling up the casino tax bill? To get the bill into hearings?" He looked down, reached for his briefcase, stood up, and backed to the door.

"Yeah, Bernie, that was me. You know, Faust had one small cottage standing between him and completion of a vast estate around his castle . . . one lone holdout. A little touch of the torch, and it was all his. I need you to carry the torch, just like you promised. And, if that tax announcement doesn't happen by the time these option contracts expire, you're torched."

"For Christ's sake, Chris, you've gone from smart and aggressive to greedy and vain . . . and beyond. How in the hell can you use Faust as an example?"

"I like that, Bernie. How in the *hell* . . . cute play on words!"

"For God's sake, Chris, step back and look at what you're doing. You're turning into a certified psychopath!"

"Isn't that just like you, Bernie! Don't weak people, little people like you, always have to use some big scientific words. Yeah, use a big medical word to describe someone you don't like, someone you can't stand up to, people that you fear."

Then, a mad empress deposed, Weiner stood up and threw her purse across the room, where it smashed against the wall, spilling its contents on the floor. Then, she raised her briefcase over her head and hurled it after her purse where, hitting the wall with a thud, it too opened and strew papers across the floor.

Her ranting continued, "Listen to me, Bernie. If you don't pull this off, I will hire someone to cut off your cock. I promise you I will. Leaving you drugged out in a sauna like Berkhardt would be too easy on you. And I'm going to tell them to leave your balls hanging, just as a reminder that there used to be something down there. And guess what? John Bobbitt's surgeon won't be near where you're going to be. You'll be using the sewing kit from room service to try and re-attach that little vienna sausage. When I'm done with you, you're going to have to squat to piss, Bernie. And you know what? I've sucked on that little cock enough times that when my folks slice it off, I can tell the cops what to look for. 'Looks kinda like a penis, only smaller!'"

Chris Weiner shook her head wildly, her eyebrows arched higher than seemed physically possible, her eyes bulged, and she howled while Cartwright stood motionless, in shock.

Then, Weiner shrieked again, "Like a penis, only smaller! Don't you love it, Bernie?" Weiner still shrieked, and Cartwright backed the last few steps to the door of the conference room and, reaching behind him without turning his back on Weiner, hand trembling, he groped for the knob.

"I've got contacts too, Chris," Cartwright shouted. "Good contacts. I know how to get things done. I didn't get to this point in my life without getting into some rough stuff myself. Even the managing partner of the top law firm on Wall Street has had to get tough sometimes, just to survive. I've still got money, power, and connections . . . and a little bit of self esteem, no thanks to you. You'll see how much power I have. I've still got the number you gave me for your two buddies from Brooklyn. Just wait."

Bernard Cartwright turned the knob slowly, opened the door, and backed out, dazed, leaving Chris Weiner, standing alone, staring at the closed door in all her fury.

46

Harwood's exhaustion failed to afford him a night of solid sleep and, as had consistently been the case, he tossed and turned all night. He was in his regular half-awake state when the doorman's buzz rattled him from his light sleep.

It was three o'clock. He rolled out of bed and stumbled to the hallway, pressing the prominent black button in the intercom, and heard the elderly night man's feeble voice.

He sounded like he just woke up, too, Harwood thought. "Huh? Who? Yeah, what's he look like? Yeah. You checked his I.D.? You're sure? Okay, send him up."

Harwood felt his way back to the bedroom, put on a T-shirt, a pair of pants, and wondered why Tony was here at this time of night. Rinsing his face when the doorbell sounded, he went to the door to find an agitated Tony Battaglia.

"What are you doing here at this time of night?"

Tony Battaglia, out of pure excitement, raised up on his toes, like a small boy trying to drink from a too-tall water fountain. "I got it figured out, Stan! I got it figured out!" he exclaimed.

"Couldn't you have called? I've got a phone you know."

Absentmindedly, Harwood had not invited his friend to come in. Battaglia pushed his way past Harwood and planted himself in the middle of the living room. "I had to see my man Stan in person this time!"

Harwood waved him to a large beige couch. "Sit down, Tony. Relax. Now, what is it, exactly, you've got figured out?"

Battaglia sputtered, "We're going in the wrong direction, Stan. Totally wrong direction. We've been fooled. I got it figured out. It ain't O'Malley and it ain't Irish . . . it can't be."

Before he could continue his analysis, a lyrical voice issued from the bedroom hallway. "What is it, Stan? Is everything okay?"

The inquiry was followed immediately by appearance of a shapely silhouette in a sheer babydoll.

"Uh . . . Harwood stammered, but even before he made a sound, Tony recognized the voice, if not the profile, of Maria Krautchik.

Krautchik threw an arm across her chest and took a step back into the shadow of the hallway.

"Uh," Battaglia mimicked unconsciously, "looks like a bad time, Stan. I'm sorry."

"No, it's okay, Tony."

Tony stood and moved toward the door, but Harwood quickly grabbed him by the shoulder. "Hey, Tony," he offered, an incipient smile crossing his lips, "she's a member of the team. Now come over here and sit down."

From the hallway came Krautchik's disembodied voice, firm, but nevertheless sleepy. "It's okay, Tony. You stay, and I'll get you guys some coffee." She immediately reappeared in a man-sized, full-length robe, brushed her hair back with her fingers, and gave Tony a mechanical wave as she headed to the small kitchen.

"You're sure it's alright?"

"Sure, of course," answered Krautchik and Harwood simultaneously, and the three chuckled.

"No coffee for me, I'm just gonna stay a minute."

Maria Krautchik joined Harwood on a small settee, sitting cross-legged, pushing her robe down between her legs, and draping an affectionate arm around Harwood's shoulder.

"We don't have him nailed yet, Tony," Harwood advised. "But everything says O'Malley. You need money and connections to kill somebody. The Irish link is undeniable. Who else could have put this together?"

Tony pulled out hand written notes. "Anybody . . . anybody . . . *but* O'Malley," he answered.

"You sound convinced, my friend. And you must be, to show up here at this hour."

"I've been thinking about this a lot. You know how much I care about

President Williams, and I just kept thinking what a tough spot he's in, and how could I help. So, listen Stan, I figure O'Malley ain't smart and he's probably crooked. He's got known IRA connections. He's got, what do you call it, motivation. He was humiliated by his being dropped off the ticket. We know the killers were Irish, or at least spoke with Irish accents. They had Irish mud on their shoes, and wore Irish wool suits."

"You got it, Tony."

"But it doesn't work. Listen, if I wanted to kill you, would I use the Mafia just because I'm Italian-American? Would I use Italians who could be linked to me? Would I use my friends in the fitness business around town? Would I *want* to get caught? Think about it . . . wouldn't I make absolutely sure they *didn't* have Palermo mud on their shoes? Would I hire guys with Italian accents, sharkskin suits, and black hair?"

"Maybe, maybe not."

"Wrong, Stan. Just like my Italian description, these Irish guys weren't real, they were comic book characters!" Bataglia panted excitedly, "Unless O'Malley was doing an in-your-face with this killing, it would never look like this. It's like he is bragging that he did it. O'Malley still hasn't appeared, and we've got two hundred agents in England and Ireland, and fifty more checking Irish leads here."

"Net it out, Tony."

"Well, I don't know where O'Malley is, but there's no way he arranged this. The IRA wouldn't work like this. The first thing they did was deny any involvement. When they make a hit, they don't issue a denial, they usually take credit. Somebody wants us to think it was O'Malley did this. This smells, Stan."

"Could be. What else?"

"Well, what's that word you used in my office one time, when you were trying to talk me into helping you meet with the President? It's like something you're so close to that you can't see the real situation. Para-something."

"Paradigm?"

"Yeah, that's it. What's it mean again?"

"It's like some strongly held belief, like something people get attached to, in the face of contrary evidence."

"Bingo!" Battaglia gushed. "Paradigm, that's what you're suffering from. The shoes were muddy with Shannon mud on purpose. The FBI was blown away at how much fiber evidence there was. Why? Shouldn't they have been suspicious about this? I think the killers rubbed their suits on the seats and pulled off fibers on purpose. The killers wore gloves. There were no fingerprints. But there's these fibers and mud all over. It don't add up."

"I'm with you, Tony," Krautchik concluded. "I think we're heading in totally the wrong direction."

"But sometimes vengeance killings aren't going to make sense," countered Harwood.

"This one, at least with O'Malley as the prime suspect, *really* doesn't make sense, honey. Tony's right."

As they talked, Battaglia studied the couple sitting across from him. He realized that his impressions of them had been confined. First, he had thought of them only as individuals, with no identify other than self. Further, at the White House, each was a paragon of professionalism. Their respective demeanors were never actually stifling or uncomfortable, Tony thought, just professional, that's all. Now, his mind, at first startled by her appearance, then further surprised by their physical closeness and the word 'honey', raced to redefine them. Sitting here, unself-conscious, hair mussed and eyes bleary, they seemed more real, more human. He allowed himself a deep and warm sense of satisfaction for whatever force had united them. He reminded himself to light an additional candle.

"Tony?"

"Yeah, Stan . . . and one other thing," Battaglia added, "These guys were so careful about no fingerprints—but then, if they didn't want to be identified, why didn't they wait in their cars until the helicopter got there or, why didn't they come late and walk straight to the waiting helicopter? Instead, they just stand around this office building, right in front of people, talking in their Irish accents, getting recognized. They *wanted* people to think that they were Irish. They were planting evidence. And, if they were so ruthless to kill the pilot, why didn't they set the plane on fire or blow it up? 'Cuz that might've destroyed the mud or the fibers! Look, Stan, you know that I can't stand O'Malley. I think he's a disgusting, low-life politician. For that matter, he might even be capable of something like this. I'm not saying he *couldn't*, I'm saying he *didn't*. This looks like a total frame-up to me. O'Malley . . . he ain't smart, but he's smarter than to do this . . . he's got street smarts, at least."

Harwood played devil's advocate. "Maybe O'Malley's smart enough to do it this way so that it looks so much like he was involved, everyone will think that it couldn't be him."

"Wow . . . too complicated for me, Stan."

"Maybe he wants you to think just what you're thinking . . . that he didn't do it. Maybe he figured if it was obvious that the killers were Irish, then he wouldn't be a suspect. Reverse psychology."

"O'Malley? No way. That's too deep for me, and it's definitely too deep for him. I still say this was somebody else. We're wasting our time looking for Irish killers. We gotta start thinking about who else did this, or who wanted it done."

"Stan, Tony is really onto something."

Stan Harwood smiled at Maria, squinted his still sleepy eyes. "Okay, so maybe you guys are right. What then?"

"Well, who else mighta had a reason to bump off Calvin? Let's go over it again. Maybe it'll jump out at us."

Harwood had always adored Tony's naiveté, and his brilliantly simple insights. But he realized that as their friendship had grown and deepened over the years, his affection for his stubby pal became increasingly tempered by respect.

"Let me give it a shot," Harwood began. "And I hope you've got a few minutes."

"I gotta be in by six," Battaglia laughed.

"Okay," Harwood began, "the IRA, or some other Irish connection, with or without the jilted Vice President, they start the list. Anybody on the campaign team who the President went around, without even telling them. While it seems preposterous, you'd have to put Whittingham, Cartwright, Bensalem, and a bunch of others on the list. How about the KKK or some other group that institutionalizes hate-mongering? They wouldn't be happy to see Calvin as Vice President, much less as President. How about any damned Democrat in the country? They'd gone from fifteen points ahead in the polls to ten points behind? How about anybody who doesn't like Congressional Medal of Honor winners? What about right-wing businessmen who gave millions to the Republican Party—or maybe even a big Democratic donor who may not like what's happened? Black power groups who don't want a 'Tom' in the White House. Blacks that want to create a power base by killing Calvin and claiming it was a white conspiracy. And the FBI still doesn't have any warm leads on Speaker Berkhardt's murder. We know he was rubbed out by someone very smart, but we don't know who did it or why. What if Calvin's assassination and Berkhardt's death are somehow linked?"

"Well, that's some good guesses, but I still know it ain't O'Malley or the IRA."

"I admit, Tony, your theory's a lot more plausible than I first thought. Sounds like tomorrow we'd better look at making a course correction. Now, can I go back to bed?"

Harwood pulled an afghan from the back of the settee, and tossed it to Battaglia. "Listen, why don't you just crash on the couch? We can get back into this tomorrow, huh?"

"No, I don't think so, Stan."

"No?"

"No, not tomorrow." Tony looked at his watch, and stretched out on the couch. "Today."

Harwood grinned. He and Krautchik moved toward the bedroom, turned the light out, and disappeared. Tony Battaglia lay in the darkness, listening to faint, undulating sounds of pleasure emanating from the bedroom, pulling the afghan more closely around him, adjusting his pillow, and drifting off to sleep.

47

Lewis Calendar had been reading non-stop for three days. He was not relaxed at home, but, typically, he devoted his energy to those activities he thought were constructive, self-improving. Plus, he had read little other than business periodicals and stock analysts' reports for years. Though this hiatus was an involuntary one, he was determined to broaden what he told Sally was his 'mono-dimensionality'.

"Damn, Sally," he shouted from his customary perch on the den sofa, "Come're . . . have you seen this article in U.S. News?"

"What article, darling?" came the lilting reply from the next room.

"This thing about the Speaker of the House. Come here. This is incredible!"

Sally Calendar came up behind her husband, put her arms all the way around his neck, and looked over his shoulder. "What is it, sweetheart?"

"Listen, Sal. This is an article about that guy, the Speaker of the House, that they found dead in that sauna. The police called it accidental, but since then they've backtracked. They won't say why, but they're looking at it again, perhaps as a murder."

"I know," Sally said, "I heard about it."

"Yeah, but I bet you didn't hear this! They're apparently stumped for a motive. Now, listen to this:

A White House spokesman refused to confirm that the accidental death determination had been definitively overruled, although he conceded that the Bureau 'is continuing to take a careful look at all the evidence.' The source refused to comment as to a probable motive, stating that it was 'too early to begin that kind of idle speculation.'

However, an aide in the Speaker's office maintained that the 'Speaker had no personal enemies. His family life was great. He got along with everyone.' One source, *speaking on the condition of anonymity, told U.S. News that 'This thing has really turned around. It smells bad. Most attention is being focused on the Speaker's legislative agenda. So far, it's the only thing we have that makes any sense to look at.'*

"Nothing strange there, Lew."

"But listen to this, Sally.

'A spokeswoman for the Speaker's office confirmed that, as would be expected, Berkhardt had a long list of issues he was actively working on, but that the only controversial ones were the long-standing impasse on water rights legislation and imminent hearings on hotly contested casino tax legislation.'

"Did you hear that! 'Imminent hearings on hotly contested casino tax legislation.' That's it! There's something going on between this tax legislation, the options' pricing, and the Speaker's death."

Sally shushed in Calendar's ear, "You've been watching too much X Files. Not everything is a government conspiracy."

"Man, what an idiot! It's been right in front of me the entire time. Duh . . . trading 101. It's one thing to take market risk... that's what we get paid for. But we don't get paid to take political risk. I've known about this situation for months . . . tax . . . no tax . . . how each side is positioning with intense lobbying. I have way, way underestimated the importance of this. Listen, Sal, this is the first time I've felt like I'm glad I was fired. I'd have never read this if I was staring at the damned computer options screen. Screw those guys! This is bigger than a hundred million hit in the options market. I'm calling Washington!"

Lew Calendar rushed to a phone across the room, and frantically punched numbers. Sally had seen him like this before, many times, in fact. Nothing would deter him, she thought. It's his blessing and his curse. The only thing to do was to leave him alone until he was satisfied or he burnt out. She silently left the room.

Two hours later Lew Calendar burst into Sally's office and performed a little victory dance.

"Yes, Sally, yes!" he shouted. "I've been talking to Washington . . . seems like every damned department down there, our Senator's office, our

Congressman's office, the White House, anyone who'll listen. God, what an experience! Talking to Washington is like showing up for a 'round the world cruise and finding out you're rooming with Sisyphus! But, Sally, this is it! I talked to the Speaker's office, three times in fact, and finally got someone to listen to me. Get this: the Speaker had told his key legislative people that he'd decided to come out formally against the casino tax. He was going to cancel hearings, at least until after the Inauguration . . . wanted to bury it for good. Sally, this is it! Somebody wanted those casino hearings to go on. Somebody wanted that law passed. Because if the casino tax law passed, every one of these stocks would sink like a stone. That someone was willing to pay an outrageous price for puts, because they *knew* the prices were going to fall. And that somebody killed the Speaker to see that it would happen!"

"And now what?" she asked.

Calendar emitted a hearty laugh, grabbed his wife by the shoulders, and gently shook her. "Now what? Now pack your bags, and head for the Metroliner. We're going to Washington!"

48

Tamara was not protective, she was efficient and she was professional. She had been Stanley Harwood's secretary since he had been in the White House, and he could not function without her, as he had told her many, many times. Harwood sat in his small office, rendered even smaller by the stacks of reports, files, papers, and binders occupying every square inch of the cramped space.

Tamara's buzz startled him. "Mr. Harwood, I have a man on the line who demands to speak with you. He's called four times in the past hour, but refuses to leave a name or number. I didn't want to disturb you with this, but the man, he's absolutely insistent. I'm a little concerned because of his attitude . . . he sounds really agitated, sir."

"Has he said what he wants?"

"He won't say, sir. He's very strange . . . and he speaks with an accent."

"What kind of accent?"

"I'm sorry, sir. I don't know accents."

"Put me on hold and politely ask him again about the nature of his call. Then casually ask him about his accent."

When Tamara returned, less than a minute later, she was more informed. "He said to tell you that the accent is 'old sod' and told me to ask you if you remembered the phrase "You can't do this to me."

Harwood flinched. "Put him through, Tamara, right now."

He hung up on his secretary's intercom line and waited for his phone to ring. It had not finished its first ring, when he answered, "Stanley Harwood."

"Hello, Mr. Stanley Harwood."

Harwood recognized the voice immediately. "Yes, sir. How are you?"

"Good," came the monosyllabic reply.

"Where are you? Everyone is looking for you."

"Police too, from what I read, eh? A couple of weeks ago I was very unpopular, and now, it seems, everyone wants to have a chat with me. It's nice to be wanted for a change."

"You need to get to someone you can talk to, sir, someone who can help, who you can trust."

"I have, Mr. Harwood," came the response from the phone. "I have."

Harwood could hardly understand the low, muffled voice, accompanied by a panting wheeze. "Good, sir. Can you tell me who it is?"

"I'm talking with him right now."

"Uh, well, sir, I guess . . . ." Harwood stuttered. He was unaccustomedly dumbfounded.

"Can you get out for a face-to-face meeting, Mr. Harwood?"

"You name it, anytime, any place," Harwood replied.

"Look, Harwood, I want to set some ground rules for our get together first. You agree not to tell anyone about our meeting, including the police, the FBI, or the President. You agree that only under court order or subpoena will you disclose our meeting to anyone, unless I agree before hand."

Harwood was eager to meet with O'Malley, but he was chary of making a bad situation worse. "I can't afford to be an accessory, obstruct justice, that sort of thing, of course."

"I haven't been indicted, arrested, or charged," O'Malley whispered. "Not only that, but I haven't jaywalked since you last saw me."

"I'm in. Where and when?"

"You know the Library Lounge, by Lespinasse, off the lobby of the St. Regis? Be there in ten minutes. If you're late, I'm gone. Do not tell anyone, or bring anyone."

"For God's sake, you won't be recognized there?"

"Just get here."

"I'm on my way."

"Ten minutes."

"Give me fifteen and it's a deal," Harwood replied.

"Deal."

Harwood checked his watch continually during his near jog out of the

West Wing, up the access drive, and out the tall iron gates separating the gawking Pennsylvania Avenue tourists from the White House grounds. Skirting the park, he arrived at the seventeenth minute after hanging up the telephone on the conversation with the famous fugitive. He doubted if a cab could have possibly been faster to Sixteenth and K, silently cursing Washington's Byzantine zone system and its indecipherable fares, as he rushed along.

A liveried doorman opened the door as Harwood reached the porte-cochère. Angling across the lobby past a massive arrangement of fresh flowers, he grabbed the huge brass door handles and stepped through the French doors into the Library Lounge. Harwood recalled his distaste for the thin rows of fake tomes on the three-inch deep shelves, the recorded jazz, and the redolence of cigars.

The bartender interrupted Harwood's scanning of the room. "May I help you?"

"Uh, yeah," replied Harwood, squinting to adjust his vision to the interior light. "I'm looking for a friend of mine."

"From Boston? There's a gentleman in corner over there who told us to be on the lookout for someone."

"That's him," Harwood cried, and made his way across a flowered carpet to a set of low stuffed chairs, covered in green flocked chenille. O'Malley's seat was snug up against a low coffee table, facing the corner.

Still standing, Harwood looked down, blurting out, "Is that you, sir?"

"Sit down and shut up," O'Malley replied. "Did you come with anyone?"

"We made a deal. I stick by my deals," Harwood said.

Harwood could not keep from examining and re-examining the Vice President's face. "I hardly recognize you, sir. "

Vice President Cornelius O'Malley wore a white straw hat and dark reflective sunglasses. He had a month-old beard, dyed coal black.

"I've lost thirty pounds, I've got Tampax stuck up under my lips and stuffed in my cheeks, and I've got cotton shoved up my nose. It's a wonder I don't suffocate. I can hardly breathe."

"That accounts for the strange voice, I guess." Harwood was amused by the absurdity of the situation, but maintained, against odds, a stern countenance. "It's a great disguise."

"Don't ever try it, it stinks. In fact," said the Vice President, "don't try a lot of the things I've done."

As Harwood's eyes adjusted to the dark corner, he slowly took in the thick pancake makeup and distorted features of the man slouched deeply in his chair. Appalled, he reverted to a drink order to break the tension. "Like to order a drink, sir? How about a scotch?"

O'Malley sucked in a breath through closed teeth. "No drinking, Harwood. I'm done."

"Holy moly, what's going on?" Harwood cried.

"After that meeting with you and the President, I stayed at the Observatory mansion for two days. I wasn't sober for a minute. I couldn't tell the difference between day and night. I asked them to take me up to Boston, and I drank two beers and a half a quart of scotch on the flight up. I checked into the Four Seasons, and gave the Secret Service the slip . . . right out the back of the restaurant, hiding in a service linen cart . . . just like in the movies . . . with a little help from my boys up there, of course. I stayed lost in the South End, drunk for another couple of days, and the boys kept me hidden. Then a friend flew me to Ireland. After a day, still drunk, I asked him to come over and fly me home. Up to this point, everyone lived by the code. No leaks."

"You had everyone stumped. The press has been going absolutely crazy."

"Good for me," O'Malley said with a laugh that reminded Harwood of the old O'Malley, the sober O'Malley, the man who served his state for many years loyally and effectively. "But in the meantime, I nearly died. It turns out my friend had already planned to check me into the hospital. I tried to protest, but I was too sick, and deep down inside I knew I had to get help quick, or I'd be another dead Mick, standing stiff in the corner with a beer stuck in my fist, surrounded by old, drunk friends, singing Irish freedom ballads. I was not ready for that, I was damned scared, I'll tell you, Mr. Harwood. A single friend saved my life."

"A Mr. Roger Houle, I assume?"

"Yeah, you got that far at least. At that point I had no money, no family, no ID, no nothing. Roger took me to St. Patrick's Hospital in Dublin. They're famous for their discretion with foreign clients and, as far as I'm concerned, it's the top-notch dry-out place in the world."

O'Malley again laughed the laugh of his past—robust, ingenuous, and pure—himself touched by the comic nature of the situation. He poured himself some bottled water, took a long drink, and gently shook his head as if to ask, self-condemningly, "Where have I been . . . what have I done?"

Harwood swallowed hard. The O'Malley of old was showing through, he thought, and how gratifying it was. He was surprised how quickly his contempt melted into sympathy. For the first time, he saw the Vice President as an afflicted man, a man whose soul had been infected by power and his mind by alcohol. Harwood reflected on his father's Jekyll-and-Hyde personality, controlled . . . possessed by alcohol. The memory was too clear for comfort.

For a moment, the men sat silently, each introspective, partaking in a kind of cathartic self-counseling. And, as the seconds passed, their inward examinations brought them closer to each other.

"Well, anyway," O'Malley continued, "Houle checked me in under an assumed name, wrote a big check, and called daily to check on my status. When I got coherent, I told them I had amnesia. I swear I don't think they ever did know who the hell I was. Get this, they even took my fingerprints and ran them through the international missing persons computer database, and the Interpol print database. They came up negative!" The Vice President chuckled, "The second most powerful man in the world, a heart beat—in this case another fifth—away from the Presidency, totally anonymous, and his prints don't register in the computer."

"No one recognized you?" Harwood asked.

"Harwood, I looked pretty bad. Yeah, they must have suspected something but, if they did, they were discreet. Anyway, by law they can't reveal their patients' names or anything about them. I tell you, Harwood, you wouldn't have known it was me. My clothes were filthy, dirty and torn. My beard was nearly two weeks old, my face scratched. I was dehydrated, had DTs, and was malnourished. They thought my pancreas was going to quit at any moment. One of the reasons my friend took me to get help was that he didn't want to declare a corpse when he cleared customs in the U.S. You know what they say, Harwood, that God invented whiskey . . . ."

". . . to keep the Irish from ruling the world," Harwood answered. "I've heard it before, Mr. Vice President, except then I thought it was cute.

Now it's different. This is absolutely unreal," Harwood said.

"Yeah. Weird. Weird like a Vice President getting dumped from the ticket just a few weeks before the election."

Harwood stared at the Vice President's contradictory face: drawn and gaunt, yet ludicrously puffed from the cotton stuffed in his gums. "I'm sorry," Harwood exclaimed, "but it was, and still is, the right thing to do."

"I know, Stan. I know."

Harwood ignored the response. "How did you get back into the U.S. undetected, and how did you keep from being recognized?"

"Stan, when you've got 'friends' like mine, you can do a lot." The Vice President stuck his index and middle fingers in the air, wagging them to make quote signs as he said the word "friends." He continued, "Some people think they're friends by giving you another drink, and some think they're friends by knocking the same drink out of your hands. The trick is knowing the difference. My true friend brought me back to the U.S., this time through Canada. I got back to Boston and hid out, hid from some of my other-type 'friends'. By the way, they want to get ugly."

"I just said I believe that dropping you from the ticket was the right thing to do," Harwood said. He was resolute. "I'm not going back on that. I'll help you, sir, but I won't debate history."

To Stanley Harwood's surprise, the Vice President repeated himself. "You were right to drop me from the ticket." And, O'Malley conceded, "I don't want to debate this either. I'm at a genuine disadvantage. It's a little tough debating with this friggin' Tampax stuffed in my gums. Do you know what it's like to sit in a dentist's chair all day? Have you ever had a dentist pack your mouth with cotton and then ask your opinion on Internet stocks? It's pure hell, but it sure helped me change my accent! Hey, Harwood, how 'bout this? I overheard one of the staff at the hospital in Dublin guess that I was from Scotland. That's a good one, eh?"

After this bone-chewing, Harwood was ready to get to the marrow. "Speaking of accents, sir, the investigation into Calvin's assassination puts you at the top of the list of suspects, either directly or indirectly. The guys who shot him had Irish accents."

"Harwood, I'm coming in from the cold and, for God's sake, I hope I do better than Leamas. I had nothing to do with Calvin's death and I can prove it. This Irish thing is nothing but a load of blarney."

The Vice President's voice rose quickly and large sweat beads began to issue from his forehead, overpowering the pancake paste, and slowly oozing down his face. He raised his voice, "I can't understand people! I've talked to all of my, how should I put it, friends. They swear they had nothing to do with it. Hell, this is not their style. This is absolutely insane!" Then, suddenly self-conscious of his loud voice, he stopped abruptly and slumped down in his chair.

"I don't see now how we could've bought into it in the first place," Harwood granted. "Actually, it was Tony Battaglia, the White House fitness guy, who first came up with the idea that the whole thing was a diversion."

"After, you spent a couple of million dollars sending hundreds of agents around the world."

"No doubt. Where does this leave us?"

"I think I can help. But I need your help, too."

"What kind of help?"

"I need protection. And I need indemnity. First Henry Berkhardt, now Calvin. I could be next. And I don't want to end up in jail."

"Why should you be a target? And, sir, if you had nothing to do with this, what makes you think you might go to jail?"

"Listen, Harwood, I've been taking money over the past several months, keeping some, distributing the rest on the Hill. I don't know exactly, but I've got reason to believe that it's one of our donors."

"You mean a Republican contributor?" Harwood asked, his voice hardly disguising his shock. "Job to do what?"

"What do you think? Do favors. Affect the outcome of legislation . . . make something happen that someone needs to happen. That's what politics is all about."

"I hope not."

"Okay, so earlier this year, Bernie Cartwright comes to me," the Vice President explained. "He wants to discuss legislative stuff, so I say sure, let's talk. Turns out he's all hot about the proposed federal casino tax . . . thinks it's great idea . . . it's not getting enough attention. He wants me to actively support it, and I say 'sure, let me take a look at it.' No big deal."

"But it was a big deal, right?"

"You got that right. Bernie's got all these papers, reports, draft speeches, tax analyses spread out all over the small conference table in my office. When he leaves, he gathers up all his papers and I notice a plain brown envelope on the table. I say, 'Hey, Bernie, you left an envelope behind' and he says to me, 'That's not mine, it must've been there before.'

Stanley Harwood grinned and started nodding his head.

"You can see this one coming, huh?"

"Yeah, sort of like a 747 taxiing in my closet."

"Well, I leave the envelope sitting there for a while, and then go back to the table, pick it up and open it. It's full of used hundred dollar bills, a hundred of them to be exact. I lock it in my desk drawer and leave it there . . . at least for a while. A couple of weeks later, here's Bernie again . . . wants to meet me for lunch. He wants to know if I think the tax is a good idea, and I say 'yeah, I think I can help you.' Half way through lunch he jumps up, says he forgot a meeting, picks up his papers and rushes out the door."

"Let me guess . . . there's another envelope on the table."

"Exactly, same as before, ten grand."

"So I'm starting to get the picture. I tell him I'll help, I meet with him, and wouldn't you know it, the envelope fairy leaves something behind every time. So, now I'm wondering how long this can go on without me actually doing anything. Well, it goes on and on, like a bottomless well . . . except each time, Bernie he keeps getting more and more agitated. So I share a little of the cash . . . I'm not greedy. I make a couple of calls, low key stuff. Hand out a little money on the Hill, pick up some big tabs for friends up there. And the envelopes keep coming, except after several weeks, Bernie doesn't leave them behind anymore, they come by FedEx to my office from New York."

"Absolutely, positively, huh?"

O'Malley pulled out a wrinkled FedEx envelope and handed it to Harwood. "Here, I kept a few of these, just in case. Maybe it'll help you find the source. I just opened 'em up, checked the bills' serial numbers to make sure they were random, and I even had a few checked for ultra violet dust. They were all totally clean. I pocketed the cash and burned the brown envelopes inside the FedEx envelopes. All this cash is probably totally untraceable. These people have got to be very careful, very experienced."

"So now what?"

"I want to come clean, Harwood and I have some good leads, but I've got to have some protection."

Harwood was firm. "I am in no position, Mr. Vice President, absolutely no position, to offer you anything at all. Even if I did, it wouldn't mean anything legally. And, at this point, it's hard for me to believe the President would pardon you, particularly if there's complicity in the murder of government officials."

"Stan, I called you because you understand these things . . . you connect the dots better than anyone over there. You're smart and you know how to get things done. Plus, you've got the President's ear. I've done some bad shit, I know, but I'm not into killing. This thing somehow got bigger than anyone expected. Hell, I don't know what's going on, but I've got some ideas. I want to help, but I can't spend time in jail. Can't the President let me do a Spiro Agnew and disappear out to Palm Springs to play golf? I'll find my own Walter Annenberg. I hear they've got some AA chapters out there that are full of stars!"

Connie O'Malley grunted an uncomfortable, self-conscious laugh, half at his black humor and half at having prostrated himself to a thirty-eight-year old White House staffer.

"Here's what I'll do, Mr. Vice President. No promises. But on good faith, I'll do what I can with the President. That's all I can offer."

"I'll take what I can get at this point, I guess. I'll have my attorney call you. His name is Jacob Walters. Take the call."

"O'Malley, Walters is the tops in Washington! Why didn't you send him instead?"

Connie O'Malley reached to his face and took off his sunglasses. Laying them in front of him, the glasses clicked as they struck the square glass-top table. "I had to see you face-to-face. Look at my eyes, Harwood. Look closely."

Harwood leaned toward O'Malley, and stared directly into the Vice President's eyes.

"What do you see, Mr. Harwood?" O'Malley asked.

"I'll tell what I see, Mr. O'Malley. I see clear, white, crisp eyes, not the yellowish, bloodshot eyes I've always seen before. You look good . . . despite the chipmunk cheeks and makeup. I'd guess your skin is clear too."

Connie O'Malley nodded. "It is. Twelve steps. God grant me the serenity to accept the things I cannot change, courage to change the things I can, and wisdom to know the difference. I got help, but I need more. See if you can help me with a deal. Please."

Harwood grinned, "You know, sir, the last time I saw you, you were being, how shall I say, escorted, physically, out the Oval Office of Hoban's great Georgian neoclassic residence."

"Yeah, right," O'Malley agreed. "Look, Stan, I'm no philosopher. I'm not like the President. I'm a street guy, not a professor. Always have been, always will be. Now I'm tired. But I'm clean. I'll get on board, join the team. I just don't want to go to jail. A few kickbacks, a little cash here and there. It's in my blood, I guess. But I didn't kill anybody. I haven't done anyone any harm. Do what you can. Please."

"I'll do the best I can, sir. Tell Walters to call me."

49

Tony Battaglia and Stanley Harwood had become, by virtue of convenience and circumstance, *de facto* roommates. Tony now had plenty of time to help Harwood, hours at the White House fitness center having been curtailed during the crises and related investigations. For that matter, the center was nearly empty, day after day, with the occasional visitor coming only to chat with Tony rather than work out. Maria Krautchik, similarly dedicated, maintained a schedule of late nights and early mornings, her too staying over at Harwood's apartment more and more frequently, though, unlike Tony, she was not consigned to the couch.

Battaglia's unorthodox insights had earned him a spot on the White House Crisis Management Team, established by Williams to give him a single point of contact on the status of the investigations. Offices had been cleared down the hall from the Oval Office, and the Team could be found, at any hour, on the telephone with Interpol, the Secret Service, the FBI, or Capitol Hill, or working any of the sundry leads and inquiries that continuously deluged the White House switchboard.

The President had endowed Stanley Harwood with the chairmanship of the *ad hoc* Team, and Harwood assembled the FBI's Maria Krautchik, Special Agents Snowden and Milbury of Treasury's Secret Service, Attorney General Shaer as an *ex officio* member, and a number of researchers and staff gleaned from staffs at the White House, FBI, and Treasury.

Harwood took particular effort to assign meaningful tasks to Battaglia, and the little man was up to everything that came his way, always exceeding Harwood's highest expectations. The men's mutual affection for, and trust in, President Williams had fully welded the bond between them, that weld tempered by the turbulence and consequence of their shared duty.

The night Battaglia arrived at Harwood's co-op in the middle of the night to spout his now-vindicated theory on the "Irish" killers, he had characteristically crashed on the couch. It became an act repeated often. The three friends finished their work at the White House, and drove to Harwood's place, speculating on evidence and motives during the short trip out Massachusetts Avenue, into Harwood's garage, up the elevator, and into the apartment, until, finally, exhaustion conquered enthusiasm. Then Harwood and Krautchik, retiring to his bedroom, left the retired weight-lifter seemingly comatose on the couch.

They were less accustomed to visits in the late hours, than to the frequent phone calls that interrupted their cherished rest. But then, it was not unusual for the graveyard-shift doorman to buzz them in the middle of the night to announce that someone had arrived with critical information on the progress of the investigations.

This time it was no different, at least that's what Harwood thought. "Sorry to bother you, Mr. Harwood," came the standard apology from the doorman. "I've got a Peter L. Snowden, Special Agent Snowden, down here . . . wants to come up."

"Huh? What time is it?"

"Two o'clock, sir."

"Snowden? Have you checked his I.D.?"

"Yes, sir. Driver's license and government I.D. with picture. Department of the Treasury, Secret Service—Special Investigations."

"Okay, send him up."

The doorman hung up the phone and motioned the visitor in the direction of the elevators. "Fifth floor, 502," he commented tersely. Before the man could leave, the old man asked, "Hey, since when does a Secret Service agent have an accent like that? Where you from?"

"Ireland," replied Willie, towering over the uniformed doorman. "I'm Irish."

Before he reached the elevators, his friend approached the doorman silently from behind, sharpened knife held firmly in a black-gloved left hand. With his right arm crooked around the doorman's head, it took only seconds for him to leave the doorman gurgling; his throat stabbed so that his violent screams were rendered silent. As he writhed on the floor, the air forced from his lungs whooshed through the cut in his throat, before it could get to the vocal chords and form words of distress.

"Nice job, Kelly," observed Willie, referring to Nick by a made-up name. "Stomp your feet around in the blood a little. Make sure you leave some good prints. And pull a couple of threads off your coat and drop 'em on the floor there."

Small discharges of air still emitted from the old man's throat in soft, vain whispers for aid, as the short man marched through the blood, looking down at the semi-conscious doorman who stared up at him through glazed, half-slit eyes.

"Should I do him a little more?" Nick asked.

Willie, furious, grabbed his short partner by the collar, and whispered, "Goddammit, Kelly, use the fuckin' accent, would you!" he whispered. "Why the hell did we practice it? Don't stick him again, you dumb shit. He's gotta live to tell 'em it was Irish guys."

Watching the oozing blood form a rusty cowl around the doorman's head, Nick smiled. "I can't help it. I get so excited when I do someone, it's hard to remember. Plus, there ain't nobody around."

"We're Irish, you Brooklyn asshole. Start acting like it!" Willie hissed through clenched teeth.

Riding the elevator, Nick asked, "Why do we hafta cut this time. I mean, I like cutting and everything, but we could just shoot him at the door and be done with it, ya know?"

"No fuckin' noise."

The men emerged from the elevator, looked up and down the hallway, selected a direction and proceeded, checking door numbers as they walked. Reaching 502, they stood carefully away from the peephole, heads leaned in toward the door, listening. After half a minute of silence, the tall man nodded, and his buddy tapped lightly on the door.

Seconds later, as the door swung open, to reveal Tony standing in white boxers and strap T-shirt, Battaglia blurted out. "Hey, man, why can't you use the phone like . . . ." His sentence was abbreviated by the men's knife-slashing attack.

Tony reeled back, shouting for Harwood, his forearms washed red and wet from the torrent of slashes. Screaming, he lunged for the tall man, grabbed him, and threw him over the sofa. The smaller attacker slashed furiously at Tony's face, head, and throat.

Tony fought back, grabbing the wrists of the little man, tossing him to his back and dropping a knee into his face.

"Augh," cried the man, as he struggled to release Battaglia's hands from his throat, "help me Willie!"

Willie recovered, leaping at Tony as Harwood and Krautchik emerged from the bedroom to see the blood-smeared men wrestling in the middle of the room.

Harwood wrenched the big man from Tony, now painted in scarlet. Tony spun, and grabbed the smaller man, twisting his arm and bending his wrist until there was a loud snap. The man wailed in pain. Krautchik screamed and ran for the phone.

Surprised by the appearance of the others, the intruders scrambled their way to the door, leaving the blood-drenched Battaglia panting on the floor, fists clenched, red streams gushing from his face, neck, and arms.

50

The sky overhead was coal black, the sun's challenge appearing only as a faint yellow glow, spreading horizontally behind the Federal buildings downtown.

Ralph Waldo Emerson Williams sat alone, reading, in the Oval Office, a worn Bible in his lap. The dark circles under his eyes bespoke nights without sleep.

For they are spirits of demons, performing signs, which go out to kings of the earth and of the whole world to gather them to the battle of that great day of God Almighty. Behold, I am coming as a thief. Blessed is he who watches, and keeps his garments, lest he walk naked and they see his shame. And he gathered them together to the place called in Hebrew Armageddon. Then the seventh angel poured out his bowl into the air, and a loud voice came out of the temple of heaven, from the throne, saying, 'It is done!'

His contemplation was terminated by the intercom.

"They're here, Mr. President."

"Thanks, Emily. Send them in."

Five dour countenances appeared at the doorway. The Team had assembled at the White House immediately after the attack at Harwood's apartment. They entered, took seats, and waited for the President to speak.

"I never thought I'd actually see the Apocalypse, but, folks, if this isn't it, it must be as close as it gets," he began.

The Team sat motionless, each one duly respectful, but more numb and afraid than deferential. No one spoke.

President Williams seemed to address himself as much as the assemblage. "I have attended the funerals of two great men. And, this morning, I spend an hour sitting by the bedside of another great man who, only by God's grace, was taken off the critical list this afternoon.

"Speaker Berkhardt, who served Arizona faithfully for thirty-eight years, was a loving husband and father, and orchestrated hundreds of egocentric, dysfunctional lawmakers into a body that could reason, discuss, and actually get things done. Sure, he had flaws and sure, he made mistakes, but maybe that just underscored the humanity of a fine man and fine servant to the people.

"Rec Calvin . . . classic, almost prototypical soldier, statesman, gentleman, and gentle man . . . he took a risk at my request, relying on my assurances, indeed my exhortations, and suffered a violent death. Then, I come close to having to bury my best friend, a man of grace and love, who has shaped my mind more than my body . . . Tony . . . to whom a negative or critical thought is more foreign than his third cousins in Sicily."

Williams dropped his head to his Bible and flipped pages for a few moments to a page marked by a small yellow adhesive note. He read aloud. "Matthew Twenty-five, forty," he began.

And the King will answer and say to them, 'Assuredly, I say to you, inasmuch as you did it to one of the least of these My brethren, you did it to Me.

He carefully closed the Book and, his head still down, began to cry, "I feel like this has been done to me, as much as to them. I feel poisoned, I feel shot, I feel stabbed."

The President's shoulders heaved, tears ran down his cheeks, cascading into his lap, and he whimpered. "And there's blood on my hands."

It was Stanley Harwood who, after a full minute that seemed an eternity, rose deliberately from his chair, and walked over to the crying President. He took the President's hands, pulled him gently to his feet. Then, he stepped back, as if to gauge the distance, extended his arms, put them around his shoulders, and gave Williams a tight hug.

After another eternal minute, he slowly disengaged, and stepped back. "Humanity is a burden, Mr. President," he said. "Love and sensitivity, they are burdens, too. But, what wonderful burdens they are! Sir, you're an inspiration to all of us. This office has had too many smiling hypocrites, preaching holiness, Teflon men, manipulative men, vacuous men . . . men biting their lower lips in magnificent displays of sincerity. This city is filled with men who spout adherence to meaningless laws, while they profit on the temple steps from trading in sacrificial animals . . . you didn't get to the Oval Office without realizing that.

"You, sir," Harwood continued, "are what this office needs, what this country needs, and what this team needs. Nothing is going to bring back Berkhardt or Calvin. Thank God, Tony will make it. Great leaders aren't remembered because they were perfect. Their greatness is forged out of adversity. They look ahead, not back. They feel pain, they make mistakes, they get hurt, but they recover and lead again."

Harwood backed up slowly to his chair and sat. The President wiped his eyes with his sleeve. "Thanks, Stan," he smiled. "I never knew you could compete with William Jennings Bryan in the oratory category."

Williams sat down, and looked each member in turn, carefully in the eyes. "Do you know what Tony whispered to me in the hospital this morning? He started to say something, and I pulled my chair close, and leaned my face close to his. I could hardly hear him, he talked in the softest whisper. He mumbled something like 'green branch', but I really couldn't understand it. So I got even closer, he forced a slight smile and said, '. . . sounded like a green branch.' Then he said, 'Go get 'em boss', and fell back to sleep. What could 'green branch' mean?"

Stan Harwood let out a truncated laugh, breaking some of the tension.

"Stan?" the President asked.

"Well, sir, Tony once told me about a Rumanian weight-lifter who was pushing more iron than his body could stand. Seems he went into this sort of half-squat to press the weight over his head. He grunted, made some huge effort to stand, and his entire body began, at first, to tremble. Then, as he struggled to push the weight up, he flushed bright red, shook violently, and then his leg snapped in two. Literally. Everyone said later that it sounded like a new, green tree branch had broken. It was a crisp, high-pitched snap that resounded all over the arena. Years later, that sound—a large, green tree branch snapping in half, was still the talk of the weight-lifting circuit. For some, it was haunting, for others it was humorous."

Harwood sat still with a half-smile on his face, the President asked, "And . . . ?"

"I'm sorry, sir, but if Tony said that, I know he's going to be okay. During the attack at my apartment, Tony grabbed this little guy's arm and sort of flipped him, then jumped on him. They were struggling, grunting and groaning, when all of a sudden, I swear, the guy's arm must have broken in half. It sounded exactly what you'd think a green tree branch might sound like when it snapped under pressure. As if you had a large, fresh tree limb lying on the ground, and, if you put your foot on one end and pulled up on the other end up as far as it would go, the green limb would continue to bend for a long way, much further than an old, dead limb. But when the green limb finally gives way, it has its own unique snap. That was the sound when Tony and these guys were wrestling. Like Tony's old pals, I guess the sound is either disgusting or amusing, depending on who you are and where you sit. Right now, I find it kind of amusing, myself."

51

His short partner lay in shock in the back seat, groaning, a blood-soaked towel wrapped around his arm and wrist. "Okay, Nick, hold on," Willie said.

Despite Nick's pain and loss of blood, the tall killer carefully observed the speed limits making his way to Greater Southeast's emergency room. He pulled to an abrupt halt in the circular driveway, and dragged Nick from the car. With Nick slumped against him, he hurried past the receptionist, down the hall, tossing the little guy on an examination table. As a nurse approached, Willie stuck his index finger in her face and demanded, "Fix this guy up. I'll be back."

Leaving Nick moaning on the gurney, Willie fled to his car and drove to a pay phone at the edge of a convenience store parking lot.

Bernard Cartwright sat, depressed and confused, his world collapsing around him. When the phone rang, he snatched it from its cradle, not wanting to speak to anyone, but in an automatic move to cease the painful ringing.

"Hello?"

"Mr. Cartwright, it's your 'Irish consultant'."

"What do you want?"

"Hey, as I said, you got problems, we got solutions."

"I wish I'd never met with you. Go away."

"It's a little late for that."

"What the hell does that mean?" Cartwright demanded.

"Now, that's not a very nice tone of voice to use with your subcontractors."

"You aren't my subcontractors! Leave me alone."

"Aw . . . we thought you'd be happy that we fixed your little problem. See, we're self-starters."

Cartwright gulped hard and stretched his neck. "What in God's name are you talking about?"

Willie chuckled to himself at Nick's creativity. "Let's take the fucker out, then go to Cartwright for some money," Nick had suggested. "We'll do the hit before we've got the deal. It'll be kinda like guaranteeing a contract. A little bit of hit and a little bit of extortion."

Willie growled, "You said this Harwood guy figured things out, that he was putting together the pieces. You said something had to be done."

"That was just talk, you crazy bastard!"

"Maybe not that crazy."

"What the hell are you talking about?"

"Your man. We took him out."

"You what!" Cartwright screamed.

"Sliced him up pretty good. 'Cept for Nick's arm, it went okay. The doorman'll be eating through a hole in his neck for awhile, but he'll live . . . and testify that the killers had Irish accents. The Micks strike again, huh?"

Cartwright squeezed his eyes shut, his face contorted, and his entire body heaved. "Go away! Never call me again, you hear me?"

"Sure. Now, what about our money?" the killer laughed.

"What money?"

"Two hundred thou, old bills."

Cartwright slammed the receiver against the desk, putting a deep dent in the mahogany, and groaned as if punched in the stomach. Still bent over, he returned the phone to his ear, and screamed, "You guys are insane! I had nothing to do with this, and you're not getting any money!"

"Two days," came the threat. "Two hundred grand, or you'll hear Irish accents."

"Fuck you," spat Cartwright.

"Hey, know how many lawyers there are in this country? A million fuckin' lawyers! And, if we don't get paid quick, you're gonna need a few of them guys."

Cartwright rubbed his eyes. They burned, as if splashed with a caustic liquid.

"Hey, Mister Bigshot, you shoulda told us that Pillsbury doughboy was a fighter, and we'd just shot him. That muscle-bound shrimp was tough!"

"Short and muscle bound?" Cartwright whispered. "A thick-necked guy with dark curly hair?"

"Yeah. Shit, we shoulda planned this one better. One tough cookie, that Harwood. Fucked up Nick pretty good. Jesus, the fuckin' bone was sticking right out of his arm."

"You idiot lunatics didn't even kill the right guy! That wasn't Harwood, that's the President's best friend! A professional weight-lifter!"

"A legit strong man, huh? No wonder. Nick'll feel better knowing it wasn't some office puke. Harwood musta been the guy who came running in during the hit. Want us to go back? Nick wants to have cards printed up: 'We don't charge *you*, 'til the job is done and *through*.' Get it? It rhymes."

"My God . . . please go away. Far away for a long time."

"Sure, Mr. Cartwright. Soon as we get our two hundred grand. And we'll go back and finish Harwood, or take off twenty-five grand. One seventy-five, we go away."

"Go to fucking hell!" Cartwright screeched.

"Ooooh, tough words. Forty-eight hours. Erin Go Bragh, Mr. Cartwright. Ha, ha, ha . . . ."

Bernard Cartwright, former Wall Street lawyer and current Republican presidential campaign chairman, winced and shook his head, as Willie's laughter faded away.

Returning to the hospital, the tall assassin pulled into a distant space in the emergency room parking lot and began checking his watch every couple of minutes. After forty-five minutes, he eased his car to the front door and, leaving the car running and the driver's door open, he entered the building. He scanned the Saturday night waiting room, jammed with friends and family of car accident victims, knife fighters, the drug-overdosed, and the drunk.

Marching down the hall, Willie furiously opened doors and pulled aside curtains, shouting, in an Irish accent, "Kelly! Where are ya?"

Finding Nick in a surgical recovery area, Willie dragged him to his feet, as a nurses and orderlies descended upon them. Pushing them aside, he supported his semi-conscious friend down the hall toward the exit and waiting car.

A bold nurse shouted, "Stop! This man is badly injured. You can't move him!" Then she grabbed Nick's good arm, instigating a brief tug of war, lasting only until Willie smashed his fist into her face, blood spewing from her nose and mouth, and drenching her starched white uniform as she lay spread-eagle on the polished linoleum floor.

A crowd of visitors and emergency room employees trailed the men to the exit, when a billing clerk ran from an office, stood in front of them, arms akimbo, and demanded, "You can't take that man out of here. We haven't gotten his insurance information yet!"

With one arm supporting his groaning friend, Willie pulled a pistol from his trouser pocket, and shoved it in the clerk's face.

"Here's my insurance information. I'm covered by the forty-five caliber HMO special."

The clerk plummeted to the floor. Willie stepped over her, dragging Nick behind. The automatic doors opened, and he turned, waved the gun, and fired a shot into the floor next to the cowering clerk. "Bill me for the co-pay," he laughed.

As they stumbled out, Willie heard sirens wailing and saw flashing blue lights racing from across the parking lot. Leaving Nick tottering on the sidewalk, he ran around the car and, one foot inside, aimed at Nick.

"Sorry, buddy," he whispered, then pumped a shot into Nick's chest, leaving the gasping little man standing saucer-eyed and bobbing like a drunken Popeye doll. Willie's tires squealed as he fishtailed around a corner and disappeared.

52

"Let's get some order out of this chaos, Team," said the President. "Stan, can you summarize where we are?"

Harwood pulled a massive folder from a leather document case beside his chair. "First, about the Vice President," he began. "He's broken immigration laws, with all his comings and goings. And, he's admitted taking money from Cartwright. But as to complicity in murder, the FBI thinks he's clean. He's cooperating fully, hoping for the best. He's knows he'll be charged and, so far, he's okay with that. I swear, he's like a changed man. The money he took has been accounted for. He deposited most of it into a dummy bank account in New York, with a Social Security number from a dead person. The FBI is tracing the source of the money now."

"Will that be a dead end?"

"Maybe not. Looks like everything came through an accounting firm, a storefront bookkeeper in New York. Their number is disconnected, and the office wiped clean. But the agents say they've got plenty of leads. They're just getting started, really."

"How deep do we think this goes, Stan?" asked the President.

"There're lots of unanswered questions. O'Malley claims Cartwright first approached him and that O'Malley took it from there. His says he was supposed to come out publicly in favor of a casino tax, and issue a press release . . . also, make some speeches about how a federal tax would provide a great new revenue source—billions apparently—and wouldn't harm anybody but a bunch of big casino companies. He promised Cartwright he'd urge the Speaker to at least schedule hearings, and, ideally, come out in favor of the tax. He's a little vague on some stuff. Says he even handed out cash at cocktail receptions, so things are a little blurry, I guess."

"I'm glad he's helping, and just as happy he's clean and healthy, " Williams offered.

"He's on the wagon, but I'm not sure if 'healthy' is an appropriate adjective," Harwood said. "Let's just say the trend of the line is in the right direction."

"What's he know about the murders?"

"According to him, nothing," Harwood continued. He says he had three meetings and several phone calls with Cartwright. In the second meeting, he promised he'd play ball. Later on, some more money changed hands and Cartwright blew up at him for not doing more."

"You believe him?"

"So far he appears credible, and he's passed two polygraphs. He said his deal with Cartwright sounded pretty harmless to him. Says he told Cartwright that he's into the ponies himself, and pursuing the tax would be like getting paid to do something he might have done anyway. Innocent stuff, he thought."

"Deadly innocent," remarked Williams.

"And all the more ironic since O'Malley never did anything, other than spread a little money around on the Hill. He never even met with Berkhardt, and didn't take any public position."

"Whoever bought him didn't get much for his money," the President observed.

"His money, their money, or her money," Krautchik observed.

President Williams smiled. "Right. So where's that leave us with Cartwright?"

"I read both his depositions," said Harwood, "and watched a video-tape interview. He says he doesn't know anything . . . claims O'Malley's brain is pickled. The guy gives me the creeps, though. Here's this famous lawyer and, every time he's asked a question, he takes about a minute to answer, only then after consulting with his high-priced attorneys. He spends most of the deposition wiping sweat off his face with a monogrammed hankie."

"But right now, it's O'Malley's word against Cartwright's," said Krautchik.

"Yeah," Harwood said, "but something's going to get smoked out pretty soon. Plus, some people might think that O'Malley's word against Cartwright's is a poor match, but as for me, I'll take O'Malley's word any day."

"God, what a mess Cartwright turned out to be. Debacle is a euphemism. Is he fully out?" Williams asked.

"Yes, sir," Harwood answered. "Your memo's been distributed to everyone, and his office is locked and quarantined, guarded by two FBI guys full time. We even installed an extra door lock, so it's a two-key entry system now. We're not going to have any Fawn Halls or Vince Fosters. The hard drives from his office and home computers are at the FBI lab, and we've got a collection of floppy disks from both places. We've also got all his phone records: home, office, cell, calling card, everything. The analysis is just starting. We should hear something within forty-eight hours."

"Is that everything?"

"Pretty much . . . other than bank and financial records, and we'll have those soon."

Krautchik interrupted, "The coroner has officially reversed his finding of accidental death on the Speaker. it's now officially a homicide. A team from Justice informed the family yesterday."

"Listen," the President said, "connect a couple of more dots for me. How does Calvin's murder fit into this?"

Stan Harwood spoke. "We've discussed this until we're blue in the face . . . here's the best we've got. Somebody desperately wants a casino tax. Through Cartwright, they buy O'Malley, thinking he's got a lot more swing than he does, or maybe than he cares to use. O'Malley sits on it, having taken their money. Then, suddenly, O'Malley gets booted from the ticket. Now they're in real trouble. They've got no one in a position of influence, no one that can make anything happen. Maybe they figured with Calvin dead, we'd somehow take back O'Malley. Or they're the kind of people who get really pissed and, just to prove how tough they are, they take out Calvin. A vengeance killing."

"Either way, it's irrational," said Williams. "They're either crazy or they've got one hell of a lot at stake."

"Maybe both," Harwood continued. "We're coming up empty on everything else . . . still running down leads, but it's dead end after dead end. No Democratic conspiracy, no KKK, no separatists, blacks, no embittered Republicans. The casino tax is the most promising thing we've got."

"Vengeance," the President speculated, "is a huge risk, I mean, just for being mad. I'd feel better with a more concrete motive. How about the Speaker situation?"

"That makes more sense, sir," said Harwood. "He was the key to any tax legislation. He could schedule hearings or not . . . do darned well whatever he wanted. He'd decided to stick the issue in his pocket, letting it die. He told his chief of staff he was against it, and that was that. Having him out of the way, these people could get something done on the Hill."

"What about the Indian sacred lands issue?"

"Working with BIA and Interior, the Bureau has interviewed the caciques—that's kind of like their secular chief—of every Southwestern tribe that has a major claim. Berkhardt was the Indian's ally, and none of the caciques nor anyone on the Speaker's staff can imagine anyone who's so opposed to land repatriation. The major obstacles, as it turns out, are with departments in the federal government."

"Mr. President," offered Krautchik, "we've culled hundreds and hundreds of leads these past few days. I've set up a database and been up all night doing keyword searches and sorts."

"And?"

"A New York casino stock trader has called a couple of dozen times. He's hit every law enforcement agency in the country, including a number of calls to the SEC. The guy has actually moved into the Hotel Washington. He personally visits the White House guardhouse every day begging to see someone. Says he knows who did it."

"Maybe he's just another crackpot crime theorist."

"We ran a background," said Harwood, "and he's totally clean. No mental illness, no axes to grind, except he lost his job over this casino thing."

Williams was amused. "No mental illness and no axes to grind? Must be the only one in Washington" he deadpanned.

"Yes, sir," replied Harwood, restraining a grin. "We're interviewing him this afternoon."

"He's made it easy enough by moving in a block away. Does the man have a name?"

"Lewis Calendar, Mr. President. Until he was fired, he was a top gun, blue blood investment guy. He's screaming to anyone who'll listen that there's a major money player manipulating the market."

"Sounds like Aesop's fox . . . sour grapes," observed Williams.

"Maybe, but this might connect with the tax and Berkhardt's death. Maria's talked with the SEC. They're only a couple of days into it, but say they smell smoke. No fire, yet, but enough empirical data—stock price movements, that stuff – to assign three more analysts to the project."

"Lots of stones to turn over," the President said.

"Yes, sir," said Harwood. "And when we flip them over, we're going to find some creepy, crawly things underneath."

53

Despite his ample self-assuredness and sophistication, Lew Calendar barely believed he was at the White House, sitting with a cup of coffee, talking with two real-live agents. Personal vindication was far from his mind. He wanted to tell his story to some independent party—someone other than Sally—who'd listen and, he prayed, believe.

A lined legal pad and several sharpened pencils sat neatly arranged in the middle of the conference room table. In front of Milbury was a small tape recorder. Next to Calendar's chair sat a large briefcase. The case had been taken from Calendar upon entering the building and, he assumed, thoroughly examined. In fact, in its thirty-minute absence, every page had been carefully photographed, and the case itself examined with infrared camera and x-ray. Fingerprints were taken from the handle and a couple of places inside the case.

"Thanks for coming in, Mr. Calendar," Harwood began.

"I'm Stanley Harwood and this is Agent Tom Milbury, with the Secret Service. I head up a small task force that coordinates information and communicates directly with the President. We're looking at the assassinations of Speaker Berkhardt and Senator Calvin, as well as an attack on Mr. Anthony Battaglia, a White House staff member."

"I've read about all that, Mr. Harwood. It's a relief for someone to take the time to listen to me. Everyone else in the world thinks I'm crazy."

"Mr. Calendar, I assure you we're interested in what you have to say. I'm afraid we can't share with you any details of our investigation, but I'm sure you understand."

"Absolutely! I want to help. I've tried to work this puzzle myself, only I'm missing about three quarters of the pieces."

"Before starting," said Harwood, "I'd like your permission to tape this session. You may, of course, refuse, and I stress that you are appearing voluntarily, and are yourself under no suspicion in relation to these events."

"Heck no, tape away! Heck, I've spent the last week on the phone and taking taxis around Washington trying to get to this point."

Harwood emitted a small, sincere laugh. "Yes, sir, we know. It's not every day we encounter folks with your kind of perseverance, Mr. Calendar. Now, Agent Milbury is going to turn on the tape recorder, and I'm going to ask some questions. Just relax and tell us your story in your own words. If you don't understand something, just say so."

"Got it!" replied Calendar with unrestrained enthusiasm.

A small red light showed on the tape recorder when Milbury pushed the 'record' button.

"Mr. Calendar, you are appearing here voluntarily, at your own request?"

"Yes, sir."

"Please state whether these facts are true: and, please don't nod or say 'uh huh' or 'uh uh', because the tape doesn't pick that up very well. Just true or false, yes and no, okay?"

"True!" cried Calendar. Harwood, grinning, glanced at Milbury. They knew they had a live one.

"You were born in Morristown, New Jersey, your age is thirty-nine, you attended high school and college in Massachusetts, then the University of Pennsylvania's Wharton Graduate School. Your current residence is 4876 Winding Oak Way, Short Hills, New Jersey. Until September eighth, you were a senior partner with Amerco Securities, 114 Wall Street, New York City."

"Yup . . . I mean, all true."

"Until terminated by Amerco, you managed a segment of their equity trading business, specializing in casino stocks."

"Well, it's casino stocks that got me here . . . got me in trouble, but I trade all kinds of lodging and entertainment stocks, or used to. I trade Marriott, SFX, Westwood One . . . even had a big position in Gaylord once . . . the Grand Ole Opry folks, you know. Thank God they finally got a guy like Mike Rose in there."

"Yes, okay, Nashville . . . now, you bought and sold stocks, bonds, and options contracts on casino and entertainment companies."

"Nearly all options of one kind or another."

"Your termination was due to large losses in casino securities."

"Yes, true."

"You told our phone investigator that you'd lost about a $110 million and, by the way, we've confirmed that with Mr. Patrick Sternberg of Amerco. Mr. Sternberg, according my notes, had nothing but the highest regard for you—and your integrity."

"In our business, Mr. Harwood, high regard and a buck gets you ten shiny dimes."

"Not unlike a lot of places, Mr. Calendar. Now, how did you come to call us . . . with your legendary perseverance?"

Well, I started in utility bonds, but there's no action there.

Calendar snapped his head to the side, closed his eyes, and feigned a loud snore to emphasize his point.

I moved to oils, large cap stocks, but predictable stuff. Then I figured I could make a lot in casino stocks. I took a huge risk. I mean, the market caps of Exxon and BP are nearly two hundred billion each, and that's before the Exxon-Mobil and BP-Amoco deals. Shell, Arco, and Chevron together are maybe another four hundred billion. And the market value of the entire casino industry—everybody in the business—is probably thirty billion. But, they're a lot more volatile than other stocks, and quick swings in price are the traders' friend. Plus, when I got in, nobody else was paying much attention to them. I was the one-eyed man in the kingdom of the blind.

The casino industry was growing like hell. Our investment banking guys, the light bulb heads, wanted a presence in the trading market, so they could pitch investment banking business with a little credibility. Drexel and later DLJ controlled the business, and the underwriting spreads were really attractive. Even after the industry stopped growing, merger speculation—they call it 'rationalization'—Mirage, that stuff, kept volatility and trading volume strong.

Calendar looked across the table at Milbury and Harwood, their faces blank, emotionless. He wondered if he might as well be speaking Latin.

"Uh, if any of this throws you, just say so and I'll slow down. Otherwise, I'll just move along."

"We'd be kidding, if we said we understood everything, but we'll figure it out. Just keep going."

Calendar picked up his briefcase and withdrew some computer summaries.

Beginning around May, the relationship between casino stock prices and their options began changing in a way that couldn't be explained by the normal volatility of trading and risk. Simply, the shares reflected their intrinsic values—a normal buy-and sell marketplace—but put and call price started getting out of line. I didn't smell a rat then. I smelled money. This can happen in any market, but it usually only lasts only a day or so . . . sometimes just a couple of hours. The object of the exercise—I call it that rather than the 'game'—is to take advantage of temporary anomalies in the market . . . exploit non-economic, dis-economic relationships between related securities, that is, stocks and their options. So, I started increasing my position, expecting the market would right itself naturally.

In this business, you're satisfied to make a few cents, over and over again, a billion or so times—and pretty soon, like Ol' Senator Dirksen used to say, it's big money.

By early July, I thought I was in the catbird seat, waiting for someone to cry 'ouch', and cover their positions. But there's no correction and my partners start shitting bricks. But, I am so damned sure of myself, I just add to my positions, taking more risk on the same side of the market.

Now, it's late July and my partners fire a warning shot across my bow. They're scared, and they're more scared that I'm not scared. In truth, I'm scared, but I'm trained not to show it. They should know that by now, but they don't. Go figure.

Calendar continued to consult his printouts, flipping through pages to hone his recollection.

By mid-August, I'm the talk of the entire firm: Lew Calendar has lost the touch. The arrogant son of a bitch will sink the whole ship. He's finally getting what he deserves. He's got problems with white lines, martinis, his marriage, you name it. Nobody's looking at the realities, and I don't guess they should. All that matters is can you generate a buck. And I agree with that. I not only wasn't generating any bucks, I was sending them out the door with red ribbons. A hundred million of them! Well, the friggin' markets never correct like I say, I lose another ten million, and I'm canned. They close out my positions, take the loss, and I'm on the front of

Investor's Daily *and the* Wall Street Journal.

"You're registered at the Washington Hotel as Steven Browne? Is that to dodge Fortune and Forbes?'

"Exactly! A couple of hundred million isn't that much, but, if you add in the name of Lew Calendar, the fair-haired, boy wonder of Wall Street, and toss in casino stocks . . . now *that's* a story!"

"So, Mr. Calendar, why are you the only one on Wall Street who's stepped in this pile of stuff and dirtied his wingtips?"

"Oh, there're others who've been burned—I know a bunch of them— but they got out, couldn't stand the heat. A few hundred thousand of losses, maybe more, and it's saya-friggin-nara. At this point, they're looking a lot smarter than me."

"Do you have any information that actually proves that there's foul play going on? Other than the prices of these stocks? Has anything illegal actually taken place?"

Calendar smiled. "Taking positions without adequate capital, moving funds around to create the appearance of capital, or presenting fraudulent financial statements, hidden borrowing against securities . . . all that violates some law or regulation, SEC, OCC—that's the Controller of the Currency— or the Federal Reserve Bank.

"But specific knowledge of manipulation of these markets?"

"It happens, maybe not on this scale, but it happens. Troubles at companies like Glittergrove, Systems of Excellence, Citron, and Healthcare International have been covered by the Journal. Prosecutors have claimed mob influence in other stock manipulations recently."

"You think there's organized crime here? Russian maybe?" Milbury asked.

"Anything's possible, of course, but it doesn't seem like their kind of work. First of all, the numbers here are really big. To create this kind of imbalance, it takes hundreds of millions, if not billions . . . not just a few million here and there. Stock manipulators usually deal with penny stock stuff, over-the-counter, pink sheet companies, lots with phony high tech names. They go after small companies with little or no substance—maybe like a Heartsoft— sometimes no actual business. They pump them up through disreputable broker-dealers, then let the air out—like mining stocks in the old days—here today, gone tomorrow. 'Pump 'n' Dump' they call it. Or they're doing IPOs, usually by merging some fancy-named company they created into an already public shell company. The stocks I trade are big, New York Stock Exchange companies with CEOs that are reputable lawyers and MBAs."

"But still, no hard evidence?"

"No, but you need to understand how powerful this financial information is. Maybe it's jungle drums or smoke signals to you, but it's plain English—in capital letters—to me. These numbers are all I need to know somebody's screwing with these stocks. Why? Who? I don't know. Except, I can tell you, as sure as my name is Steve Browne—a little joke there, guys, just to see if you're still listening—Lewis Calendar, Junior, that it's not anyone in the casino business, and it's not the mob. And I'll bet good money that it's not anyone on the Street."

"I think you already have bet good money, Mr. Calendar."

"Uh, good point."

"I'm impressed with your insights," Harwood continued, "but help us out here. We've got unimaginable resources at our beck and call. We've got the FBI, SEC, Treasury, CIA, Interpol, you name it. But where the hell do we start?"

"Every trade I make, every time I sell or buy, there's a contra trade—someone on the other side. Most of my trades have been with big legitimate houses, you know, Merrill Lynch, Salomon-Smith Barney, those types. No way they're going to intentionally get into something like this, but there's no way they're going to surrender customers' names to me either. So I've been digging, using up my old chits, trying to figure out where these trades are originating."

"Exactly what we need," Milbury said.

"Okay, but I've got information coming out of my ears." Calendar pulled out a hand-written list of names. "Here are the places I've heard these trades are originating. Try this on for size: Andorra, St. Kitts, Nevis, Gibraltar, Belize, Antigua, Bahamas, the Isle of Man, the Channel Islands, Monaco, and Switzerland, of course, Guernsey and Jersey—must be the dairy Mafia—Sark, Malta, and Panama."

"Time for a world tour," Harwood joked.

"I'll narrow things down, because some of this stuff has come from good sources. I'm told these trades are being directed from three specific places. First, a legit Grand Cayman trust company. A customer is probably executing trades through them. Another trader I play squash with talked with his clearance people—the back office guys. They say a numbered trust account at a Panamanian bank gives orders to the Cayman bank. They whispered that we should start with the Commercial Trust and National Trading Company of Panama. TNT it's called, probably for good reason."

"I recall stories about Panamanian banks washing Colombian cartel drug money," Milbury ventured. "Maybe this is a laundering scheme."

"They'd certainly have the cash, but it doesn't make sense. Why would they draw attention to themselves like this? They'd rather buy a couple of billion of T-Bills. It'd probably never be noticed."

"Banks and trust companies in the jurisdictions you mentioned are like sand at the beach," Harwood said. "I'd hate to check them and their securities trades at random."

"I think that together we can do it! Listen," Calendar continued "I realize what I've been through is nothing like what those guys—Battaglia, Berkhardt, and that poor Senator Calvin—experienced. If I thought so, I'd be the self-centered bastard that half the Street thinks I am. Whoever's doing this is one smart cookie. You'd have to sit where I've sat for the past several months to appreciate that. I've lost a ton of money, but tracking down the person who poisons, shoots people, stabs them, and slices their throats . . . that's ultimately what this is all about."

"Mr. Calendar," Harwood said, "you may be the one who'll end up getting the hero's medal here."

"That's fine . . . but let me get onto the rest. The second group of trades is supposedly going through a penny ante storefront broker in LA called Wonderink Securities. I'm told they're executing trades for numbered accounts in the Channel Islands and Bahamas. There's supposed to be a guy named Mickey or Johnny who executes the trades, but he's just a cover. Orders originate at a New York law firm called Tyler & Cohen. I checked, and couldn't find such a firm. Wonderink, on directions from the law firm, executes trades and debits funds at a L.A. bank. The bank, in turn, draws against letters of credit on a Bahamas accounts."

"Whew," cried Milbury. "Are we going to be able to sort all this stuff out?"

"Well," replied Calendar, "it's multi-level for a purpose. As for the Gordian Knot, I'll give you the biggest knife I have, but you'll have to do the cutting."

"Well spoken, Mr. Calendar. What else?" Harwood asked.

"I've researched Wonderink. It actually exists. A hole-in-the wall, three-branch outfit. One guy claims Wonderink has a close relationship with a Panamanian bank of questionable reputation. That has to be TNT."

"Who's the third group?"

"Orders have also come from a big, legitimate Canadian bank. Seems they act as an agent, just holding and disbursing funds, giving orders to buy and sell. It's said their client is a Channel Islands company."

"The Canadians should be cooperative," Harwood said. He turned to Milbury. "Tom, we'll need to talk to people at Treasury and State about how we act in these jurisdictions. We'll also need highest level support at the SEC and the IRS. Thanks a lot, Mr. Calendar. If it's no burden, we'd appreciate your staying in Washington and being available, if we need you."

"As a retired man, I'm rather enjoying my time here. My wife is seeing the Smithsonian for the first time in twenty years. We're even thinking about pulling the kids out of school and bringing them down. And again, with no disrespect to the guys that got killed, I'd like to get my own reputation back. So I've got a horse—I guess maybe a miniature pony—in this race, too."

54

Bernard Cartwright did not understand—could not understand—the forces at work on him: joining the first Williams campaign, moving to Washington, glowing in the inebriation of a new type of authority. For more than four years, he had paraded in the corridors of power, summoning a meeting or telephone conversation with a cabinet member, general, senator, or congressman on a moment's notice. Or even a whim.

Cartwright was proud. And, like in most men, that pride, at best, simmers. At worst, it is a cauldron of hubris boiling over in self-destruction. Now, his White House office was under armed guard, while he sat, nearly cataleptic, in his home-office lair, with dozens of messages from Chris Weiner and reporters clogging his answering machine.

Washington power differed from that which cloaked Cartwright as an eminent Wall Street law partner, recognized for brokering mergers between America's largest firms. When a mega-deal was underway, whether between computer, health care, or telecommunications giants, he always successfully marshaled and deployed his forty years of knowledge and experience.

Here, two hundred and twenty miles south, Cartwright's power was more associative than actual. His ability to maintain respect was a function not of what he knew or could produce, but of whom he stood next to or was seen with at political and social functions. Intelligence and experience were *useful* tools here, to be sure, but not *important* tools. In the District, Cartwright's power was a mere mental *trompe l'oeil*. An evanescent, surreal illusion of worth and significance, fated to remain one-dimensional, always pleasing the eye, sometimes pleasing the mind, but never pleasing the soul.

Bernard Cartwright, Yale scholar and ever-enthusiastic alumnus, brilliant lawyer, devoted leader of countless civic and charitable efforts throughout his career, poured another glass of wine and gulped down half of it. The '93 Opus One was by now nearly tasteless, his tongue sensing only residual tannin, his glass now a vehicle for continued self-medication, a delivery system for the mind-numbing alcohol.

His pride was like a larva, at first insignificant, but chemically coded, through some sort of genetic promise, to assume a radically different form. It lay in wait, assuming the guises of self-esteem and self-confidence, until accorded an opportunity to form a chrysalis of arrogance. And, if and when the environment became favorable, it metamorphically transformed into fully-winged, mature hubris, that, with no ability to reflect in the mirror of truth, sailed blithely on the winds of power. Thus adorned with hubris, Cartwright glided, believing that the winds were *his* winds, convinced he was endowed with the power to control its direction, thus his destiny—until those same winds turned violent and foul, buffeting him to the ground, breaking his wings, and defiling all his transitory glory.

Human conflict is as old as man himself, reaching into the most secret places of the human heart where self dissolves rational purpose and where pride reigns. History is strewn with great leaders who failed. Lee at Gettysburg. Or Wellington, great in generalship, failed in politics and government. Great leaders are self-confident, never prideful. And, in defeat, they still understand the dimensions of their own humanity, whether in the glow of success or the gloaming of failure.

Bernard Cartwright was not endowed with an ability to reckon his own humanity, nor could he comprehend the humanity of his fellow man. His inability to relate to, and revel in, the dignity and aspirations of the human spirit may have been a curse, or it may have been the absence of a blessing. It did not matter. Cursed or unblessed, Cartwright was, once allured by the arcane attractions of America's capital, inevitably vulnerable to its sirens.

But in Washington there is no Circe to warn, to tell him to fill his ears with wax or tie himself to the mast. Beckoning with songs of sex, money, and politics, the enchantresses of power drew his vessel, inexorably, toward the rocks.

With an unsteady hand, he clutched his glass, draining it before setting it down on the mahogany desk. The same hand punched the buttons on his phone. He leaned back and listened to the disembodied robotic voice of the telephone company: *You have . . . fifty-six . . . new messages.*

Jesus, twenty-six messages since I checked them an hour ago. Gotta be half from Weiner, half from the press. Maybe one from Suzy. Message number . . . one . . . sent at . . . one . . . fifteen . . . a.m . . . *Bernie, I'm telling you, you'd better call me quick! Where the fuck are you, anyway? I'd better hear from you tonight! You hear me, goddamit?*

Even in his stupor, Cartwright noticed how his wine consumption failed to render Weiner's voice any less strident. She was brassy, brilliant, and beautiful. But the abrasive, dissonant sounds that issued from her mouth, that soft, wet mouth. What a contrast: the sensuous, magical mouth and the whining shrieks. Now, her screeching and her scheming were over. And he would be through with his own deceit: his own pretense, his perfidy, his grand masquerade.

So, me and Weiner . . . rumors surrounded Foster? Was that thick-legged co-dependent enabler really sleeping with him? No such rumors about me . . . not lying in some Capital park . . . no questions about me being moved, the bullet's trajectory, the lack of blood. My White House office ransacked by the FBI. By now, everything found. But here, at home, my office and my windows are locked from the inside. Here I may be devastated, destroyed . . . but I have my own solitary security . . . my own peace . . . my own solution to the complicated puzzles . . . not like New York . . . here in a labyrinth . . . devoured by the mighty Minotaur on the Potomac . . . no more lies . . . no more doubt . . . .

Cartwright was deep in the labyrinth, but there was no Ariadne for this Theseus. His ball of thread was the 1993 Opus One, two cases received as a gift from his former law partners. With no savior to lead him from his self-constructed maze, his solution was a central nervous system depressant . . . more gloriously disinhibiting wine.

He reached for the phone again, awkwardly, to re-play his messages, then abruptly stopped, gazing at the most recently opened bottle. It, like the previous two, was empty. He reached under his desk, pulled another from a cardboard case, briefly contemplating the label before stripping the lead cover, clumsily pulling the cork, and spilling wine into his lap. He had not approached the phone during its incessant ringing, touching it only to check messages, every one betokening, reinforcing his fall. He suddenly wondered why he would want to hear Weiner's voice again. Ever. Cartwright pondered the inefficiency of listening to the messages again. That would not be a good use of my time, he thought.

Irrational. Drunk. Depressed. Discovered. Destroyed.

Cartwright had not eaten nor slept in nearly forty-eight hours. Nor had he showered, shaved, or changed clothes. In the earliest hours of this pilgrimage, Bernard Cartwright prepared detailed lists allocating his most valued possessions. He had not noticed that each was a tangible symbol of his own lifelong struggle for material possessions and prestige: engraved plaques, sterling plates and crystal bowls commemorating achievements; photos with Presidents and foreign dignitaries; the 1960 300SL Roadster.

He threw his head back, mouth agape, staring at the ceiling. Its detailed molding spun in a blurry haze. Were he sober, he thought, this spinning would have made him sick. But he was too drunk, insensate, and sad to comprehend that, were he sober, he would not be sitting, head back, staring at a spinning ceiling.

At length, he sat up and ran his fingers through his tousled hair. He rubbed his unshaven face, more to determine if it was sufficiently abrasive to rasp the skin from the heels of his hands, than to gauge the age of the whiskers. He propped his elbows on the desk and buried his face in his hands.

For several minutes he remained nearly motionless, save a single glance to see if it was still there, polished and gleaming. It had not moved. It would not move on its own. He was neither surprised nor disappointed. Surveying the walls, President Williams' campaign chairman examined the certificates, photos, and hunting prints. Then, fixing his eyes on a small door across the room, he stood, stumbled to a closet, and rocking to and fro, considered its meager contents. Finally, he pulled dark blue sweater from the top shelf, and pulled it over his head, bracing himself with his hand on the corner of his desk when he nearly fell.

The renowned Wall Street attorney centered himself over his desk chair and let his weight fall freely into it, like a sack of wet sand, nearly toppling the chair. He looked down at the white 'Y' on his sweater, then slowly lifted his arms, examined the worn elbows, and picked clumsily at a loose strand of yarn. But for his pathetic absurdity, he might have appeared comic in his college letter sweater, now several sizes too small, clenching his torso and riding up over his porcine belly.

Abandoning his meaningless fingering of unraveled threads and moth holes, he dropped his head on the desk, looked for it again. It was still there, its twelve inches of satin stainless steel and its wood grip no further than the hand of an outstretched arm.

No more . . . fake . . . old . . . tired . . . failure . . . no matter . . . Suzy . . . confused . . . Chris . . . New York . . . pain . . . worthless . . . O'Malley . . . Washington . . . Calvin . . . so what . . . loss . . . losses . . . my friend the Smith and Wesson . . . the most expensive model . . . nothing but the best . . . fuck gun control . . . .

Cartwright sat up as much as his tired and drunken body would allow. He placed his hand over it, feeling its strength and power rush into him. Then, slowly, indeed as if in slow motion, his hand grasped it. His mind, barely communicating with the rest of his body, somehow sent instructions to his index finger which groped the wood grip and cool steel for the trigger guard.

The three-pound Smith & Wesson Classic Model 629 revolver lifted, the barrel moving gradually, gently, toward his head. He stabbed it against his right temple, then lazily scratched his head with the muzzle of the eight-inch barrel, as if to address a nagging itch, then dragged the .44's muzzle determinedly toward his mouth. He spun the six-chambered cylinder, then extended his arm, considering the weapon, admiringly. Then, opening his mouth only enough to admit it, he pushed the barrel into his mouth, closed his eyes, and sucked. His wrist rolled over, pointing the muzzle up at the roof of his mouth and, beyond, his brain.

Cartwright Roulette. A new game, but no game at all. Played only once. Russian Roulette is for pussies: one full chamber with five empty. Cartwright Roulette: six full chambers with none empty. Just spin the cylinder. Everybody's a winner.

The index finger of his right hand contracted slowly and deliberately.

Suzy was visiting their daughter, son-in-law, and six-month-old granddaughter in Philadelphia. Cartwright had dismissed the housekeeper, instructing her to stay away until she heard again from him personally. Thus, no one heard the sound of the cartridge exploding and propelling its lead payload through his head, scattering bits of brain, skull, and hair across the ceiling. Nor was there a witness to Cartwright's slumping onto the floor, where the cerise ooze from his head quickly spread, soaking his sweater, and transforming the white Yale "Y" to a russet-brown.

55

"Stan," Krautchik shouted, "we've just got a big break. We got a guy that attacked Battaglia!"

"What happened?"

"Remember when Tony broke one of the assailant's arms, you asked for a follow-up on that as a lead? Well, I sent out field teams and set up a telephone team. We visited hospitals, and called the ones we couldn't get to immediately, plus every orthopedist within a hundred miles."

"How'd you hit on the guy?"

"About three a.m., two guys came into Greater Southeast Community Hospital. Witnesses say they looked different from the regular Saturday night crowd: well-dressed and cool. One, a tall guy, spoke with an Irish accent. The little guy doesn't say anything, just looks kind of sick. Later, when he talks with the doctor, guess what? No Irish accent."

"The guy's got a broken arm?"

"Turns out 'broken arm' is a euphemism. Both his lower arm bones, ulna and radius, are snapped completely in half, and one bone is sticking straight out of the skin. The nurses took one look at the him and called an orthopedic resident on duty to operate on him immediately. After nearly an hour, they'd put one pin in his arm, and were waiting on an expert hand guy to come in."

"How'd we get them?" Harwood asked impatiently.

"Not them . . . him," Krautchik corrected. "Okay, this tall guy says they were in a bar fight, but the nurse noted that neither of them had been drinking. They're really calm, and there's no alcohol in the little guy's blood work."

"So where are they now?"

"The little guy's in custody at Greater Southeast, critical care. The bullet hit the upper part of his chest. They think he'll make it. The other guy got away."

"Slow down, Maria. What bullet?"

"Okay, the doctors were looking at some X-rays, getting ready to do more surgery on the little guy, when the other guy comes back—opening doors and pushing back curtains—looking for the little guy. The nurses are having a fit. So he finds his friend in surgical room, pulls him out, and starts walking him toward the door. Well, when our phone calls got a match at Greater Southeast, we called the blues. They were there within five minutes and, damn, they showed up with lights flashing and sirens screaming. That cowboy stuff just pisses the hell out of me, Stan. We explicitly told 'em, no lights, no sirens. Unmarked cars, if possible."

"Duh! Let me guess . . . the marked cars and blue uniforms come screaming in while the big guy is taking the little guy out. One guy splits, leaving his friend behind?"

"Precisely. The one with the broken arm is kneeling on the sidewalk outside the door, holding his arm, and coughing up blood. Seems his friend put a goodbye slug in him."

"Silence insurance. And the big guy?"

"Streaks across the hospital parking lot and disappears around a corner. A witness says he was driving a white or beige four-door, 1996 or later. Big help."

"The little guy?"

"They tried to get a statement, but no luck. It'd only help if he could direct us to his friend. No D.A. in his right mind would make a case on a statement from a guy full of Demerol who'd just gotten a pin in his arm and a bullet in his chest. We're running prints now."

"Keep out APBs from Philadelphia and Richmond. Cover airports, highway rest stops, train stations, everything. And get a sketch artist over to the hospital,"Harwood said. He paused, then added, "With O'Malley talking, and close to an arrest on Cartwright, it's looking a lot better."

"Plus, we're making progress on Calendar's stuff," Krautchik noted. "The SEC has already tied some big option trades to a couple of offshore accounts, right where Calendar said they'd be."

"Good work, darling. See you tonight."

"Big kiss . . . bye."

56

From the nurses' station they could look down the hall and see the swarm of uniformed officers and a several others in suits and ties congregated outside his room. Agent Snowden took the lead, "This way, gentlemen."

The phalanx of security personnel parted as the President and Harwood neared. Williams acknowledged their silent nods with a simple "Gentlemen . . ." and, as Snowden held the door, they entered Battaglia's room.

"Damn, Tony," Harwood quipped from the doorway, "you look like something from a grade B horror movie . . . *The Mummy's Crypt* or some damn thing."

The President was shocked to see his best friend's head, neck, and arms completely wrapped in gauze bandages, save holes for his eyes, nostrils, and mouth. Harwood's quip gave Williams a moment to recover. He walked straight to the bed and leaned far over so he and Battaglia could make eye contact without Tony having to turn his head. "Hey man, what'd they think you were, a big chunk of Gorgonzola?"

"Yeah," Tony said in a lock-jawed mumble through his bandages. More like *spiedini*, Sicilian shish-kebab."

"How're you feeling?"

"Glad to be alive, boss. But, I'm not hurt as bad as I look from all these bandages. The docs are worried about infection, so they keep me wrapped up pretty tight."

"We've been praying for you, Tony," Harwood said.

"Well, don't pray for me. Pray for Senator Calvin's soul, and for his family."

"He was going to be President, Tony. We'd made a deal with him that

I would resign after a couple of years, automatically making him President," Williams confessed suddenly.

"I wondered about that, Mr. President. I'll tell you, something down deep inside me told me that there was something else going on."

"Really?" Harwood asked. "We'd kept it completely confidential. In fact, we promised the Senator that we wouldn't tell anyone. I'm even surprised the President is sharing this now."

"Tony, I'm telling you this because I feel responsible for what's happened. Stan and I thought Calvin deserved a shot at the Presidency, and being black, he wouldn't get it any other way. Despite his obvious credentials, his color would never allow him to get elected. Putting him on the ticket would assure a win, and allow us to do this for the people."

Tony waved a bandaged arm and instructed, "Pull those chairs over here close. I want to tell you guys something, and my voice doesn't carry too well with all these stitches in my lips and cheeks."

Harwood slid Tony's I.V. aside a few inches, allowing him to bring his chair next to Williams', and the men leaned over to listen.

"What is it, Tony?" the President asked.

"I helped you guys get this done by arranging for Stan to meet with you, Mr. President. I thought it was the right thing to do. I still do. And I love both of you like brothers. I trust you."

"And . . . ?" Williams asked, waiting for the other shoe to drop.

"You screwed up."

Williams and Harwood were not prepared for criticism from their weight-lifting pal who less than forty-eight hours before had been near death.

"I guess that's obvious," Harwood responded, "given Calvin's assassination and the attack on you."

"No, you guys don't understand what I mean. You know, one reason I am so fond of you two guys is that you respect me. I'm a professional weight-lifter without a lot of schooling, but you treat me like I'm equal."

"You are, Tony," Williams insisted.

"I know I am. You guys give me credit for being bright. Hey, I know I don't use a lot of big words or think a lot of deep thoughts, but I'm smart enough. Listen, my grandfather kept a little farm in Sicily . . . goats, grapes, some olive trees. He came here in thirty-seven . . . he knew what was coming. In 1938, Mussolini finally turned Italy completely fascist, by taking elections away from the people. They just stopped holding elections. Mussolini and his buddies saw the government as having its own power . . . all on its own. It wasn't something that was responsible to the people . . . it had its own form, its own life. And the government somehow got the idea that it knew better what was good for the people than the people knew themselves."

"Man is because the state is," Williams added. "Without the state, man is nothing and can become nothing, rather than the other way around. Without the structure and authority of the state, men comprise a formless mass, without discipline or purpose. That's the philosophical basis for fascism."

"Okay, so all this happened like in little steps, so that people hardly noticed they'd lost all their power to a handful of bad guys. Yeah, Mussolini made a big deal about trains running on time, but he never asked people whether they'd like to trade on-time trains for democracy. My friends, you took for yourself the power that belongs to all those people out there. It was one thing to kick O'Malley out. That's okay, he was a disaster. And bringing in Calvin, hey, that's a brave thing to do. Also, I agree with you about Calvin's situation. He damned well should have been the candidate for one party or the other . . . I'd been honored to have had him as my President. You're right, if the man were white, he'd have probably been president already. But when you strike a side deal to make him President—or at least offer him the job without the voters knowing what you're up to—then you put yourself above the people. That's how the Fascists in Italy started."

"Oh, my God, Tony, is that what we've done?"

"Calvin might not have taken the VP job, if he hadn't been promised the Presidency."

"He wouldn't have . . . he'd already turned us down," Williams responded.

"So you guys talked him into joining the ticket in exchange for a promise that he'd be President. And that cost him his life."

"And almost yours," added Harwood dourly.

"You didn't mean for stuff to turn out this way," Tony added. "You were trying to do right. But you know about the highway to hell?"

"Yeah." Harwood answered, "Paved with good intentions."

"Now what, Tony? What would you do?" Williams asked.

"Come clean with the American people. Tell them about the deal, apologize, and ask for forgiveness." Tony twisted and stretched his arms out, as if to relieve pain. "Peter asked Jesus how often to forgive and Jesus said up to seventy times seven. This is a great country. The people can face that."

"They'll throw us out of office," Harwood claimed.

"That's for them to decide, Stan. Throw the light on things. And one more thing, guys," Tony said. "Leave the Senator on the ticket."

"Really?"

"Yup. Doesn't he deserve to be elected Vice President?"

"Yeah, but . . . ."

"No 'yeah buts,'" interrupted Tony. "Just run with Calvin."

"Can it be done?" asked Harwood.

"You guys are smart, you figure it out," Tony laughed.

"Not that smart, apparently," Harwood replied.

"And, pray for guidance and wisdom . . . don't forget about the power of prayer."

"And if we get elected, what do we do about a VP?"

"Like that's the worst of your problems . . . ." Battaglia gibed.

"Anthony Battaglia, you are something!" Williams cried.

"I may be something, but I'm not Anthony. I'm Giovanni on my birth certificate. When I was little, I guess I looked like a Tony to some folks. Plus, the non-Italian kids I went to school with thought Giovanni was Tony in Italian. It's really John."

"And you've gone by Tony all these years?"

"Yeah, it doesn't bother me. I know what my name is. When my mother was in labor, she said to my father, 'We're going to have a new life pretty soon.' And my father replied, 'Yeah, a new light.' They'd already picked out another name for me, but right then, my mother says, 'He's going to be Giovanni. Like the Gospel of John, he'll bring light and life.'"

"And so you have," said Harwood.

57

President Williams was numb. Somehow the dominant emotion was the very lack of it, like staring too long at an insoluble puzzle, the mind becoming flat, non-functioning. When Emily buzzed, he knew, with stale anticipation, who had arrived. Others might have been energized by the prospect of answers. But the magnitude—and tragedy—of recent events continued to stifle his enthusiasm. And the challenge of Tony's profound insights was more than a little unsettling. The entry of the Team forced the President from his stupor.

Harwood's expansive smile and confident demeanor betokened his optimism. "Mr. President, you know everyone, with the exception of William Bryant," he said.

"Bill is a senior investigator at the Securities and Exchange Commission. He's spent a long time investigating and prosecuting complex securities fraud cases."

"Too long, I think sometimes, Mr. Harwood," Bryant offered.

"Thanks for your assistance," Williams said.

Stanley Harwood started, "Everything's coming together quickly, Mr. President. I'll let Maria give you the overview."

"Fine." The President's voice was emotionless. "Ms. Krautchik, what do you have?"

Maria Krautchik rocked slightly in her chair. Williams noticed her eyes linger on Harwood. "First, we're holding a Nicholas B. Tesso. He was taken into custody at the Greater Southeast emergency room. We don't have a print match yet, but we've got plenty of blood evidence from Stan's apartment, the emergency room, and Tesso himself. Plus, I expect we'll get plenty of hair and fiber evidence, too."

"Is Tesso talking?"

"He's spilling his guts, hoping for a lighter sentence. And protection. The guy is so afraid of his partner, he's told his attorney not to request bail."

"So he and this other man attacked Tony?"

"Absolutely. Tesso's identified the tall guy as a William J. Cosicio. Tesso's not admitting to either the Berkhardt or Calvin murders, but we've told him we've got phone logs linking him with Cartwright. He admits they talked with Cartwright, but can't seem to explain why."

"And the casino angle?"

"Looks like that Calendar fellow was dead on. When State intervened for us in these foreign jurisdictions, well, some of these so-called secret accounts and trades quickly became not-so-secret. The SEC says that maybe billions went into the scheme. And the way it was structured, by using options, it could've returned twenty—maybe even fifty-to-one—on the investment."

"Where'd the funding come from?" the President asked.

"Mr. President," said Harwood, "I'd like Bill Bryant to take over here. He's the expert on this."

"Fine. Mr. Bryant?"

"Thanks. Mr. President, it's pretty complex, but, simply put, some entity has taken huge positions in casino stock options, all on the 'short side' . . . that is, betting the stocks will fall. The trades were executed through a number of institutions. Sometimes the orders came indirectly through separate intermediaries."

"Say again, Mr. Bryant," asked the President.

"It's like telling someone to tell someone else, to tell still someone else to call a broker and make a trade. Multiple levels of insulation. It usually just slows us down a lot. We call it 'peeling the onion.' It's not difficult, just takes time to strip away the layers. We're having to get lots of phone logs, plus faxes, emails . . . everything. Anyway, we hardly have the onion totally peeled, but we're far enough to be able to get to the big picture."

"So, let's jump ahead," the President interrupted. "O'Malley's said he was taking money from Cartwright to influence casino tax legislation, influence that would either make the tax happen, or make it seem likely."

Harwood confirmed, "Yes, sir. Speaker Berkhardt was a roadblock, bottling up hearings, dragging his feet on legislation."

"That's a reason to kill a man?" the President asked.

Harwood's responded quickly. "Lots of people have been killed for less."

"So, whoever was in cahoots with Cartwright invested massive sums—betting Cartwright and O'Malley would pull it off."

Bill Bryant jumped in, "So this Calendar guy is sitting there, trading these stocks . . . but there's big money on the other side, playing against him. And they know something he doesn't, at least they think they do. They think they've got it fixed so these stock prices will fall out of bed."

The President thought for a second. "Okay, so who's this stock fraud person?"

Stan Harwood, frowning, cautioned, "We can't jump to conclusions, but Bill can give you what we've got."

"At the middle of the onion is a group of Los Angeles and Aspen based accounts. It's a little confusing, because some of them are trust accounts, others are nominee accounts, and so on. But their very structure concerns us, because it indicates an intent to conceal identity . . . to obfuscate."

"Mr. Bryant, net it out," The President said impatiently. "Do we know who's controlling these accounts?"

"Uh, er," Harwood sputtered, "we're pretty much there, sir."

"And?"

"This is difficult, sir, because the accounts have been traced to a Ms. Chris Weiner and a company she controls, Weiner Oil."

The President slumped in his chair, his eyes closed, while the others glanced at each other uncomfortably.

Finally, Williams took a deep, slow breath, then exhaled, as slowly and as deliberately. He stared, his face a mix of incredulity and anguish, at Stan Harwood.

"My God," he said. "That woman is our largest contributor. I heard rumors about her and Cartwright, but it didn't make sense. Now it does. This is sickening."

"Yes, sir," Harwood responded. "For what it's worth, she's also one of the biggest contributors to Moore and the Democrats."

"Small solace. In the end, it isn't about Republicans or Democrats looking bad. It's about the kind of people one chooses to associate with and how one chooses to make that association. I like to think that the leaders of my party are people of honor." Williams buried his face in his hands and the others heard a muffled, "Goddam."

Stanley Harwood shifted in his chair, and spoke. "Mr. President, I've had a lot of self-doubts through this entire thing, how we—I mean, I—might be responsible for Calvin's death, for placing him in harm's way. But, I know we did our best. O'Malley was a good choice for Vice President at one time, and so was Cartwright for campaign chairman. But each was doing a terrible job, and should've been cut a long time ago. If men have so little integrity that they choose to get involved in affairs and stock manipulation that end in murder . . . well, that's something that we—you, Mr. President or anyone else—can't be responsible for. I, for one, am not going to kick myself for the machinations of evil people . . . and," added Harwood surveying the room, "neither are any of you."

"I'm upset," he continued, "but there are limits to what well-intentioned men can do. If anyone's hands are dirty, then mine are filthy. But, we can't be blamed for the evil in the hearts of people like Chris Weiner."

The group emitted a collective sigh of relief as the President, squaring his shoulders and straightening his back, asked, "Okay now, our avaricious, murdering benefactor, where the heck is she?"

"We're tracking her as we speak, sir," Harwood replied. "We think she's actually in D.C. She arrived on her private jet last night. And as long as we keep things totally confidential, she's got no idea that we're on to her."

"Why's she here?"

"Maybe to cover some trails. All we know is that a black limousine picked her up at the airport."

Krautchik broke in, "A tall man met her, they got into the limo together, and off they went. She had a suite at the Grand Hyatt, but never checked in. Her pilot and plane are still sitting out at the airport, presumably waiting for her call. We've got taps on phones at the Hyatt and the private jet terminal at the airport. So far, no sign of her."

"The man who picked up her up at the airport has to be our guy," Harwood said. "The helicopter people in Birmingham identified a tall man and a short man. Tony broke a short guy's arm, and a tall man dropped him off at the hospital. This has got to be this William Cosicio."

"So you think Ms. Weiner is responsible for the deaths of the Speaker and Senator Calvin?"

"Mr. President, I'm afraid that's the most logical conclusion."

"So, how do we find this demented oil czarina?"

"We're running Weiner's and Cosicios' names and descriptions through every hotel and motel—and law enforcement agency—within a hundred and fifty miles. Unfortunately, right now we've got no idea where they are. Since the hospital fiasco, they must've gone to ground. Maybe she's with him, we just don't know. We've contacted every limo service in town, but there's been no match yet, Mr. President."

"What about Cartwright?"

"Nothing, Mr. President. It's strange, but no one's heard a thing in two days. The District police and FBI have checked his house. It's been dark and locked. They're covering it twenty-four, seven. Maybe he's on the lam, sir. They were preparing a warrant for his arrest this morning."

"As far as Cartwright's concerned, something really smells bad. And I know something about this Chris Weiner," Williams counseled, "and I can guarantee that this is not the kind of person who can stay underground for a long time. We'll dig up something here pretty soon."

58

With Nick Tesso squealing loudly, hounds on the tails of Weiner and Cosicio, and Cartwright likewise flushed from cover, President Williams was exhilarated. Of course, the frightful assassination of Calvin still consumed him, but he was—finally—more determined to devise a way to honor the Mississippian, than to brood or grieve. The press, the opposition, and the voters anxiously anticipated the announcement of a new Vice Presidential candidate.

The RNC and its financial pillars neared panic.

Harwood, consumed by the murder and stock manipulation investigations, nonetheless deliberated alternative re-election strategies in the face of the turmoil he had unwittingly spawned. In response to Tony's recommendation—and castigation—Harwood had become, at least to the degree time allowed, an expert on the federal electoral process.

Battaglia's insights were, as always, as simple and profound as they were uniquely honest. Now, Stanley Harwood struggled for the answer to Tony's challenge. Finish what you've started, Tony insisted, as honorable men would.

How to trump the Democrats, honor Calvin, and have the Republicans keep their integrity intact? Meanwhile, run the killers to ground. President Williams was still more than a little confused as to how they might respond to Tony's concept.

"Stan, the Democrats will take this as a real 'in-your-face' . . . and so might the voters. This is either the smartest or the dumbest thing a President's ever done," Williams laughed.

"Very possibly both," replied Harwood, who consulted some papers in front of him, and continued. "Let me read a draft press release:

After much consideration and deep prayer, I have decided to proceed to the

general election without naming a replacement for Senator Reginald Calvin. If the
Republicans earn a majority in the Electoral College, I will ask them to re-elect me
President, and elect Senator Reginald Calvin Vice President. I will take no action
with respect to the naming of another Vice Presidential candidate until after the
popular election, balloting by electors in their respective states, and the counting of
Electoral College votes at the joint session of Congress in January. I ask that you join
me in honoring the legacy of Senator Calvin, decorated war hero, dedicated public
servant and preeminent leader of men. We should do no less.

"We can pull this off?" Williams inquired.

"The Constitution just says the VP has to be natural born, thirty-five and a U.S. resident for fourteen years. Obviously, electing a dead man isn't something the framers contemplated. So, one could maintain that if a restriction is not mentioned in the positive, then it's not a restriction. Thus, constitutionally at least, Calvin *can* be elected."

"Right now, O'Malley's on some state ballots and Calvin is on others," Williams observed.

"It matters, but only indirectly," Harwood replied.

"The popular election doesn't legally bind anybody to anything. The popular election just establishes the members of the Electoral College," Harwood continued, "who then vote for President and Vice President. So, whether a state ballot says 'Roosevelt', or 'McKinley', nobody's directly voting for the name on the ballot. And we know the gap between the legal and the ethical: Al Gore and Buddhist nuns, need I say more?"

"Well, we're certainly not covering up anything here. In fact, this is designed to do the opposite."

Harwood paused, then said, "In short, we're asking the voters to direct the Electoral College to choose Calvin as Vice President. The College meets on the first Monday after the third Wednesday in December. Their votes are then sealed and sent to Congress. If you like controversy, then this is the election for you!" Harwood said.

"We don't actually inaugurate a dead man?"

"No, we can go pretty far, but not that far. The Senator really would have to be alive to take the oath of office."

"Stan, right now we're ahead by just about the greatest margin in history. Only Minnesota, Idaho, and Massachusetts look doubtful. And the District, of course. But everything, depends on how we handle this. Everyone is expecting us to name a new candidate. The whole world is waiting for the other shoe to drop."

"It'll drop this afternoon, if you approve my "Tony Plan.""

"How about O'Malley?" the President inquired.

"Whatever happens, he's still Vice President until Inauguration Day. He's all set to make a statement supporting our position. And there's no coercion in this, either. He wants to do the right thing."

"Fine. You know, when I said I wanted to take care of him, I meant it."

"He knows that now, Mr. President. Better late than never."

"So, are we heading toward a Constitutional crisis, Stan?"

"Well sir, first, the Electoral College has to be willing to vote, then send its votes to the Hill. I'm sure they'll do that, I mean, they are *our* electors. Then, Congress could do one of three things. First, open and count the votes and declare Williams and Calvin the winners. Second, refuse to open the ballots. Third, they could go to the Supreme Court for direction. But Congress is trapped. They can't refuse to open the ballots, send them back to the Electors, or go to the Court until they open them and see who's been elected."

"There's another wild card: the Twentieth Amendment says 'Congress may provide for the case of the death of any person from whom the Senate may choose a Vice President, whenever the right of choice shall have devolved upon them.' I talked with a professor of constitutional law at Georgetown this morning, and he thinks there's a possibility that the Senate might try to choose the VP themselves, claiming the 'right of choice had devolved upon them.' Confusing enough?"

"Yes, but I'm still concerned that the voters might reject the idea of doing all this just to get Calvin recognized with an asterisk . . . making Calvin a sort of Roger Maris vice president."

"That doesn't mean we shouldn't give the people a chance to honor a great man, who certainly would have become President."

"I agree about honoring Calvin, but the press will see this as manipulation—to put the country through this, regardless of the greatness of the man. Just yesterday, the NAACP questioned whether we were pandering."

"I say Tony's right. To hell with 'em," Harwood cried.

"I think that's what Rec would say, and Mrs. Calvin is completely behind us on this."

The President quickly played out various contingencies in his mind. Then, his face suddenly brightened, as if he had reached a satisfying conclusion, and he blurted, "Good for Tony and good for you, Stan! To hell with the press, to hell with the negativists, to hell with the ax grinders. Helen Keller said the greatest curse was to have sight and no vision. Let's go with it!"

59

Each year five million tourists walk the grounds of this icon, Arlington National Cemetery, this great symbol of national service. Most do not come close to the two hundred and fifty thousand permanent residents. Instead, the transients spend their time honoring the large white sarcophagus of the unknown, and the resting-place of a mythicized president, his demigoddess wife, and his too-mortal brother. They crowd the gift shop and the lower, more accessible areas, rarely seeing most of the six hundred and twelve acres and their almost unimaginable number of graves.

Indeed, the visitors are humble. If they were not possessed by its sense of quiet dignity and reverence before their arrival, it soon comes upon them. The dominant features of the immaculately groomed grassy landscape are the thousands—no, tens upon tens of thousands—of small headstones, an expansive orchard of white marble markers stretching, seemingly for miles, in long uninterrupted rows.

Throughout the cemetery, larger, custom-designed monuments sit silently, side by side, each providing more tangible evidence of a legacy of service, courage, and loyalty. These grave markers are those of officers. For over a century, men interred in the officers' sections have been allowed to design their own monuments. This privilege ultimately became so exploited by officers' families, that the graves' size and ornamentation raised fierce objections from enlisted men's families, resentful of the contrast of the large, finely decorated monuments to the small, uniform white stones marking the resting places of their loved ones. Today, a general's grave marker—say, a large, dark, granite obelisk—appears somehow insignificant, even unseemly, next to a rolling green meadow of neatly arranged, small white stones. Indeed, the contrast serves only to heighten the honor of the privates who perished in such great abundance in our nation's conflicts.

Here and there, the finely groomed landscape of markers is punctuated with sprays of fresh flowers. Always evident throughout the cemetery, are freshly dug graves, beckoning their ultimate occupants, individuals whose funeral services are likely scheduled the next day for the Cemetery chapel. By some, forest green canvas tents have been erected to afford shade and a sense of shelter to the attending mourners.

Elsewhere are recent graves, covered with fresh dirt, no grass yet intruding. Perhaps, if a grave is but a few weeks old, a few blades appear on their way to the eventual conquest of the brown blanket above the body. Then, but for the date and whiteness of the headstone, these new grass-covered graves join the others in a solemn, but reassuring, mass anonymity.

"I'm not sure what you guys have to show me, but I know it has to be good." She was in a good mood as they walked toward the waiting black limousine.

"Thanks, Ms. Smith. We do our best."

Weiner had a driver from Signature drop her off under the Delta Shuttle sign on the commercial side of Reagan, rather than enable the tall man to see her jet at the FBO. As the driver approached the baggage claim area, Weiner noted the new garish steel and glass pagodas, with their repetitive, pale yellow archways. This geodesic Angkor Wat was offensive, but probably functional, she thought.

Exiting the FBO's courtesy vehicle, she looked up to see a long, black limousine a short distance away. As she approached, the tall man emerged from the limo and greeted her. He offered to carry her bags.

"No thanks, I got 'em," she said. As they approached the waiting limo, its engine idling, Weiner adopted a complimentary tone. "I told you once I think you guys should franchise. You bring real creativity to a field that's really lacking fresh ideas. Now, listen, I want to get to my hotel pretty quick. Traveling from the West Coast wears my ass out. I'm exhausted."

Willie remained impassive. He opened the passenger door of the limo, and Weiner carefully placed her bags on the floor in front of her seat, and climbed in. After walking around the limo, he opened the door, joining her in the back seat. "Let's go," he directed the driver in a low growl.

As soon as they were underway, Weiner leaned slightly forward to try to identify the driver. Assured that he wasn't Willie's regular companion, she leaned slowly back, turned to her backseat companion, and inquired, "Where's your buddy?"

Willie thought, *Jesus, if the cops had announced Nick's arrest, what the fuck would I have done? The little shit . . . getting his arm broke, and having to go to the hospital. And then the fuckin' cops descending . . . looked like a K-Mart special sale with all the blue lights flashing. As usual, timing is everything. This time, I'll have planning, timing, and luck. A lot of planning, a little luck, and some good timing thrown in . . . that's what Nick used to say . . . you get those three, you can do something in this business. Where the hell do you suppose they got him? Man, I hope that shot killed the little turd.*

"Willie . . . are you there? I just asked you a question. Where the hell is Nick?"

"Uh, yeah, I'm here. I was just thinking about something. Uh, yeah, he's . . . ah . . . tied up for a while. I got this limo from a local company. They're supposed to be very reliable. I asked for their best driver."

"Yeah, okay, great. So what's up with Nick? He laid up or something? Sick . . . hurt? Hey, he's not in the slammer, is he?"

"Nah, no big deal . . . he's just taking some time off. A couple of rough jobs recently. He's gonna sit tight for a while. You work hard, you know how it is."

"So tell me, Willie. I got some other business in D.C. so I brought the balance with me. It's here in the bag, fifty grand. But we could've met in Chicago to make the final payoff. Why'd you have to see me here?"

"I told you, this is important. Plus, you said you might have a new job. I like to do job planning face-to-face, if possible. You'll see. This fits into everything we've been doing. I couldn't describe it to you on the phone. It's gotta be a surprise, Ms. Smith."

The man's impassivity concerned Weiner. As he spoke, he never turned his head toward her and there was no animation in his body or inflection in his voice. His words were flat, monotonic. This did not seem to be the Willie that Chris had previously worked with.

"What's up, Willie? Something's not quite right. You're quiet . . . too quiet . . . and Nick . . . you still haven't told me exactly where he is."

Her backseat companion looked down to a small console of buttons on his armrest, and pushing a switch, closed the soundproof window dividing the driver's and passenger's compartments.

"Can't be too careful," he cautioned. "Look, there's nothing wrong. Nick's still in Washington, and he's not planning on leaving anytime soon. He really wanted to be here, but, like I said, there's no way he could make it."

"We don't have a fuck up, do we? Tell me right now if we have a problem."

"We don't fuck up, so relax."

"Where the heck are we going, Willie?"

"You'll see."

"I'm not used to getting indirect answers. Read my lips: where the fuck are we going?"

Finally, the tall man turned toward Weiner, his face and voice brightening simultaneously. "We're going to Arlington, Ms. Smith."

"Arlington what?"

"Arlington National."

"Arlington National what?"

"Arlington National Cemetery."

"The cemetery? That's where you're taking me? The fucking cemetery?"

"Yeah. We got something we want to show you. You're going to be friggin' amazed by this."

"It's two o'clock in the morning, and I've been flying for four and a half hours, so it'd better be good. I want to hear some more about this, Willie."

"Well, you know how we did that Speaker guy—pretty creative, huh—and taking out that Senator Calvin was a masterpiece."

Weiner was increasingly anxious, and through with compliments. "Yeah, great job on the Speaker. It took the F.B.I. all of seventy-two hours to figure that one out. You should've just shot him on the street. Plus, I wouldn't call the Calvin job the cleanest I've ever seen. For Christ's sake, did you have to kill that poor helicopter pilot?"

"That wasn't us . . . that was some Irish guys hired by O'Malley! Ha, ha, ha, ha . . . ."

"Very fucking funny."

The limousine passed the perennial construction adorning Reagan, rolling North to the George Washington Parkway, past the Roaches Run Waterfowl Sanctuary, Columbia Island Marina and Lady Bird Johnson Park.

Weiner looked out at the path paralleling the roadway, now empty, but normally busy with cyclists and hikers. Across the Potomac, the Lincoln Monument glowed. Easing to the left lane, they drove slowly past a sign indicating the "Women in Military Service for America" monument.

Weiner had no reason to consider the sign ironic. At the foot of the deserted Memorial Bridge, the driver circled, heading across the cobblestones toward the Cemetery, before abruptly turning right, circling again and heading south on the Parkway.

"Hey," Weiner cried, "We're heading back to Reagan!"

The distance from Reagan National Airport to the closest point of Arlington National Cemetery is but a mile and a quarter, as the crow flies. But between the two is the Pentagon—the wounded Pentagon—lying snug up against the Cemetery, but for the intrusion of busy Washington Boulevard, itself a part of the nexus of roads and highways that funnel the multitude of bureaucrats, civil servants, and lobbyists to and from their offices across the Potomac.

As Weiner spoke, the limo circled right again, following the Washington Boulevard / Columbia Pike sign, passing only a few yards from the Cemetery. A third of a mile from where the Boulevard makes its near one hundred and eighty degree turn north along the southwestern border of the Cemetery, the limousine suddenly jerked to the right, into a service driveway, past a row of silent Deere backhoes and dozens of other pieces of parked maintenance equipment, resting on the opposite side of a security fence. The vehicle passed through an open gate in a chain link fence, passing by a sign declaring "No Digging. Call 697-4478." Again, any irony was lost on Weiner.

Rolling slowly across a gravel parking lot, the limo stopped behind a brown van. The driver blinked his headlights twice. In front of them, beyond a thin strip of trees and across the highway, sat the Pentagon, its scars still visible. Behind them loomed Ft. Myers' South Gate and the now-partially-occupied Federal Building Number Two, headquarters of the U.S. Marines and BUPERS, the Navy Bureau of Personnel. Here, during the day, hundreds of thousands of men and women worked, and hundreds of thousands of cars passed within a few yards. Here, in the middle of the night, this hurricane's eye lay deserted, eerily tranquil, but for these men at their frantic task.

"Where in the hell are we?" Weiner demanded.

"This is the back side of Arlington, Ms. Smith. This is where we got something to show you."

The tall killer stepped quickly out of the limo, and sticking his head back inside said, "Come on Ms. Smith, this is it."

"I don't think so . . . changed my mind, Willie. I'm not getting out. Whatever you got, it'll wait until tomorrow. I don't like the looks of this place. Now, let's get out of here."

"It'll only take a minute. You gotta see what me and Nick have cooked up for you this time."

"No fucking way. I don't like the looks of this. Come on, we're gettin' out of here."

Willie began to climb back into the limo. "Yes, ma'am, whatever you say."

As quickly as the words left Willie's lips, his accomplice, who had just left the wheel of the limo, jumped from the driver's seat, opened the back door, and plowed into the back seat, knocking Weiner flat. She struggled to escape his grasp, the collar and sleeve of her dress tearing away as the driver pinned her down. "Got her!" he shouted.

Willie opened the front door and pulled a roll of duct tape off the front seat. "Keep her down!", he shouted, as Weiner pushed her way out from under her assailant.

The driver renewed his hold, spun her around, and dropped a knee into her chest. He smashed her face with his fist, then pressed the palm of his hand down firmly on her mouth. Blood streamed from her nose.

Weiner retaliated with a bite, followed by a stream of invectives, flailing and kicking. "You motherfuckers . . . what the fuck do you think you're doing . . . I'll fucking kill you . . . you assholes . . . help . . . hel . . . !"

The short strip of duct tape that Willie slapped across her mouth stifled her last 'help'. Two more pieces of gray tape, each nearly a foot long, were applied quickly over the first, covering Weiner's mouth and extending beyond her jaw line.

"Mmph . . . ooo 'uckers . . . mmph . . . ." Weiner's screams and shouts were so muffled that she may as well have been shouting down a well on some abandoned farm on the Eastern Shore. As the limo driver continued to hold her down, fighting her flailing arms and legs, Willie quickly pulled long strips off the roll, taping Weiner's hands behind her back.

As the desperate woman kicked and tried to roll away, her black wool skirt rose to her waist. Willie, took a few seconds to admire her smooth, brown, well-muscled thighs ending at a pair of sheer white lace bikini panties. "Too bad we're in such a hurry. We coulda got real close . . . we coulda had some fun together." Then, without further musing, he quickly tore off more strips of tape and bound her ankles together. After a minute, the muffled curses continued, but she lay motionless on the gravel lot.

As the two men restrained their captive, two others, dressed in Army lieutenant's uniforms, jumped from the back of the van parked in front of the limo. "Pick her up, Frank!" Willie shouted. "Com'on, you guys, quick, this way."

One of the 'Army officers' remained by the vehicles, as the others dragged the oil heiress along a grassy strip behind a row of trees that separated the cemetery from the highway. A black iron-rail fence sat atop a thigh-high flagstone wall. A twenty-foot section of fence had been unbolted, and moved slightly aside.

The men tossed Weiner over the stone wall through the gap in the fence, allowing her body to slam to the ground on the other side, then scrambled over after her.

"Which way?"

"Right down here, follow me," said one man, and carrying a small flashlight, he led the men a short distance, with Weiner wriggling and squirming for her life, the men running as fast as they could, dragging her behind. Shortly, they stopped, and the leader cast his light on two long, thin aluminum grave covers lying next to a large dirt pile.

"Here it is . . . pretty nice huh?"

The men stopped, chests heaving from their short run, and lifted the ladder-like covers from the empty grave. The van driver scanned it with his flashlight.

"How deep ya get it?" Willie asked.

"It was already finished . . . dug out . . . ready for some poor sucker tomorrow, I guess. We just took a couple of feet out of the bottom. It'll look fine when we fill in a little and smooth it out."

Willie pulled a small flashlight from his coat pocket and aimed the beam at Weiner's face. Now she lay still, but her eyes were wide with simultaneous fear and realization. Her mouth taped shut, she panted, wheezing through her nose, her chest rising and falling with each terrified breath.

Willie straddled the prostrate woman. "Goddam . . . you got too dangerous, lady. I don't like it when clients get all emotional and stuff. That's when they lose it . . . make mistakes, ya know? I hate to lose a good client, but thanks for the last fifty grand. I just wanna say I appreciate customers who make good on their promises." He grinned, turned to his associates and, without emotion, ordered, "Chuck her in."

The van driver grabbed Weiner's hair with both hands, and lifted the top of her body off the ground. The limo driver took her legs, swung them to the edge of the empty grave and together they rolled her in. In a second, she tumbled, landing face up in the bottom of grave number 69-5499-2-A, just a stone's throw from Patton Drive.

Willie put his flashlight beam on her face, listened to the unintelligible, horrific sounds that came through the duct tape. He studied her for a moment, focusing on the eyes that alternated between supplication and abject horror.

Weiner struggled furiously, if vainly, against her bonds, wriggling futilely in the dirt at the bottom of the freshly dug grave.

Seemingly satisfied at his appraisal of the situation, Willie calmly instructed the men, "Cover 'er up." They grabbed the shovels lying nearby and went to work, quickly and efficiently, while Willie stood at the graveside, watching the first few shovels of dirt rain down on Weiner's contorted face and writhing body, before walking deliberately back to the waiting vehicles.

For fifteen minutes, the men worked quickly and efficiently, barely noting the slow covering-up of the frantic body, rolling and fighting to free itself from the tape. They moved shovel-full after shovel-full of brownish-red dirt from the pile next to the grave on top of the casino stock queen. Even as

359

she was fully covered, the bottom of the grave looked like a small earthquake in action, as the last of her vain squirming took place fully under the dirt.

Soon she was still.

Having transferred a couple of additional feet of earth back into the pit, they carefully examined the new grave bottom, assuring that it was level, and that the night's disturbance would not be noticed in the light of day, when it came time to lower a new casket on top of the person who wanted to be the richest in the world. Then, they stepped back to survey the gravesite, replacing the covers, and smoothing out the footprints with their shovels and a tree branch that they had secured from a nearby oak.

When satisfied with the appearance of the scene, they ran, carrying their tools, scrambling across the wall, and replacing the piece of fencing. They hustled back to their vehicles and climbed in. As the van pulled away, from the front seat of the limousine, the driver turned around and asked his sole passenger, "Ready Willie?"

"Yeah, let's get out of here."

As the limousine headed north on Washington Boulevard, its occupants became conversational. "Who was that broad, anyway?"

"I dunno. Just another job . . . you know how it is," Willie answered.

"Seems kinda strange, you know. Where'd you ever think that one up?"

Willie leaned back and stretched out his legs. "Ah, there's nothin' new under the sun, man. I read that one in the paper . . . some guys down in Memphis did it once. Got caught though."

"Having those guys dressed as Army guys was a nice touch. Good cover."

"Yeah, well, we had to think of everything. Damn, we were only there twenty minutes or so, but you never know when one of these Ft. Myers' guards is gonna show up. Man, Nick would've appreciated this job, how quick it was planned . . . his kind of stuff."

Willie mused for a moment, then remarked, mostly to himself, "Ya know, I gotta find a way to take out Nick. That guy is suddenly real dangerous."

The driver turned his head slightly so he could hear better, but Willie went silent.

Finally, the driver broke the quiet. "Still seems kinda strange, you know."

"What's that?"

"I dunno. It somehow don't seem right. Her bein' in there with all those heroes. You know who all's in there?"

"Nah. Tell me."

"That Calvin guy . . . the black guy that got shot. You know about him . . . he's in there."

"Yeah, I hearda him," Willie smirked. "So what . . . who else is in there?"

"Well, there's all kinds of presidents and senators and stuff. And remember Audie Murphy, the movie star guy that was a war hero . . . he's in there."

"Never heard of him."

"Well, there's all kinds of astronauts buried in there, too."

"Like?"

The driver paused to think. "Well, like, you know…Alan Shepard, Gus Grissom, John Glenn . . . and that Neil Armstrong guy that walked on the moon."

"I don't think those guys are dead."

"Well, if they're not, they soon will be . . . and, when they are, that's where they'll be."

"Astronauts! La de fuckin' da," Willie opined.

"Yeah, well they got all kinds of guys from the Supreme Court in there too."

"Like?"

"I dunno . . . who the fuck knows those guys names? I just know they're important."

"If you can't remember their name, they ain't important."

"Yeah, well what famous people's names do you remember?" the driver insisted.

"The important ones," Willie replied matter-of-factly.

"Like . . . ?"

"Like Mario Cuomo. People who did things for people," Willie answered.

"And what did he do for people?" the driver asked.

Willie was quiet for a long while, finally saying, "Just go fuck yourself, okay?"

The driver was unperturbed, but persevering. "Well, I still say it ain't quite right sticking that broad in there."

"Give it a rest, huh."

"You know, puttin' her in someone else's grave. Maybe the guy was a war hero or something."

"So . . . his casket will lay down easy," Willie offered. "Hey, wouldn't you like to spend eternity on top of a good looking broad like that."

"Willie, listen to me. The guy that goes in there tomorrow . . . he mighta lost a leg in Vietnam."

"Speaking of legs," Willie interrupted, "You see those legs on that bitch? And that crotch! I was startin' to get horny, struggling with her, man. If we'd had a little time, I'd have jumped down in there and done her."

"Yeah, she was okay," the driver replied solemnly.

"You had to know her, I guess. That cunt was so mean, she'd have admired me for taking the initiative."

60

The Democratic candidate for the presidency was in a foul mood. "Give me some fucking answers I can understand," snarled Frank Moore.

Bill Miller, the Deputy Campaign Chairman was tired, but he was not confused. Everyone else might be perplexed, but to him it was simple. He would explain it . . . again. But he would not suffer harsh words from the Democratic candidate. Especially a man whom he was convinced had suffered a fatal blow from a Republican masterstroke. Moore had long since been trumped by integrity. Now, he was trumped in political strategy.

"I will review how it works technically. And if I hear a single word of personal attack on any individual—Republican or Democrat—I will quit." Miller looked around the room, his eyes lingering on Frank Moore longer than anyone else, adding rhetorically, "Is that clear?"

He proceeded, "It's purely theoretical as to whether a dead man can be elected. There are lots of cases on the books, but most aren't applicable here, or they're from little towns or counties."

A junior staffer could not restrain himself. "What about the state ballots?"

"*Is anybody* listening *out there?*" Miller demanded. He glared around the room again to stifle further questions.

"Pay attention," he groaned. "The names on the popular ballot don't make any damned difference. The general election is a hollow proxy, a vote for electors that are committed to the candidate."

"Is that legal?" Moore timidly interrupted.

"If the Republicans win, the electors will undoubtedly follow Williams' wishes and elect Calvin VP."

Frank Moore frowned a frown that said, Yeah, I know the friggin' facts . . . I know we're twelve points down in the polls . . . and, I know that Minnesota and Michigan don't look good.

"What the hell is up with Mr. Potato Head . . . without an 'e'?" Moore asked.

"O'Malley is still the Vice President until the January inauguration. Whether we win or lose, he won't be in for a second term. From what I hear, his bags are packed and he's just trying to decide whether to take his graphite driver to Federal prison camp at Eglin."

Miller continued, "Okay, assume Williams wins. The electors could dishonor Williams' wishes by refusing to vote, or by electing O'Malley or some other living candidate. But party regulars aren't going to do that to a sitting President who's offering up a paean to an assassinated, African-American, Vietnam Medal of Honor winner. So, assume for now Williams wins the general election and the electors vote for Calvin. Williams' press release says he's not doing anything until the Electoral College votes go to the joint session, in January."

Moore's frown, the one that had been chiseled on his face since the meeting began, would have deepened, were it possible. He remained mute, his expression his only communication.

Miller, undeterred, continued to lead Moore's campaign team through the process:

"Everyone needs to realize that any person with standing—and that's about anyone in the country—could litigate this mess at any point in time. It would go to the Supreme Court immediately, and what the Court would do is entirely speculative at this point. I just hope we've got the good sense to let some other group file the legal papers before us. We're talking about a black guy whose body got blown into about four separate pieces on national TV. If we file suit—this far behind—we'll end up looking like the guy who crapped in the punch bowl."

Miller did not see Moore drop his head sheepishly.

"Anyway, when the electors' votes reach Congress, Congress could refuse to open the ballots, or it could act like Calvin's a viable candidate, open and count them. Then, Calvin would be Vice President-elect. Now, even if Congress ordered the electors to re-vote, they could still refuse. That would create—or in this case further—a constitutional crisis. I mean, what's a Republican-appointed Attorney General going to do, put the electors in jail?"

"This is fucking stupid," Moore shouted. "It's an outrage. They are shoving a pie right into the face of the American people!"

Only Bill Miller's incredible combination of loyalty and patience had kept him in the campaign this far. For too many months, he had suffered Moore's hostility. "That's right, Frank. How does it taste?"

"Goddamit, Bill! Are you going to help, or what?"

"As soon as we're through here, I will help a lot. I'm going to walk out that door, give my Florida telephone number to Sara, and pray to God you don't dial it, because you will be interrupting my sleep, golf, and piña coladas."

Every face at the table stared down, as if diligently consulting some important notes. "I will proceed now, thank you very much," Miller added.

"If Congress sends the ballots back to the electors, unopened, Williams could ask the electors to vote again, or play hardball and tell Congress to stuff it. With the support he's got up there, I predict Congress will count the ballots and certify Williams and Calvin as the winners.

"Now, the Twelfth Amendment says, 'No person constitutionally ineligible to the office of President shall be eligible to that of Vice President.' But, I don't see how that helps us. In any event, the Constitution wasn't designed to consider every alternative. Stuff that falls in the gray areas is a matter for mature and reasonable men to discuss, negotiate, and agree on. Or, more likely, call 1-800-SUETHEBASTARD.

"So the Republicans win, the electors choose Calvin, they send their ballots to the Hill, and Congress certifies Calvin as Vice President-elect. Of course, he's ineligible by virtue of being dead. Then, the Senate probably picks the VP.

"A last possibility has this going all the way to Inauguration Day. When Calvin fails to take the oath of office, the office is declared vacant. Amendment Twenty states that the VP's term ends at noon on January twentieth. If, at twelve-oh-one there's no VP, the office is considered vacant, in which case Williams could name a new VP, subject to confirmation by the Senate."

Moore became conciliatory. "Okay, good analysis, Bill. What do you personally think will actually happen?"

"I think it virtually certain that somebody will sue somebody, so as usual, the lawyers will do better than anyone. The entire issue is legally moot until Congress opens ballots and only then if Calvin wins the VP slot. To put it short and sweet, I think Williams will win, the electors will choose Calvin as VP, and Congress will open and count the votes. That will make Calvin Vice President-elect, for history to remember. And that's Williams' whole point, of course. Calvin never actually becomes Vice President, but that's not what this is about. Finally, whether the Congress chooses someone, the thing goes back to the electors, or the President appoints someone, Williams will ultimately get the VP he wants. It's a win-win-win for him. He's got no downside."

"How about some fuck up in the legal process?" Moore inquired hopefully.

"Not likely, if they carry the popular vote the way it looks now. Plus, even though about twenty states legally bind their electors to voting for whoever wins the popular vote, only five of those have any penalty associated with what they refer to as 'unfaithfulness'. Anyway, though O'Malley will be on a bunch of ballots, he's quit the race legally, so that frees up his electors to vote for Calvin."

"How about this whole thing backfiring?" Moore asked. "Having this fucking prestidigitation blow up in the goddam scoundrels' faces?"

Miller chuckled, and scanned the room to see if anyone dared respond. After a brief collective silence, he declared, "Great question, Frank, one I've thought about a lot. I've come to this conclusion: if it were anyone but Williams and Calvin, this wouldn't stand a chance . . . there'd be such furor that a President wouldn't dare try it. But, Williams and Calvin are, or were, two men . . . indeed, two gentlemen . . . of unquestioned integrity. Their reputations for probity are such that I don't think that any ill will is going to be ascribed to this move. The voters and the press are going to take it for what it is: a bold, if outlandish, move to afford some measure of lasting honor to a great general, Senator, and man."

As Bill Miller finished his sentence, Conrad Weller, the campaign's legal counsel, rushed into the room, ecstatic.

"We did it Frank! Just like you wanted! We just filed a motion in D.C. District Court asking the Court to force the Republicans to put an end to this preposterous charade and formally name a living person as Williams' running mate."

Bill Miller abruptly threw his papers into his briefcase, stood, and marched to the door. Half out of the room, he turned and snapped, "I'm leaving this punchbowl. And Frank, I don't think it's any accident that you're wearing a brown suit today. Now I *know* who I'm voting for, and he ain't in this room!" Swinging the door closed, he disappeared.

Though it seemed physically impossible, somehow Frank Moore's frown deepened further, and he sat, slumped with arms folded, and glowered.

61

On the first day of November, the Washington sky was gray and cold, a fresh northerly wind chilled the city. The men, oblivious to the changing weather, wore no coats nor sweaters, strolling the grounds in their shirts and ties. For a long time, they did not talk nor look at each other. Their pace was not sufficient to keep them warm, but still, they did not feel the cold. They just walked.

We do not like silence. We: Western cultures. Silence is presumed inactivity. To Americans, silence is not golden, but gold tarnished. It represents opportunities lost: to say something. Anything. To be profound or inane. To sing along, make observations, express feelings, ask questions. To hear oneself speak. Merely to make sound.

Background music in elevators and restaurants is the stuff of stand-up comics, but it is missed when the occupants must descend, floor after floor in total silence; or sit at their tables, accompanied by only their thoughts. Quiet is disconcerting. A jackhammer, a jet, a truck, shoes scraping on the ground, doors slamming shut, the clearing of a throat—any sound is welcomed so long as it crowds out the silence. Because silence is the essence of self.

But for these men,—perhaps because of their shared experiences, perhaps their respective natures,—the silence was not uncomfortable.

Finally, the older man, never lifting eyes from the path, never altering his pace, spoke. His words were as much directed at himself, as intended for his walking mate.

"Tony went home today," President Williams said.

"Yes, sir. I got a message."

"They still have twenty-four hour security on him."

"I don't think they'll be back, after what he did to that fellow's arm."

"Then again, you just can't be too sure. You heard about Cartwright?" the President asked.

"Yes, pretty ugly."

"Suicide's rarely pretty. What happened?" Williams asked.

"Mrs. Cartwright came home to find the police staking out the house. She'd been off visiting her family, and when she went in she was struck by a foul odor. She traced it to Cartwright's study, but it was locked from the inside. She retrieved a key, unlocked the door, and found him on the floor behind his desk. He'd shot himself in the head. It was a real mess. He had a space heater on underneath his desk, and it'd been blowing heat on his body for three days. The police went in after Mrs. Cartwright—to check on things—just when she discovered the body, and they found her . . . well, I guess the stench and pieces of brain all over the walls and ceiling must have overcome her. The cops found she'd, uh, moved her bowels, vomited all over herself, and passed out on the floor of the office."

"God, I'm sorry I asked."

"I wonder if Cartwright's somehow more to be pitied than censured?" Harwood asked.

"At some level, everyone is."

The gravel path crunched beneath their feet and the cold wind cut through their shirts. President Williams took his hands from his pockets and folded them in front of him.

"Tony says the final count was two hundred and fifty eight stitches and sixteen pints of blood."

"How much blood's in a body?"

"Fourteen pints, the doctors said. But, for a while in the emergency room, he was leaking it faster than they were putting it in. They had to keep catching up. Tony said he wanted to replace the lost blood with Chianti, but the doctors wouldn't do it . . . said they insisted on a real blood."

"One tough nut, that guy," Harwood offered. "If I'd answered that door, I'd be dead right now."

For another long period, their only companions, distant ones at that, were the ubiquitous squirrels, sniffing, digging, and burying on the White House lawn.

"Mr. President, we never talked about my sister, I mean since that day that you and the Attorney General met with me."

"I figured you'd talked enough. I feel close to you personally, at least as close as anyone gets to Stanley Harwood. I didn't want to gouge an open—or maybe partially healed—wound by bringing it up."

"Sir, I just want you to know that whatever happens, well, I finally feel that's behind me. And I owe that to you." Harwood gulped hard, restraining a mass of emotion.

President Williams did not elicit the unspoken words, the rest. *It's always about the rest, isn't it,* Williams thought. *The rest . . . of course, isn't that what it's always about . . . not the said, but the unsaid . . . not the obvious, but the subtle, the inferred.*

"You know," Williams said, "the Attorney General asked me if I didn't think that there was some element of transference in what you said and did. I told her I didn't even know what the word meant."

Now, the President grinned slowly, a warm smile crescendoed. "She thought you had demons to exorcise, Stan. If she was right, I think they're well on their way to being expelled."

"I've had a lot of help. Like I said, the way in which you . . . ."

The President interrupted, not from any lack of sensitivity to Harwood's message, rather to spare them both the emotion that Williams knew would result from Harwood's finishing his sentence.

"I understand you've been getting a lot of, er, support from certain members of the Team," Williams remarked, beaming.

"Uh, yeah. Some folks have brought me a long way."

"I'm glad that she... er, that *they* are so dedicated."

"Yes, sir," Harwood chuckled. "Now, we've only got a couple more days until the voters choose you to serve a second term, and Mississippi's Reginald Edward Calvin as your Vice President. It seems like everyone understood that we were trying to do the right thing."

"Except for *the Post,* of course. Anyway, I'm gratified," said the President. "No, that's a terrible understatement. To have the *L.A. Times* and the *New York Times* unconditionally support the ticket . . . well, I'm still amazed.

And the piece in U.S. News was just about as insightful and accurate piece as I've ever seen."

"And this would have been nothing without Tony's inspiration and integrity," Harwood added.

Williams rubbed his hands together. "Stan, I'm getting cold. How about we sit in Tony's office for a while?"

As they wound their way to the small sweat-stained office in the White House basement, they did not speak. Once seated in the small office, finally Williams broke the silence. "Seems rather like a shrine for some reason, doesn't it, Stan?"

Harwood leaned back and took in the room. "Yes, sir. I'm glad it's a kind of shrine, and not a sepulcher. Pretty soon, though, Tony will be back dispensing his own unique brand of Italian wisdom and good humor."

"You know, he's not comfortable being injured and having people waiting on him. He likes to serve others."

"*Cui servare regnae* as you say, Mr. President. "

"Right. So now how do we lead?"

"There is a plan for all of us, we just have to listen."

"To what or whom?" Williams asked.

"Him, sir. Listening to Him is praying," Harwood replied. "Most people think praying is asking for things . . . for yourself or others. But I think it's being completely still and quiet and listening to Him."

They sat together, they listened together, and they prayed together.

The President finally interrupted the silence, "Stan, do you read mythology? Lots of folks remember who stole fire from heaven . . . ."

"Prometheus. And he paid a heavy price for it, too. His liver looked worse than O'Malley's." Harwood caught himself, "I'm sorry, sir. Black humor. I couldn't resist."

Williams laughed. "It's okay. Anyway, O'Malley might tell that one on himself one day. Still cooperating, and still no alcohol." The President continued, "Do you know who the first woman was?"

"Eve?"

"Biblically. But the Greeks had a different 'first woman': Pandora. When Prometheus stole fire from the gods, Zeus got mad, as god-kings will do, and gave Pandora to Prometheus' brother. Then, Pandora opened a jar she had with her, allowing all the evils in the world to escape. By the time she closed it, only a single thing remained."

"Hope," responded Harwood slowly, savoring the words, as if tasting a new wine.

"After everything—the assassinations of Berkhardt and our dear Senator Calvin,—hope is our spiritual yeast . . . it's our final victory. Hope let's us prevail over ever-present man-made evil. Hope and service together are a pretty powerful combination. The Senator didn't accept our mission with any thought of being served, but to serve. He gave his life in ransom for many, Stan."

"And I hope we're honoring that . . . that's certainly the very least we owe him. Mr. President, I have always regarded myself as a positive type of person, but I must say that despite what's befallen us over the past weeks, I've never been more positive about America's future. I really admire you, sir, for what you've had the guts to do."

"Thanks, Stan. It's strange to realize we're going to win this election— in a landslide. Heck, I'm staying in Washington for another four years. And since you're my *de facto* Chief of Staff anyway, I thought maybe we should go ahead and make it formal. I've already discussed it with Charlie, and he's completely on board."

"Thank you, sir. You know, right now it's still pure cacophony out there. Everyone born with a larynx has an opinion on this. A lot of them are still demanding that you name your Vice President before the general election . . . not to mention the Democrats' lawsuit."

"It helps to have Connie O'Malley backing our decision. I swear there's a straight-arrow in there somewhere desperately trying to get out."

"You've probably heard that there's quite a constituency developing for Mrs. Calvin."

"Yes, indeed. I talked with her this week," the President replied. "She's completely behind us, and shared with me that there's even a 'Draft Ellie' movement going now to get her housekeeper on the ticket. Apparently, 'Draft Ellie' buttons and bumper stickers are appearing all around town."

"Lord knows Ellie would do a better job than some VPs. And Governor Moore wants to meet," Harwood added. "I probably shouldn't read between the lines, but he talked about 'new and mutual leadership with greatness shared by all.' He as much as said that he wants to throw his hat into the ring as your running mate."

"Despite Calvin's crossing party lines, Moore's a whole different kettle of fish. Plus, I'd have to learn to tolerate his mix of anger and aphorisms," Williams chuckled. "That in itself would be tough."

"Mr. President, it's going to be an old-fashioned landslide. Every poll— black, white, orange, or yellow—confirms that the voters are behind your serving four more years."

"Or maybe for *two years*, if we can find the right man, eh, Stan?" Williams teased.

"Exactly." Harwood carefully considered the President's torso. "Looks like you're still wearing the Kevlar vest, sir."

"I'm afraid I've pretty much gotten used to it. Phyllis has convinced me to wear it through the Electoral College vote. I promised that I'd keep it on until the College's five hundred and thirty eight votes go to Congress."

"We've still got to look beyond January, not the least of which is picking another VP candidate," Harwood said, adding "Mr. President, you once told me you originally came to Washington with a vision and that, along the way, you'd lost that vision. What about now?"

Before the President could answer, they heard light footsteps approaching Tony's office.

"Who's there?" shouted Harwood. "Who is it?"

As the footsteps progressed toward the office, Stanley Harwood stood. A figure emerged into the brightness of the doorway "Maria! Man, we wondered who that was."

"Hi, Stan. Hello, Mr. President." She gave a big hug to Harwood, and nodded affectionately to Williams. "I didn't know anyone was down here. I came down here to . . . well, I saw the light and thought I'd see who was here."

"Where were you heading, Maria?" Williams asked.

"Here, Mr. President. Since Tony got hurt, I've been coming here just to sit. It's really peaceful. The hospital wouldn't let me visit, so this is as close as I could get. When I opened the hall door, I certainly didn't expect to find anyone else here. Kind of scared and kind of relieved, I guess."

"Yeah, us too," replied Harwood.

"Look, if you two are talking, I can go back upstairs," Krautchik offered. "I didn't mean to interrupt."

"Not at all, Ms. Krautchik," the President said.

"Anyway, I've still got a lot of stuff to look at tonight, so I've got to get going anyway. Stan, why don't you walk Ms. Krautchik back upstairs. I'm going to sit here for a couple more minutes."

"Yes, sir."

Maria Krautchik stepped back into the hall, Harwood following her out. They had almost reached the end of the darkened hall, when a voice echoed behind them.

"Stan?"

Turning, they saw the President, standing in the hall outside Tony's office, the light of the office cast upon him.

The President regarded the two dimly-lit figures. He was not surprised to see Harwood's arm around Maria's shoulder, and hers around Harwood's waist. They did not disengage.

"Did you say something, Mr. President?"

"Yes, Stan," replied Williams, his voice echoing down the long hall. "You asked me a question that I didn't answer."

"Sir?"

"I told you I'd come to Washington with a vision, and that I'd lost that vision. Then you asked 'what about now?'"

Stanley Harwood and Maria Krautchik stood silently in their half-embrace, waiting.

"Light," said the President.

"Sir?" said Harwood.

In the yellow glow from Tony's office, they could see the broad smile, the beaming face of the President of the United States of America.

"That's the answer to your question. Grace and truth are born of light. Rec was a light shining before men. We need to bear witness to that which lights every man that comes into this world. From light comes hope. From hope comes the desire to make positive change where others see darkness."

"Yes, sir . . . exactly," answered Harwood.

"Good night." The President turned and re-entered Giovanni Battaglia's office, and stood in silent awe before the framed Olympic gold medal, gleaming in the reflected light of a desk lamp.

Williams whispered to himself, hardly a sound coming from his lips, "Light shining before men."

At the same time, Stanley Harwood opened the hallway door for Maria, nodding and repeating to himself, almost inaudibly, "Light."

We thought we ranked above the chance of ill.
        Others might fall, not we, for we were wise—
Merchants in freedom. So, of our free-will
        We let our servants drug our strength with lies.
The pleasure and the poison had its way
        On us as on the meanest, till we learned
That he who lies will steal, who steals will slay.
        Neither God's judgment nor man's heart was turned.

Yet there remains His Mercy—to be sought
        Through wrath and peril till we cleanse the wrong
By that last right which our forefathers claimed
        When their Law failed them and its stewards were bought,
This is our cause. God help us, and make strong
        Our will to meet Him later, unashamed!

—Rudyard Kipling